RACING TOWARDS DESTINY

Lena Gibson

Black Rose Writing | Texas

This is a work of fiction. Names, characters, businesses, places, events, and incidents are either the products of the author's imagination or used in a fictitious manner. Any resemblance to actual persons, living or dead, or actual events is purely coincidental.

ISBN: 978-1-68513-641-3
LIBRARY OF CONGRESS CONTROL NUMBER: 2025932433
PUBLISHED BY BLACK ROSE WRITING
www.blackrosewriting.com

Printed in the United States of America
Suggested Retail Price (SRP) US $21 .95 / CA $24.95

Racing Towards Destiny is printed in Minion Pro

*As a planet-friendly publisher, Black Rose Writing does its best to eliminate unnecessary waste to reduce paper usage and energy costs, while never compromising the reading experience. As a result, the final word count vs. page count may not meet common expectations.

Praise for
Racing Towards Destiny

"Racing Towards Destiny is an adventure, a coming of age story, and a love story wrapped into one engaging plot."
–Gary Gerlacher, author of *The AJ Docker Medical Thriller* series

"When life throws you a curve, the only way to keep from crashing is to lean in."
–Cam Torrens, award-winning author of the *Tyler Zahn* series

"A wonderfully written, sports romance that I couldn't put down."
–Anna Daugherty, award-winning author of *Outside of Grace*

"This novel explores driving on all its levels: from motorcycle racing, to being driven, to driving one's own life."
–Susan Sage, author of *Dancing in the Ring* and *Silver Lady*

"A heartfelt story of love, loss, and the struggle to be your very best self."
–Gail Ward Olmsted, award-winning author of the *Miranda Quinn Legal Twist* series

"Racing Towards Destiny is a testament to the power of taking control of your life and finding love in the most unexpected places. A must-read for anyone who believes in the magic of new beginnings and the excitement of life on the edge."
–Janis Robinson Daly, best-selling author of *The Unlocked Path*

"For neurodivergent Anna and overshadowed Isaac, new beginnings often come disguised as endings. Add in a villain worthy of Lena Gibson's meticulous plotting, and you've got a satisfying beach or a cozy night by the winter fireplace read."
–Karen K. Brees, author of *The WWII Adventures of MI6 Agent Katrin Nissen*

For MotoGP racers and their loved ones

RACING TOWARDS DESTINY

CHAPTER 1

Anna

Today was Anna's biggest nightmare. The intermittent buzz of office chatter, humming lights, and clacking keyboards created an unbearable racket, making it impossible for her to complete her work. She winced and scanned the busy room, her hands clutching the side of her head, lost without her headphones. Listening to familiar, repetitive music kept regular office noises from intruding.

Yesterday, her boss had suggested she'd be more accessible without her headphones. Sandra had smiled and moved on, perhaps having no idea what horror she'd unleashed on Anna. How could anyone work with this din? Her brain had always been different, too stimulated by sensory information. That came with being on the spectrum.

Anna examined her organized cubicle, her post-it notes color-coded and her pens upright in a jar. Everything else remained bare, except the postcard she kept of a European village with polished cobblestone streets. This bland workstation wasn't how she'd pictured her life.

She rubbed her temples, trying to massage away a budding headache. When she was young, she'd dreamed of being a published author. Her thirtieth birthday loomed on the horizon, and instead of being the driver, she'd spent her life as a passenger.

She glanced away from her computer screen toward the far-off window, took a deep breath, and shoved back from her desk to take a moment for herself. Standing relieved the tight feeling in her neck and shoulders from hunching toward her screen. She had to get out of here, if only for a few minutes. She'd get some tea.

Sandra's slick voice reached her as she neared the conference room. Anna's steps faltered, and she stopped, open-mouthed, in the doorway.

Her boss's presentation was, word for word, what Anna had agonized over for weeks and pitched to Sandra just days ago. Those were her slides on the screen. After belittling it, Sandra had stolen her work and was now presenting it as her own to their biggest client. It wasn't the first time someone Anna trusted had betrayed her. Tears threatened, but a surge of fiery rage kept them at bay.

Sandra noticed Anna at the door and shot her a triumphant look, her jade-green eyes dark and flat like a reptile's. Mr. Jones leaned back in his chair while Anna stood rooted in the doorway behind him, unable to enter, her throat constricted. His fingers steepled together in front of him as Sandra finished discussing *Anna's* proposed marketing campaign.

"It's brilliant, Sandra. You've outdone yourself again. You're a genius. This is just what my company needs. Based on our previous conversation, it isn't at all what I thought you were working on. This is better." He smacked the table for emphasis, and Anna jumped at the unexpected loud noise.

"It just came to me the other day," Sandra said with a toss of her honey-gold hair. "I redesigned everything and wanted to surprise you. I'm so glad you like it." She unnecessarily smoothed the front of her crisp navy-blue power suit.

"Mr. Jones," stammered Anna. The big man half-turned, his thick eyebrows arched. "Actually…" She wanted to tell him it was her work. Her ideas. But how could she do that? The blood drained from her face as reality set in. She couldn't change what Sandra had done.

Her boss smiled her snake smile, her flat lips curving away while Mr. Jones had his back to her. Perhaps daring Anna to continue, knowing she wouldn't. This wasn't the first time Sandra had taken advantage of Anna, and she was sick of it.

When no words followed, the client's gaze flicked back to Sandra.

"Anna, can you get us the champagne from the kitchen? And a couple glasses. There's a dear." Sandra turned. "Marcus, we need to celebrate."

This couldn't be real.

"But…" Tongue-tied, the rest wouldn't come out. Anna had never imagined this happening. Her stomach ached—she didn't deal with confrontation well. She'd worked on this strategy for a month. Given up every weekend and countless hours of her own time, often staying at the office until nine or ten o'clock. When Sandra told her she'd wasted her time, to scrap everything, and restart, Anna was devastated.

She'd picked herself up and thrown herself into the next idea, vowing to do better. A red haze settled in front of Anna's eyes. This time, she wouldn't just sit back and let it happen.

"This marketing strategy was my idea." Her voice shook with suppressed fury and traitorous tears fell, but she spoke with a rare confidence. When Mr. Jones turned to face her directly, her face burned with embarrassment. She struggled to look him in the eye—something so difficult for her but expected in the business world. When calm, she could force herself, but upset, it became almost impossible.

She held her ground at first, then darted a glance at her boss, who stood, one hand on her hip, her face a false mask of confusion. Sandra's unbuttoned top button had become two.

"What are you talking about, Anna?" said Sandra with a derisive laugh. "You influenced my eventual choice of color scheme for the slides, but that's hardly the campaign. Don't be so unprofessional. One day, when you're more experienced and have earned it, I'll give you more responsibility. For now, you should go back to your spreadsheets." She motioned with her hands like a mother shooing a pestering child.

When Anna didn't move, Sandra stared, her face appearing disappointed or maybe annoyed. It was difficult to tell the difference. Reading other people's emotions wasn't Anna's strength.

"This was my idea. How could you? I quit." Her boss's betrayal was the last straw at a job she hated. Great gulping sobs burst from Anna's throat, which threatened to close. Oxygen seemed in short supply. She couldn't feel anything besides her flaming cheeks and needed to leave before things became worse. Already the embarrassment made her stomach ache. It would be a miracle if she could prevent a conflict-induced meltdown.

"I don't know what to say," said Sandra with a shrug. "Good luck."

Anna stumbled backward. Behind her, Sandra's voice resumed, overlaid with Mr. Jones's deeper voice, but Anna couldn't make out their words as she fled. Spinning, she ran to her cubicle, grabbed her laptop, and scanned her desk for her few personal effects. She snatched the postcard and her jar of pens, stuffing them into her laptop case, and headed for the elevator. Hushed whispers followed, the news outracing her, as gossip always did. The hum of the too-bright lights had never been more incessant.

She needed the solitude of her car and her music. Now. She pushed the call button six times, the tightness in her chest intolerable while the wait for the elevator became interminable. Her shoulder blades twitched while she willed the elevator to climb faster. She dared not look behind, already feeling the stares burning into her.

She breathed a sigh when the doors opened with a ding and she stepped inside. Traveling downward, she focused on twirling the ring on her right hand, waiting for her stop on the parking level. Her grandmother had given her the ring to help her cope. Sometimes her talisman worked—the magic of a gift from the person who'd tried to teach her self-worth. Each floor Anna passed, she held her breath, hoping the elevator continued without stopping. This early in the afternoon, she made it all the way to the bottom alone.

She couldn't believe she'd quit. Adam would be so happy. Her brow furrowed. Wouldn't he? Her boyfriend was always after her to take a different job. This would be the perfect chance. He'd always said she'd never be able to handle a high-pressure competitive marketing job, and she'd just proven him right. It was galling to admit. The first big account she'd worked on, the first time she would have won a major client, and she'd been duped.

Anna could almost hear Adam's words when she got home. He would say, "You're not designed for business, Babe. You should take a less challenging position that won't make you feel inadequate. They don't appreciate your differences the way I do." She blinked back tears and pressed the back of her icy hand against her scalding cheeks.

He was right about that part, at least. They didn't. She'd told no one at the company she was neurodivergent, though more observant co-workers may have figured it out. It wasn't anyone's business as long as she did her work well; that's all the company cared about. Until today, she'd been a model employee.

She ran to her white Civic and jumped in, turning on her music. She let the sound block everything else while she concentrated on breathing and control. Two songs later, she was ready to go.

Before leaving her parking spot, Anna sent Adam a quick text to say she'd be home early and that she'd explain when she got there. She clutched the wheel, her hands still trembling. She still couldn't believe she'd left her job, no matter how she disliked it. She hadn't meant to get into marketing, but the idea had appealed to her creative side and paid the bills. What was she going to do? She had little savings because she'd used everything as a down payment on the townhouse last year.

Adam stayed on her mind as she drove. He'd convinced her that buying instead of renting was the way to go, and she'd bought the place so they could live together. He'd had nothing to contribute because of bad luck with his investments, but she hadn't minded sharing her nest egg. After all, he was her boyfriend. They'd been together for four years now and were serious. Weren't they? She frowned, a sudden realization dawning. Somehow, he always changed the subject when she brought up marriage. That didn't seem committed.

Though Adam hated her job because it kept her so busy, she had the new and disquieting thought that he might be unhappy with her rash decision to quit. He liked her steady paychecks. As a community college anthropology professor, he made a pittance. Her lungs compressed, and she inhaled several times to regulate her breathing. She drove the rest of the way home, rehearsing. She'd say quitting was an opportunity—a gift of time to figure out what she wanted.

Anna's throat ached from holding back sobs, and she couldn't wait to shower and wash this horrid day down the drain. After dinner, she'd veg in front of the TV for an hour or two in her pj's, have a bath with a favorite book, and go to bed. A relaxing evening for a change. Tomorrow she could come up with a solution, update her resume, and do preliminary job searches online.

Her shoulders tightened again. She now had no income and bills to pay. She swallowed hard and forced herself to relax. The hard part of job hunting would be not taking the first offer that came along. If she wasn't careful, she would end up in the same box.

She parked in her spot, taking another minute to regroup. She would explain to Adam so he understood Sandra was the villain—one who'd left her no option but to quit or accept that her boss could cheat her at will. Anna checked the time. It was just five o'clock. She hadn't been home this early in years. She frowned at her phone. Her text to Adam remained unread. Well, no matter, she'd explain in person. He'd be surprised she was home, but hopefully, it would be a pleasant surprise.

She checked the flip-down mirror to determine if it looked like she'd been crying, wincing at her creased forehead. It had been like that several times in recent months. The line seemed permanently etched on her face, even if she wasn't yet thirty. Not quite. She still had several months left in her twenties. Deep down, she must be worried about Adam's reaction. She rubbed at her forehead, smoothing the wrinkle away.

Anna hurried up the stairs, unlocked the house, and rushed inside. Adam's gray car sat outside, but the house echoed and seemed empty, with no blaring TV or music playing.

"I'm home." She dropped her shoulder bag with her laptop on the bench by the door and kicked off her heels, tucking them into their proper place in the hall closet. She wiggled her toes and flexed them, loving the feeling of freeing her feet from her confining work shoes. Looking down, she wanted to be rid of the awful clothes that weren't her either. She was tired of trying to fit into what she should be instead of accepting her differences.

What had she been doing the last six years at that company? She must have been sleepwalking, going through the motions of living. She'd worked so hard, but it was only now that she dared to admit she hated her job. Leaving would be a positive thing. She would make it the best decision of her life.

There'd been no response to her announcement of being home. She checked the kitchen, the living room, and the den, but he wasn't in any of them. Maybe Adam had gone for a walk. She didn't know what he did after he got home from work hours earlier than she did. Maybe he'd walked to the store to pick up dinner. She checked her phone. Her message was still unread. She frowned again and took a breath, smoothing her face once more.

Darting upstairs to change, she walked into their bedroom and stopped, aghast.

She covered her mouth at the sight of Adam's bare ass as he dove off the bed toward the corner. It took a second to register what was happening and who the busty blonde in her bed was. He'd been having sex with Tiffany, his most recent grad student. Sex. In her bed. How cliche.

Anna stood frozen, her hand still over her mouth. There was no one to imitate, no one as a guide. This was out of her league. How dare he? She probably shouldn't be shocked by another act of betrayal. This is what she got for playing it safe.

"Jesus, Anna," Adam said, grabbing a pillow and covering himself with a cushion as he stood awkwardly beside the bed. Tiffany scrambled in the rumpled sheets, covering her nakedness. She wouldn't meet Anna's stare, but at least she had the grace to blush.

Anna's cheeks burned, mirroring Tiffany's response. The taste of bile filled her mouth. She'd been a fool. How had she never considered the possibility of Adam cheating?

"How long?" Her voice sounded high and wrong. Shriller than she'd have thought possible, further unnerving her. She couldn't meet Adam's eyes and stared a foot to his left.

"Anna, go downstairs. We'll talk about this later." Adam motioned to the door.

She flicked a look at his face, unable to speak. How dare he speak to her that way?

"You shouldn't be here." He pointed to the exit. "Get out."

"No, I don't think I will." She fought her desire to give in to him. While she couldn't stay in this house with him longer than it would take to pack, she would stand her ground. Even if the townhouse was hers, she was done. She would sell it. She'd never wanted this life in the first place.

Anna turned her back, stood on tiptoe, and grabbed her suitcase from the top shelf in the bedroom closet. Throwing it on the bench seat by the closet, she filled it with random handfuls of clothes from her drawers and from the stuff hanging. She had no idea what she packed. Some of this and some of that. All of her clean underwear, some of her sweaters. Jeans. She needed jeans. Shorts. She liked shorts. She wasn't really thinking. Maybe her purple ball cap.

She glanced out the window at the slate-gray sky and made a note to grab a rain jacket from the hall closet on her way out. Mid-March in Seattle could be wet.

It was difficult to process, but she kept moving. She collected her passport from the drawer in her bedside table along with her other important documents, stuffing them into her purse.

"Where the hell do you think you're going with your suitcase?" Adam attempted to block her exit by standing in the doorway to their bedroom. She glanced down pointedly at the throw pillow he still held and raised an eyebrow.

"Away from here. Away from you." Her voice quavered despite attempts to remain calm.

"I'm going to go," said Tiffany, finding her voice at last as she slid off the bed, still clutching Anna's blue sheet to her chest. She bent and scanned the floor for her missing clothes.

"Don't leave because of me," said Anna. "Oh, I almost forgot my toothbrush and my conditioner." She returned to the bathroom, collected her travel kit from under the sink, and added a few items.

"Anna, be reasonable. You can't leave. You have nowhere to go. Let's talk about this." Adam acted like she was the one who was in the wrong.

It was official—this had become her worst day ever. Well, the worst day since her grandmother's accident. Any success in her life she owed to her grandmother, and now that she had died, Anna's only support system was gone. Were her failures today a sign of that loss?

Anna stared at him, the jar with her overnight face cream clutched in one hand and her toothbrush in the other. Her fist tightened, clenching the toothbrush like a weapon. "Yes, Adam. Let's talk. Explain this. Give it a shot."

She indicated the rumpled bed that reeked of sex, half-dressed Tiffany, and his scattered clothes strewn across the floor. How was he going to explain? "Was this accidental?"

"I'm so sorry. He said he was single." Tiffany wiped a tear from her cheek.

Anna felt for her but couldn't spare the energy to address the girl.

"Babe, if you were ever home, you'd know you haven't satisfied me for some time. You have put on a few pounds since you started your desk job. Besides, I don't think the male of the species was designed to be monogamous. If you look at this objectively, you'll see that by having sex with someone else, I'm taking care of myself, so I can be a better partner." Adam had gone into lecture mode like she was one of his students.

Anna rolled her eyes. How could she argue with someone who believed such ridiculous logic? She let out a long breath before she turned on her heel and collected her favorite pajamas. Her best T-shirts and two unread books from her bedside table. She'd need more, but it was a start.

"Anna, put that shit away. You're acting like a child."

Tears filled her eyes, but she didn't look at Adam as she blinked them back. He didn't get to see her cry. Her hands shook as she shoved her mauve bathroom kit into her suitcase and zipped it closed.

"Anna. Stop." Adam stomped his foot.

That was a simple emotion to read. Good, let him be annoyed.

She carried the suitcase past him and down the stairs without another word. Reaching ground level, she scanned to see if she wanted anything else. Nothing. There wasn't one piece of her life in this place she wanted to keep. The things she cared about, her colorful Depression glass from her grandmother, a couple of old family pictures, and the flowers her grandmother had painted had been declared too tacky for their new home. They were in storage with most of her books, and she could get them later.

It was as if she was seeing the living space of the townhouse for the first time. The dull, brick red accent walls and otherwise stark black and white decor. The lack of bookshelves. She cringed as the place assaulted her eyes, and she blocked it out, the way she always did. It contained nothing soft. Nothing feminine or pretty. Nothing soothing. Everything in their house screamed Adam. Why hadn't she spoken up about how much she hated it?

Her vision blurred as she neared the door, tears almost overwhelming her eyes. Somehow, she held them in. She only had a matter of minutes until she wouldn't be able to cope. This second confrontation had been too much, leaving her on the brink of overload. She couldn't let Adam see this particular meltdown. Clinging to her last shred of dignity, she grabbed her jacket and jammed her feet into her sneakers. She collected her hiking shoes, slung her laptop bag over her shoulder, and yanked the door open.

Without warning, Adam stood in her way, wearing pants at last. Her muscles tightened, and her free hand balled into a fist. She'd love to hit him, though, of course, she wouldn't.

"Anna, you're not going anywhere until we've talked." He snatched her keys from her hand and backed into the living room.

How dare he? A fog of anger gave her a few more seconds of strength.

Tiffany sidled past, now fully dressed. "I'm sorry," she whispered.

"I don't want him. He's all yours." Anna meant every word.

Tiffany fled, scuttling to her car down the block, leaving the front door ajar in her haste.

Anna turned. "My keys. Now." Her voice shook. She needed to get out. Already breathing had become difficult, ragged.

"Fine." He threw her keys back, which she fumbled and caught before they hit the floor. "When you're ready to talk like a grown-up, I'll be here."

She flung herself out the door, down the stairs, and into her car. Starting it, she swiped at her tears and drove, stopping three blocks from home to sob.

She couldn't go back, but she had nowhere to go and no one to call. Her grandmother had passed eight years ago, and she had no one else to turn to. Anna had never felt more alone, and she gave into the grief of more of her life wasted, letting it out. Though she lost track of how long she cried, her tears at last subsided into a few hiccups. Wrung out, Anna allowed herself a few moments to breathe, and composed herself. Her face must still be blotched, red, and puffy, but she regained control. She rolled down the window to get some air and sat for another fifteen minutes, calming herself by concentrating on the rhythm of her regular breathing.

While she tried to figure out her next move, the smell of spicy food caught her attention. Meltdowns took an immense amount of energy. She would feel better if she ate. Her stomach grumbled in response.

Across the street stood a Mexican restaurant, so Anna moved her car into their parking lot and entered the establishment. The background music was subdued, and only two families and three couples occupied well-spaced tables in the front section. She slid into a quiet corner booth.

Ordering chicken tacos, Anna ate mechanically, not tasting her food at first while her thoughts whirled. Her first step would be to figure out where to stay tonight. At first, nothing came to mind. A hotel? That seemed so… temporary. She didn't want a solution for a night or two, but something with potential to last.

How had she ended up with a life she didn't want? She hated her job, and Adam treated her like a child. She wasn't going back to either. Good riddance.

Seeking calm, she closed her eyes. Once upon a time, she'd dreamed of writing a book. Several books, in fact. Writing while sitting at cafes in Europe, seeing fresh places every holiday. It was something she and her grandmother had talked about when she'd started university. Anna had wanted to make a living as a writer. Somehow, she'd been convinced her dreams were too difficult or unattainable. She'd never gotten off the continent or made it past scribbles she'd never had the guts to share with anyone.

Goosebumps rose on her arms. What if she tried to be a writer? For once, she'd have time. No matter how awful her day had been, there was no reason she couldn't change her life.

With the new possibilities abuzz in her head, the rest of her dinner was delicious.

As the sun set in a blaze of cotton candy pink and soft orange, she paid for her dinner and left the restaurant. She stood facing the glow and refused to let herself be crippled by fear. What would she do to become a writer if she didn't have to play it safe? Like a bolt of lightning, it came to her. She could start over somewhere new. Her mind flashed back to the postcard from her cubicle. That was the life she wanted.

Not daring to think too hard, she hopped in the car and drove. She sold her almost new car at a used car lot, called a cab, and got dropped off at SeaTac airport. With the cash from the sale of her car tucked deep inside her purse, she wheeled her suitcase inside the airport, checking that her passport was accessible.

With a deep breath, Anna studied the Departures board and bought a one-way ticket to Barcelona—the first flight leaving for Europe. In three hours, she'd be on a plane.

CHAPTER 2

Isaac

Isaac shut his laptop and leaned back, slumped into his seat. He glanced out his bedroom window at the lush countryside, which was misty and cool this time of year. He relished these days as the Spanish summer would soon scorch the hillsides golden and brown. Another MotoGP season approached. Something inside told him this could be his last, and he didn't like the uncertainty. He didn't have a contract for next year and might not receive an offer to sign one. For the first time in his adult life, the future was uncharted.

He pulled out the journal his therapist had given to him two weeks ago. He'd suggested that Isaac write about his relationship with his brother. Until today, it had remained blank, but it was time to do something about his discontent. He wrote in his almost illegible scrawl.

My brother is a legend. A star. The Ronaldo of motorsports. The greatest motorcycle racer of our lifetime, maybe ever. I ride too, but I live and race forever in his shadow. One day, not too far in the future, he'll retire, and so will I. He has twelve MotoGP championships, several that he ran away with almost uncontested. I scrapped and fought tooth and nail for my championships at lower levels but have never come close in the premier class. That's my brother's domain and never once have I rivaled my brother's feats. I'm proud of what he's accomplished and the small part which I played.

I love Vince and cherish these years we've had together. Training and traveling the world, from racetrack to racetrack. He's my best friend. But when we stop, he'll still be the brightest star in motorcycle racing history. What will I be? Vince Vasquez's little brother? I need to find out what else I can be. I want more. There has to be more to life than living for my brother.

Isaac's chest clamped, squeezing the air from his lungs. Ever since childhood, the family's life had revolved around Vince, his talent, and his dreams. After a prolonged illness, their father had died six months ago, leaving Isaac wondering about his place in the world and thinking about mortality. If he wanted something more than racing in his life, he'd need to make changes.

"Ready?" His brother appeared in the open doorway. Vince's dark wavy hair was as unruly as ever, forever stuffed under one helmet or another. Isaac appreciated that his brother's expressive face wasn't guarded in the way it was at the racing paddock, or artificial, as it was in front of the TV cameras that dogged his heels from late March until the end of November. At home, he was a different person, someone the rest of the world seldom saw.

"Get a move on. I want to do the usual twenty-four-kilometer loop this morning on the road bikes then hit the weights when we get home. The dirt track can wait until this evening. The season starts in two weeks." Vince's eyes gleamed.

"Coming." Isaac closed the journal. He tried not to draw attention to it as he stowed it inside his desk before following his brother into the long white corridor of Vince's villa. He'd lived with his brother for almost his whole life, even now at age thirty-two. That was something else that might need to change in the not-too-distant future. Should he get his own home?

Ideas about owning his own place brought all his recent wants bubbling to the surface. He longed for a connection of his own, someone to settle down with. The problem was, he was so busy, it had been years since he'd had a serious girlfriend. Not one had lasted more than a few months in the off-season. Isabella had been the closest, and that had been what? Eight years ago? Maybe he should move out. He could afford it. He wasn't rich like Vince, but his racing years had left him more comfortable than their middle-class upbringing.

"Hurry up," Vince's impatient voice came from halfway down the stairs. "Race you into town."

Isaac's musing continued, unconcerned about being left behind, as he leaped down the stairs three at a time. He wasn't the only one without connections. His brother had never had a serious girlfriend either, or if he had, he'd kept it secret. Vince had devoted his time and his heart to his one true love, MotoGP. If he retired, he wouldn't be single for long. All Vince would have to do is crook his little finger and flocks of women would swarm the villa. Okay. Maybe not that bad, but Vince never had a problem finding women when he wanted to date.

Lifting his ultra-light steel road bicycle from where he stored it on the garage wall, Isaac pictured an American body spray commercial with women emerging from everywhere, chasing his brother in a horde. He snorted at the absurd image. Vince would have his pick from the most beautiful women in Spain. Hell, from all over Europe. Isaac shook his head. Maybe the Americas too. Vince was good-looking, had a sense of humor, and was outrageously wealthy. What more could a woman want?

Isaac grimaced. If they were anything like himself, the list was easy. Someone to talk to, be friends with, and enjoy spending time together. Well, that and attraction.

However, the women Isaac dated often had a crush on his brother, and it was impossible to blame them. Isaac lacked spontaneity or his brother's full-throttle laugh, preferring to be quieter in his supporting role. At some point, the women he dated always wearied of being third. They all learned that Vince came first, and motorcycle racing came second. Few young women were willing to put themselves that far down the ladder.

Isaac gripped the handlebars and leaned forward. The rush of spring air as he pedaled his bike still invigorated him, even after all these years. He followed Vince down the windy roads to the village of Cervera, their hometown. White villas and terracotta roofs came into sight. Not everywhere was as beautiful as the village on the rolling tree-studded hills of Lleida. Nor as peaceful—the perfect counterbalance to their busy travel schedule in the racing season.

The fresh air whizzed past as they coasted toward town. It had been a challenge they'd engaged in for at least fifteen years—who would tap the brakes first? It wasn't a surprise that Vince often made it all the way to the bottom. Isaac had a better sense of self-preservation than his brother and, depending on road conditions, slowed on the corners. But not today. This part of the ride didn't even count toward their mileage, and their training circuit wouldn't start until they left the village.

They arrived at the town square just as a bus filled with one of the first waves of tourists for the spring stopped outside the cafe. Despite its picturesque location, Cervera wasn't a hotbed of tourism, especially this early in the year. Some of those who found Barcelona hectic might make it this far by bus, searching for somewhere quiet. His hometown was that, which was why he and Vince always returned.

This time of year, the travelers would be older, retired people, and most of the dozen arrivals fit that description. It was too soon for university students or working-class vacationers trying to find peace or stretch their vacation dollars. Vince's eyebrow quirked, probably because this wasn't just another bus full of old women.

Toward the back was a young woman—a hot young woman. Isaac and Vince stopped their bikes and dismounted, watching one particular newcomer with interest.

The young woman stepped from the bus, her long blonde hair pulled back in a ponytail, while errant wisps framed her pink-cheeked face with its full red lips. Her lips gave Isaac a slew of bad ideas. Her gaze swept the square, eyes sparkling as she looked around as if she saw more than a sleepy village square in the off-season.

"Maybe I'll look for her after our ride," said Vince, his attention fixed. "A quick fling for a week or two before the opening round in Qatar might be just what I need."

With no other locals standing nearby, it wasn't a shock when the newcomer turned and walked toward them.

"She's cute," said Isaac, just as her dark eyes made contact with his. A current shot through him, straight to his groin. Had she heard?

The young woman smiled, lighting up her face. "Excuse me," she said in heavily accented Spanish. American perhaps. "Does anyone here speak English?"

He breathed a sigh of relief. She'd probably learned a few phrases on the plane and wouldn't have understood either of their comments in Spanish.

"I do," said Isaac, stepping forward. Vince shot him a surprised look. It wasn't like him to be the first to speak. "We do," Isaac amended with a small smile for his brother. "How can we help?"

Breath whooshed out of her as she swiveled to face both of them in their biking helmets and black and red spandex. "I'm looking for a place to stay for a week or two. Someplace that won't cost too much."

"They almost always have a room or two at the Inn." Vince's English was the better of the two of them, and he'd proclaimed his interest first. That's how the bro-code worked.

Isaac couldn't help a twinge of disappointment at Vince's slick offer of advice. He found it interesting that she didn't have a reservation. These days, most travelers arrived with a destination and a room they'd booked online.

"Would you mind pointing me in the right direction?" She smoothed her wrinkled skirt and stretched, perhaps limbering up after the bus ride from the city. Her movements reminded him of an athlete and showed off a slim figure with curves in all the right places.

"I can show you." Isaac turned to his brother. In Spanish, he said, "Don't leave. I'll be back in less than five minutes. I'm still going on the training ride."

Vince responded in their language. "I'll wait. Ask her round the house later for a drink with me."

Why didn't his brother ask her himself? They weren't in middle school. Still, Isaac nodded. What harm could it do? Vince seemed serious. Pretty. American. Temporary. That checked a lot of boxes for his brother.

"Can you watch my bike?" Isaac asked his brother in English so the girl would understand. "I'm Isaac Vasquez, and this is my brother, Vince Vasquez." He paused a heartbeat to see if she recognized his brother's name, though as an American that might be a longshot. European women were more likely to follow their particular league of motorcycle racing.

Her cheerful smile remained the same. "I'm Anna."

"Do you have more luggage?" said Isaac, expecting to collect a couple heavy suitcases from the bus luggage compartment.

"Just the one." She indicated a small hard case by her feet.

"I'll take it," he said, crossing the pavement to collect it. Up close, her eyes had flecks of yellow in the brown that gave her an exotic look, like a rare bird. He hefted her suitcase, discovering it weighed less than expected. She couldn't have much in it, which was intriguing. Most people over-packed for long trips. Maybe she was here on business, though he couldn't imagine what business would take a week or two in Cervera in March, the off season.

Her ponytail swished back and forth when she hefted her laptop bag over her shoulder before picking up an airport shopping bag from Barcelona. He'd bet there was a story behind traveling this far with just carry-on baggage.

"Maybe you can also direct me toward a store or two. I brought a toothbrush, but my trip was spur of the moment."

For a second, he didn't recognize the expression. Americans had odd ways of saying so many things. Her trip had been unplanned. What would it be like to be so carefree? His life was accounted for in specific increments. He measured his time on the motorbike in blocks of forty-five minutes, laps by seconds, and races to the thousandth of a second—infinitesimal differences mattered.

"The inn is this way," He extended his hand, offering to take her shopping tote bag since she'd insisted on keeping her laptop. She hesitated a second but handed it over, though he was a stranger. It, too, was light. Perhaps not much more than a couple books inside.

As they strolled down Primera Calle, or First Street, she said, "Is there anywhere in town to buy books in English? I hadn't thought of that before I left Seattle."

He shook his head. She must plan to spend time reading if the books she had weren't enough for her week or two. He understood, as he was also an avid reader. "Perhaps online. You could read on your laptop."

"I have an iPad too. It's more portable," she patted her laptop case. "Thanks. That's a smart idea, even if I like the feel of paper books better."

"Bigger cities, like Madrid or Barcelona, will have several bookstores with English titles," he said, ambling at her side. He wanted to ask her to go to the city with him one day, but Vince would be upset if he thought Isaac was moving in on the pretty American. The bro-code meant if Vince was interested, Isaac backed off. It was kind of one-sided.

The white-washed Inn stood only two blocks from the town square, with a wrought iron arch out front that read, "La Posada." In Spanish it meant simply, the Inn—not the most original name, but it fit. The building was a two-story villa in the village's heart that had been converted to a bed-and-breakfast about ten years earlier. Because it was spring, they should still have rooms, even without a reservation.

He could have left Anna at the entrance, but wanting to make sure everything worked out, he accompanied her inside. A bell jangled as they crossed the cool tile floor and the temperature dropped by several degrees. Goosebumps rose on his bare arms. Though cool now, old buildings like this were a respite in the summer heat. An image of himself and Anna flashed through his mind—the two of them snuggling by the fireplace and watching a movie together. What was wrong with him?

Quick footsteps clicked toward them from the hallway ahead and the clerk arrived in the burgundy and tan lobby. Isaac smiled at the familiar young woman who slid behind the counter. He'd forgotten that

Catarina Navarro worked here—taking over when her father had undergone cancer treatment. She'd been one of his friends growing up and Vince's girlfriend for about a month, several years ago. They'd parted on amicable terms and remained friends. Not an easy feat, even for someone like Vince.

"Isaac," Catarina said with a grin.

She came forward and kissed him on both cheeks. Though a common European practice, his face flamed with the pretty American at his side. Would she get the wrong impression about himself and Catarina? Despite Vince's declaration, Isaac couldn't deny his attraction.

"Who is this?" Catarina rested her hand on his arm.

He stepped back to put a little more distance between himself and his friend. "This is Anna," he said, switching to English once more so the newcomer wouldn't feel left out. "She just arrived on the bus and was hoping to find a place to stay for a week or two." He looked at Anna for confirmation as he handed back her luggage. "This is Catarina. A friend." Was he babbling?

Catarina smothered a laugh and winked at him. He hadn't meant his interest in Anna to be so obvious. "Yes, we're old friends. I've known Isaac forever. He's like a brother." She turned to Anna. "We've got four rooms available." Catarina pulled her long, black braid over her shoulder. "You can take your pick, but the upstairs ones are nicer." Her hand, with manicured bright red nails, reached for the tote, and he surrendered it. He passed the suitcase to Anna.

Before he turned away, Isaac said, "Catarina will be more helpful with shopping than I could be. You should ask her for the best places to go."

"Shopping?" Catarina's eyes twinkled, "My specialty." She draped her arm around Anna's shoulders as she led her away. "Maybe we can go shopping together in a couple of hours when I'm off, and you're settled."

Anna shot Isaac one last look over her shoulder. He nodded, and his face warmed.

He hadn't asked Vince's question, and now it was too late, but he wasn't sorry. He shouldn't care if she dated his brother—but he did. He didn't move as the two women headed for the stairs, unable to rip his gaze away.

Anna turned back and said in accented Spanish, "I'm not interested in a date with your brother." She took a deep breath and clutched the handrail. "But if you ask me out for dinner, I'd say yes."

She'd understood Vince's words. And his own. Heat rose up his neck and face, but before he could speak, Catarina chortled. "You're turning down Vince Vasquez? I think we're going to get along famously."

Before Isaac stammered something awkward or ridiculous, Anna and Catarina turned the corner of the staircase, and she was gone. He wouldn't tell Vince the last part. He'd say that he'd forgotten to ask, which was true.

Isaac left the Inn with a spring in his step and returned to his brother, thinking about Anna's declaration with a smile. He wouldn't ask for that date, but her unexpected preference filled him with pleasure.

"Well," said Vince, passing Isaac's bike back. "Is she coming over later?"

"I didn't get a chance to ask," said Isaac. "Catarina has taken her in hand. By this evening, they'll be best friends. This might be the last we see of her."

"Catarina is coming on tour with us this year," said Vince absently as he mounted his bike and pedaled toward the mountain road they favored for daily conditioning rides. "I talked to HRC about her last week. They hired her as my new umbrella girl because she wants to get back into the racing world and travel. Unlike some girls at the venues, she won't bother me or be a distraction. She knows I'm serious when racing. Not like the other one."

Vince had asked for the other umbrella girl to be let go. The first problem had been that she'd kept talking to him on the starting grid. Anyone with sense would know the MotoGP riders concentrated before races, visualizing each corner and replaying braking markers for each part of the track. Instead of providing shade and giving him peace, she'd chatted incessantly and snapped her gum. She'd lasted two races.

Isaac wasn't surprised Vince had gotten someone safe, someone familiar, to accompany them this year. Too many women on tour were 'helmet chasers' who tried to sleep with the racers. That sounded great in theory, but it wasn't in practice. They weren't Isaac's type of woman. He'd rather find someone with whom he had something in common.

Vince would be considered a prize, but he'd never been interested in the circuit girls either. He might casually date at home or in the city, never on the road. He maintained that racing and dating didn't mix. The championship came first. Some riders might welcome the idolization, but Vince had been unimpressed when one had snuck into his trailer, waiting in his bed stark naked. She'd lost her job on the spot. Women like that were unnecessary distractions.

Isaac had never had trouble. Most of the time, his umbrella was held by one of his mechanics, or his mother if she joined them for a race or two. He'd long since stopped thinking life was unfair. It was just how things were. Vince got special treatment, and everyone worked around him. Isaac couldn't even begrudge him for it. Nobody worked more relentlessly to succeed than Vince.

CHAPTER 3

Anna

Anna breathed in the clear air of Cervera, relishing the quiet which had eluded her since she had left her old life. Barcelona had been hectic and busy, even if parts were postcard worthy. Despite being in a foreign country, Anna had been disappointed. It had seemed much like any other big city back home, except with more people and older buildings. Finding anywhere peaceful to sit and write in such a noisy throng had been impossible. Barcelona was also more expensive than she'd considered when she'd chosen Spain as her destination. The snap decision to head into the countryside had seemed inspired.

Cervera was lovely with the promise of spring. There were new green leaves on the trees and the picturesque old city on the hill enclosed by a wall from the thirteenth or fourteenth century. Though only an hour and a half from Barcelona by bus, it was a different world. The village might be the perfect place to write, but she wouldn't be able to stay long unless she found a job. Preferably one that wouldn't monopolize her time. She'd wasted enough time on things that didn't matter.

She smiled at the idea of a possible new friend, Catarina. When they met up to shop, she would ask her for job advice. She'd come to Europe without sandals, a bathing suit, or enough underwear. Her only major purchases in Barcelona had been an electrical adapter for her chargers to plug in and a new SIM card for her phone at the airport.

Anna had also converted the cash from selling her car into Euros, leaving her bank account in Seattle alone. It held enough money for six months' worth of townhouse payments, because she couldn't expect Adam to pay the mortgage. By the end of the summer, she would deal with the remnants of her old life and find someone to help her sell the place back in America. She didn't plan to go back to that life, but she could return to North America if she chose. Maybe she'd choose a new city or somewhere quiet in a small town.

Anna glanced down at her phone and her Messenger notifications. She had eighty-seven unread messages—all from Adam. She'd muted him at the airport before she left. Now that she had Wi-Fi again, his latest messages were stacking up. She had a feeling they'd say variations of "*Where are you?*", "*Stop being childish*", and "*Come home.*" She didn't want to talk to him. If she spoke to him, she would stammer through, and he wouldn't respect what she had to say. He might even mock her for being "difficult" and "too emotional." With shaking hands, she deleted the messages unread and blocked him. With luck, she could avoid him forever. Maybe she'd hire a lawyer to oversee the sale of the townhouse.

Someone knocked on the door to Anna's room and she jumped, fear skittering through her for a second. In the days since she'd left Seattle, she startled easily, but her nerves should settle now that she had arrived in such a peaceful place. Cervera seemed like somewhere she wanted to stay longer. A familiar town would go a long way toward calming her jitters. She'd feel better when strange surroundings were no longer a source of stress. This was a new start.

She opened the door and smiled to find Catarina outside in the dim hallway. Anna felt less self-conscious about speaking English while in Spain. Catarina's English seemed good, Isaac's had been even better, and his brother with the fiery eyes had spoken fluently with very little accent.

Despite Vince's handsome face, she'd found his intensity unnerving. Isaac was more her style. She also appreciated his height, finding him more attractive than his brother. She might want to change her life, but she wasn't about to change who she was. A fling in Europe might be fun, but she'd never been that kind of girl.

"You ready?" said Catarina, tossing her dark hair, no longer in its braid.

The language barrier didn't seem to be a problem, which reduced the tension Anna had carried in her shoulders since she'd boarded the plane three days ago. She'd taken Spanish in school and been fluent on paper, but her anxiety stemmed from not having had many opportunities to speak it in the last ten years. Her skills were rusty.

This morning, the young men had spoken too fast for her to understand every word with her limited language skills, but she'd caught Vince's lingering look, the word "date", and the possible flash of disappointment in Isaac's eyes. It had been brief, but she noticed only because she was used to tracking emotions as a matter of course. Reading people took work. But he'd also called her pretty.

"Are you sure you don't mind coming with me? If it's easier, you can just point me in the right direction. I'm just looking for clothes, a bathing suit, and underwear. Nothing exciting." Anna hoped Catarina still wanted to go shopping, but only if it wasn't a burden.

"It's a perfect excuse to have fun this afternoon," said Catarina, waving away Anna's hesitation. "I'm looking forward to this. Nothing happens in this town all winter, so this is the most excitement I've had in weeks. It's also one of the warmest days so far this year, and an afternoon outing is just what I need. Plus, who doesn't love sexy new underwear and bras to make you feel brand new? I'll take you up to the Castle too and show you the view."

She and Catarina strolled into the upper-walled village where Anna soon lost her bearings. They took in quaint shops designed for tourists and functional ones that sold everything from colorful produce to decorative stationery, and a small pharmacy where Catarina also picked up a few things. They shopped for about an hour and a half and visited the Castle before Anna called for a time-out.

She didn't love shopping, but this had been both practical and fun. She'd seen lots of the old town with narrow, winding streets, small courtyards filled with beautiful greenery, and spring flowers tucked in unexpected places. Many of the streets were made of cobblestones polished smooth by hundreds of years of foot traffic—just like her postcard. It was astounding to think how long people had inhabited cities in this part of the world. Seattle had nothing older than Ward House, built in 1882. Here, a plaque said they built the Castle of Cervera prior to 1026 CE. The only Europeans in North America at that time would have been the Vikings.

"I'm beat," she said. "Can we stop for a coffee or tea? Maybe a snack?"

Catarina led the way back to the more modern part of town to a sidewalk cafe, where she rattled off an order for two pastries and two coffees.

"Make mine a black tea with sugar, please," Anna said to the server.

He nodded and headed inside to get their orders.

"How long are you staying in Cervera?" Catarina sat, resting both of her cloth shopping bags at her feet.

"I'm not sure," said Anna as she sat across from her companion at the cozy round table. "I'd love to stay for several months because I want to write, but I don't have money to stay longer unless I find work. Do they need any more help around the Inn?"

Catarina shook her head. "I'm actually heading out of town soon for the racing season and my younger sister has already spoken for my job at the Inn while I go watch motorcycles." Her eyes gleamed.

Anna's heart sank. Her first friend in Spain was leaving.

Catarina continued, not noticing Anna's disappointment. "What kind of job did you used to have? I know everyone in town. There might be something similar. I could put in a good word for you."

Anna frowned at the suggestion and shook her head. "I appreciate it, but no thanks. I worked in marketing for the last several years, but I'm not interested in that kind of job anymore. Do you race motorcycles?" She couldn't imagine her fashion-conscious new friend with her perfect eyeliner and crimson nails racing.

Catarina chuckled. Being laughed at was one of Anna's personal hang-ups, but nothing about Catarina indicated she was laughing at Anna, so she relaxed. "I was an umbrella girl on the racing circuit for a couple of seasons almost ten years ago. I'm going again this year." She cocked her head to the side. "I'll get to travel all over Europe without paying, as long as they're happy with my work. There are also two trips to Asia and one to the Americas. If you're interested, I bet I can get you the same kind of job. Some teams hire their own grid girls instead of relying on the ones brought in for the events by the racetrack owners."

"Racing circuit?" said Anna with a shake of her head. "What's a grid girl?" Though Catarina had spoken English, her words had still been a foreign language.

The chocolate-filled pastries arrived with two hot drinks in white cups with saucers and a creamer-size pitcher of milk. Both women fixed their drinks and spent a moment savoring the aroma.

"Motorcycle racing," said Catarina, blowing on her piping hot coffee. "I thought you knew."

"Why would I know about racing?" said Anna, raising her eyebrow. Placing her cup on the saucer, she hid her sweaty palms under the table. Had she missed something important?

"Because of Isaac and his brother." Catarina paused, perhaps waiting for Anna to clue in, but she just shrugged. What should she know? "Vince Vasquez is one of the most accomplished motorcycle racers of all time and the current world champion. His old rival, Victor Rossini, retired a few years ago with nine championships. Rossini was famous worldwide, but Vince has an unprecedented twelve. He hopes to get one more this year, then decide if he'll retire."

Vince and Isaac Vasquez. Famous. Anna's fantasy about getting to know Isaac flickered and died out. If he was someone important, he wasn't likely to be interested in someone like her for anything long term. Like his brother, it was probably just a one-night kind of thing. Plus, it sounded like he too, was leaving.

"I just met them in the town square when I got off the bus. I couldn't see anyone else besides tourists. When I wandered over, they spoke

English. Isaac was nice and offered to show me where the Inn was," said Anna. "Vince told Isaac to ask me to have a drink with him. I think. They were speaking Spanish, so I might have been mistaken." Tears of embarrassment welled up in her eyes. "I had no idea either of them was famous."

"Don't get upset. How were you to know? You aren't from here." Catarina patted Anna's hand, then laughed, an infectious sound that reminded Anna of sunshine and picnics. "The province's most eligible bachelors invited you to hang out, and you didn't even know who they were. I love it."

"I've barely heard of motorcycle racing," said Anna, also recognizing the humor. The tension in her shoulders relaxed. "Just Indy cars and F1. That's about it. And even then, I've never paid attention." She vaguely recalled hearing about some sort of monster trucks, too, but that hardly seemed like racing.

"I can't wait to tell them you've never heard of the great Vince Vasquez." Catarina chuckled as she added another dollop of milk to her steaming coffee.

"If Vince is the champion, what does Isaac do?" Anna couldn't help herself from asking. She wanted to find out anything she could about the younger, taller brother with dreamy eyes. Something about him had appealed to her at first glance.

"He races too, but he underestimates his abilities. He thinks he's only there because of who his brother is, but that isn't true." Catarina stopped laughing as her tone became more serious. "He earned his own ride at the top level and has been moderately successful. He doesn't think it is a big deal, but he won both Moto3 and Moto2 on his way up through the ranks and is consistently a threat for the top ten. For another ten or twelve finishes, he was on the podium." She sounded proud, like an older sister, not like a love interest. "He's most competitive when it rains."

The mention of rain brought Anna back to Catarina's job suggestion. "What would I have to do if I became an umbrella girl?"

What did being a grid girl entail? Other than holding an umbrella, which sounded easy.

"Races are every week or two, though there is a month off in the middle of the summer and we'll all come home. They start in Qatar, then most races will be in Europe for a few months. There will be a race in Argentina, one in Texas, and another in Mexico City. In October and November, there's a race in Australia and a few more in Asia, before we finish up in Spain again. The best thing is, all that travel is paid for if you're with a racing team. You should come. There's almost always at least one day to sightsee."

Catarina's voice picked up speed and her eyes widened. "I bet Vince can get you a job with his brother. Isaac would never ask for his own umbrella girl to travel with them, but Vince can make it happen. You would get paid to look pretty, smile, and wave." She grimaced. "Your feet will ache from wearing heels on the tarmac for so long and your arm will get sore from holding the umbrella, but other than that, it's easy. Just don't talk to Isaac on the grid, or any of the other riders, and you'll be a hit. Before long, we'll have converted you to a super-fan."

"Why would Vince help me?" Anna's brow furrowed. Would there be strings attached to a favor from Vince? She didn't want to lead him on. But Catarina would be asking for the favor, so maybe this would work. It would be nothing like her previous job and she needed the money. The adjustment could be difficult, but she could do it. Plus, Catarina's excitement was infectious. Starting over was about new experiences.

"Trust me. I can convince him to do it for his brother. They're close. Besides, he owes me. I'm returning this year as a favor to Vince. He was tired of all the hot sports models throwing themselves at him." She laughed and crossed her hands over her chest. "The poor popular racing star."

"Is his ego that huge, or are the girls that crazy about him?" Anna tilted her head. She'd found Vince mildly attractive in a generic sort of way, but Isaac was unforgettable.

"It's real," said Catarina, with a gleam in her eye as she took another sip of hot coffee. Maybe Catarina was interested in Vince.

"Isaac is more my type," said Anna, stirring a teaspoon of sugar into her second cup of tea. Cursing her forthright nature, she met the other woman's eyes. Anna hadn't meant to confess that. "Not that I'm looking for a relationship," she added, the words tumbling out as her face flamed. "I just broke up with someone, but if I had a type…" She was babbling and she clamped her lips shut to make herself stop. Adam had told her that kind of chatter was off-putting.

"Isaac is a cutie. You could do a lot worse," said Catarina with a smile. "If Vince can get you the job, are you interested? I don't want to get him involved and then you decide not to go."

The idea of wearing tight clothes and smiling for the camera was daunting, but with her scant bank account, Anna needed to do something. She wanted to make her writing plans work, but she needed money to live. "One race every week or two? Travel with the team? Downtime to write? Count me in." She was proud she hadn't stammered.

Catarina picked up her phone from the table. "I'll ask Vince right now." She read her message aloud as she texted. *'Wondering if you can pull strings to get my new pal Anna an umbrella girl gig with Isaac's team. It would be fun to travel with someone besides you serious racers, crotchety old mechanics, and snooty sports models.'*

She set her phone down and ripped her croissant into lady-like pieces, which she ate, one at a time. Anna copied Catarina's method, savoring the melted dark chocolate in the middle of the buttery pastry. She would need to start running again if all the food was this rich. Especially if she'd be on camera. Her stomach fluttered. What was she thinking?

Catarina's phone chimed less than two minutes later, and she read the incoming text aloud. *'Why don't you and Anna come to my place after six? I'll talk to Isaac's team boss between now and then.'*

"That's as good as a yes," said Catarina with a smile as she signaled for more coffee.

•   •   •

Catarina and Anna drove up the hill that evening, pulling up to a gated villa ten minutes from the village. Anna had crossed and uncrossed her ankles several times during the short drive. Her heart raced at the idea of the job. What was she doing? It was unlike her to be so impulsive, but it was too late to turn back. Maybe the answer would be no.

They arrived at the specified time, Catarina punched in a code, and the gate swung open. Like most of the buildings since Anna had left Barcelona, the Vasquez house was a clean white, rambling structure with long, half-cylinder terracotta roof tiles arranged in a series of long domed tubes like buildings in a Mediterranean movie. Her mind flashed to the opening chase scene from *Skyfall*, a Bond movie.

The color of the roof matched the local stone that lined several flower beds, the stone path in front of the house, and the lower section of the walls. The hillsides were pale green with new grass and dotted with darker green leafy trees of a variety unknown to Anna. Everything was beautiful in its simplicity.

Beyond the house, instead of a lower lawn, the slope led to a dusty track that followed the curve of the hill and wound out of sight. A plume of orange dust hovered in the air and the buzzing sound of dirt bikes reached Anna's ears as she stepped out of the car onto a paved driveway. The high-pitched noise resonated in her ears and chest, but not in an unpleasant way. She hadn't considered the noise of racing bikes. She would need to wear earplugs—if that was allowed.

"Let's go watch," said Catarina, grabbing Anna's arm and tugging her down the path toward the homemade dirt bike track. Were these bikes similar to what the Vasquez brothers rode when racing? Bikes this size didn't look that dangerous or powerful. She would Google it later to satisfy her curiosity. She hadn't looked up the Vasquez brothers yet. What would she find?

"These bikes are just for training," said Catarina, almost like she'd read Anna's mind, or perhaps she was skilled at guessing from Anna's facial expressions. Some people had exceptional social skills, unlike her. "These are 250cc dirt bikes, just for home. The guys race on paved tracks with 1000cc bikes that carry speeds of over three hundred and fifty kilometers an hour on the straights." Catarina sounded excited to share her knowledge.

Anna's jaw dropped. 1000cc meant nothing to her, but the amount of speed sounded daunting. These bikes must be toys compared to the powerful racing bikes. Watching the homemade track below, 250cc seemed plenty fast.

As they approached, one of the riders skidded around a corner, flatter than seemed possible, carving a rut in the hard dirt which sprayed upward in a wave of pale sand and gravel. Anna didn't know which brother it was, and she didn't understand how the bike defied gravity, moving at that insane angle. He must be out of control and about to crash. She hoped that whoever it was didn't get hurt.

The rider made it around the corner to her surprise, knee and elbow scraping the ground, the rear end of the bike skidding. Somehow, the rider recovered, and he pushed the bike upright as he flew toward the next corner, soaring through the air over the crest of the hill, and was gone, fresh dust hovering over the track in a cloud while the sound faded to a more muted level.

"Vince." Catarina's eyes shone as she yelled to be heard over the noise of the approaching second bike. "Don't tell him I said so, but nobody saves his ride the way he can. Anyone else would have been on the floor with that move."

Anna knew nothing about racing or motorcycles, but Vince's move with his knee and elbow had been impressive. "He must have incredible core strength." She hadn't realized she'd spoken aloud until Catarina replied.

"Exactly. Nobody rides like Vince Vasquez, even if they all try." Her voice hushed as she spoke into Anna's ear. "He's totally ripped. They both are. You should see their training regimen. We'll have to go with them to a hotel pool or to the beach in Portugal."

Anna's cheeks flamed, imagining Isaac in far more detail. Immediately, she was wracked with guilt before remembering that she was single.

Catarina nudged her with her shoulder, "Don't feel bad. There's nothing wrong with admiring from a distance. We all do."

Anna wasn't sure if it was better or worse to be one of many admirers.

Catarina leaned over the barrier built of old tires around the track. The second rider slowed up nearby and stopped with a wave. Isaac pulled off his dirty black-and-white checkered helmet and grinned. Anna's stomach lurched. Covered from neck to toe in orange dust, with his hair disheveled and flushed from exercise, he was oh so sexy.

Anna's heart hammered as she tried not to visualize his hard, defined muscles. Stop it, she told herself. Her cheeks flooded with heat. Who was she to think someone famous might be interested in her? Nobody. She must have imagined his interest earlier. Besides, she couldn't afford that kind of distraction or to be disappointed. She'd practically asked him out. What had she been thinking?

"What brings you two out here this evening?" Isaac's voice sounded pleased at the surprise. He directed his question to Catarina in English, but his eyes flicked to Anna while he spoke. She appreciated that once again, he used English to make sure she understood, and she smiled. His eyes lingered on her. Maybe her interest in him wasn't one-sided. At the very least, she could use another friend.

"I asked Vince for a favor, and he said to come by after six to discuss it," said Catarina, checking the time on her phone with a quirked eyebrow. "He's running late. Did you know that I'm coming on the road with you two this season?"

"I did," said Isaac with another quick glance at Anna. "Vince mentioned it earlier." He hesitated. "I see you two are hitting it off." His smile was gentle this time. "I thought you might." Isaac locked his dirt bike in a shed trackside and joined them on the sloped pathway.

"What do you think his chances are this season?" said Catarina.

They walked toward the house and Anna looked back as Vince skidded around a distant corner of the track below, once more making dust fly.

Isaac turned, his eyes following his brother on the track. "He's in the best shape of his life and, barring injury, I don't think anyone can touch him."

Injury? Anna hadn't considered how dangerous motorcycle racing might be and added that to her list to research. Knowing a few facts and figures wouldn't hurt. She hated the idea of anyone getting hurt.

"Last year's rookies will be better this year, plus there's a special rookie this year. They're wild cards, since last season wasn't really indicative of their potential. The one this year, Luka Catala, could be the real deal," said Catarina as she slipped her arm through Anna's, including her in the talk, even though she knew nothing about this sport yet. She added another name to her mental list. Luka Catala. She might be up half the night reading about MotoGP and its riders, but she planned to be prepared.

"I know. Plus, Yamaha improved their bikes in the off-season and Suzuki is back after a seven-year hiatus," said Isaac, his brown eyes flashing as his words tumbled faster and faster. He ran his hands through his messy hair in an attempt to fix it.

Racing seemed to be a passion for both of her new acquaintances. That Isaac would be passionate about his chosen sport was a given. In Catarina, it was intriguing.

Anna refocused on Isaac as he continued. "They're always a few things that make the championship hard to predict. Like a hot rookie or a rider who had bad luck the last few years, but everything comes together the following season. Other than the couple of years he lost to that arm injury, in my opinion, Vince is still the best."

His opinion about his brother would be biased. But Anna remembered the intensity in Vince's expression earlier. Someone with that passion could be driven to succeed at almost any cost.

"The Honda is one of the top bikes again," said Catarina. "And Vince knows it better than anyone, even if it is a new model with all the latest upgrades and technological additions. He'll make it soar."

"It'll be good to have you with us," said Isaac with a smile, sliding briefly into Spanish, which Anna couldn't follow as well. Something about keeping his brother dancing? Then to Anna, he said, "Catarina knows racing. Sorry if we got too excited and talked about it too much."

"It's okay. I don't mind. I enjoy learning new things." Talking like this seemed easier, side by side, instead of face to face. Not so overwhelming.

"I admit, I follow you two every year. You're our hometown guys. We're proud of both of you. This season could be the most fun in years." Catarina's broad smile included Anna and warmth filled her chest.

Isaac opened a white door on the side of the house, and they walked through the corner of a large open kitchen to a courtyard patio on the far side of the house, away from the track. Anna looked around, wishing she could see more of their beautiful home. It resembled something from a designer catalog with navy, soft brown, and sea blue accents. It had a restful feel.

"Make yourselves comfortable. I'll be right back. I just want to wash up. Vince has ten more minutes or a perfect lap before he quits. Then he'll join us."

Anna and Cat sat and enjoyed the peace of the villa. Within minutes, Isaac returned with a glass pitcher filled with what looked like lemonade and ice, carrying a stack of blue plastic cups in the other hand. He'd changed his clothes and washed his neck and hands.

"Lemonade?" He placed everything on the low table in front of the seats. "I'd offer you something stronger, but we don't keep anything alcoholic around when we're training."

At Anna's nod, he filled her glass, and three more. He handed one to Catarina, took a third, and left one-half full for his brother. Isaac sat down next to Anna. She couldn't help but be aware of him wherever he moved. She hadn't been this interested in someone for a long time. She and Adam may have just broken up, but she couldn't remember the last time she'd found him attractive. Maybe staying with him was another thing she'd done to play it safe. Why had they stayed together? Habit?

In the distance, the sounds of the remaining dirt bike ceased, and the evening became peaceful. In the west, the rosy glow of sunset spread across the sky while they visited.

"See," said Isaac. "Vince is going to harass me for quitting early. No surprise that he drives himself the hardest of all." The three of them chatted about inconsequential things, like movies and siblings, until Vince joined them fifteen minutes later. He must have had a quick shower because his dark brown curls were damp, and he'd changed.

Vince carried his phone in one hand and held it up as he said to Catarina, "Your wish is granted. She's got the job." He sat down on Anna's other side, giving her a long calculating look.

"Thank you for finding me a job." Her tongue became tied in knots. She didn't know how to interpret his look. Was this where he'd flirt or ask for something in return?

CHAPTER 4

Isaac

She has the job. She. Anna would come on the road during the racing season. Isaac glanced from his brother's shining eyes to Catarina's. So pleased with themselves. His chest tightened as he glanced at Anna, who sat between himself and Vince, looking down, her hands curled around her icy glass of lemonade. Should he smile and play along or throw something in frustration? On one hand, this lovely girl with long blonde hair and quiet demeanor would travel with them, so he might get to know her better, which was something he wanted. On the other hand, Vince must have orchestrated this because of his own continued interest.

Guilt shot through Isaac because he hadn't mentioned Anna's words about dinner with him to his brother. Perhaps Vince thought he'd have a chance for that fling, especially now that he'd done Anna a favor and gotten her a job. Isaac's lemonade tasted like disappointment, so he set it down.

"Well done. You two seem proud of your maneuvering." Isaac fought to keep the bitterness from his tone. What was the point in showing his annoyance? Especially when Vince and Catarina were delighted. Now that Anna would be available at home and on the road, her dating Vince seemed inevitable. While she said she wasn't interested in Vince, his brother had a charisma few could ignore. Isaac would need to push his own attraction to the side. Still, his eyes were drawn to her like magnets.

Anna twisted a ring on her right hand, some braided silver thing with an orangish-yellow stone. Amber, perhaps? She bit her lip as she looked over at Catarina, maybe looking for help. She seemed embarrassed at the attention and his heart went out to her. He didn't want to step aside for Vince. Plus, her preference should matter, and she'd said she wasn't interested in Vince. Hope surged through him. He could try to get to know her and see where his attraction went. There must be a story about why she was here and in need of a job—he would find the courage to ask.

"Thank you for finding me a job." Her voice was quiet as she spoke to Vince. "I have some savings from my previous job, but mortgage payments don't leave me much to live on."

Vince waved off the thanks as he stood up. He rarely sat for long, preferring to be active. "I'm putting steaks on the grill. You two will join us for dinner?" His confident tone left little room for debate.

"We couldn't," said Catarina, but she made no move to leave.

"Just steaks and salad. Nothing fancy. We're in training." Vince winked at Catarina. "How about if I let you make the salad? Otherwise, it might be just steaks and lettuce."

Catarina laughed. "Anna?" She waited, probably for her new friend's approval, before answering.

Isaac's hope surged once more when Anna shot a furtive glance at him and nodded. Catarina jumped up, following Vince toward the kitchen, leaving Isaac and Anna on the patio alone.

"Mortgage payments in America?" He couldn't keep himself from asking as he double-checked her ring finger. Bare. Not married.

"It's complicated. I left my job and everything else earlier this week." A single tear escaped and trickled unnoticed down her cheek. Did everything include a boyfriend?

Isaac wanted to put an arm around Anna to reassure her that everything would work out, but she seemed guarded, and self-contained. Without more information, he couldn't help any other way.

Maybe one day she would explain what had made her leave her old life to come here.

"What kind of work did you do?" He couldn't imagine what would make someone leave everything behind to move to a foreign country in a matter of days. He'd bet she was educated and been a professional in an office before coming here. An umbrella girl job would be very different. Was she on the run from someone or something? Maybe she was in trouble.

Her cheeks flamed, and he backpedaled.

"I'm sorry. You don't want to talk about it. I understand. I didn't mean to upset you.

"You didn't upset me. What happened did. I'm not ready to talk about it yet." Her eyes pleaded with him to change the topic. "While I'm here, I plan to be a writer."

She shifted in her seat and stared down toward the dirt track below. He could have kicked himself for making her uncomfortable. He wouldn't press her, but he could ensure she had a friend. They had one common interest he'd learned so far.

"Maybe we can find a book to read together. It's been a long time since I read anything in English, and I could use the practice." He smiled to encourage her, hoping she'd accept. He hadn't read in English for pleasure since high school, but he'd made the suggestion without thinking too hard.

He often read thirty to forty books a year, mostly biographies and mysteries, but in Spanish. English was only for work. It was the second, third, or fourth language of most of the racers. That and racing were their common languages.

"Why would you do that?" Her yellow-brown gaze was so direct that it was impossible to look away.

"I can't usually find anyone to discuss books with. Everyone I know discusses racing twenty-four-seven." Isaac's heart pounded as if he had just ridden full-throttle down the home-finish straight, not asked a pretty girl to spend time with him.

Vince wandered over from the grill, spatula in hand, and shot a pointed look in Isaac's direction as if to remind him he'd called dibs. This was none of Vince's damn business.

"That's a great idea." The spots of color on Anna's cheeks deepened, and a dimple appeared on one side when she smiled. "Like a two-person book club."

Isaac's body reacted, and he shifted in his seat. He swallowed and nodded, ignoring his brother for a heartbeat, then turned to Vince. Dealing with a more mundane question gave him a moment of distraction. "You get two umbrella girls this year? Or have you promoted Cat to your personal assistant?"

"Anna's joining your team," said Vince, his dark eyes looking thoughtful.

Isaac felt his eyebrow shoot upward. That was outstanding.

"Catarina has her job lined up already, but assistant is a great idea." Vince called inside to Catarina. "Hey, Cat, would you like to shadow my assistant with a view to the job for next year? If not with me, with someone who could use your keen racing insight and superior organizational skills?"

Catarina appeared in the doorway with a radiant smile. She came out and peppered Vince with questions about the possibility while he stood at the grill.

Isaac blocked out their playful banter and instead asked about Cervera and what Anna had seen this afternoon with Catarina. He soaked up every word, even though he didn't understand everything she said. He was just happy to hang out with Anna.

•　　•　　•

Thursday morning arrived and Isaac and Vince departed for the start of the MotoGP racing season. They arrived at the airport early, leaving them time to spend with Catarina and Anna. Isaac spent most of the time walking with and chatting with Anna as they gathered snacks and wandered the shops. She seemed excited about traveling, having never been anywhere except North America and now Spain.

In the bookstore, they selected three titles. Unfortunately, they didn't have seats together on the plane. He took a seat with Vince in business class and shifted uncomfortably when Catarina and Anna walked past to take their seats in coach. It seemed unfair, but that was how the team had booked the flight.

The six-hour flight from Barcelona to Doha, Qatar, was uneventful, but when he landed, he looked out at the darkened expanse of sand and his pulse quickened.

The beginning of the season always put a spring in his step, the excitement and possibility of a new season. It was always unpredictable and never went according to script. Isaac planned to soak it up this year as it might be the last. He frowned. His racing bucket list still had one unfulfilled item. He wouldn't win a championship, but it would be fabulous to win a race. Just once to be a MotoGP race winner. He shook off the unrealistic idea. That might not be in the cards this year, not with Vince still racing.

There would be a new championship hunt for Vince, and the competition would be fierce. Word around the racing paddock implied that this would be the breakout year for the young Spanish prospect Luka Catala. There was also an Australian rider, Austin Spencer, who'd won the title a few years ago when Vince had been out after successive arm surgeries.

At the ripe old age of thirty-five, the media considered Vince past his prime, practically a dinosaur. Last year, he'd only won nine races, less than his dominant performances of the past, and Isaac had read predictions of fewer than three victories this year. Everyone who said that hadn't seen what kind of shape Vince was in or the fire in his eyes. His brother was here to fight for the title, as usual.

Many of the flights arrived in Doha at about the same time from all parts of the world as the racing teams collected people from across the globe. Not just riders, but bosses, crew, and media personnel. It was a tight-knit community through the racing season, even if they scattered in the off-season.

"G'day," said Austin Spencer, as though Isaac's earlier thoughts had conjured him. His easy-going drawl sounded friendlier than it was. Something about the other man had always irritated him. Perhaps it was the Australian's swagger or smug smirks that trumpeted he was better than everyone else.

Isaac nodded. "Spencer. Good flight?" The other man's eyes skated past him and followed someone beyond Isaac's back. A woman for sure, based on the way Spencer's eyes gaze lingered.

"Hey, wasn't that Spanish chick on tour with us seven or eight years ago when I was new?" Spencer's square chin tossed toward the woman in question. A half glance confirmed it was Catarina as she and Anna wheeled their suitcases toward the buses outside waiting to take them to their hotel with the rest of the Honda crew.

Isaac clenched his jaw and shrugged. "Catarina. Yeah." The man used to hit on her day and night. She'd never given him the time of day. There'd also been something about some of the other girls complaining he came on too strong.

"That's a tasty piece with her, too. I'll have to introduce myself to the ladies tonight. The sooner the better. This season is looking up already." Austin Spencer strolled after them, leaving Isaac waiting for his delinquent suitcase.

He restrained himself from peering outside like an idiot, dying to confirm if Anna and Catarina had made it onto the buses without being accosted. Spencer's words set his teeth on edge, although the Australian wouldn't be the last man to notice Anna and Catarina. They were a striking pair who'd turn heads, especially in his crowd. Motorcycle racing was dominated by men, though there were women who raced in Moto3, the lightweight class. He'd known four in total, but no one had stayed more than a couple of years before moving on. Now, there was a women's league or WorldWCR for short.

There were a few other women around the track, just not many. Several teams included a female mechanic or two, and a few riders brought their wives and girlfriends on a regular basis. All of them were off limits. Fabiano Perotti's sister, who was his assistant, was also left alone. Messing with the Italian rider's sister would be unprofessional. Umbrella girls were a different story and would be fair game.

Catarina would have no trouble fending off men on her own—she'd always been able to look out for herself. But something told Isaac that Anna wasn't used to that kind of attention. He watched the exit where everyone else had gone, hoping for another glimpse. Anna and Catarina were more than beautiful, they were smart and interesting to talk to. The other night at Vince's had solidified that opinion. Maybe he'd matured enough to appreciate those qualities. His mom would be happy.

Isaac had yet to learn Anna's story, but they'd picked up double copies of three different books in Barcelona before their flights so they could read together. They'd each chosen one that looked interesting, and Catarina had picked another for them in the spirit of fun. Isaac had invited Catarina to read along, but she'd just laughed and said it sounded too much like work. He'd asked to be polite and had been relieved when she'd declined. He couldn't help it if he preferred the idea of hanging out with Anna with no one else around.

The first book they'd selected was about a 1920s gangster in America—a Prohibition rum-runner. He'd read for half the flight, enjoying the fast-paced story, even if the odd English word was unfamiliar. He planned to read some more later. With the time change, it might be tricky to sleep.

Isaac jumped when his bag arrived with a thunk onto the conveyor in what was probably the last batch from the plane. It reminded him of his job—he was here for more than a book club.

He hefted the suitcase and headed for the labeled team bus out front, carrying just his personal items. He'd shipped his racing gear ahead. His pit crew, crew chief, and Anna should be waiting already, as well as the second crew that made up his entire satellite racing team. He'd overheard Catarina offer to introduce Anna before boarding her own bus with Vince and the factory Honda team. He cursed his tardiness. If he'd been out there first, he'd have taken care of the introductions, and stood next to Anna for a few extra minutes.

Climbing aboard, the door whooshed closed behind him. He must be the last aboard. His teammate, Yoshi Sozui, nodded from one of the front seats on the right. Isaac nodded back and took the seat across from him, beside his chief engineer. The drive from here to the hotel would be brief, and because it was still just dawn, there wasn't much to see of Doha, besides tall buildings and bright lights. During the day, the scenic city sported turquoise water, silver skyscrapers, and pale desert sand. So much wealth concentrated in one place made for a modern, beautiful city.

Anna looked up from her seat farther back, where she sat alone. She mouthed something, and he raised his eyebrow so she would repeat what she'd said. He'd rather move back and sit with her, but it was too late and would be rude to Angel and Yoshi.

"One hundred three." She held their book up.

It took a second to register. That must be her page number. Digging through his carry-on, he checked and reported his progress in return. "Seventy-three." She smiled and sunk lower into her seat, her eyes already back in her book as the bus rumbled onward.

"New friend?" said the crew chief in Spanish. Angel's deep-set eyes peering out from his weathered face missed little, on or off the track. Though he could never replace Isaac's late father, Isaac respected the older man and his opinions, about more than just racing.

Isaac nodded. "Just friends." He might be interested in more, but it wasn't what he expected. He still didn't know where Vince figured in the equation, or if he cared what his brother wanted.

"Uh-huh," said Angel with a slow smile. "I wondered what was up when your brother asked for her to come along. Not what I expected from an American. Quieter. She seems intelligent too." He changed the subject. "How was your off-season? You and your brother get much training in over the winter?"

"Don't worry. Vince had me up early every morning," laughed Isaac. "I'm not sure I've ever been in such good shape." He flexed his right biceps, making Yoshi laugh and show off his own.

Angel's bushy gray eyebrows rose. "That's saying something. You Vasquez brothers are always fit."

When Isaac talked to the crew chief and the rest of his personal team, he always spoke Spanish, as that was everyone's language. What would it be like to be surrounded by people whose words flew by so fast that he'd be lucky to catch one word in four? It might get lonely. After giving Anna a chance to settle in, he would be sure to seek her out to chat. He didn't want to come on too strong and scare her off, he wasn't a Spencer, but he would keep finding excuses to talk to her. She would need someone with whom to practice her Spanish.

He returned his attention to his crew and chatted about the bike and its new features. They used English for certain words or brief bits to include Yoshi in the bike talk. While their bikes were a year older than the factory team rides that his brother and Luka Catala rode, they were competitive bikes, and what Vince had ridden for his twelfth championship last year.

Counting Vince out of the championship would be a mistake. Isaac looked forward to the reporters taking back their words and writing stories about the great Vince Vasquez instead of speculations about retirement.

Because they'd reached Doha first thing in the morning, they drove straight to the hotel to sleep instead of sightseeing in the city, like they might in other cities. All racing activities here took place at night, even practices. It was early Friday morning, and on race weekends, the schedule was Free Practice One, or FP1 and FP2 on Friday, FP3 and FP4 Saturday evening with qualifying later that night. The warm-up and the race would be on Sunday after the Moto2 and Moto3 races— the intermediate and lightweight classes. In most cities, the MotoGP races were afternoon affairs with as many as a hundred thousand fans in attendance, depending on the venue.

Here in the desert, they lit up the Lusail circuit like daytime and rode at night when the scorching heat wouldn't be a factor. The reversal of day and night played havoc with Isaac's internal clock, so he always ate dinner fare instead of breakfast when they arrived, a light mid-day meal in the middle of the night between practices, and breakfast when he first got up at dusk. Eating the proper food helped him to feel normal. He'd have to share his trick with Anna. He caught himself watching her several times during the short ride, but she was engrossed in her book and to his disappointment, she didn't look up.

After check-in, the riders attended their first press conference, signed a few autographs, then had dinner. Isaac sat next to his teammate, his friends, and his brother before the public part of the evening wrapped up. The feeling that something was missing persisted. Anna hadn't come down to eat. As Catarina stood, he stopped her with a hand on her arm, "Anna didn't come down. Is she okay?"

"Why don't you send her a text? Here's her number." Smiling, she shared Anna as a contact. "She won't mind my sharing her number with you." She glanced across the busy restaurant to a raucous table where Austin Spencer held court with his cronies. Empty beer glasses littered the table. "Don't worry. I didn't share it with him, even though he asked. Twice." Her lips flattened in disapproval.

As soon as Isaac excused himself from the table, he sent Anna a quick message.

"It's Isaac. Did you get food? Missed you at dinner."

Immediately dots appeared as she typed.

"Room Service. Angel suggested it when I said I felt overwhelmed by traveling."

Flying was hard on everyone at first, but it became routine—at least it had for Isaac. It had been part of his life since he was thirteen, and they'd traveled almost every weekend for his brother's racing schedule. Vince had been a phenom even then and had raced at a high level from age sixteen onward, making history as the youngest rider in history to win a MotoGP title when he was just twenty.

Leaning against the elevator wall as it shot upward, Isaac asked, *"How's the book?"*

"Enjoying it," she said. *"More romance than I expected for a gangster."*

"Me too." He pondered his next words as he stepped off onto the eleventh floor, where his room was located. *"If you need anything, let me know. See you tomorrow."* She would have orientation first. At that time, Angel would assign her the other odd jobs she'd do for the team. Had she received her schedule yet?

"FP1, tomorrow. We'll be at the track. If you want, I'll show you my bikes." He hit send before he reconsidered. That was something a friend would suggest, right?

Her response was quick. *"Sounds good. Thanks."*

Isaac tossed and turned, unable to sleep with his internal clock messed up. After an hour, he pulled out their book and read. Through the wall, the violent sounds of an explosive action movie played in Vince's room. He must not be able to sleep either. Isaac would be welcome next door, and on any other night, he'd have gone, but for once, he wanted something of his own and this gangster book had been his choice. He read until he yawned, and his eyes blurred, then shut off the light. In the darkness, his phone flashed beside his bed with a message.

"Page 300."

He smiled as he put his phone down. They were going to need more books.

CHAPTER 5

Anna

When Anna woke on Friday, it was the first day of her new job. Her eyes flew open, and she jumped out of bed. It had been years since her last "first day" and for once, she was looking forward to working. It had been a long time since she'd had that feeling. Because of the night races, the pre-race press conference had been at dawn—right after arrival yesterday—and thankfully she'd been excused.

Her chest tightened at the idea of all the people she'd meet and the responsibilities she'd learn today. The feeling was a mix of nerves and excitement. Everything was changing so quickly. She didn't regret the choices she'd made in her life; that was pointless. Her life had been stagnant, and she'd been wasting her time. Now she was ready to live.

Angel had been helpful, giving her a printed copy of both her schedule and Isaac's for the weekend, including a time and place to catch her ride to the track. Plus, a stack of team clothing. Her skin tingled when she donned the new white t-shirt and navy cargo shorts, each with the team logo. A thrill shot through her about being part of a team, an unfamiliar experience. She'd always preferred to work alone— even when technically part of a marketing team, she'd been on her own—but this time, the idea of working with others was invigorating.

She'd avoided looking at her umbrella girl outfit, leaving it thrown on the bed in a crumpled heap as long as she could. At last, she held it up and cringed. She'd shown little skin in public other than at the beach, and even then, she'd been uncomfortable. Adam hadn't encouraged her to look sexy, and she'd often felt invisible around him. His recent comments about her desk job adding to her weight didn't help. Perhaps later she'd feel more confident about wearing clothes like this. But right now, his cutting words were too recent.

Worrying about the Sunday clothes made her late for breakfast downstairs in the busy hotel dining room. She was one of the last to arrive in the Honda section that held over two dozen mechanics, engineers, and technicians of various kinds—other teams had their own area today.

Most of the job titles meant little to her as Angel introduced her to the crew while they stood beside the long buffet table. Her hands shook as she grabbed hot tea and sweetened it, distracting herself from the buzz of noise and press of people by stirring. Taking a breath, she focused on meeting people's eyes and learning some of their names. She didn't understand most of what they did, other than they were part of Isaac's crew, and therefore her team. But she'd learn.

She glanced at Isaac. He and Vince wore similar team polo shirts, Isaac's in white with blue and green, and Vince's white with orange and black. Both rode Hondas, but they seemed to have several unique sponsors.

She'd looked up their teams last night to learn about the differences. Vince's team was the factory team which entitled him to more upgrades and the latest bikes. Isaac's was a satellite team with last year's bike and was considered an independent team. She'd also discovered that the brothers had a massive online following and their own fan clubs. Many young women professed their undying love, particularly to Vince. It seemed that Isaac hadn't exaggerated his brother's popularity, even if he'd downplayed his own.

Collecting yogurt and a spoon from the breakfast buffet, Anna's throat constricted as she turned towards the tables, uncertain where to sit. It was like high school all over again. She should have come down sooner. She breathed a deep sigh when Catarina waved for her to join her, two people away from the Vasquez brothers at the long table.

Isaac caught her gaze and smiled, causing her stomach to flutter. He made her nervous—in an exhilarating way. She liked that he wasn't loud or intense. He seemed easy-going and pleasant. She watched his long supple fingers as he took apart an orange, unable to help her fascination. That was how her brain worked, uninterested or mildly obsessed.

"You settling in?" said Catarina as Anna sat.

Like Anna, she wore team colors in a polo shirt and navy shorts. Somehow, her Spanish friend seemed stylish, even in generic clothing.

Anna nodded, checking the time. She didn't have time to eat more than her yogurt and fruit. She'd spent too much time stressing over the umbrella girl uniform on her bed, eventually trying it on. She didn't have to wear it until tomorrow, but the idea was a blight hanging over her morning that she couldn't shake.

"Questions so far?" Catarina spread jam over her roll before taking a bite.

Anna shook her head and smiled, forcing herself to forget about her problem with the uniform. It was kind of the other woman to check-in. She would have liked to talk more, but it was close to departure time. Anna wiped her palms as she finished eating and glanced around. Several riders and crew bosses had left the room, which seemed to be a signal for everyone. Time to work.

"First days are tough, but you'll be fine. Angel will be good to work for. He's a kind man that Isaac looks up to. Sit with me tonight at dinner," said Catarina in a quiet voice as she got up to follow Vince to her shuttle—headed for the track. "I'll want to hear about your day." She left with a smile and a confident stride.

Anna didn't feel that way herself, but she attempted to give her own walk a similar confidence. She passed the Australian rider with his off-putting smirk and ignored his rude stare.

"Hey, America. What's your name?" He called after her. She pretended not to hear and climbed onto Isaac's shuttle with the rest of their team.

Once she arrived at the track, the full Honda group separated into four distinct garages, one for each rider. Instead of calling them garages, she learned they called each section a box. All the interior panels matched the team and manufacturer colors and looked to be portable and fastened into place. They must be set up again at each venue. Looking down the long row, she counted at least twelve other non-Honda teams. If each had two riders, that meant twenty-eight competing in each race. Counting was calming and easier to focus on than all the unknowns.

Isaac disappeared out the back of the box, and when he returned, he'd changed into tight-fitting cobalt blue, bright green, and white riding leathers covered with logos and writing across the top half—including down the sleeves.

While Isaac had been gone, the crew had uncovered two identical-looking motorcycles that matched the colors Isaac now wore. Up close, the bikes seemed huge and more powerful looking than any motorbikes she'd seen. She looked around, unsure where to stand. Everyone seemed busy, bustling through the garage with familiar jobs. The scent reminded her of the parts department of a car dealership: rubber, oil, and gas.

She jumped at a repetitive staccato noise and turned. Two men in team shirts were inflating tires on a compressor of some kind. Another screech of a power tool added one of the new tires to the back of a motorbike. The burst of sound was over quickly. Calming her racing heart, she glanced at Isaac.

After meeting her gaze, Isaac called her over and patted the blue and green tank of the closest of the two motorcycles. "These are my beauties," he said when she'd joined him.

"Why are there two bikes? They look the same." She bit her lip, hoping it wasn't a stupid question.

"Mostly to save time." He didn't quite look at her as he spoke. "The guys can have two bikes ready with different settings or tires." He crouched down to look at something lower on the bike. He glanced upward and met her eyes. "We use different tires for rain or for different temperatures. The harder tires are for the hottest or roughest tracks." He seemed about to say more but stopped short.

Was there something he wasn't saying? She ran through what she'd learned last night. Ah. She sucked in a breath. He also had a second bike in case he crashed the first one in practice or qualifying, making it unrideable for the race. That's what he was avoiding mentioning. She flushed. He must not want to think about the risk, even if it was always present. Either that, or it didn't even cross his mind. After all, as a motorcycle racer, he must be an adrenaline junkie.

"How do you like the bikes?" There was pride in his voice as he raised his eyebrow.

She bit her lip. She didn't want to ask too many questions all at once. Adam said that was annoying. "They look fast." Now that she'd seen them, she believed they could reach the insane speed of three hundred and fifty kilometers per hour. What would that feel like? Would she ever get to feel the speed?

As if reading her mind, Isaac grinned in a slightly crooked, daredevil way, so different from his usual composed expression. "They are really fast. Maybe one day when you're more comfortable, I can take you for a slow lap." He checked over his shoulder for Angel, who had joined them and said, "A very slow, cautious lap."

Angel laughed and handed her a thick folder with a wink. "This should get you started for this morning. Today is for observation. Tomorrow, we'll use you at the autograph sessions and on race day we'll keep you busy with all three races. I need Isaac now, but if you have questions, feel free to ask any of the crew." He turned to Isaac, saying, "I think this will be your best year yet. This bike is what your brother won the championship with. It's the best bike we've ever had." The two switched to Spanish as they moved across the room.

Anna wasn't sure where to start, so she sat at the back of the garage on the first seat in a row of half a dozen chairs. She read the information packet, making notes about Isaac's team sponsors. While she had time, she looked them up online. Though some of them were familiar, many were not. Most of these were European beer and motor oil brands, others were tires, the usual energy drinks, or well-known tech companies such as Lenovo and HP. From a marketing perspective, wearing sponsorship logos and painting them on bikes, helmets, and grandstands seemed gaudy but efficient. Everywhere the fans looked, or the riders went, they advertised their brand.

She settled in to read more about her duties. She would help at autograph sessions with the stacks of pictures and her umbrella if Isaac needed shade. Every time the media interviewed Isaac, she was responsible for the prep work, making sure he arrived at the right place at the correct time for cameras from Britain, Spain, and Italy, the three most common feeds. MotoGP had a world-wide following. She hadn't expected televised practices and fans in the grandstands today or tomorrow, but from the noise outside, the crowd seemed substantial.

On race day, she seemed to have several assistant or publicity duties besides umbrella work, which suited her fine—organizing lines, markers, and fan photos for signing. All that sounded easy. They would pay her for six to eight hours of work for four days each race week, plus all food, lodging, and travel expenses. She wouldn't get rich on her wage, but it should be enough to live on if she was careful.

Product placement for pre and post-race interviews included helmets, hats for after the race, and water bottles. Extra important if a rider placed in the top three or was the top independent racer for a race. They'd assigned someone to show her tomorrow so she could do it for qualifying and subsequent events. Getting things ready would make her feel useful. Everything listed about regular racing operations seemed very particular, which she didn't mind—at least the expectations were clear.

She would help at other weekend autograph sessions, like the one after the qualifying sessions on Saturday, and provide shade at other events for riders, Honda dignitaries, and MotoGP alumni. Sometimes, like this Sunday, she'd be asked to hold a grid sign to mark the starting rows for the Moto2 and Moto3 races. She licked her dry lips. With her concern about what she was supposed to wear, it seemed too soon.

Anna watched Isaac with her peripheral vision while he spoke with Angel and his crew, that fluttery feeling in her stomach returning whenever her eyes met Isaac's—which happened too often to be accidental. Once, Angel back-handed Isaac's shoulder to regain his attention, and she ducked her head with a smile. Still, she didn't want to be too much of a distraction and studied the information packet while listening to the voices in the garage and the sounds of unfamiliar machinery.

Spanish, with odd bits of technical language in English, made for a strange conversation around her but she soon blocked it by keeping her head down and concentrating on learning her new job.

The section just beyond the temporary garage was called the pit lane, and the riders couldn't exceed 60 km/h. Anyone working in pit lane during the race needed to wear a safety helmet. That didn't include her as she'd return to the box after the race was underway. Startled, she looked up when an announcement came through a ceiling speaker.

"Pit lane will open in ten minutes. Ten minutes until FP1."

A timer started counting down, the bright red numbers easy to read in the dim evening light since massive overhead lights lit the track and its surroundings like bright sunlight. Anna walked to the front of the garage to check out what was happening outside. At the entrance, a faint breeze of warm air scuttled swirls of pale sand across the edge of the pit lane.

Beyond a dividing fence lay the Lusail International Circuit starting grid, where she would stand before the race on Sunday. Staggered diagonal rows of three start lines per row filled the area. Beyond the starting area, a ring of emerald-green turf surrounded the track, making the desert appear lush and inviting and, in the distance, the city lights sparkled like jewels against the growing darkness.

While she stood there, the pit crew rolled one of Isaac's bikes outside to prepare for the first practice session. Much smaller bikes had been whizzing around the track earlier, but she had paid little attention to their buzzing. When the timer ran down to the last minute, the crew started his bike with a separate device. Isaac tugged on his helmet, fastened the chinstrap, and tightened his gloves with Velcro strips. With his full outfit on, he looked serious and ready for business.

"What's the funny lump on the back of his suit?" She asked one of the young men who was adjusting something on the second bike. She couldn't remember his name yet, either Manuel or Miguel.

"That's his airbag. In case he crashes." The young man with the ponytail winked. "I'm Miguel. Welcome to the team."

She'd never heard of airbags in clothing, but she was too self-conscious to ask for more information, even if Miguel seemed friendly. The airbag in Isaac's leathers must be like the inflatable kind in a vehicle.

Several more bikes started nearby, and Miguel took a pair of earplugs from his pocket and rolled them before inserting them into his ears. "It's about to get loud."

He arched an eyebrow, and she took a set from her pocket, too. She'd been worried people wouldn't like her wearing ear protection, but it looked to be standard practice. Even Isaac had stuck some in before putting on his helmet. Anna slipped hers in as bikes started all down the pit lane. Even with protection, the roar of the bikes filled her chest, but it was a bearable rumble instead of a piercing whine.

She bit her lip and turned away from the helpful mechanic. The idea that the riders rode so fast and crashed fairly often must add to the excitement, but to her, it just seemed dangerous. She'd watched a couple of horrific crashes online last night before stopping. It was too scary to think about watching real-time accidents. Every few years, a MotoGP racer died. Had any of them been Isaac's friends?

She shook her head, not wanting to think about crashing as she watched the beginning of FP1. Within seconds, riders streamed past, nice and slow. Isaac and Yoshi joined them. Many of the racers swerved back and forth, weaving the bikes as they worked their way toward the main part of the track. She'd have to ask the reason for that later. She soon lost them from sight around the corner. The bike sounds faded but didn't disappear as they returned in less than two minutes.

Turning to a TV screen in the box that showed the riders as they circled the track, she watched in fascination to see the riders in action. She got caught up in the racing and lap times more than expected. It was suspenseful and mesmerizing to watch the laps as the speed increased. She sucked in her breath several times as riders came close to each other or wobbled at high speed. Once Isaac came half out of his seat, and she found herself clutching her folder so tightly, she had indentations in her hand.

For the first lap or two, each rider rode at a moderate speed, somewhat less than full out. After that, they did what the commentators called flying laps, where they rode faster and had incredible lean angles as they flew around the track, pushing themselves and their bikes to the limit. Her hands grew damp as she waited for someone to crash, but the only rider to fall slid across the track as though in slow motion and walked away unscathed with only dusty, scuffed leathers.

There wasn't much to differentiate most of the riders to her undiscerning eye, except for Vince who pulled her gaze on every lap, as did his young teammate. They had a similar riding style that seemed more off the bike than on, as they clung to the seat and handlebars by some miracle. From what she observed, Vince's abilities were incredible. It was no wonder he was a twelve-time champion. Twice she watched with awe as he saved what should have been sure crashes that seemed to be taken in stride and barely affected his lap times. Those around her seemed unfazed by his near misses—they must be his normal.

With her heart in her mouth, Anna watched the riders in their bright colors whiz by, often too fast for her to follow who they were. She couldn't take her eyes away from the screen. The noise remained constant as the riders staggered themselves into position around the track. She'd have to learn the teams and their numbers to follow them better. She found herself getting into the racing spirit, even if Isaac wasn't on the screen very often. Vince and Luka were on the screen about half the time, because watching them was such an exhilarating show.

She knew little about racing, but the men on bikes were incredible. Motorcycle racing wasn't just daring; it was also athletic. No wonder the riders had to be fit. The idea of asking Isaac to go to the pool with her flashed through her mind. Since Catarina had suggested it, the possibility had stayed with Anna.

Each rider's best lap time appeared on a ranked scoreboard. Vince stayed consistently in the top three, as was the brash Australian she'd met last night. Vince, Austin Spencer, and Luka Catala jockeyed for top position while Isaac hovered between eighth and tenth, sometimes higher briefly before being knocked back to tenth as everyone's times improved lap by lap.

When he returned to the pit after twenty minutes, the crew sprang into action, removing his used tires and replacing them with new ones on his main bike while he sat on a chair and discussed tire selection and the curves with Angel. There were no flirty looks now. He was in a different zone—entirely focused on his job. She was prone to hyper-concentration herself. Perhaps this was what it looked like from the outside.

Everyone in the box let Isaac and Angel talk, keeping busy with their own duties. She had nothing specific to do yet, so she stayed out of the way but drifted closer to follow their discussion. This debrief was another facet she found fascinating.

Isaac stayed in the box for only a couple of minutes before he remounted his bike, once more swerving his way up pit lane and zooming onto the track. Several other riders had come in and gone back out, too. It seemed to be part of the process. Ride. Debrief. Ride more as the countdown from forty-five minutes ticked toward zero.

Next door, another rider arrived, revving his engine much louder than the others. He stopped his bike with a shout and threw something, perhaps a glove, across his box, where it smacked against the thin partition that divided their garages.

Anna's eyes opened wider at the stream of fluid Spanish cursing that erupted from the emotional rider. Translating the gist of his tirade, she learned his bike was crap, the track was dirty, the engine was too slow, his tires were wrong, and he didn't like the brake settings. That was quite the list of problems. She wouldn't have understood, except that he repeated his opinions several times at full volume. It had started in front of his bike and included expansive hand gestures as his rant continued deeper into his box.

His crew remained quiet, perhaps shocked or offended, as they listened. Maybe it was a regular occurrence, though it seemed peculiar behavior. She wanted to peek and get a better look at who was acting this way so she could steer clear.

The boxes on the other side had been quieter. She couldn't hear Yoshi, with whom they shared a garage, or Luka and Vince. She glanced around Isaac's team. Isaac hadn't acted like that when he'd returned, even if he'd suggested adjustments to the bike. Which was normal?

Miguel, the young man with the ponytail, caught her eye and mouthed the name, "Xavi Martinez."

She crossed to crouch beside the mechanic and whispered, "Does he yell like that a lot?" It bothered her that this Xavi would be so abusive to his team. Even hearing that level of frustration made her bite her lip and her breathing raspy. Directed her way, she'd have been triggered. She couldn't imagine Isaac reacting that way if he was unhappy. If so, she didn't want to deal with it.

The young man threw back his head and laughed. "Pretty much always. His team lets him get the emotion all out before they talk to him about their suggestions. It lasts about five minutes, then he calms down. You watch, on race day he'll be totally different. Cool as a cucumber and all business."

Given the volume and length of the outburst, Anna was skeptical. She'd have to see it to believe it.

After an intense forty-five minutes, FP1 ended, and she found herself wound tight from the tension of the practice. Her shoulders ached, so she stretched and unclenched her fists. If she was this swept up from practice, she'd be a wreck on race day. Vince finished second and Isaac tenth. He congratulated the team when he returned to the box to debrief once more with his crew chief, seeming pleased, if she read him right. Isaac seemed easier to read than most people, perhaps because she paid better attention, or maybe he just didn't mask his emotions. From his hand gestures, he and Angel discussed his approach into several of the corners, which he knew by both name and number.

"Anna, can I get your help?" Isaac said once he'd finished. She hopped up from the chair where she'd been sitting, her folder under her arm. He gave her his helmet, and she placed it on a shelf near the TV beside a second one. He handed her his gloves and a tall plastic water bottle, and she followed him out the back through a short maze of winding turns that opened up outside.

"How can I help you? You didn't need me to carry these," she said when they stood behind pit lane in front of a long row of trailers painted with various team colors. She shuffled her feet, not looking at Isaac. Was she supposed to go back inside now? The expectations were unclear, and she didn't want to do something wrong. Plus, without the distraction of the others around, she was very aware of how her body reacted to Isaac's proximity. She felt an insistent attraction being so close, and she didn't want to do something embarrassing.

"I thought you might want a break from the noise," he said, removing his earplugs with a heart-stopping smile. "Or something to eat. Since you ate little at breakfast."

He'd noticed her rush at breakfast? She took out her earplugs and looked around.

She hadn't paid attention until he mentioned it, but it was much quieter here. The first free practice had finished, and another was about to start. Her schedule said the Moto2 bikes would soon have the track.

"This one's mine," said Isaac, indicating a white, blue, and green trailer with a set of steep stairs with a white handrail leading up to a metal door. Now that she was paying attention, his team colors and logo marked the trailer. "You can come here anytime, whether or not I'm here. Even just for a break from the noise." He hesitated and looked down, his boot scuffing the sand from the asphalt. "Want to come in? Do you want a Coke or some water while I get changed? Maybe lunch?"

She nodded, and he turned and climbed the stairs.

She hesitated before following with a smile. It seemed like more than an offer of friendship, something not extended to a regular employee, but there shouldn't be any harm. She liked Isaac and was excited that they could hang out for more than book club discussions. Luckily, there had been nothing in the information packet about rules restricting friendship, or even dating, between team members.

The inside of the trailer had been designed like a camp trailer, with a slim foldaway table opposite a sink and a narrow counter with a row of overhead cupboards. Beyond the sitting area, the back opened into a bedroom with a double bed. He could nap while waiting for the next practice. It must be nice to have a room on wheels, so he didn't have to go back to the hotel to change or rest.

"Help yourself," he said, waving to a small fridge under the counter as he retreated down the hall and closed the bedroom door. He soon returned in his team shirt and shorts, making them a matched set. Anna liked the idea, feeling somehow satisfied that their clothes went together. They had a few hours before the next session, and she hadn't been sure how she would fill her time; read perhaps? Her schedule had said lunch and a three-hour break until the MotoGP riders were once again on the track for FP2.

"Want to watch the Moto3 practice with me after lunch?" Without looking at her, Isaac took a platter with sliced deli meat, chunks of orange, yellow, and white cheese, and chopped vegetables from the fridge. He added two bottles of water and removed two plates from a top cupboard and set them on the table before looking at her. It looked like he wanted her to stay and warmth filled her face.

"Don't I have to report back to Angel?" She wanted to stay, and not just because the array of food looked appetizing, but she didn't want to get in trouble.

Isaac raised his eyebrow. "What does your schedule say?"

Her voice was quiet. "That I'm free until FP2." Butterflies flitted back and forth in her stomach as she met his chocolate-colored eyes. They were a soft brown, more like milk chocolate than dark—friendly compassionate eyes. Isaac had brought enough lunch for two. He'd planned this, and she wanted to stay.

A sliver of guilt stabbed through her. She should probably be writing, but she brushed it aside and sat. Last night, she'd outlined several chapters of the story she planned to write before she'd read. Perhaps there would be time for writing later. If not on the weekend, maybe on the plane or once they returned to Spain between races. It might be harder to write in her downtime than expected. Still, she would try as it was important.

"How do you like motorcycle racing so far? Any questions?" Isaac grabbed several cubes of cheese. He popped one in his mouth while he waited for her answer.

"What's with the swerving in pit lane?" She sat across from him at the skinny table on a cushioned bench. Heat flooded her cheeks because her response had been too abrupt and possibly from left field. She hoped she didn't seem rude.

He allayed her fears when he laughed. "New tires or fresh rubber is slippery. We do that to rough them up before laps. Fewer crashes. What else did you notice?" His tone was warm. Perhaps he was pleased she'd paid attention.

"You seem happy to be in the top ten and Angel mentioned it several times while you were on the track." She reached for a piece of yellow cheese. "Is the top ten significant?"

"They combine our free practice times. The riders with the ten best times have an advantage and go straight to the second qualifying session." He hesitated, perhaps to make sure she was following. "That's Q2 on your schedule late Saturday. Do you know what qualifying is?"

She shook her head. He didn't seem bothered by teaching her, and with something so new, he shouldn't expect her to know this yet. Was he always so patient, or just with her?

Isaac continued his explanation. "Q1 is for all the riders who weren't in the top ten. The two with the best times join the top ten in Q2 to compete for the top twelve positions for the race on Sunday. The fastest rider gets pole position, the position farthest up the grid as an advantage. Second and third also start on the front row, and so on."

Filing away the new information, she'd be better informed for the rest of the weekend. Since arriving at the track, she'd surprised herself by enjoying everything more than she'd expected. If a practice was thrilling, a race would leave her breathless.

"Have you ever had pole position?" The question felt odd on her tongue with the new lingo.

He shook his head with his same calm smile. "Not since Moto2. Vince used to get it all the time. Still does on his favorite tracks, like the Sachsenring in Germany and the Circuit of The Americas in Texas."

She hadn't asked about Vince, but his conversation often looped back to his brother. Of course, he'd started from the front. "So, your practice position determines your race starting position." Interesting.

"Are you sure I'm not boring you with this stuff?" Isaac raised one eyebrow.

It was a sexy look, combined with his wide smile and tousled hair.

"I want to learn about racing so I understand what's happening. Also, so I can be proficient at my job." Thinking of her primary job and what she would have to wear, her smile faded.

His voice was quieter when he said, "What's wrong? Do you regret coming?"

She shook her head. How to explain? She didn't want to cause a problem, but she wasn't sure she could deal with this. All of it was beyond her comfort zone, but she was trying.

"No, I mean it," Isaac said, his voice soothing. "You can tell me. I won't judge or get you in trouble. I might even be able to help."

Tears pricked her eyes, but she didn't let them fall. "I don't think I can wear the tight crop top and miniskirt on the grid." There, she'd blurted the words. "It's even smaller than I imagined." She swallowed, her face burning as she stared out the window instead of meeting his gaze. "I came here as an umbrella girl, and that's the part I'm scared of. Everything else is terrific."

"So, don't wear it. Wear your team clothes, like now. You should have a few sets. It won't bother me." He shrugged and snagged another piece of carrot that crunched loudly in the now quiet trailer. In the distance, the buzzing sounds of bikes on the track became more apparent.

"Won't I get in trouble?" Her voice trailed off as she swallowed. Her throat tightened. She didn't like to do things wrong.

"I bet Catarina has a tip or two that could help dress this up or keep this shirt and wear a longer skirt. As long as you have team colors, you're fine. She might even have one you can borrow." He hesitated. "You'll be beautiful no matter what you wear."

Tears threatened again with the compliment, but she fought them back. It had been a long time since she'd felt noticed. He'd called her beautiful. The happiness those words created washed over her, and her shoulders loosened as he continued.

"I'll be proud to have you on the grid next to me, and it will have nothing to do with what you're wearing. Besides, I've never had my own umbrella girl. You're a big step up from Miguel or my mom. That's who held it most of the time last year."

She looked at his face to determine if he was serious. "Your mom?"

He laughed. "She most certainly didn't wear a crop top, either. Wear what you're comfortable in. Text Catarina right now. Ask. It'll make you feel better, won't it?"

She picked up her phone from the bench beside her.

"My grid outfit is too skimpy. Isaac suggested you might help modify it. Please?" It seemed too formal and stiff, but she hit *Send*.

"Of course," came the instant reply. *"Hanging with Isaac, huh? Good work, girl."*

Anna's face burned again as she put her phone back and looked at Isaac, who sat crunching celery with that raised eyebrow. "She'll help. Thank you." She didn't explain the blush.

"Finished eating?" At her nod, he said, "Ready to watch Moto3? We can stand on the wall and watch for a bit. Then maybe walk on the path outside of the fence so you can see more of the track. The grandstands aren't full tonight, but there's a sizeable crowd up there. By Sunday, the grandstands will be packed." His excitement was infectious.

At her nod, he got up, checking the time. "They should start soon." He held out his hand, and she took it without thinking as they left the trailer. Her skin tingled at the contact in a pleasant way. He didn't release her hand until they climbed the wall that overlooked the home stretch. From there they watched the smaller bikes, most of them ridden by younger riders, as they whizzed around the track, buzzing like a swarm of bees as they moved around the track in clumps, often three or four abreast as they sped into corners. It looked wild.

She took Isaac's hand again, when they headed out around the track. Several times he waved to the spectators in the grandstands, and as they ambled, he talked about his Moto3 days when he was younger— his teammates, his favorite tracks, and the highlights. Through all of it, she couldn't help but think how pleasant it was to walk and talk together.

This friendship, or whatever it was, was progressing rapidly. She smiled and glanced at him from the corner of her eye. Wasn't this why she'd taken this job—at least in part?

CHAPTER 6

Isaac

Vince might be annoyed, but Isaac hadn't been attracted to someone like this in ages. Maybe ever. Anna had asked smart questions at the track and seemed to be observant and a quick study in the box. She was becoming a racing fan in front of his eyes. Warmth filled him. Maybe his love of racing could be something else he could share with a partner. He'd always emulated Vince in keeping racing and dating separate. Perhaps that wasn't necessary. Maybe he needed something different than his brother.

Isaac sat with Anna and Catarina for dinner and when they returned to their rooms, he joined Vince for a movie. They'd watched thousands of movies like this together over the years. It had become something they could do in their downtime on the road when their energy was spent. It took little thought and was comfortable.

This particular action movie didn't hold his interest, though Vince seemed engrossed. Should Isaac bring up the topic of Anna? His brother hadn't said anything about her since the day they'd met, but that didn't mean anything. They were guys. In the end, Isaac said nothing and watched the explosions and action sequences on the screen. If Vince had seen them holding hands, he would have already asked what was going on if he cared. Knowing Vince, he might wait until they were home, or for Isaac to talk to him about Anna on his own. Isaac suppressed a sigh, turning it into a yawn. Eventually, he'd have to talk to his brother.

The next day's practice sessions were similar, and Isaac squeaked into Q2 for the first time in a long time for a dry race. Qualifying had never been his strong suit, but this bike was faster and smoother than anything else he'd ever ridden. He loved how it held speed on corner entry.

Anna helped for all four practices and was much more than just a decorative umbrella girl—more like a general assistant. She helped engineers, mechanics, and Angel as well, making her an extra set of hands, indispensable in a dozen small ways. It was hard to believe she'd never done anything like this before. She always seemed to be in the right place to help, even with the media events and crowds.

Isaac's heart skipped a beat when she came out Sunday evening before the races, wearing a modified team T-shirt with the sleeves removed, a navy-blue skirt that fell to her knees, and white knee-high socks. Instead of stilettos, she wore black loafers. The look suited her. Catarina had outdone herself. They'd assigned Anna to hold the Row 3 sign for both the Moto3 and Moto2 races and his eyes tracked her movements until it was time to focus.

Anna was clearly taking her job seriously and didn't speak to him on the grid, holding his umbrella steady and providing shade. Not that he needed it for a night race, but he didn't complain. Even in racing mode, it was pleasant to have her nearby.

Minutes counted down before the race, and Isaac went into his pre-race routine, inserting his earphones to listen to music and block everything else out. His world shrank as he visualized the track, the twists and turns. With two minutes left, he switched to earplugs and tugged on his helmet for the sighting lap. Returning to the grid, he maintained focus, waiting for the warm-up lap. By the time everyone cleared the grid, his focus had narrowed to getting a fast start.

He sat in ninth position after qualifying; at the bottom of the third row. Both guys ahead on his side of the track were fast starters. He planned to follow them up the outside as they shot toward the front.

Making gains on the first lap and getting away from the grid without a crash would be the real trick, as everyone aimed for the same stretches of free tarmac.

With his eyes riveted on the starting lights, the world moved inward again, and his heart rate skyrocketed. Blood pounded in his ears and sweat dripped down his face inside the helmet. But that was inconsequential. There were only the lights, the track, and his bike.

When the red lights disappeared, his bike shot forward as he stuck to the plan, following Spencer on his Yamaha and Vince's Honda up the far right, going around several riders with more sluggish starts—those who hadn't timed the start to perfection. He slotted himself into fifth by the first corner, getting away with the lead pack.

It was one of those rare days when Isaac became one with his machine, an extension of the bike. Adrenaline pumped through him as he fought for position, to keep what he'd earned. He traded places twice with a Ducati, keeping in front by the smallest of margins, but eventually pulling away through a tight twisting section. The buzz of another bike followed, hot on his rear wheel as they flew down the home stretch. An automatic part of his race, a quick check of his pit board, which flashed at the edge of his vision. Xavi was the rider on his tail.

The laps flashed by and they stretched the field, leaving the main pack behind though the leaders had cleared off in front, running a pace too fast to follow. Though places to overtake remained rare on this track, and Xavi couldn't show him a wheel, the race results remained uncertain. Isaac couldn't afford to deviate from the main racing line where the track became dirty, slippery. The fiery Spaniard must be waiting for Isaac to make a mistake. Isaac gritted his teeth and stuck to the racing line, keeping his race mistake-free.

All of a sudden, ahead of him, Spencer tucked the front of his bike, and slid off the track in a spray of sparks headed for the gravel trap. Isaac avoided the resulting dust cloud and continued, hoping Spencer wasn't injured, though he didn't watch to find out. He'd be the next on the ground if his concentration lapsed.

Only three riders remained in front of him, Luka, Fabiano Perotti—one of the factory Ducati riders, and Vince. Right at the edge of the track, Isaac's pit board read P4, L2. Xavi 0.4. Fourth position, lap 22 of 24—two laps to go. He must have put a bike length between himself and Xavi if the other bike was almost half a second behind. He braced himself. Xavi would have another go before the finish line. Isaac needed to be ready to defend his position with two laps remaining.

The top three were too far to catch, but fourth was a fantastic result if he could keep it. Vince and Luka were so far gone he couldn't see them except in the distance on the home straight as he flew past the teams and the packed grandstands. The teammates wore the same colors and were indistinguishable at this distance. He couldn't tell who was ahead, but he hoped it was Vince. Refocusing, he leaned in perfect synchronicity with his bike as they went into turn one for the last lap.

When Isaac crossed the finish line, he couldn't believe it. He glanced up at the screen to be sure. Vince had won, but Isaac had placed fourth. He pumped his fist skyward. That would show the doubters.

He waved to the boisterous crowd, his heart slowing as he did a cool-down lap, waving to the Vasquez fan club grandstands, then headed for pit lane. He received an electronic message from the officials on his dash, *'Top Independent. Go to parc ferme.'* Fourth. His best race result in three years. Pulling up in parc ferme, where the victors were parked, he threw himself off his bike and hugged his brother.

"Great race." With pride oozing through his pores, Isaac squeezed.

Vince pounded Isaac's back as he said, "Great job yourself, little brother. Nice to have you here with me. Dad would have been so proud."

It was true. There hadn't been many post-race celebrations of this kind, with them both in the winner's area. They posed for photos, first with Luka and Fabiano, then just the brothers. When Vince released him, Isaac turned to Angel, standing by the fence. The older man grabbed him by the back of the neck and tugged him closer.

"Terrific race, Isaac. Fantastic focus." He released Isaac but leaned in to speak in his ear. "I brought your good luck charm down here to celebrate." The older man nudged Anna toward the barrier of parc ferme.

Her eyes glowed and her grin stretched across her entire face. His heart filled that someone could be this happy for him. He wanted to kiss her, though he didn't want to scare her with his enthusiasm, nor did he want their first kiss to be so public. Instead, he vaulted the flimsy barrier and caught her up in a hug. For an instant, he was worried he'd overstepped her boundaries as her body stiffened in his arms.

Then, she threw her arms around his neck, "You were fantastic. Congratulations. That was the most fun I've ever had."

He lifted her from her feet and spun her around in a circle, giving her a squeeze before putting her down. He wrested his gaze from her full lips. Not yet. Instead, he said, "Let's go cheer for Vince at the podium."

Isaac looked over to the camera crews. They didn't care about him anymore, but the top three were giving TV interviews. Then there would be trophy presentations and another set of autographs, at least for the winners. Taking Anna's hand, they followed Angel to join the rest of the team in the area on the track below where the podium presentation and celebrations would be. Everyone spilled out of the boxes, the track becoming crowded with Honda crew—three of the top four riders today had ridden Hondas. He kept ahold of Anna's hand, making sure not to lose her in the crowd.

If his brother had noticed his marked preference for Anna's company before today, he hadn't mentioned it. He might have seen them holding hands again, so Isaac would bring it up tonight. Tomorrow at the latest—before they arrived home. He couldn't bear the idea that he might create bad blood between them for stealing the girl Vince had claimed, though there'd been no sign that Vince was still interested in her by the time they'd flown to Qatar.

Isaac watched Anna as the Spanish anthem played and his pride swelled. Her small hand seemed the perfect fit for his. His fingers laced together with hers seemed right, satisfying.

After their duties and the crush of celebration with the crew, Isaac's head swam from drinking champagne. He hadn't overdone it, but the bubbles had gone straight to his head, and his skin tingled all over. Anna had been quiet but nearby. The room narrowed once more to a single focus, the way it had during the race, but this time, to the beautiful woman at his side. It was almost time to make his move.

"When's the bus back to the hotel arriving?" he asked Angel.

"The boys are getting ready right now," the older man said. "You want to say a few words now, so they won't be looking for you later?" Angel was no dummy.

Isaac grabbed another glass of champagne from the table and raised it in the air, and Angel banged a wrench against a metal table to get everyone's attention.

When they'd turned to Isaac, he said, "A toast to my fabulous pit crew." Cheers erupted. "Thanks for finding the perfect set-up this week. This was my best race in years, and I couldn't have done it without all of you." They cheered. He took one sip and put the glass back down. He didn't want to lose what clarity remained.

"Ready to talk about the book," he whispered to Anna on the bus ride back to the hotel. He hadn't relinquished his hold on her hand and didn't want to. His thumb traced the back of her hand as if getting her used to the feel of him.

"You want to talk about the book tonight?" Her eyebrows arched.

"I'm not ready to say goodnight," Isaac half-whispered. "I want an excuse to see you to your room." His fair skin flushed with warmth. It might be the alcohol or residual heat from the exertion of his race. Or it could be from being near her all night. She rested her cool fingers against his lips, and his skin broke out in goosebumps. Did she know how desperately he wanted to kiss her?

"You can make sure I get to the right place." The sweet candy scent of her seemed intoxicating. He couldn't wait much longer for a taste.

Once the door to her hotel room closed and they were alone at last, the daring feeling subsided. He didn't want to mess this up. "Will you go out for dinner with me later this week in Cervera?" He wanted a plan in place for the future. So, she'd know this wasn't about just tonight—that he wanted more.

Her hand caught his again. "Of course."

He tugged her closer with light pressure on her lower back.

She offered no resistance and looked up at him with trusting eyes.

"Can I kiss you?" He struggled to keep his voice lighthearted and moistened his lips, shuffling one foot. He hadn't been this nervous about the race.

Anna put her arms around his neck and looked him straight in the eye, something she seldom did. "Please."

The one word was all he needed.

His thumb brushed against her jaw and her breath caught, which was nearly his undoing. Her skin was so sensitive. The first touch of his lips to hers was soft, but sure. He'd thought about this for days. She seemed more certain of this than he'd given her credit for as she kissed him back, teasing his lips as the kiss deepened, her tongue darting to meet his. A groan escaped his throat, and she kissed him harder.

He tangled his hand in her soft hair, clasping the back of her head as he tugged her closer. His body seemed electrified from their contact. He had no idea how long they stayed together, but when they stopped, he rested his forehead against hers. He'd never experienced a kiss like this—one that emptied his head and took his breath away.

"I don't want to scare you. But I'm really hoping I can get to know you better." His chest constricted. What if she didn't want something serious?

She rested her palm against his chest, the heat seeping in while his heart thumped. "I'd like that."

"Until tomorrow, then." He swallowed. If he didn't leave her room now, he would try to stay all night. It might be fantastic, but he wanted to be the kind of guy that got to know someone first. He didn't want her to think this was purely physical and that he just wanted to get her into bed. He wanted to be the kind of man who had a relationship.

"Tuesday?" she said, lifting her eyes to meet his gaze.

"Tuesday is perfect." Monday they'd travel home. Date on Tuesday. Unable to resist, he cupped her face between his hands. She quivered, and he kissed her again. Long and slow, enjoying her lips, showing her he considered her precious. He pressed his lips to her forehead as he wrenched himself away. "Goodnight, Anna."

"Goodnight, Isaac." With messy hair and swollen lips, she was stunning.

He walked out, unable to wipe away the grin that stretched across his face. He still knew nothing about her past, but he wanted to take the time to find out everything.

•   •   •

Isaac fidgeted in his seat next to Vince on the plane, his palms sticky. They were due to land in Barcelona in less than an hour. He'd waited until they were almost home before saying something.

He drank some of his ice water before turning down the volume on Vince's TV and breaking the silence. "Anna and I spent a lot of time together this weekend."

"I noticed." Vince didn't look away from the superhero movie he was watching. "I take it she still isn't interested in going on a date with me."

Isaac shook his head. Swallowing. It really shouldn't be this difficult. "We're going out for dinner on Tuesday. A date."

Vince turned, his face expressionless. "I was wondering if you were going to tell me what was going on."

"I really like her." Isaac kept his voice steady. No pleading.

"She might be a distraction." Vince's voice was flat. "You know that, though." He paused, then shrugged. "Lots of other fish out there for me."

His brother wouldn't put up with a distraction of that kind, but Isaac didn't care. He'd been plenty focused on race day. "This is probably my last year in MotoGP. I have to look out for what comes after."

Vince nodded. "That makes sense." His eyes flicked back to the screen. They seldom talked about life after racing or settling down, but since their dad had passed, Isaac got the impression that Vince was determined to race for as long as possible. Another championship would ensure a contract extension. Isaac's life might look drastically different without racing, but he wanted to figure out what it could be. For Vince, the idea was unfathomable. Racing was still everything.

"You aren't surprised?" The conversation didn't seem done.

"It surprised me you volunteered to walk her to the Inn that first day. And you started a book club. In English. Now, I'm just surprised it took you so long to ask her out." Vince nudged his shoulder. "She seems more your type than mine, anyway."

Isaac shook his head. "Thanks." He didn't need permission or Vince's blessing, but it didn't hurt.

Vince waggled his eyebrows. "You think the red-headed flight attendant is staying over in Barcelona? She mentioned her shift's over when we land. You might need to arrange your own ride home."

CHAPTER 7

Anna

Anna dropped to a walk gasping for oxygen, sweat dripping down her face and soaking into her running clothes. She kept striding along the quiet roadside, her arms swinging at her sides. As part of making her life healthier, she wanted to be in better shape, but this was her first workout since she'd left Seattle. Being outside might make exercise more enticing. Back there, her cardio had been on the exercise bikes at the gym, not in the countryside. This was preferable.

She surveyed the green landscape, admiring the beauty of the hills. Catarina had dropped her off out here and said to follow the road back into town. No way to get lost. Anna had asked for a five-mile route, and she wasn't far from Cervera now. Perhaps the distance had been a little ambitious, but exercise often helped clear her mind.

Dinner with Isaac two nights ago had been pleasant. She reminisced as she ran. They ate baked chicken, roasted vegetables, and shared a chocolate dessert. Their hands gravitated across the small table, toward each other at every opportunity, his touch sending a current buzzing through her.

Over dinner, they dissected the gangster book in detail. He'd noticed interesting things about the story, and she'd shared what she'd liked about the writing. He looked at her with interest when she said she'd outlined several chapters of her own story, and he offered to read it when she was ready—her first potential reader. The idea made her slightly nauseous, but if she was going to be a writer, shouldn't she get used to the idea of someone reading her words?

Anna had started a dozen stories over the years, but hadn't finished a book-length manuscript before, always convincing herself that what she'd written wasn't good enough. This time would be different. She had an idea for a twisted fairytale that had promise, and she wouldn't let her insecurities get in the way. She'd noticed several fairytale retellings on the market, but none like hers. Her idea was unique.

After dinner, Anna and Isaac walked hand-in-hand through the nighttime streets of Cervera, where he'd shared stories about growing up there and some of the crazy things he and his brother had done when they were younger. She got the sense that he was trying to help her get to know him and put her at ease—and it was working. The kiss in the hotel room had promised more, and she felt ready.

She hadn't told Isaac much about her life, though she mentioned that she'd left her job in marketing. She still didn't want to talk about Sandra and her betrayal. What was more important was that she'd never liked her job and needed something different. She told him about her dream of making a living someday as a writer. Adam's name hadn't come up. She wasn't avoiding the subject. He just wasn't relevant anymore. Not really. Though, perhaps at some point, it would be proper to share how they'd broken up. Everything back in the States already seemed like a distant lifetime.

She quickened her pace. She and Isaac had plans again tonight. He was coming down to the village for a walk and they'd find some place interesting for dinner. He'd probably been everywhere before, but they could still see what they found together. She pictured Isaac escorting her back to her room afterward. That's what she needed to do with all this extra energy.

She'd mentioned the date to Catarina earlier, and her friend had said, "Wear your fancy new underwear."

Anna had flushed but intended to heed her friend's advice. She hadn't been able to get sex off her mind since. If everything went how she expected, she'd ask him to come inside. A thrill raced through her.

She'd been tempted last time but had hesitated for a second. He'd been a gentleman and said goodnight. If she'd judged the look in his eyes correctly, when she asked, he wouldn't refuse to come back to her hotel. Butterflies danced through her stomach.

Anna's concern was that she'd never been the biggest fan of sex. Every time, it had been underwhelming. She'd memorized the number of dots per ceiling tile in Adam's old apartment and the bumps on her bedroom ceiling in the townhouse. If their chemistry when they kissed was any indication, she and Isaac together could be incredible. She took a deep breath and broke into a run once more. A final push to get back to the village.

She'd have to hurry to shower and let her hair dry before Isaac arrived. The nagging feeling that she should talk to him about Adam, her parents, or her neurodivergence almost made her change her mind about sex. Shouldn't he know everything important about her first? Isaac was curious about her past, but talking about much of it was still too raw. Maybe soon. She ran faster, once more emptying her mind of unwanted thoughts.

•　　•　　•

Just before seven, Isaac rapped on the door of her room. Anna jumped up from her bed where she'd been sitting. She'd been ready for fifteen minutes, and the seconds had ticked by so slowly. When she opened the door, he grinned and gathered her up in a hug. She liked that he was so affectionate, even if she typically didn't like to be touched. He was the exception. His firm body wrapped around her in a way that didn't seem invasive but protective.

"I'm four minutes early," he said in her ear. "I hope that's alright." He set her down. "I couldn't wait any longer." Smile lines creased the sides of his eyes.

Every time she saw him, she found another piece of him to like. She grabbed her phone and tucked it into her purse. "I'm ready. Where to tonight?"

He jammed his hands into his pockets. "I have a suggestion. Feel free to say no."

She raised an eyebrow, mirroring his favorite questioning expression.

"I want to cook for you, back at the house." He looked so earnest.

She bit her lip. That wasn't the original plan. "Will Vince be with us?"

"Vince is out. He left this morning and said he won't be back until Monday. He was all mysterious about where he was going." Isaac caught her fingers. "We don't need to worry about him for days."

Heat worked its way up her body and face. He wanted time alone with her, too. "What are you making for dinner?" She shut her door, checked that it was locked, and took his hand.

"Secret family recipe." He grinned and hauled her down the hall at a fast walk, his eagerness reminding her of a teenager. "I even brought the car tonight."

"That was kind of you," she said, letting him pull her into a run as they bounded down the stairs and trotted through the lobby. "Slow down. I already ran today, and I'm not dressed for a run up the hill to your place." She chuckled to take the harshness out of her words. She waved to Lola, Catarina's younger sister, at the front desk on the way out.

He whisked her outside to his small navy-blue sports car parked just down the narrow street. Of course, he drove something fast. He held the door, and she slid in with a smile. Nobody else had made her feel special the way he did with small things, like opening her door. It was old-fashioned and sweet. The ride up the hills to the home he shared with Vince was over before she had time to become nervous.

Isaac parked in a separate garage near the house with several covered motorbikes on one side, four road bikes, and three more cars.

Seeing her interest, he said, "Mostly Vince's collection."

They walked between the back of the house and the garage, where she glanced over her shoulder at the muted sunset spreading across the west, staining the sky in bands of soft shades of pink and orange like something from a romantic movie.

"Can I help make dinner?" She didn't particularly like cooking, but she also didn't want to be bored while he was occupied. Plus, she wanted to be near him.

"You can chop and keep me company," he said, shooting her a sideways glance as they entered the kitchen. "The rest is underway." Getting a cutting board, he pointed her toward the knives as he set a selection of vegetables in front of her. "I'm making my mom's recipe for garlic chicken. I just have to put it in the clay baker and bake it. It's been marinating for a couple of hours."

"What would you have done if I'd said no to dinner?" She couldn't resist.

"Eat it tomorrow. Did you want to say no?" He gave her another sidelong glance, his eyes twinkling.

She shook her head. He was fun to tease. "No. I enjoy being here with you. Maybe this time you can give me a tour of the house." She returned his sidelong glance as she chopped the tomato into wedge-like sections. The fluttering in her stomach started again. She wanted another kiss, one that would make her lips sizzle and set her ablaze.

"Give me ten minutes to get this in the oven while you make the salad. Then I'll show you around." His smile seemed brighter than the sun. He seemed so relaxed and at home in the kitchen, his motions fluid and his face happy. He must like to cook, which was handy, because while she was a functional cook, she preferred to eat.

With the chicken in the oven and the salad on the island in a large wooden bowl, Isaac led her through the house, her fingers tingling from their contact. While there were some things that were a given for bachelors living on their own—like a massive TV hooked up to a gaming system—there were other unexpected things, like beautiful art on the walls. The house was light and airy and open with lots of large windows which looked out on the gorgeous Spanish countryside. They'd painted the walls in gentle colors, while the furniture and art provided splashes of vibrancy.

"Did Vince decorate the house himself? Or did he hire someone?" she said as they left a sunken living room with comfortable blue chairs. This would be the perfect place to curl up with a book on a rainy afternoon.

"We did it together. Do you like it?"

She nodded. "I let someone else decorate my townhouse, and I hated it. I just didn't have the guts to tell him. Being in the living room hurt my eyes, so I pretended not to see the jarring colors, but being there put me on edge." She braced herself for Isaac's questions, but he didn't push. Good, she didn't want to talk about Adam.

"If you hate my room, you'll have to tell me. I'll change it." He squeezed her hand.

Warmth suffused her. He would do that for her? He led her upstairs to a long hall. "Vince's rooms are that way." He pointed toward the wing of the house overlooking the dirt bike track. He tugged. "Mine are over here." He hesitated and opened a door on the left, and she walked through. He stood in the doorway behind her, perhaps waiting for her reaction.

The suite contained a sitting area, a small office with a wooden desk, and a bathroom with a double shower and a soaker tub. His king-size bed fit in the spacious room done in cream and varying shades of pale blue and green. The colors reminded her of Isaac, soothing and calm.

An enlarged and framed photograph of Isaac and Vince from several years ago hung on one sidewall. They wore championship T-shirts that read 2019.

Seeing her interest, Isaac came up behind her, close enough that his heat radiated onto her. "That was the year I won the Moto2 Championship, and Vince won his sixth MotoGP title."

"Look how young you were," she said without thinking. He made her comfortable enough that she forgot to be on guard and blurted out the first words that came to mind. Would he become defensive, like Adam would have if she'd mentioned his age?

Isaac swung her around, his hand resting on her lower back. The room suddenly grew warmer. "So, I look old now?" The corners of his eyes crinkled.

She laughed. "Older. But it suits you."

"You know what else suits me?" He didn't wait for an answer as he cupped her face in his firm hands. "You do," he whispered before he kissed her. His words, as much as the touch, made her shiver.

When they came up for air, she had to fight to make her words coherent. "What about dinner?"

"The oven's on a timer. I'm not a fool. I knew I couldn't bring you up here without getting distracted." This time when he kissed her, she gave herself to the sensation. His hands lit her on fire, and she trembled at his touch. His lips devoured hers, kissing her so thoroughly she ached for more. Her mind emptied, and she lost track of everything except how her body came alive.

She hadn't been aware of moving until, unexpectedly, she bumped against the edge of the bed. He stopped kissing her and waited, perhaps for a sign. She wanted his hands on her skin. She'd thought sex would be later, but now was better because she didn't have time to worry about it through dinner. Sliding one hand inside his untucked shirt, she almost gasped at the heat of his skin and the hard, defined planes of his muscles. He kissed her neck and her collarbone until she whimpered.

"You taste so good," he said, nibbling the side of her neck below her ear, sending shivers coursing through her body.

She arched into him, pressing closer, wanting to feel more of him. When he slipped his hands beneath her shirt, she whispered, "Take it off."

She raised her arms, and he tugged her shirt off, letting it fall onto the floor. His arms wrapped around her bare ribs, and he leaned, so that they tumbled to the bed with her on top. She threw back her head and laughed. His hands were suddenly everywhere, one cupping her butt, the other in her hair, his mouth on her breasts where they spilled out from her lacy bra. The hand on her butt tugged on her thong underwear.

"Fuck, fuck, fuck." The way he cursed sounded like praying.

He tugged her bra down on one side and nuzzled her breast, his tongue leaving wet circles that tingled, before he took her nipple into his mouth and sucked. She cried out as desire unfurled deep inside her, its heat spreading.

This was already the best sex ever, and they'd just gotten started.

Isaac was hard beneath her, and she rubbed against him, wanting to feel all of him. He switched his mouth to the other breast with a groan and touched her in different places, his hands roaming. When she started shaking uncontrollably, he returned his mouth to hers, as if knowing she needed his kisses most of all.

Without pausing, he rolled her over, pinning her beneath his fit body, yanking his shirt over his head, stopping their kiss for only seconds. His lips were swollen, and his eyes were heavy-lidded with desire. Did she look the same? She felt wrecked, and this wasn't anywhere close to over. She needed more.

He unclasped her bra with a quick flick and freed her breasts at last, and he cupped them in his hands, almost worshipful. First one, then the other, the heat sending shivers through her once more. She shrugged the straps aside, and he returned his attention to making love to her, one sensitive piece of skin at a time. When his hands moved lower, it was with purpose. He slid a finger underneath the edge of her underwear, sliding it through her slickness. She gasped.

"You're so wet." His fingers swirled over her most sensitive parts, which were swollen with need. "Do you want me to keep going? Should I make you come?" His voice had a husky quality that was new.

She nodded and sucked in her lower lip, unable to keep her hips still, writhing against his firm touch. She should be embarrassed, but she wasn't. He smiled and kissed her forehead before returning his attention to her pleasure. It didn't take long before her vision darkened at the edges. She closed her eyes and was met by an explosion of sensation while colored lights like fireworks exploded in her mind. Her body shuddered as she came and when she returned to herself, Isaac's finger slowed, but still touched her sensitive core.

She'd never had an orgasm caused by another person, and it left her shaken. This was what all the fuss was about.

His next kiss was gentle. That could be the end of their play. By now she understood he wouldn't push her to do anything she didn't want to, for which she wasn't ready. She slipped her hand between them and caught the waistband of his pants. She unbuttoned the top.

His hand caught hers. "You don't have to." His breathing was ragged.

"I want to," she said, her voice sounding rough. "Take your pants off."

He laughed before giving her a quick hard kiss and rolling off the bed to undress.

She took the opportunity to slide out of her skirt and her sodden underwear, tossing them to the floor near the rest of their clothes. His athlete's body was amazing. He didn't have an extra ounce of fat and was all planes and angles. She scooted farther up the bed and he lay beside her, his warmth touching all along her side. She explored him with her fingers while once more they kissed, this time slow and sweet, leaving her just as turned on as before.

When her hand reached for his cock, the first touch was tentative, but she liked the sound he made deep in his throat when she slid her hand along, up and back down. It gave her confidence, so she did it again, and then slid down, kissing his solid chest and his abs, all the way down.

"Do you know what you do to me?" he groaned, one hand resting on the back of her head. He didn't exert pressure; it was about connection.

"I have some idea," she said, taking a firm hold and taking him into her mouth. She stroked him deep into her throat, in and out, making him cry out each time. He was hard like steel and smooth like silk. Another rush of heat shot through her. She'd never ached for someone to be inside her so badly—it had become a need, not a want. Still, she continued to stroke and suck, but with her other hand, she touched herself. She was still wet.

"Isaac, do you…?" Her voice trailed off as he rolled away and reached into the drawer beside his bed.

"Condom. Now." He reached for the box and removed a packet, ripping it with his teeth. With shaking hands, he unrolled one onto his length while she watched, unable to look away.

Lying beside her, he kissed her again, his mouth relaxing her like magic. When he rolled on top of her, he looked her in the eyes and smiled as he slid inside her. She gasped at the pressure and thrust her hips against him to take more, stretching to fit all of him. She'd never been this in tune, this close to anyone.

It should have been awkward. It was their first time having sex with each other, and they shouldn't know how each other's bodies fit, but somehow, it was instinct—everything worked. They moved together. Slow at first, then faster and deeper, each thrust bringing them closer to bliss. The world faded again, leaving Anna with the feeling of being cherished, her body worshipped. Sparks flickered against her closed eyes, and she cried out.

"Oh yes, come for me." Isaac's voice was raspy. He, too, must be on the brink.

She shivered all over, her body obeying his words, heat flooding through her. Seconds later, he cried out and came too, thrusting into her with abandon as they rode their climaxes together.

A minute or two later, when she'd caught her breath, she said, "The tour was excellent." Isaac rolled away with a laugh.

"You don't think you're funny." He stroked the hair from her face. "But I like your humor. You're fun to be around."

"My brain's a little different." Her voice tightened. How would he react to being told she was on the spectrum?

"That's what I like about you." He caressed the flare of her hip. "Your skin is like silk." He kissed her again, this time soft and slow. "You aren't like anyone else I know."

"I have a diagnosis for that," she said. "Autism spectrum disorder. ASD, for short." With her guard down, she blurted the first thing on her mind. She tried not to cry as she waited for his reaction, her chest aching. What if telling him brought this relationship crashing to a premature end? She didn't think Isaac would be like that, but it was always a fear.

"Big words that just mean you're smart, unexpected, and forthright," he said. "If you want to talk about it, I'm happy to listen, but it changes nothing. Even if we only met two weeks ago, I've never been more interested in anyone. I haven't dated a lot because too many women I've met are superficial or phony. I love that you're an open book and that this..." he motioned between them, "is easy and comfortable."

It was true. She and Isaac had a connection that went beyond the physical, and it wasn't hard work. She smiled. Isaac felt it too. Perhaps they'd been meant to find each other at this exact time in their lives.

Though Anna had never wanted to talk to anyone else about it, over dinner she told him about struggling to fit in, her distress in social situations, and what could happen sometimes when she was overwhelmed. How would he react to a meltdown? They were no longer common, but they happened.

He listened without speaking, waiting until she finished, then he kissed her again. "Promise me that if you're overwhelmed, you'll tell me. I'll do what I can to help, even if it's just to find you somewhere quiet to recuperate." His warm eyes met hers and his unexpected offer snapped another piece of their puzzle together.

He didn't seem bothered by anything. How had she gotten so lucky?

CHAPTER 8

Isaac

Anna's revelation about her diagnosis didn't faze Isaac as he lay in bed later that night, Anna sleeping next to him. Nor had it been much of a surprise. He looked over to where she slept. She'd rolled onto her side, and he rested his hand on her hip, liking the feel of her naked in his bed. He could get used to this.

His best friend growing up had been on the spectrum, and some of Anna's quirks were similar. It didn't bother him. She liked to know plans and follow a routine, though tonight, she'd shown she could also be spontaneous. Looking forward to tomorrow, he drifted off to sleep.

•   •   •

Golden sunlight streamed through the seams of the blinds when Isaac woke with a smile to find Anna sitting up and reading his copy of one of their books from his bedside table. Seeing his eyes open, she marked her place with her finger and closed the book.

"Will you please drive me back into the village this morning? I hadn't planned to spend the night," she said. "And I have nothing clean to wear today."

He'd found her a spare new toothbrush last night, but she needed clothes–among other things—if he was going to enact his plan. He hoped to convince her to stay another couple of days while Vince was away. Now that she was here, he didn't want her to leave because he didn't know when they'd have the house to themselves again. He relished the peace and beauty of Cervera and wanted to share that with her. Maybe he could help her fall in love with Spain enough to stay longer than the MotoGP season.

"I can run you down to the Inn after breakfast," he said, his words coming out slowly. He rested his hand on her arm, feeling her warmth. "If you like, you could pack a bag and stay here for the weekend while Vince is away." He held still and let her process his suggestion.

She chewed on her lip, hesitating. "I won't be in the way?"

He sat up next to her. "Never. We could spend the weekend together. I can take you for a ride on one of the old dirt bikes with a double seat. I have a spare helmet you can use."

"What about your training?" She didn't quite meet his eyes as she fidgeted with the edge of the sheet, running her finger along the piping near the top.

He didn't want to come across as desperate. If she didn't want to stay, that was one thing, but they'd had a wonderful time so far, and he was reluctant for it to end so soon. "We'll bring your laptop. When I train, you can write. That way, we can hang out together later. Maybe watch a movie?" A faint pleading note crept into his voice. He'd have to be careful. He didn't want to pressure her into anything she didn't want. He had a suspicion that had happened to her in the past.

"I'm not imposing? You want me to stay?" At last, she met his gaze.

"I do." He kissed her softly. "I can't bear to give you up yet. This way, we'll only have a couple of nights apart before we leave for Indonesia."

"I'll stay," she said, her eyes narrowing. "On one condition."

"Anything." A grin tugged at the corner of his mouth.

"If you change your mind, or tire of me being here, you tell me." She seemed so serious.

"Anna, mi corazon, I won't get tired of you in three days or three hundred. I promise." He infused all his sincerity into his words. He would help her understand her value.

"I mean it." She bit her lip again. "I've been told I'm high maintenance."

"Whoever told you that is an idiot," he said, "But, if it makes you feel better, I agree to your condition. Plus, if you change your mind at any time, I promise to drive you back to Cervera whenever you want."

Her dimple reappeared, and her smile lit up the room. "Then, I'd love to stay."

After breakfast and a quick trip into Cervera, Isaac got out the dirt bike and helmets as promised and took Anna for a quiet ride on the mountain road above them and into the neighbor's fields. There were no animals there to disturb right now, and the neighbor had given them permission to ride on his property. At first, Anna clutched him tight around the middle, but she soon relaxed and seemed to enjoy herself. It filled him with warmth that she enjoyed spending time doing something that was such a major part of his life.

Everything about their weekend together went like that and was full of firsts. The first time they made pancakes together. The first time they showered together. Their first movie. Everything about the weekend felt magical.

The best part was they filled the days with everyday things and having Anna with him made them better. He didn't have to invent things for them to do—they just happened naturally. Isaac hadn't realized how lonely he'd been until Anna changed it, giving his life a zest it had been missing for a long time.

Isaac trained extra hard on his runs, the road bike and the dirt bike, just knowing when he finished, he'd get to spend more time with Anna. They went running on Friday and Sunday. They ran the first kilometer together while they warmed up, and then she waved him forward. When he got home, she'd showered and was relaxing on the patio with her notes. The rest of the time when he trained on his dirt bike, she wrote. She hadn't let him see what she'd written yet, but said she was making progress.

She'd write for an hour or two, print the pages in his room, edit, type her revisions, then print again. The next day, she'd revise and then add on with new writing. She said that writing her way into a scene kept up her momentum. He glanced over to where she was blushing as she typed. He'd bet there were naughty scenes in her book and was intrigued to read her manuscript once it was ready. He'd never heard of the story she was using as an inspiration, *The Twelve Dancing Princesses*. A twisted fairytale wasn't his typical kind of story, but the idea of seeing what occurred in her mind was fascinating.

Sunday after dinner, Isaac drove her back to the Inn an hour before Vince was due to return. His brother would be tired, and he didn't want Anna to feel as if she was underfoot. He and Anna had already made plans to have dinner on Tuesday and about what they could do together in their downtime in Indonesia next weekend. There were a couple of places he wanted to share, as she'd never traveled to that part of the world.

That night, his room felt emptier than ever. He missed her scent, her feel, and he wanted to talk to her. They'd spent the last four days together, but it wasn't enough. Grabbing his phone, he texted her his opinion about the intro to the book she'd chosen. He smiled when she texted back right away. They traded messages as they dissected the first couple of chapters. When at last he was too tired to keep his eyes open, he drifted off to sleep still on an Anna high.

•　　•　　•

In Indonesia, Anna met him at the hotel pool for a couple of hours between practice sessions on Friday. The warm water and the leafy palm trees surrounding the deck seemed exotic enough that it was like they were on a vacation for something other than work. He hadn't always found time for leisure and racing, but instead of making him stressed, he found it was the opposite. He excelled at compartmentalizing time on and off the track and was more relaxed before riding because of his fun downtime.

Vince swam lengths of the pool while Isaac and Anna floated and swam circles around each other, making each other laugh. Once, unable to resist, he wrapped himself around her and kissed her in the shade. Her enthusiastic response made his heart race. It didn't matter that others might see—his happiness bubbled out of him when they were together.

At the end of the day, Isaac and Vince sat with Anna and Catarina at dinner. Isaac filched fries off Anna's plate, and, in return, she stole a few bites of his spicy chicken. Vince was quiet and as soon as he'd eaten, he left. Isaac and Anna stayed with Catarina and told stories about growing up. Anna shared nothing about her parents, just that her grandmother had raised her. The rest remained a mystery.

Where had her parents gone? Had they died? It had been her grandmother who'd helped her cope with her autism and to navigate the resulting social difficulties. His own childhood had been filled with vacations to other countries and motorcycle racing from a young age, but his parents had been a major influence.

Early Saturday morning, Isaac accompanied Catarina and Anna to a nearby beach for an hour for a walk before heading to the track for FP3. He couldn't think of a time he'd been so relaxed. This was how life should be.

His results for the first three free practice sessions on the Pertamina Mandalika circuit were better than expected. Isaac marveled at his new bike, pleased at the consistency with which he could set fast lap times. He found himself slotted into the top ten, once more going straight to Q2.

Before the afternoon session and qualifying, Vince strode past Isaac's box and motioned him out the back with a toss of his head. What did he want?

Isaac followed. His brother's request was surprising this close to the next session on the track. They climbed the stairs and entered Vince's trailer.

"Everything okay?" said Isaac, looking around the trailer that matched his own.

"Are you tired?" said Vince. "I'm worried about you."

"Tired? Not especially. Why? I've never felt better." Isaac's forehead bunched, feeling tense. It wasn't typical of Vince to ask about his well-being. Where was he going with this line of questioning?

"I'm concerned because Anna monopolizes your time," said his brother, his dark eyes intense as always.

"We've spent a lot of time together," said Isaac, choosing his words with care, "But it's not unwanted. If anything, I'm monopolizing her time."

"You're sure?" said Vince, his dark eyes riveted on Isaac.

"Yeah. We like hanging out. I'm good," said Isaac, a little puzzled by Vince's concern. Sure, he and Anna stayed up late some nights, but they couldn't seem to leave each other alone. The sex continued to be fantastic. Vince should understand that part, even if the relationship part was foreign territory.

"I just mean, women out here on the road are a distraction. She could affect your racing."

"I won't let her have a negative impact. In fact, I'm racing better than ever," said Isaac, getting annoyed with the discussion. Since when did he discuss his love life with his brother? It was none of Vince's business what he did with his time.

"I also wouldn't want you to get too attached. After all, she could be gone anytime," said Vince. "This is seasonal work."

That had better not be a threat. Vince had gotten her hired. Would he have her fired? Instead of saying that, Isaac said, "You don't have to worry about me." He didn't want to argue and kept the edge from his voice. The sooner they changed the subject, the better. He rotated his head, his neck cracking. Vince chose not to have a special person in his life and had always preached about the single life, but for the first time, Isaac felt a pang of sympathy for his brother. Vince had let no one get close to him, and until now, neither had Isaac.

"Of course, I worry. You're my brother." Vince grabbed an energy drink from the fridge and held one up for Isaac, who shook his head. Vince drank half in a few long gulps. Setting down the can, he said, "Hey, I noticed you've been taking a slightly wider line into turn six this season, like I suggested. How's that feel on the bike? Last year, that helped me get an exceptional drive out of that corner as well as turn ten."

The abrupt change of subject back to a more typical conversation lifted the tension that had settled like unwanted fog in the confined space. Isaac struggled to let it go, but they soon fell back into their comfortable conversation area. Racing. They compared notes on a couple more corners before Isaac left to change for FP4 and Q2.

On the track, he fell into a rhythm, trying out his chosen tire selection for the race tomorrow, letting the tires get worn, and testing their responsiveness. Overall, he was pleased with the result. Returning to the box, he took on fluids and stayed in the zone, putting on his headphones to block out the bustle around him and to remain focused.

Before he knew it, it was time for qualifying, and he removed his headphones and switched to earplugs. Anna handed him his helmet, which he took with a small smile. They weren't fooling anyone who didn't know about their new relationship status, but in the garage, they'd kept everything professional. She could have been any other team member. They'd keep it that way in public until after the race tomorrow. No matter the race result, he resolved to kiss her in front of everyone afterward.

His brother wasn't an expert on romance. Isaac was determined to do this his way. Vince be damned.

CHAPTER 9

Anna

Anna clutched the umbrella with both hands, her arms shaking slightly with the effort to keep it steady. The Indonesia sky had become ominous, grayer than the forecasted sunshine had indicated. She tore her gaze from the worrisome sight and stood to the side, smiling for all she was worth. The roaming TV cameras weren't for her, and she didn't change her gaze for them. She didn't interrupt Isaac or attempt to speak to him while he was in race mode. Several riders on the starting grid had similar pre-race routines, while a couple of others talked and joked with people around them.

Four separate camera crews wandered between the riders, perhaps looking for someone to interview as they conducted their pre-race shows. Celebrities with special passes moved through the crowd, often stopping to chat with each other. She spotted Keanu Reeves in a ball cap and sunglasses.

Vince ignored all reporters, and none of them tried speaking to Isaac, at least not that he noticed. Twice she shook her head and signaled that they should move on rather than disturb him. They had better luck at the back of the grid with some of the newer riders. As the clock wound down, the cameras moved off to the side and out of the way. When there was one minute left on the timer, everyone except the riders left the grid.

Visors came down, and the riders got ready for their warm-up lap. Even as she left, her focus remained on Isaac. How would he do today?

This week, he'd qualified seventh and now sat on the third row. Yesterday after the fast-paced qualifying session, as soon as he'd finished debriefing with Angel, he'd hauled her back to his trailer. They'd had sex. Not the patient, slow kind they'd had until now, but fast and urgent. It had left her trembling with aftershocks from the intense orgasms. They hadn't even made it to the bedroom. Qualifying had lit a fire within him. Her stomach fluttered. Would the race do the same?

Those that had cleared the grid joined the rest of the team in the box, huddling around the largest screen to watch the race. Anna sucked in her breath when the riders returned to the grid after their single lap, everyone tense and focused. This was it. Miguel squeezed her forearm, anticipating the start. She shot him a nervous smile.

The green and red flags waved, then left the track.

As a collective group, the team held their breath, leaving the garage silent and filled with pent-up nervous energy. Nobody wanted to miss this. Starting lights showed at the top of the screen, then blinked out, and the riders shot forward. She didn't care about the other riders. She concentrated on following Isaac's movement, tracking how his bike leaped ahead of the others on his row.

Vince got the holeshot, which she'd learned meant going around the first corner in the lead, but more importantly, Isaac had gotten a clean start, shooting up the inside of the track. He slotted into third as the initial positions settled into the race and the riders flowed through the first half of the lap, while the crowd cheered.

Anna couldn't take her eyes off the TV. Conversation and movement resumed around her, though everyone watched while they worked. Those responsible for Isaac's pit board communication checked their headsets, got the portable sign ready, and headed for the wall, ready to keep him updated about his track position. Isaac had mentioned that it was easy to lose track of how many laps remained and how many riders had passed—the pit board helped. Several of the more experienced crew kept tabs on the weather and the circling dark clouds.

"Get the second bike ready with rain tires," said Angel in Spanish. He looked at Anna when her head swiveled with a jolt, on slight delay as she translated. "Just in case, mi carino. Don't worry, our Isaac is tremendous in rainy conditions." His tone was reassuring.

In the background, the noise of the power tools whined as the crew jumped to follow Angel's directions.

She'd been told about Isaac and the rain before by Catarina, so she sent a quick text to her in the garage next door. *"Rain makes it even more dangerous, doesn't it?"* Her lip trembled as she sent her message.

"Isaac is good at this. Trust him. He's killing it out there, btw." Catarina's text eased Anna's tension a little. He had experience and was a world-class racer. His team was full of experts. A little rain wouldn't be a problem. Probably.

Lap after lap, the riders circled the track. Swapping positions and making daring passes left Anna breathless with fear and excitement. She loved knowing who the other riders were, not that she could identify them all with their helmets off, but she'd learned the teams, their names, and their numbers. Vince had run away with the race, and so far, the rain had held off, though the wind had picked up and the air temperature dropped. Now that she was off the grid, she wore a blue team jacket with Isaac's name on the back. Still, she shivered.

With three laps left, Isaac remained in third. Anna glanced at the menacing clouds as drops of rain appeared in pit lane and spotted the camera lens tracking the riders on the course. She clutched her pencil so tightly it hurt her hand, hoping for no more rain.

Several riders behind Isaac slowed their pace, widening the gap between the front three and everyone else. Sections of the track darkened as the rain intensified. White and red flags waved on the course, which Marcus Birch, the British commentator whose feed matched the screen, declared rain flags. But the riders continued.

"What does this mean?" She turned to the surrounding team, hoping someone would explain. Before they got a chance, a KTM rider mid-pack suddenly swerved on the wet track, bouncing out of his seat as his bike skidded sideways and then cartwheeled across the ground, spraying chunks of metal and plastic left and right. The luckless rider flew through the air, landing hard on his shoulder, but somehow missed being hit by his careening bike. She gasped involuntarily as the rider lay crumpled on the ground for several seconds. Two additional bikes detoured off the track to avoid the accident.

"It's a flag-to-flag," said Miguel, answering her question, his attention still on the fallen rider who pushed himself to his feet as race marshals in their bright orange vests sped toward him.

Miguel's explanation didn't help. She still had a lot to learn about racing.

The image on the screen flashed back to Vince at the front, his head tucked in, still lapping faster than everyone else, throwing his bike through the corners with abandon. A man possessed to finish before the rain descended in earnest. The camera panned back to the group of riders jostling for fourth through eighth. Where was Isaac? Her chest tightened, though it still listed his name in third at the side of the screen while the fallen riders' names slid down the order, disappearing off the bottom of the list. He must be safe.

"I don't know what flag-to-flag means," Anna said, still not taking her eyes from the screen, her shoulders tight. Why hadn't they shown Isaac, so she'd know that he was safe?

"The riders can come in and swap bikes. This close to the end of the race, some will gamble on staying out on track unless the rain becomes harder. Others will risk making up time on wet tires by changing. It's about track position and the weather. Everyone will judge it differently." She hadn't seen Angel approach, and he patted her on the shoulder.

A Ducati in fourth lost traction with his rear wheel as he rode off-line. He skidded across the track as his bike slipped, sliding into the gravel, spraying it everywhere.

Two laps remained.

The three front-runners, including Isaac, all stayed out on track in the rain. She breathed a sigh of relief when they showed him—still upright and on track. The lap times had slowed, but they were still out there. Just after they passed the entrance to pit lane, the rain picked up, and the wind blew in gusts. Several other riders came into the pit from mid-pack. The final group and stragglers came in, too. The riders hopped off one bike, jumped onto their waiting, second bikes, and they putted back toward the track in a slow-moving group, being careful not to exceed pit lane speed limits.

Vince, Spencer, and Isaac were more than halfway around their penultimate lap when the heavens opened. Cascades of white water streamed down in sheets, water pooled on the track, and the soggy riders slowed to a crawl. It was a miracle anyone could ride in these conditions.

All riders had changed bikes, except the three leaders.

"I can't believe those three are still on slicks," said Angel in Spanish.

"Slicks?" Anna felt tears gathering. Everyone in the room radiated stress that she couldn't ignore as it seeped into her already tense muscles.

"Slick tires. Smooth," said Angel. "Rain tires are bumpy, grooved. Look how much faster those riders can go." His calm tone kept her tears from falling as she watched the screen. The riders on rain tires rode much faster than the leaders on their slicks, water spraying up from their tires.

They watched as Vince, Spencer, and Isaac slowed still more, maneuvering their bikes gingerly through corners as the rain bounced upward off the track, pelting the riders from above and below. They no longer appeared concerned with taking the best line. It was just about staying vertical. Water sprayed around them, ruining their visibility for the cameras and for themselves.

Behind them, and closing, came the rest of the spread-out field—riding three times as fast as the leaders, with Xavi in front of the chasing pack. Even on rain tires, Luka Catala slid out of contention in turn two when he misjudged a corner. Then another rider went down. Conditions were nightmarish.

Anna wiped her hands on her skirt as the three at the front inched their way around the track on their final lap. Would they finish top three or be caught and swallowed up by those charging on rain tires?

The racers turned onto the home stretch—Vince, Austin Spencer, and then Isaac. Behind them, the others gained with every passing second.

Spencer hydroplaned through a large puddle of standing water, losing ground, and Isaac passed him in a spray of water. Vince crossed the line first. Isaac, second. Then the first pack of riders on rain tires sped past, leaving Spencer limping across in ninth. He'd rolled the dice on slicks and lost. Xavi finished third for the final podium position.

Anna let out a huge breath as everyone on the team jumped up and down in excitement.

"Take his hat and go meet him," said Angel, a wide smile on his creased face. He nudged her toward the exit.

Anna met a race official beside parc ferme and collected the bright yellow finishers hat, with "second" embroidered on the side. She brought it to Isaac, who was taking off his helmet. He grinned as he took it. The rain continued with a whooshing sound where it poured off the overhang, but parc ferme was covered. She took the helmet and set it down beside the bike and the marker with the big number two. Second position was a fabulous result, tying his best finishes ever. He must be proud.

Isaac launched himself at his brother, and they shared an enthusiastic hug, slapping each other's backs as they jumped up and down, celebrating their hard-won finish. The rain stopped as quickly as it had started, leaving the ground steaming and wet. Anna couldn't hear Vince when the brothers stood face to face, but whatever he said made Isaac grin. He stepped back, tugged on his hat, and then threw himself at the waiting team over the thin divider separating parc ferme from pit lane.

Anna stood back and let him celebrate with the pit crew. The fanfare in parc ferme was boisterous, and she had difficulty making out individual words and phrases—it was just noise. She drifted to the side as the finishers celebrated. Xavi was crying, tears running down his already wet cheeks. The emotional rider seldom finished on the podium. It was some time before he settled enough for his post-race interview. He must be excited about finishing third.

Her job finished, she turned to leave when Isaac came to her. He lifted an eyebrow, perhaps questioning if she was okay. She nodded, and he picked her up and swung her in a circle. She gasped in surprise that he still had so much energy after the grueling race. Setting her down, he kissed her hungrily. "I'm so glad you're here," he said at last.

"Congratulations." To her left, she caught a flash of Vince's frown and she blanched at the anger on his face. Was that directed at her?

Isaac kissed her again. "How do I look?"

"Fabulous." She handed him his cap, which had fallen off in his team celebration. He always looked great to her.

Xavi finished his interview with the British Racing Network, which meant Isaac would be next. He smiled and adjusted the hat in preparation.

She stood to one side with Angel as the reporter asked Isaac about his race and his decision to stay out on slicks.

"It was just a fluke that I didn't go down. I got lucky." He turned to face her, and the intended double meaning in his words sunk in. Warmth filled her, and she couldn't wait to be alone with him, though it could be hours before they left the team, and he completed his media duties. She would relish the slow burn of anticipation.

During the celebrations, she sipped champagne from the enormous bottle the team passed around, left over from the podium celebration. Her handling was a little awkward, and she dumped champagne on her shirt. Excusing herself to wash up, she slipped out the back and crashed into Austin Spencer, coming from a garage farther down the row.

"I'm so sorry," she said, stepping back. "I didn't see you."

He swayed on his feet then grabbed her arm. Was he drunk? He held her in place when she would have continued to Isaac's trailer. "Where do you think you're going?"

"Just to wash up." She tugged her arm but couldn't break loose. "You were having a great race. Too bad about the rain."

He ignored her comment. "I notice you and little Vasquez have something going on."

She froze. His normal smirk was gone and in its place was a sneer. His grip on her arm hurt. It became hard to think or breathe. "Let me go."

"When you get tired of playing with Junior, give me a shout. I can offer more than a quick fuck in the trailer between sessions. I've had a lot of experience pleasing women."

Had he listened to them yesterday? The creep.

His free hand slid under her skirt and cupped her ass and she pulled farther away. Her skin crawled.

Tugging her arm free at last, she fled up the stairs. Her cheeks flaming, she opened the trailer and stumbled inside, not looking back until the door was locked. She collapsed on the bench seat and took deep breaths, trying to calm herself. When her stomach stopped churning, and Spencer was gone, she unlocked the door.

A few minutes later, Isaac joined her, his hair tousled and his grin wide. She didn't want to ruin his celebration so remained quiet. She would forget what had happened with Spencer. He hadn't hurt her, and she would stay away from him. He wouldn't touch her again—he wouldn't get another chance.

She smiled as Isaac came closer and pulled her against him. He bent down for a long, lingering kiss that chased everything else from her head. "I can't wait to be back in the hotel," he said. "I'm sorry if the celebration got too loud." His eyes showed his concern, but she waved it off.

"It was okay. I just spilled champagne and didn't want to be sticky." She looked down at her damp shirt. It wasn't quite a lie.

He laughed and tossed her one of his team t-shirts to change into. It was a little too big, but it smelled like him and was an improvement over her soaked one.

He changed into street clothes and hung up his riding leathers. One of his crew would pack and prepare everything for the next race. Coming out of the back room, he said, "Let's go say our goodbyes and organize a ride back to the hotel. Time for more private celebrations." His voice became deeper, and his pupils dilated as he pulled her against him with a gentle tug. She couldn't resist him, nor did she want to.

He kissed her slow and sweet, unfurling desire in her again as she shoved the remnants of unwelcome thoughts about Austin Spencer from her mind. He had nothing to do with tonight's celebration.

CHAPTER 10

Isaac

Isaac had a spring in his step everywhere he went these days. Argentina and the lead-up to the race in Texas were much the same as the two previous rounds, with his happy life on and off the track. Isaac credited much of this to Anna, finding time in their schedules to be together. Angel's people still booked a room for Anna at the hotels, but she stayed with him. He smiled, satisfied that she'd become an oasis of peace and contentment.

Anna and Catarina met up for most meals on the road, and Isaac joined them when he was free. He'd always had a brotherly relationship with Catarina and enjoyed her company too, but Anna made his skin tingle and his heart race. He also appreciated that it must be nice for Anna to have another friend. She'd seamlessly fit into his racing world and, by extension, his life. It seemed to work for her too—she was upbeat and pleasant to be around.

The only discomfort came from the idea that Vince may have continued concerns about their relationship. Isaac had caught his brother's frown when he and Anna had shown up once at the house on a day off, and another time on their way to their hotel room. But nothing was said. Isaac let his performance on the track speak for him. If Anna was a distraction, it was the kind that worked.

He'd finished on the podium again in Argentina, behind Luka Catala and Vince, for third. Here at the Circuit of The Americas, or

COTA, he'd qualified fourth. He couldn't believe his string of luck. This was the best qualifying position of his career. He was used to starting mid-pack or, more often, toward the back. Thinking of qualifying brought Vince to mind again. His brother had turned away after a quick handshake following Q2. They'd always been best friends and celebrated each other's successes, so Isaac had felt the snub.

Maybe for the first time, Vince felt threatened by Isaac's racing consistency. After three races, he was second in the championship only to his brother, but he wouldn't let it go to his head. With eighteen more races, it was too early to be thinking of the championship. Still, it was nice to be higher than usual in the standings, even if it meant additional press appearances and responsibilities. The tension between them was building with each race, and the networks didn't help. They were billing it as Vasquez vs. Vasquez.

On race day in Texas, Anna surprised him. He assumed they would spend the morning together, but she looked nervous and claimed a mystery errand. She ordered a car and left, promising to be back before holding grid signs for the Moto2 race and her grid duties. Because she was excused from Moto3, Angel must have approved her errand. Isaac felt odd not knowing what was going on. It shouldn't be a big deal, but why hadn't she shared?

He'd been looking forward to surprising her with the fact that today was his birthday and that he'd made dinner reservations in downtown Austin. He hadn't told her about any of it in order for it to be a surprise. In retrospect, he should have mentioned his birthday, and she probably would have made plans on a different day. It was his own fault he was on his own.

With unexpected time on his hands, he went looking for his brother and found him studying race footage from last year's COTA race.

"You won by twelve seconds, and I was eighth." Isaac peeked at the screen.

"Yep." Vince didn't look up.

"What are you looking for on the recording?" said Isaac as he sat down.

"Why aren't you with that girl?" said Vince without looking up. "You're always together."

That girl? What the hell?

"We're in her home country. She had a few errands," said Isaac. What was with Vince? He hadn't even wished Isaac a Happy Birthday. They were adults and didn't make a big deal about their birthdays, but they'd always been acknowledged.

Vince raised his eyebrows. "If you can't find her, ask Spencer. He might know where she is."

"Why Spencer?" said Isaac. Anna barely knew him, and she didn't like the loud-mouthed Australian.

"I don't really have time to chat." Vince's eyes remained intent on the screen.

What pressing knowledge his brother thought to learn from that race now was a mystery. Maybe he was watching this one because his race had been flawless. Isaac stood up. "I'll see you later then."

Isaac returned to the track and watched the Moto3 race on his own, although he didn't pay attention to much of it as his mind was distracted. He hoped everything was okay with Anna.

Texas was the first time Anna was back on American soil since she'd gone to Europe. He'd interrupted a phone call yesterday that sounded like she was meeting up with someone. Perhaps she had unfinished business or family to visit. He hoped she would tell him what was going on when she returned. He respected her independence, but if there was a problem, he wanted to be there for her. If she was meeting family or someone important, wasn't he worth including? His questions gnawed at him. He and Anna weren't casual, and he continued to be slightly hurt for being left in the dark.

There was nothing wrong with Anna leaving on her own or even keeping something private. She was entitled to her own life, for as much as they'd shared lately, they were still new. He considered her as his girlfriend, but they hadn't discussed their status beyond being together. There was a lot they still didn't know about each other. Including birthdays, obviously.

Maybe Vince had a point about distraction. This ridiculous worry was a distraction, but not Anna herself. Isaac couldn't get settled and fought the urge to check in with her and make sure everything was okay. As promised, she returned in time to hold the Row 2 sign for the Moto2 race, but they didn't have a chance to talk, and Isaac couldn't settle into race mode.

He felt like a fool, but he texted Anna. *I'm in my trailer. Can you spare a few minutes to chat before the race?* He sighed in relief when the dots appeared to show her typing.

"Be right there."

Two minutes later, she knocked and entered. Once more, she wore her sleeveless shirt and race day skirt and looked delicious.

"You're wondering where I went this morning." She cut right to the chase. "Since I didn't tell you anything, and just left."

"You don't have to tell me anything you don't want, but I wanted to make sure you're okay." He searched her face for signs of distress.

"I hired a lawyer." Her gaze dropped to the floor. "I called her office last week and set up the appointment for this morning. Today I met with her in person."

"Do you have a divorce to arrange?" Isaac hadn't considered that possibility.

She shook her head. "I've never been married. I have a property to sell, and I was worried that my ex-boyfriend would try to take a share. As far as I know, he's still living in my townhouse. According to my new lawyer, common-law marriage is not recognized in Washington state. The townhouse is in my name, and I'm the one who paid the deposit, and makes the mortgage payments. The lawyer is arranging written notice that the property is being sold and will make all the arrangements. That way, I don't have to talk to Adam."

"Adam." The name felt as wrong on his tongue as when she'd said it. "Did he hurt you? Is he the one that belittled you and made you uncomfortable all the time?" His angry words tumbled out.

"He didn't hit me. He just treated me as less than him, and I see now that he took advantage of me financially. The lawyer will tie up the loose ends, so I don't have to."

"Have you heard from him since you left?" Isaac hadn't seen her messaging anyone except Catarina. He hadn't expected her past to spring up. Nor had he expected the brief zing of jealousy.

"Not since the day I quit my job, when I found him in bed with one of his grad students," said Anna. "I drove to the airport and left for Barcelona that night. I blocked his calls when I arrived."

"So, you only just broke up with him?" Isaac swallowed. Was he just her rebound guy? He wanted to be more than temporary.

"It's become clear that Adam and I were never close. It should have been over a long time ago." Anna tracked Isaac's movements as he paced the narrow corridor in his trailer. He could feel her gaze. "Come here," she said, stretching out a hand. "I'm sorry I didn't tell you what was going on. I'm just trying to close that chapter of my life. It has nothing to do with us."

He stopped in front of her. She didn't owe him anything, not even the apology. He opened his mouth to apologize for being upset about her errand.

"Isaac, I know it's way too soon to say certain things." She fumbled for words and took his hand, lacing her fingers between his. "I want to be clear. What Adam and I had is over. I didn't talk about it because it wasn't important. I have no lingering feelings, and I'm not even angry about him cheating. We weren't close, and I don't miss him." She sucked in her breath and looked him right in the eye. "I'm falling in love with you. I hope that's okay and doesn't scare you."

Her bare honesty left him shaken. She'd taken his thoughts and distilled them into something more potent. "You amaze me," Isaac said, wrapping his arms around her with a squeeze. "I'm falling for you too." He lifted her chin. "I'm not going anywhere."

Her forthright gaze met his. "I don't have a proper job or a home, but I enjoy spending time with you. I decided to deal with my past. I didn't want you to be part of my entanglement." Her eyes pleaded with him to understand.

"I'm hoping you'll find some quality time for me and a different kind of entanglement in a few hours. After the race." He went to kiss her, but she gasped and stepped back.

"I haven't messed up your race routine today, have I?" Her tear-filled eyes were so intent and serious. "We're due on the track in five minutes."

"You make me race better. You help me concentrate on what's important. One kiss, then it's race time." Her soft lips parted beneath his. When he stepped back, he said, "One of these days I'm going to win a race." He hadn't shared that goal with anyone in a long time.

"Maybe today," she said with a smile that brought out her dimple.

"Circuit of The Americas is one of Vince's favorite tracks," said Isaac. "I won't beat him here unless he has an out-of-character disaster and crashes. But one of these days, I'm going to be a MotoGP winner."

"I believe in you," she said. "Go race."

They came out of the trailer together. Vince stood at the bottom of his stairs, dressed in his orange, black, and white riding leathers.

"You might want to save that energy for the track," said Vince with a headshake.

His brother assumed he knew what they'd been doing in the trailer. Isaac grit his teeth. Vince needed to mind his own business.

Anna's smile disappeared and she let go of Isaac's hand. With a glance over her shoulder, she slipped into the box from the back lane.

He and Vince were alone.

"You don't seem to take my advice. I hope you know what you're doing, little brother." Vince stalked into his garage without saying anything else.

Isaac clenched his jaw for a moment, closed his eyes, and pictured the track. He wouldn't think about Vince right now. Just the race. He calmed his thoughts, at last, got into racing mode, and joined his team. With the countdown on to start time, he ran through the course in his head the way he had the last few races.

The race itself flew by in a flash. It was a fun course to ride with tight turns, a roller coaster hill with a blind crest, and enough straights to hit top speed each lap before hard braking. His favorite spot to overtake was at the bottom of the hill as the track turned. The course ran counterclockwise, unlike most of the other tracks, which was part of the reason Vince had been so successful here. He excelled more than most riders at left-hand turns.

Isaac finished second, having kept his brother in sight during the entire race. A feat here at COTA, where Vince had often finished ten or twelve seconds ahead of the second-place rider. There'd even been a moment with five laps to go when he'd considered chasing down Vince and vying for the win. But, with worn tires, Isaac hadn't wanted to throw away a solid second place. The way his bike was functioning, and with how he was riding, there would be other chances for victory.

This afternoon's celebration in parc ferme was more subdued than previous times they'd been together on the podium. His brother's smile seemed forced, and he'd turned away quickly to talk to his teammate, Luka Catala, who'd finished third. Isaac forgot that awkward moment when Anna stepped forward with shining eyes to give him his cap and water bottle with his energy drink sponsor for the camera.

"I have a surprise," he whispered as he lifted her for their now customary post-race hug. Maybe she was his good luck charm, like Angel insisted.

She arched an eyebrow. "What kind of surprise?"

"It's my birthday, so I've arranged to spend this evening with you somewhere nice."

"Happy Birthday." She kissed him again. "What about the team?" Her eyes had gone wide.

"I paid for their dinner and a night out, too. Just somewhere else. Lots of great live music here. They'll never miss us."

•   •   •

After the podium celebration, Isaac and Anna ducked out the back of the garage and into a car that took them first to the hotel to get changed, and then into downtown Austin for dinner. A camera crew caught them sneaking away, and a car followed when they left. At the restaurant, a camera filmed when they exited the car and headed inside. Isaac signed a few extra autographs on the way.

"Does that happen often away from the track?" she said in a stage whisper as she tossed her head toward the reporter.

"More in America than most places, other than at the racetrack. They probably think I'm Vince. Or expect him to come along soon. This is one of his favorite places too. I invited him to come tonight, with Catarina or a date, but he declined." Declined was a polite way to say that he'd been unresponsive.

Anna squeezed Isaac's arm in sympathy while they followed the server to their table.

"I don't think Vince likes me," said Anna as they sat at the table for two at the window overlooking the river and the brightly lit city on the other side.

"Vince? He likes you fine," said Isaac, opening his menu. He didn't want to talk about Vince, and his voice was more clipped than he intended.

"Yeah. Fine." Anna's words conveyed more acid in her tone than he'd heard her use before.

He closed his menu and took her hand. "Vince doesn't dislike you. His problem with us is because of me. He's worried I'll become distracted and ruin my racing career."

"Aren't you off to a great start this year?" She frowned, looking more puzzled than upset. "You're in second overall."

"My best. I've had entire seasons with fewer points than I have now. Just to put it in perspective, I'm usually happy to finish in the top ten. That I've been in the top four for all four races is a complete surprise. To me, as much as everyone."

"Shouldn't Vince be happy for you? This afternoon, he was… weird."

Of course, she'd noticed.

"You're the first woman who has ever been important to me. The only person I've dated anywhere near the track or for more than a couple of weeks. Maybe Vince is jealous." He'd never considered the possibility, but suddenly, some of Vince's scowls made more sense. His brother would deny it, but Isaac hadn't been spending much time with Vince. Isaac loved his brother, but he had to be his own person, and spending time away from his brother was important. However, it may have been too big a change all at once for Vince. When they got home, Isaac would see if they could get back in their brother groove. Try to match up more of their training again.

"Do you want me to stay away from you in Cervera? Give you more time for your brother?" Anna spun the ring on her right hand. He hadn't seen her do that in a while.

"I'll find time to train with him more, but I'm not giving you up," said Isaac. "Before I forget, my mom wants to meet you. She's invited us to dinner on Wednesday. Are you free?"

She nodded and bit her lower lip. "Will I be what she expects?"

"She's so excited I have a girlfriend, at last. I don't think you need to worry," said Isaac with a laugh.

Anna's smile chased thoughts of Vince away so he could enjoy his birthday dinner. They were brothers. They'd work it out, eventually.

•   •   •

Back at the hotel, Isaac's focus shifted. As soon as they stepped through the door, he flipped the lock and pulled Anna into his arms. She fit perfectly, and when he bent to kiss her, he forgot everything else. He wanted to taste all of her. His skin thrummed with energy as he touched her smooth skin. Attuned to his every touch, she pushed against him, deepening their kiss. One strap of her dress slipped down her shoulder, and he traced the neckline with a finger, goosebumps rising on her skin as she shivered beneath his touch.

"I don't have a present for you," she gasped.

"You are my present. I'm unwrapping you right now." He ran his hands down her sides and lifted her dress, pulling it off over her head, leaving her in a purple lacy bra and matching thong underwear. He wanted to rip it all off but instead dropped to his knees, kissing her flat stomach, his fingers sliding under the edge of her underwear.

As always, she was wet and ready, as turned on by their kisses as he was. They'd been all over each other in the limo coming back to the hotel, and it seemed like he'd been hard all night. He slid his fingers deeper, making her cry out. Removing them, he licked them and ducked his head to taste more. He kissed the lace and did something new, sucking on her through the flimsy fabric. She bucked away, but he held her close and licked her again, watching for her reaction.

She closed her eyes and twisted her hands into his hair.

Oh fuck. She tasted like candy, sweet and delicious. He dove back in, sucking until he couldn't stand not to reach her bare skin. Sliding her soaked underwear down, his tongue slid into her swollen folds, and he kissed her there. First soft, then with his tongue swirling in her wetness. His insistent cock strained at his boxers, and he sucked harder. She rocked against him, pushing him deeper. This was so fucking fantastic.

"Isaac. Oh. Oh, oh my god," she said, tightening her grip. A hot rush filled his mouth as she came. He slowed down and kissed her again, savoring all of her. He wasn't a selfish lover. He enjoyed her pleasure, but he was wound so tight and needed his own release.

With a last kiss, he undressed, her eyes fixed on him. His turn.

She dropped to her knees, where she stroked and blew him until he was incoherent. Twice she brought him to the brink, but he held back. He wanted to come, but he needed to be inside her, or this would be over too soon.

When she slid onto the bed, he rolled on a condom with shaking hands and followed. He was so ready he could have come with the first tight thrust, but he'd learned he could make her come a second time and that's what he wanted. Knowing that he was giving her pleasure too made everything better.

When Anna came again, clenching around him as he thrust deep, he could hold off no longer. He watched her face as she came down, and his orgasm rocked through him—an unstoppable train.

After cleaning up, she snuggled against him, and they drifted toward sleep. He was almost out when his phone buzzed and lit up the darkened room. It was late, but carefully, so he didn't disturb Anna, he reached for his phone on the bedside table. The message was from Vince.

"Happy Birthday, little brother. Should have gone to dinner. My apologies."

Isaac's last thought before drifting off to sleep was that it was good to hear from Vince. They might not always be as close as they had been in the past, but he didn't want a rift.

CHAPTER 11

Anna

Anna gazed out the expansive windows of the hotel room in sunny Portugal, enjoying the view. Other than her trip that had started in March, she'd never left North America, so every destination was new. There wasn't a single cloud in the blue sky, unlike spring in Seattle. Portugal's Algarve region reminded her of Spain, but with incredible sandy beaches. She smiled at the memory of this morning's quick morning dip in the ocean with Catarina and Isaac. Chilly but refreshing on this last day of April.

In the summer, southern Portugal would be stunning. Maybe she should come back for some of the summer break. She hadn't talked to Isaac about his plans for that time, but she should. Maybe they could book a hotel or condo down here for a week or two. Her funds would stretch that far if she was careful.

Vince had declined the outing to the beach this morning, though things had thawed between the brothers since Isaac's birthday. Anna liked they were getting along better, and that Isaac was trying to help his brother feel less excluded. She didn't seem to spend less time with Isaac. He'd returned to doing his longer runs, gym time, and track times with his brother, but that was time spent without her, anyway. It provided her with the opportunity to write whenever she was free, and her story was progressing. They'd postponed dinner by a week with his mother until Vince was free to join them next Wednesday.

Anna headed for the door, intending to meet the team for the second shuttle to Portimão. They were staying in nearby Faro, and she was running late after washing ocean water from her hair and the gritty sand from her skin. She hated feeling like she wore a layer of salt and sand. She spent a long time getting rid of it all while Isaac had a quick rinse then left for the track and free practice with the first group because he preferred to be early. She didn't mind catching the next shuttle, since she would still be on time.

Hurrying, she didn't pay attention to who else was present in the almost empty elevator. She pushed the button for the main level. As soon as the doors closed, she glanced at the figure in the back and met Austin Spencer's pale eyes. Her stomach clenched. So much for not being alone with him.

"Have you been avoiding me? I haven't seen you in ages." He slid closer. "Where did you go swimming this morning? I liked your sexy purple bikini."

Why was he being so friendly? Her skin crawled. He'd been watching her again. She already stood at the far side of the elevator, but with eleven stories still to descend, she wished for more space.

"Isaac still keeping you satisfied?" He inched closer, making her feel cornered. "If you were my umbrella girl, I'd have you on your back so often you wouldn't be able to walk."

She flushed hot with anger. "What my boyfriend and I do, is none of your business." She turned to face him.

"Darlin', I'm still waiting for you to leave that twig and move on to a real man. Though I have to admit, he's punching above his weight this year." He shuffled closer still and the air in the elevator became stifling. "Let me know if you need a little action on the side. Your boyfriend doesn't need to know." He stroked the side of her bare arm.

The hair on the back of her neck rose and the acrid taste of bile filled her mouth.

"This is sexual harassment. Touch me again, and I'll charge you with assault," she said, lurching to the other front corner of the elevator.

She hated confrontation but she wouldn't let him make her feel powerless. She was done with feeling that way because of someone else.

"Don't be like that," he said. "I'm paying you a compliment."

"You're disgusting. Stay away from me." Her fist was clenched, and she wanted to punch the smirk off his face.

"You're even hotter when you're mad." He smirked and sipped his energy drink.

The elevator finally came to a halt, and she scooted out the door, hurrying to join the team, where she'd feel safe.

"See you at the track." His words didn't sound casual—more like a threat.

She couldn't stop trembling. She stood just behind Angel while she calmed herself, twirling her ring and focusing on her breathing. She should tell Isaac about what had just happened, but talking about it might cause a meltdown. He said that didn't bother him, but it bothered her. Plus, they didn't have time today for her to fall apart. She would pretend things were fine. She took a deep breath. Isaac was starting from fourth again and needed to concentrate.

All week at Portimão, Vince had struggled to ride at a fast pace, and for the first time, Isaac was starting in a grid position higher than Vince. Luka Catala was on pole—the first of his career. At lunch, Catarina mentioned that Vince was in a funk about his lack of progress this weekend. He must also be bruised and hurt because he'd had two jarring crashes during practice when he'd pushed himself and his bike to the limit.

At race time, the grid became awkward. Today, Isaac shared a row with Spencer while Vince was just behind them on the third row. Isaac and Vince were quiet and focused inward, while Spencer was loud and joked with the milling reporters and a variety of team crew members. Once, he caught her glare in his direction after a sexist joke and he winked. What an ass.

The hair on the back of her neck rose, and she turned to find his calculating eyes raking over her from head to toe, making her skin crawl. Had Catarina noticed? Her friend's attention was directed elsewhere. In the pre-race bustle, it seemed nobody had noticed Spencer's attention. She watched Isaac with his headphones in, his gaze down, blocking out the world. Maybe after the race, she could go to Angel or the racing stewards to complain.

The problem was that Spencer's comments, while presumptuous and rude, probably wouldn't be enough to get him in trouble. It had been sexual harassment. She hadn't read something into his words that wasn't there. He'd been clear about his intentions. There'd been no way to misconstrue his meaning. Despite that, it still might not be enough. Angry tears stung her eyes at the injustice. She should have reported him weeks ago when he'd grabbed her in Indonesia. Now it might be too late to bring up that encounter. Plus, both times, there hadn't been witnesses.

He'd probably deny what he'd said, and it would be his word against hers. Austin Spencer was a popular figure off the track. A fixture in the racing paddock and known for being a good sport. She was just a new umbrella girl. She shifted her position so she couldn't see him. Minutes later, the back of her neck prickled again. He must be staring, but she refused to give him the satisfaction of checking. Tears stung behind her eyes, but she concentrated on breathing. She could get through this. Isaac was only a foot away but noticed nothing. He was in his own world—at least she hadn't pulled him out of his zone.

With a minute left before the race, she cleared the track, feeling better once she escaped from Spencer's line of sight, and the riders left for their warm-up lap. Maybe Spencer would crash. She could hope. Right away, she took that thought back. He was a creep, but she didn't want anyone hurt, and every crash came with the potential for injury.

Standing with the team, the race itself became exciting, as usual. The track in Portimão was nicknamed "The Roller Coaster" because of its rolling nature, which made the course different and entertaining.

The only race-related dark cloud came early on. Yoshi crashed in the third corner and had to be taken by stretcher to the med center for a check-up. Isaac's quiet Japanese teammate had barely spoken two words to her, and she didn't know him well, but she hoped he would be okay. His side of the box remained subdued as his crew waited for the doctor's results.

The front six that got away clean at the start included Isaac, Luka, Spencer, Fabiano, Xavi, and Vince. They ran nearly identical lap times, and there were few overtakes as they reeled off lap after lap with their group strung out in a line, nobody close enough to pass—leaving the chasing pack of twenty racers behind. Several times Anna grabbed for something to squeeze as riders flung themselves through tight corners and twisty chicanes.

Tire wear became an issue by the three-quarter race mark on the bumpy track and several riders slid out of bounds, including Fabiano from the front group. He stood immediately and walked off the track, his head in his hands. Everyone took it hard when they crashed. In Moto3, the youngsters often cried, unused to public failure. Even without tears, all competitors became upset with a DNF—Did Not Finish—next to their name on the official scoresheet. Her heart quickened. That left five leading racers, including Isaac and the other front runners in the championship, a fact also pointed out by British commentator Marcus Birch.

Luka stayed at the front and eked out a full-second lead with hard braking and daredevil speed that only someone with his youth possessed. On worn tires, the others had more sense. Maybe. Either that or because of their experience, they were patient and had better race strategy, biding their time. She fixed her eyes on Isaac in second, with the rest of the streaming pack behind.

Vince had slotted into the back of the lead group in fifth. He must be fuming as he set the fastest lap of the race in the second to last lap, gaining on the others. He looked poised to make a move as he closed the distance between himself and the bikes ahead.

On the last lap, Vince surged, passing Xavi and Spencer, slotting himself into third as he and his bike became poetry in motion, throwing himself through corners at breakneck speed. The commentator went nuts, ranting about Vince's masterclass in tire management and race craft.

In the second last turn, Vince pulled alongside Isaac, and Anna held her breath. Flicking right, then left, Vince ran wide and lost his drive into the final corner. The brothers flew down the home straight toward the finish line, almost side by side. At the line, Isaac maintained greater speed, finishing second. Vince had to settle for third.

Isaac had beaten his brother, an incredible feat. She did a little dance and Angel, Miguel, and the team hugged while they celebrated. LCR Honda would be thrilled. It wasn't often the satellite team beat one of the factory bikes, let alone the reigning world champion. All around the track massive screens replayed the ending for the screaming fans.

It still wasn't a first-place victory for Isaac, but it was a fantastic result. Out of curiosity, she'd asked after qualifying yesterday if he'd ever finished ahead of his brother. The answer had been an emphatic no. There had been a couple of decent race battles with his brother while Vince had been recovering from arm and shoulder surgery years ago, but every one of those had gone the champion's way.

Anna shared a look with Angel as they headed for parc ferme. The older man's face looked calm, but she caught a look of disquiet cross his features. What was she missing? He looked like he expected trouble.

Her worry seemed unfounded when they reached the victor's section. Vince seemed happy for Isaac, and they shared a back-slapping hug when they returned after celebrating in front of their fan club grandstands. Maybe Vince didn't mind his brother finishing ahead of him for a change. She felt uncharitable for thinking it might have been a problem. Of course, he was happy for Isaac.

Isaac celebrated with her in their usual way, spinning her in an exuberant circle before kissing her breathless. She didn't mind that he was sweaty. This was her Isaac, and she loved that he shared his enthusiasm. He set her down to get ready for the cameras and his post-race interviews. He couldn't stop grinning, and his eyes gleamed. She should have become immune to his gorgeous looks, but right now, she was reminded how attractive he was. Not everything in her life had been so lucky, but for once, she had a terrific boyfriend.

Standing at the edge of the area, she listened to the BRN English-speaking reporter's interview with Vince while she waited with Isaac, who would speak next. Interviews always progressed from third to first, with the winner speaking last.

"Would you say that you were more or less motivated to pass on the last lap because it was your brother ahead of you?" the reporter asked.

His camera crew stood behind him while a second crew filmed the post-race interview from further back. A different network, perhaps. She'd seen them around a lot.

This reporter often asked unique questions and offered insightful commentary about engines, racing, and the bikes themselves. The second group must also want to hear the answers.

"More. For sure. We've always been competitive," said Vince with his wide camera smile that made him seem open and approachable instead of driven and cut-throat competitive. "But, since this is the first time my little brother beat me on a Sunday, I can let him have one every fifteen years."

Let him? Nice. She tapped her toe—kind of an asshole way to look at Isaac's superb race.

The reporter laughed. "How do you feel about your brother being second in the championship? Any extra sibling rivalry at home this year?"

Without hesitation, Vince said, "I'm happy for him." He winked, "As long as he doesn't win too many races, or I might have to increase his rent." He and the reporter shared another laugh.

Like it was all in good fun.

If Anna hadn't been watching so closely, she might not have seen the flash of annoyance on Vince's charming camera facade. He didn't like to lose. Especially to his brother, it seemed. Isaac knew his brother too and his face lost its glow of happiness. For all Vince was joking, there was a nugget of truth in his words. He didn't like Isaac's success. What would he do or say if Isaac ever won a race?

• • •

While Anna waited for Isaac to finish showering before they drove to his mother's place for dinner, her phone buzzed. The name that appeared on the screen was a surprise—Sandra, her former boss. What did she want? Anna almost didn't answer, but curiosity got the better of her. It was mid-morning back in Seattle. Maybe Sandra needed something related to Anna quitting. There might be paperwork she should have filled out. Instead of just leaving the country and not speaking to anyone in HR, other than leaving a message with her new number.

With a deep breath, she answered. "Hello."

"Oh, thank goodness I found you," said Sandra, her breathy voice sounding panicked. "Where have you been? I've left you a dozen messages at home this week."

"I moved," said Anna. "Listen, this is long distance. Do you need something?" She hated to be abrupt, but she wanted to get this conversation over with.

"We need your help," said Sandra. "It was unfortunate how that all played out a couple of months ago and that our little misunderstanding led to you quitting."

The gall of that woman. Anna didn't have to swallow her anger anymore when dealing with her. This was no longer her boss. "Misunderstanding? Do you mean when you stole my work and took credit for it with a top client? When you belittled me when I stuck up for myself?" She couldn't keep the edge from her voice.

There were several seconds of silence. Had Sandra hung up?

"Uh. About that." Her former boss cleared her throat. "Just because that happened to me a couple of times on the way up the corporate ladder, doesn't make it right. I'm sorry. I should have brought you in and made you part of the discussion from the start. Your ideas had value."

An apology was something, but Anna couldn't quite let her anger go. "What do you want?" Her emotions from that day flooded back, constricting her throat. It was one thing to have the moral high ground—another to deal with confrontation—which never seemed to get easier. She blamed her parents and their angry fights. Even the thought of them made her clench her fist. She hated when thoughts of them intruded in her life. Closing her eyes, she returned her focus to the phone.

"I want you to come back to work. Marcus Jones has rejected every idea I've had for the next phase of his campaign. He says they're missing the magic. I admitted that you might have come up with the original concept and that you were the one with the vision. I need you back on the team, or we lose his business. All of it."

Anna chewed on her lip. "I'm in Spain and not coming back." It felt fantastic to say that to this woman who had made her professional life a misery.

"Oh my god. Spain? What in the world would you go there for?" said Sandra. "Please. If we have to, we can do this remotely, but I need you to help with this account, or we'll lose it."

"That isn't my fault," said Anna, still with a bite in her voice.

"I can see that I've caught you off guard." Sandra's words sped up. "Don't say a final no. Think about it. Please. I'll stall Marcus for a few more days. I'll tell him you're a, maybe."

"I don't think so." Anna didn't want to be part of that world anymore. She wanted to be a writer.

"You'll be well compensated," said Sandra. "Pretty please."

Anna hadn't expected to hear from anyone from her old job ever again. She wasn't willing to return to work the way it had been, but she could use the money. It might not hurt to agree to this one project. Still, the unexpectedness of the offer left her off-kilter. "I'll think about it. This once." Dazed, she hung up. Sandra had apologized.

Anna would run the idea by Isaac later and see what he thought, even if it was her decision. She valued his opinion, but it would have to wait until after dinner. She didn't enjoy having another secret from Isaac, but with the tense feelings back between the brothers, it didn't seem like the time to talk about herself and her issues. He had more important things to deal with.

It was close to an hour's drive east from Cervera to outside Lleida where Mrs. Vasquez had relocated after her husband had passed last year. Anna bit her lip as they pulled into the driveway but stopped as soon as she noticed. She hadn't met many of her boyfriend's mothers before. The modest white house sat outside of the historical town of Lleida. It was hillier and drier than Cervera, but still lovely with a view of the rivers.

Mrs. Vasquez rushed from the house as they stepped out of Isaac's sports car. Vince's matching red BMW sat next to the garage.

"Your brother's been here about an hour," she said in Spanish. "He's always in such a hurry." She smiled. "You must be Anna. You're all Isaac has talked about this spring." She had a thicker accent than her sons, but her English was excellent. "I apologize if I forget sometimes and speak to my sons in Spanish. You are most welcome to my home."

Anna smiled. "It's nice to meet you."

Isaac ran around the car and enveloped his mother in a big hug. She was a petite woman with shoulder-length wavy black and gray hair. Vince and Isaac favored her with brown eyes and dark hair. Vince more so, but Isaac had her warmth.

Stepping back, Isaac said, "Mom, this is my Anna. Anna, this is my mother, Carmela."

"Isaac has brought no one to meet me in many years," said Carmela, shooting him a pointed look and pursing her lips. "How will I get grandkids if he never has girlfriends?"

"Mom." Isaac sounded exasperated, but his smile remained. This was affectionate teasing.

A pang shot through Anna. She couldn't imagine having a relationship like this with her mother. Anna hadn't heard from the woman in over twenty years.

"What?" Carmela said with a laugh. "It's true. Don't worry, I like you already if my son does. I have many stories I will have to tell you over dinner." She motioned toward the house. "Come, join Vince on the veranda with a cold drink. We have tasty wine, cold beer, or fresh-squeezed lemonade."

Isaac took Anna's hand and kissed her temple. "My mom is going to embarrass me, isn't she?"

Anna flashed him a mischievous grin. This might be fun.

Anna's smile slipped a few minutes later when Mrs. Vasquez sent her to sit on the deck with Vince while Isaac stayed inside to help his mom with the food. Vince might have only been there for an hour, but he was on at least his third beer. The empties sat beside him on an end table. She didn't know him well but remembered their strict in-season diet, and how devoted he was to it. He must have given himself the day off and plan to stay the night. She girded herself to sit across from him on her own. Would he behave?

She and Vince had never been alone before, and she didn't know what to say to break the ice. Starting conversations had never been her strength. For a couple of minutes, she sipped her lemonade in silence.

"So, Anna," he drew out her name, giving it longer syllables. "Where were you before you attached yourself to my brother?"

His tone put her on edge. "I'm from Seattle." No way in hell was she talking to him about her past.

He rolled his eyes. "How much longer do you plan to stay in Spain? Till your European adventure has run its course?" He made it sound like she was free to leave at any time.

"I'm not sure." She stood up again, no longer wanting to sit with him. She blinked back tears brought on by his hostile tone. What was his problem?

She glanced through the kitchen window where Isaac and his mom were laughing and chattering a mile a minute as they set food on a tray.

He looked happy, as he always did when preparing food. She wouldn't ruin their evening by fighting with Vince or taking offense at his words. She wandered to the railing overlooking the river and the stone ruins below. She fought for control of her threatening tears. Hostile vibes and people arguing always brought back negative memories of her childhood.

Behind her, Vince got to his feet. He wasn't a big man, but he'd had a few drinks, so his footsteps were heavy as he tromped in her direction.

"I blame you." He leaned against the white railing.

Surprise made her turn and face him. "For what?"

"From the beginning, I told Isaac you'd be a distraction. You're worse than that. You're an intrusion." Alcoholic fumes filled the space between them from his breath. He leaned closer and half-whispered. "You might have Isaac fooled, but I have more experience. I see you, weaseling your way into his life. You're just another American helmet chaser. When my brother gets over the novelty of regular fucking, he'll come to his senses. See that you're just a common whore." He tipped his beer, finishing the bottle.

She backed away, her tears blinding. Why was he so hateful?

"Vince," Isaac's voice snapped from behind.

Neither of them had noticed him come outside with the charcuterie platter, which he dropped onto the low table with a thump.

"You need to apologize." Isaac's eyes blazed as he strode toward them.

Vince raised his empty bottle in a salute. "I'm just calling it like I see it. No offense to you, brother. I'm just looking out for you."

Isaac's voice dropped. "You have one more chance. Apologize. Now."

"Or what? You'll pick your slut girlfriend over your brother? You've known her for all of a minute." Vince tried to cover his inebriation with slow, deliberate movements as he set his bottle down by the others.

"Anna, I'd like to leave," said Isaac.

Her chest hurt, and the world was still a blur, but she stumbled toward Isaac. He took her lemonade and set it on the table next to the appetizers. She was so grateful that he understood she needed to get away, and was not giving his brother any chance to use it against her. Leaving was for her as much as for him. He put his arm around her stiff shoulders, but even that couldn't stop her growing distress.

Turning to his mom in the open doorway, Isaac rattled off a quick stream of angry Spanish. Carmela stood, her mouth agape. Anna couldn't follow his words but caught Vince's name and the word insult.

"I'm sorry, Mom. We can talk later." Isaac guided Anna back to the car, revved the engine, and backed out with an uncharacteristic spray of gravel. His mouth was set in harder lines than she'd ever seen.

She couldn't speak, the pressure inside her intensifying to intolerable levels. She'd passed the point-of-no-return and wouldn't last much longer. The tears kept coming, then a gut-wrenching sob. She tried to stifle the noise with her hands, but failed. She wanted to ask Isaac to stop, but she couldn't speak.

She screamed from behind her hands. The muffled sound caused Isaac to jump. He pulled the car to the side of the road and held her while she rocked, unable to do anything else. She would be embarrassed later, but for now, it only mattered that Vince and Carmela hadn't witnessed her meltdown. The heightened emotions from everyone had been negative and so intense that she'd been overwhelmed. Fighting reminded her of the tough years with her parents when they'd constantly battled about her difficulties and lack of money. First Spencer, then Sandra, and now this. She could only hold back for so long—the dam had burst.

CHAPTER 12

Isaac

Holding Anna while she cried, Isaac made a resolution. He wouldn't spend another night under Vince's roof. He would stay with Anna tonight, if she'd let him, and he'd find a place of his own to either buy or rent as soon as possible. Despite his anger with Vince, he'd stay in Cervera, though he was free to choose where to live.

He smoothed the hair from Anna's face when her crying subsided and handed her a packet of tissues from the car's center console.

"I'm sorry," she repeated several times as she took deep breaths, clearly fighting to regain control. She couldn't look at him, though she hadn't pulled from the circle of his arms. It was only now that their awkward positioning in separate seats became uncomfortable.

"Let's go for a short walk." He stepped out of the low-slung car. On her side, he helped her out. Taking her hand, he led her to the scenic viewpoint where she could catch her breath in the fresh evening air. He wrapped himself around her from behind, holding her close. "Is this okay?"

She nodded but didn't speak. Several minutes of close contact elapsed before her stiffness faded, and she relaxed in his arms. He kissed her temple.

"I'm sorry Vince was an asshole. Is there anything I can do?"

Her head shake was so minute he wouldn't have felt it if she wasn't leaning into him. "I'll understand if you aren't interested in being with me anymore." Her quiet words broke his heart.

It was like she thought being different made her defective or unworthy. There was nothing wrong with her. Who'd made her feel this way? Her mystery parents? That Adam?

"I love all of you. Even this. When you're hurting, let it out. I can handle it." He squeezed, hoping his words sunk in. She might need to hear them more than once to make her believe. "Can I stay at the Inn with you tonight? We'll pack up a few of my things from Vince's."

"Of course." Her body tightened again at his brother's name.

"He won't be there. Mom won't let him drive, not after drinking." Isaac clenched his fist so hard it hurt. "I'll move out after we return from Jerez on the weekend. We leave tomorrow." He'd do better with more space from Vince for a while, but that wasn't an option.

Anna would see Vince this weekend after all, at the track. That might be difficult.

"I'm sorry I got so upset." Her words weren't much louder than a whisper, and her cheeks remained warm and flushed.

He moved to face her so she would understand his sincerity. "You have nothing to apologize for. Anyone would be upset by what Vince said. I'm embarrassed for him."

"But my meltdown,… I hate when I get like that." Her eyes shone with new tears as she looked up, at last meeting his gaze.

"Mi corazon, you never have to apologize for how you feel. We have to be able to tell each other the truth and express our feelings." He took a breath and said, "It was more than this, though. You've been tense for days and bottling things up." His voice became rougher, and his eyes narrowed. "Has Vince spoken to you like that before?"

She shook her head. But her tight body language made him think her answer was only a partial truth.

"Who?" he said, a red haze clouding his vision.

"I can't tell you." Her scrutiny returned to the ground.

He took a breath. "Yes, you can. If it was Vince, I'll go back and bloody his nose. Anyone who speaks to you like that is out of line."

"It wasn't Vince. It was someone on the road. A misunderstanding about umbrella girls versus groupies and whether I was available for sex." Her cheeks flamed.

"Groupie? I don't know that word." He understood enough to know it was derogatory.

"Helmet chaser." Her mouth twisted. Vince had called her that too. It was so far from the truth that it was ridiculous. She'd never looked twice at the other racers. From the first moment, she and Isaac had been drawn to one another, and it had nothing to do with racing. They just suited one another.

"I'm sorry that happened to you." He swallowed, trying not to show his hurt that she hadn't confided in him yet again. Other than her late grandmother, she hadn't mentioned kindness in her past and he'd inferred she hadn't had many people to trust in her life. It might take time. "You could have come to me." He kept his voice soft, non-threatening. She needed to learn that his love wasn't conditional.

"You were minutes from the starting grid. I couldn't. Then, I didn't want to cause trouble." She bit her lip. "It wasn't worth making a fuss over me."

He took her icy hands in his. "Yes, it was. You are important. If someone is inappropriate, say so. A race is never more important. It's just a race. You are always worth it. Always." It was the truth. "I love you. I'd do anything to keep you safe." He wanted her to look up and see that he was serious.

When she looked up, trust in her eyes, he bent his head and claimed her lips; he could have drowned in her kiss. She pulled him so far under that he lost his bearings. All he wanted was to bring her closer. He'd never felt this way about someone before. Her happiness meant as much as his own, if not more. When at last he broke off the kiss, her eyes were no longer filled with tears and all trace of her meltdown was gone.

•   •   •

That night, they cleaned out Isaac's room, taking his clothing, bedding, towels, and books. There was nothing left to take after the race weekend. Looking around his empty room made his heart ache. He'd lived here all of his adult life and it felt wrong to leave under these conditions, sneaking out in the night after a fight. He and Vince had spent so many years as training partners and best friends that it was a shame this was how things had ended. He'd miss the comradeship of being brothers, but he didn't regret standing up to Vince. With a last glance, Isaac closed the door and strode out with the final boxes.

He left his dirt bike and home riding gear in the track shed. He would still practice on the dirt track at least twice a week. After all, he'd helped make it. He would just be sure to come when Vince was out on his road bike or occupied in the home gym. The thing about having trained together for so long was that Vince's schedule was predictable. Isaac was too angry to consider training together, and he wouldn't forget Vince's cutting remarks. His brother had crossed a line, and there was no going back.

Before the flight to Jerez, Isaac contacted the airline and requested that his business-class ticket and Anna's economy-class one be exchanged for two premium seats with extra leg room so they could sit together. Avoiding his brother was a bonus. He sent a quick message to Angel, mentioning an argument with Vince, without going into specifics. As his team boss, he needed to be in the loop. In the future, Isaac and Anna would have business-class tickets together.

The next two race weekends flew by in a flash, with Isaac renting a condo on a month-by-month basis near Cervera. Anna left the Inn and moved into his rental with him. At two months, it was early in their relationship for such an important step, but they were always together. It made no sense for Anna to pay for somewhere she never slept. Since they no longer needed to worry about Vince's feelings, they could spend as much time together as they wanted.

Anna insisted on chipping in for a share of the rent and food, and Isaac let her, even if he had more than enough money. All his years of living with Vince and living a moderate lifestyle meant he'd saved millions, but being a partner meant sharing responsibilities.

Vince was stone silent whenever they were in the same place, and neither of them was willing to make the first move to reconcile. Without an apology to Anna, it didn't matter. Their argument didn't affect them on the track as Vince finished first in both races while Isaac had been third in Jerez and second in Le Mans.

Le Mans had been another wet race, but one with mixed conditions from the start—Vince's specialty was judging tires and when to switch bikes. The entire field of riders had followed his lead, changing bikes during the fourth lap. The steady rain had been solid enough to leave puddles and wet patches on the track, but hadn't become the torrential downpour of Indonesia. With such a physically demanding race and challenging conditions, only sixteen of the twenty-eight riders had finished.

The eighth race, in Italy, too flew by with Fabiano winning his home race in Mugello for Ducati. Vince finished second and Isaac third. Luka Catala remained in third overall behind the brothers in the championship.

The most troublesome part of the weekends for Isaac came at the press conferences. With the brothers dominating the championship as they neared the summer break, their rivalry was the media focus, and it was obvious that their relationship was strained.

The extra camera crew following everyone in the racing paddock didn't help. They were making a MotoGP series for Amazon Prime, and the rivalry between the brothers made for an interesting angle for their story. In fact, it had become one of their overarching themes. Or, so the director said when he requested additional access to the Vasquez family in Cervera. While uncomfortable, the league wanted it, citing good publicity, and Isaac couldn't refuse.

Isaac wasn't sure how faithful the new camera crew would be to actual events, and it bothered him that their cameras seemed everywhere—a constant barrage of attention. His mind flashed back to his birthday and the camera at the restaurant and the crew in Cervera weeks ago. What had they caught on film? They couldn't know the real reason he and his brother weren't speaking. There hadn't been a camera at his mother's. Their story would be skewed.

Despite his efforts to seem civil in public, he and Vince weren't speaking. After they'd snubbed each other in parc ferme and been glacial on the podium for the last three races, their rift was common knowledge.

At the pre-race conference in Barcelona, Isaac watched Vince work the cameras and reporters with ease. His easy-going manner impressed Isaac, and he had to give his brother grudging respect for dealing with the press this way for all these years. Isaac found it nerve-wracking to have to answer all their questions while remaining calm and respectful. This was the first time he'd been a contender in the championship, and the status came with considerable pressure and attention.

The last time he'd been fighting for a title was his final year in Moto2, ten years ago. While important to the Moto2 teams, that championship had been nothing like this one. The media had manufactured most of this championship rivalry, but that didn't mean Isaac didn't feel the demand to succeed.

Vince maintained smiles and a pleasant demeanor whenever the cameras were near, even if he avoided speaking to Isaac. Isaac struggled to look as smooth on camera. The situation reminded him of an occurrence that had garnered a bit of media attention years ago. After a serious on-track racing incident, Vince and his former rival, who'd retired, hadn't gotten along for seven years. Despite mutual respect for each other's racing abilities, the two men had never been friends, and Vince had become an expert on giving diplomatic answers that gave him the high ground. This experience served him well amidst the current hostility.

Isaac fumbled for composure when the reporter's words brought him back to the present.

"We understand that as brothers and close friends, you and Isaac have spent hours every day training together. Recently, your brother moved out of the home you shared. Has this affected your training regime? If so, how?" The Spanish reporter waited for Vince's answer.

Vince glanced at Anna standing at the side of the room. She kept her chin high as she stood at Angel's side in Isaac's team colors.

"It's not my fault if my little brother can't keep up anymore and has placed less priority on training than I do," said Vince, his voice sharp. His eyes met Isaac's. "Perhaps that's why he's never won a race."

Isaac ground down on his molars and kept his face neutral. That had been a low blow.

A different reporter waded into the fray. "If Isaac can't keep up, how is he your closest championship rival this year?"

"Riding my cast-off bike is keeping him in this championship. Here, it's the bike, not the rider. Being a champion takes hard work and dedication." Vince's dark eyes narrowed as he stared down the female reporter.

She swallowed but motioned her camera crew toward Isaac. She wasn't cowed.

Was Vince implying that Isaac wasn't dedicated? After all these years of training together and racing side-by-side, the idea was ludicrous. What a jerk.

"Isaac, what do you have to say? What could be more important than training this time of year?" The BRN reporter was giving him a chance to counter.

"Thinking about a life after racing." Isaac's gaze cut to Anna's where she stood with Angel. Damn. His look, combined with parc ferme celebrations, would lead to more questions. The ones working on the special might try to get her alone and ask questions. He'd have to warn her to be careful. Unlike him, she was under no obligation to speak to them.

"What could be more important than racing?" said Vince, not giving up the topic. "More important than brothers? Ask him about his

American girlfriend." He spat the word 'girlfriend,' like it left a nasty taste in his mouth.

Isaac jumped to his feet, removed his mic, and dropped it onto the stool where he'd sat. "I'm not doing this here." His hands shook with anger. "If anyone has racing questions, I'll be happy to answer them later. My personal life is off limits." He left the room, the camera following until he was out the door, Angel and Anna following in his wake.

Angel took him aside. The older man's face showed his concern. "Vince was out of line. Next time perhaps say, 'no comment' instead of walking out. It gives your brother too much power. Now, he can say anything, and you aren't there to defend yourself."

His crew chief was right, but at the moment, leaving had been satisfying. "I know. I won't do it again." Isaac huffed a breath of air out. "My brother really doesn't like it when I don't do what he wants." He'd given in to Vince and put his brother's needs before his own for so long that he'd forgotten that Vince could be so spiteful.

"Just worry about yourself," was Angel's sage advice. "A happy rider is a fast rider."

In Barcelona, Isaac started from the front row of the grid on a scorching hot day, typical for the first weekend in June. Track temperatures stayed in the mid-forties—measured in degrees Celsius—all weekend, and almost all the riders chose the hardest tire options possible. On Saturday, the grip had gone part way through FP4, with few riders finishing the session. Sunday afternoon was even hotter.

During the race, Isaac grit his teeth and pushed hard. He almost caught Vince and spent most of the race trailing by less than a bike length as they flung themselves through corners and roared down the straights, pushing each other to their limit. Late in the race, as expected, his tires ran out of grip, becoming slippery. Cornering became an exercise of will to stay on track, and his muscles shook from the exertion. Sweat ran down his face and impeded his vision, but he stuck it out. It would be the same for Vince.

Early in the last lap, there was a moment when Vince ran wide. Isaac hesitated. He chose not to take advantage of the slight lapse because he worried about wiping out. He told himself that it would have been too dangerous. Once again, he settled for second place, crossing the finish line a tenth of a second behind his brother. Standing next to Vince's turned back in parc ferme, Isaac regretted playing it safe. The victory had been there for the taking. Why hadn't he pushed that bit harder?

With this victory, Vince had won three of four races since their fight, and the upcoming races—the last two before the summer break—were some of his favorite tracks. This had been a stellar first half of the season for Vince, with seven wins already. His brother had always trained and worked harder than anyone, but now he seemed more intent than ever on winning—at any cost.

His season looked to rival his 2019 season, his most dominant year to date. With three extra races this year, Vince looked set to shatter his previous record for the most wins, most points, and most podium finishes in a single year for any rider of any class in MotoGP history. All that success, and yet, he seemed miserable.

From what Isaac could infer from Catarina's guarded remarks, Vince did nothing except work out and train. He didn't socialize or take breaks, even at home. Now that Isaac was paying attention, in the month since Isaac had moved out, his brother had developed dark shadows under his eyes. Vince probably wasn't sleeping. He should be ecstatic and under less pressure because he'd earned a contract extension for the next two years and an option on two more, which he'd earned despite his age. By the end of that contract, Vince would be forty. His brother was getting what he wanted: More money, more accolades, and more time racing.

Several contract offers had extended to Isaac, but he hadn't decided if he was coming back next year. He turned down offers from all but his current team and let them know he was considering the terms. Angel knew what he was thinking, but management didn't—Isaac had time before they needed a definitive answer. The crux of the issue was that he didn't know how much longer he wanted this lifestyle. He'd come to grips with this being his last season before it had started, and despite his unprecedented success, he wasn't sure he wanted to keep racing. It was mentally and physically exhausting, and despite his recent on-track success, it wasn't fulfilling enough.

He dropped off his leathers in the trailer and grabbed a Coke. He resolved to talk to Anna about retirement during the summer break to learn her opinion. Isaac loved having Anna with him at home and on the road, but being together wouldn't have to change if he quit. Some of what had rejuvenated his love of racing had been her excitement and seeing it through her eyes. His bike was the best he'd had, and his racing had been the most focused and consistent of his career. Some of that he chalked up to his overall happiness.

Still, racing felt like a placeholder for his real life that he was waiting to start. What would Anna say if he decided not to race next year? She'd become a dedicated fan and followed all the stats. His most of all. Would she be as interested in him if he were just a regular guy at home? More and more, he didn't want to be like his brother, with no life other than racing.

Anna had, at last, told him the circumstances that had led to quitting her marketing job last spring. She hadn't forgiven her boss but had taken on a limited contract for a single client. After she completed that job, the company begged to have her back. To Isaac's surprise, she refused the more permanent offer. They wanted her to return to Seattle and offered her a sizeable promotion. She explained to him she'd never liked her job and told them, "Thanks, but no thanks." They hadn't valued her when they'd had a chance, and now it was too late. He admired she was sticking to her guns. She wanted to write and see if she could make that a career.

She had seventy-five thousand words written in her story and said she was at about the three-quarter mark. He could tell she got a lot of satisfaction from writing. That had value. He frowned. He hadn't figured out what he'd do without racing, nor had he written in his therapy journal since the day he'd met Anna. It was probably still back in his old room at Vince's.

Isaac glanced out the window of his trailer with its view of the back of the garages in pit lane while he waited for Anna. There was still something or someone bothering her. Twice this weekend, she'd arrived in the box shaken and upset. She hadn't told him what was happening or who she'd spoken to, and he hadn't pushed. He respected she wanted to handle it on her own, even if everyone needed help sometimes. He'd already said she could tell him things, and reminding her again so soon might seem overbearing. If he relaxed and let her choose the right time, like with the information about her old job, she might yet explain.

He watched carefully and didn't think it was Vince bothering her, nor did he think it was anyone on the team. She was popular with his crew, and Angel thought she was smart as a whip. He'd called her amazing and said she reminded him of his oldest daughter—high praise from Angel—who was devoted to and proud of his daughters who were at university.

Anna still undervalued her worth, but until Isaac understood what else was going on, he couldn't reason with her. This time, when she arrived, all thoughts of everything except her fled as he pulled her into his arms.

CHAPTER 13

Anna

The race weekend in Germany marked an exciting turning point for Anna. This afternoon she'd written the climax of her novel and the end felt like it was in sight. She could do this. She just needed to figure out what happened next to get to the ending she'd already imagined. Over the summer break, she should be able to finish writing this story. The idea of completing the draft was exhilarating. She almost texted Isaac to tell him what she'd written, but decided to tell him in person after the race. He'd asked about reading it, but she worried it wouldn't be interesting enough, especially when he was distracted by the continued media circus.

Hurrying to the track, she spotted Vince and several trailing cameras ahead of her and slowed her pace to let them get further ahead. She didn't want to speak to reporters but should be safe at this distance. This weekend, they were more intent than ever on Vince.

Germany's Sachsenring was the only track on which Vince remained undefeated for the entirety of his career. The track ran counterclockwise with eleven left turns and only three rights. Something about the way they'd designed the course had always worked for him. He was the undisputed 'King of the Ring' with a lifetime total of seventeen victories. She'd love for Isaac to be the one to take that crown away.

Anna looked left and right before crossing the back service lane. This close to race time, most riders were already geared up and inside their box garages, but lots of people scootered up and down the lane to get where they needed to be. It was fun, and faster than walking. By keeping a close watch, she'd been mostly successful at avoiding Vince and Spencer the last few weeks, which was perfect.

Rushing into the box, she smiled at Angel. He raised an eyebrow and tapped his watch. She grinned back and shook her head. She was almost late, but she'd wanted to finish that pivotal scene and had taken to slipping into the trailer to write when she had a chance. When her laptop was nearby, she made progress. If she left it back at the hotel and had inspiration, it was too far to retrieve.

She glanced at Isaac, who'd already gone deep into pre-race mode with his air pods in and his riding leathers on. His leathers were unzipped, his eyes closed as he leaned back with an icepack wrapped around his neck to keep cool. He would put in his chest plate and zip the suit when he grabbed his helmet and headed out for the first of the two pre-race laps. His departure was the signal for everyone to assemble on the grid for the countdown and final preparations.

Dressed in her usual Sunday outfit, Anna retrieved the jumbo blue and green umbrella as the countdown to race time continued. She took a deep breath, enjoying being out of the direct sunlight, glad she was wearing a sleeveless shirt and a skirt instead of riding leathers. Isaac must already be broiling in his gear. Out on the track, the heat would be insane.

Today, the riders would have to worry about overheating and dehydration, as well as tire wear and the usual race exertion. The air temperature was over forty degrees again, while track temperatures were over fifty degrees Celsius. The umbrella's shade would be welcome on the baking hot tarmac of the grid, providing a small patch of respite. Here at the Sachsenring, Isaac was starting from third while Vince was on pole, of course.

At the proper time, the crew started Isaac's bike, and he departed for the sighting lap. They met him on the grid, where she took his helmet and handed him a new ice pack for his neck. Once it was in place, she gave him his water bottle which had been filled with ice water, though the outside said Powerade—one of his sponsors. He gave her a quick flash of a grin before returning to his visualization of the course.

The warm feeling she got inside when he smiled reminded her it was only eight days until they left for the beach house they'd rented in the Algarve. She couldn't wait. She'd hoped for maybe a week or two of beach vacation. Isaac had rented a small villa for the month, insisting that they could stay there for most of the summer break. He'd bring his road bike and run for exercise, take a break from the track completely. He would save dirt-track practice until the last week when they returned to Cervera.

Holding the umbrella steady, she used a free hand to take the water bottle when Isaac finished. Angel passed him his helmet when only thirty seconds remained before all non-racers had to clear the grid. Isaac tugged it on with a serious look as he focused on the track—all business.

She watched with the team when Isaac and Vince leaped away at the start. Grabbing Miguel's arm, she watched the TV screen as Isaac got the holeshot and led the race after the first corner. Vince raced practically on his back tire, not letting Isaac get away on his own at the front. She sucked in her breath the as his reckless attempts to pass Isaac failed. It was almost more than she could watch, but at the same time, she couldn't look away.

"Vince needs to calm down or he'll take them both out." Angel's creased face set in an unusual frown. "Patience Isaac. Let him make the moves. Just race your race."

Isaac couldn't hear, of course, but Angel kept giving him quiet instructions as the race progressed. When they flashed across the line to start the final lap, Isaac still led and the two riders were in a class of their own—fifteen seconds clear of Xavi and Luka, who were fighting for third. The commentators flashed to Xavi just as he ran wide and crashed into Luka. Luka wobbled and somehow stayed upright, but Xavi's bike pitchforked first one way, then the other.

Xavi was thrown from the bike as if it had been a rodeo bronc. When the dust cleared, he sat in the gravel cradling his right hand and arm, rocking with pain. Three marshals and a medic dashed across the dusty rocks, helping Xavi to his feet and supporting him away from his dangerous position trackside. They headed for the track's medical center.

The camera hadn't stayed on Xavi long once it was clear that while injured, it wasn't serious. The race action returned to the fight at the front, and Anna couldn't take her eyes from the screen. Isaac and Vince were far too close together. How were they not crashing into each other?

Her hands ached where she'd dug her nails into her hands, and her clothes were damp with sweat. All activity ceased in the garage while everyone held their breath. Vince would do something desperate to claim victory. He wasn't the kind to settle for second. She just hoped nobody got hurt. Especially Isaac.

"Vince is going to lunge up the inside on turn seven," said Angel, his eyes fixed on the big screen. "That's where he was looking on the last three laps. That's where Isaac goes a little wide. If that doesn't work, Vince will have something lined up for turns ten and eleven too. Vince wants this bad."

"Vince always wants to win," Anna said, unable to stop herself.

"Isaac might win this one," said Miguel under his breath.

Two people threw things at him, and several others said, "Shhh."

Miguel grimaced. "I forgot. It's bad luck to say that."

Anna's heart thumped a mile a minute as if she was on board with Isaac as she willed him to hold off Vince's impending attack.

Angel's prediction came true. Vince passed on turn seven and Isaac fought back, regaining the lead in turn eight, a matter of inches separating them. Vince somehow found space on turn eleven and pulled ahead again. Isaac didn't give up, but couldn't find a way back through with Vince's perfect defensive track position on the final turns. She held her breath. Anything Isaac tried would cause a crash.

Isaac lunged on the last corner, unable to pass but sweeping up alongside his brother as they flew down the final straight. Vince and Isaac swept across the line together. It was almost too close to call. She glanced up at the official scoreboard, and her heart sank.

Vince had won—still King of the Ring.

Cheers erupted next door in Vince's garage, and Isaac's crew clapped. This had been another fantastic race for Honda, with first, second, and third. The manufacturer was dominant this year and, barring disaster, would win the constructor trophy at the end of the season.

Still, Anna wished Isaac had held on for the win. It had been so close. He'd be gutted, as Marcus Birch and the other commentators were wont to say, whenever anyone led for most of the race and didn't win. His efforts deserved the victory, but he'd been second. At least Isaac hadn't crashed, and he'd pushed Vince to the brink of possible defeat. Isaac had made Vince earn this crown. One of these days, Isaac would get his victory.

To Anna's surprise, Isaac didn't seem upset with second place. His eyes gleamed, and his grin was huge as he stood on the podium beside a subdued, though victorious, Vince. She was proud of Issac for being happy with his accomplishment. Nobody beat Vince at the Sachsenring, but maybe he was no longer untouchable.

Waiting for team celebrations to die down in the garage, before they shifted back to the hotel, Anna's phone pinged with an email from her lawyer in Texas. Standing on tiptoe, she whispered, "I'll be right back." She gave Isaac a smile of reassurance as she stepped away and headed for the trailer, where she could read and reply in peace.

Adam had ignored the first two letters her lawyer had sent. He'd been sent notice requiring him to move, and he'd waited until just before the final deadline for the third letter before responding. He'd filed a countersuit, claiming half the value of the townhouse, citing that they'd been in an "intimate, committed relationship" when it had been purchased. From what her lawyer explained, Adam now had the burden of proof to prove that relationship, as her name was the only one registered on the title.

She sighed. Of course, he was dragging this out and making it take longer than it should. He would do nothing to make her life easier. That snake had never paid a dime for the townhouse, just his half of the groceries. She'd canceled the cable, phone, internet, and electricity when she'd arrived in Europe, so at least he'd paid those bills the last few months.

In this latest email, her lawyer asked for specific details about her relationship with Adam. She wanted to know if they'd discussed marriage, children, or the future. The answer was an emphatic "no." Anna frowned. She and Adam had discussed none of those things. Neither had she and Isaac, but being in a relationship with someone for four months differed from the four years she'd spent drifting with Adam. Her thirtieth birthday was this fall, and for the first time, it felt like having a family wasn't a distant future. Maybe in a few years. She returned her attention to the email.

The lawyer had already inquired about her financial arrangements with Adam, which had always been kept separate. They'd had no joint credit cards or bank accounts—Adam would have already taken that money. They'd been together for four years, and on Anna's part, she'd been exclusive, which was one item he would use to prove they'd been in a committed relationship. Adam had been less exclusive, which was now to her advantage.

Anna hesitated. It wasn't ideal to share so much personal information, but she had little choice if she wanted to win. She wrote back that she and Adam hadn't had sex in six months before she'd left and only twice in the six months before that. She squirmed as she replayed the scene back in March when she'd interrupted him having sex with his grad student. That hadn't been intimate or committed. Nor had he tried to contact her after the first twenty-four hours of unread messages before she'd blocked him. No emails, no calls from his work for the last three months. Adam hadn't tried to get her back or made any effort to work things out. He must still be dating Tiffany, or he would have been more persistent.

Perhaps he'd also been relieved when she'd left. Still, dragging the sale out was a problem. She only had the money for three more months of mortgage payment. She needed it to sell.

Not that Isaac would kick her out of the place they'd rented, but she didn't want to depend on him with no way to support herself. She needed to have this business with Adam finished by December, or she would need to go home. She was counting on the influx of money, whether that meant asking for her old job back or taking another like it in marketing. It wasn't what she wanted, but at least she had experience.

Anna blew out a breath of air. She would hope that the sale worked out and would try not to stress. Her lawyer was working on it and was aware of the deadline. Tucking her phone back into the belt pouch she wore with her race day outfit, she left the trailer and headed back to the party. The shuttle should arrive soon to take everyone back to the hotel. Isaac was usually partied out before that, and they'd sneak away for a private celebration, even if the crew often celebrated until late. Isaac had already whispered his intention several times, letting the anticipation between them grow.

Anticipating naked fun with Isaac caused her to daydream as she tromped down the trailer stairs. With her mind elsewhere, she missed Spencer hovering near the bottom. Emerging from the shade between Isaac's trailer and Xavi's next door, Spencer grabbed her arm just as she reached the ground and spun her around. Off balance, she stumbled, and he hauled her against him as he backed deeper into the shadows.

She cried out, but the sound was lost in the sounds of the loud Honda partiers across the lane. He pushed her against Xavi's trailer, banging her head on the metal siding. Dazed, she stood shaking while he leaned in, creating a cage with his arms on either side.

"I've been waiting to get you alone," he said. "You and Little Vasquez haven't rocked the trailer yet today, so you must be all hot and bothered. Crawling out of your skin with lust. You little minx. If I take you back to mine, no one will bother us." Seeing her blank look and perhaps interpreting it as confusion rather than fear, he said, "You know. The expression? If the trailer's rockin', don't come knockin'."

"You're gross." Her voice shook. "Leave me alone."

"Or what? You'll tell? You've told no one about our other stolen moments. Why would you mention this to anyone? When I deny it, either they'll think you begged me to fuck you or that you made it up." He leaned closer. "Deep down, you know you want me."

"You disgust me." The taste of bile filled her mouth. He was repulsive.

His hips ground into hers, pinning her against the trailer wall. She flailed, catching his face with a weak smack. One of his hands clenched the top of her throat under her chin and squeezed. He was so much bigger and stronger than she was, and it became hard to breathe. She couldn't yell, and spots appeared in her vision. Was he going to kill her? Tears trickled down her cheeks.

Spencer tried to kiss her, but she turned her face away. Instead, he licked the side of her neck and face, almost to her eye, leaving warm slime sticking to her skin that felt like acid. His hand around her throat loosened.

"Let me go," she gasped, attempting to knee him, then kick him.

He blocked her kicks with a nasty laugh. "Not going to escape that easy, Sweetheart. I know all the tricks."

"Anna," called Isaac from the back of the garage. "Is everything okay? Where are you? The shuttles will be here any minute."

Spencer let go with a vicious pinch on her ass that stung. "Till next time," he whispered. He turned and strode away toward the back of the trailers.

Anna took a deep breath before answering Isaac. "I'll be right there." Nothing had happened. She'd be fine. She spun her favorite ring, focusing on it. Closing her eyes, still spinning her ring, she took another breath. She wasn't blowing off the seriousness of what had happened, but it was too much for her to handle. She needed to pretend it hadn't happened, or she'd go into full meltdown.

Spencer was gone. She was okay.

She hurried past Isaac and ran up the trailer stairs. "One sec," she called over her shoulder. "I just need to use the bathroom before we get back on the bus."

She rushed inside and washed her face and neck, scrubbing where Spencer had licked her. Even after hot water and soap, she couldn't get rid of the nasty sensation. Looking in the mirror, she straightened her hair. She needed to hurry, or Isaac might get suspicious. Drying off, she tried to keep her hands from shaking. Her neck should be red from Spencer's chokehold, but it had already faded. It just looked like she'd rubbed it.

Anna returned outside to Isaac. "Sorry, I had an email from my lawyer. I needed a few minutes and went for a short walk. Adam's being a jerk and refusing to move." Her head shook as she said, "He wants half the townhouse that he didn't pay for and doesn't want to leave."

Why couldn't she say what had just happened with Spencer? Isaac would confront Spencer, who would just say she'd come onto him. Spencer's threatened words would 'prove' Vince's allegations. Even if she trusted Isaac to believe her, others might not. They might even fire her. She'd rather keep quiet than cause another confrontation.

"Adam's an ass. Does your lawyer have a solution?" Isaac took her hand as they walked together toward the bus that had pulled up.

"I had to answer personal questions about my lack of relationship, even while Adam and I were together." She wiped an escaped tear from her cheek. "I can't believe I wasted so much of my life with someone like him." Her words brought the incident with Spencer flooding back. Her throat constricted in the same place Spencer had squeezed, and his leering face flashed before her eyes. She needed to be there for Isaac right now. He couldn't afford the drama and confrontation a public spectacle would cause. It would be all over the news. She shuddered.

"I'm glad you told me about Adam." Isaac pressed a gentle kiss to her forehead. "We can face our problems together."

Guilt flooded through her. She left her hand in his, wishing she wasn't terrified and tongue-tied. It was on the tip of her tongue to tell him about what had happened, but she couldn't find the right words in time. They climbed onto the bus, and she couldn't start the conversation—it was too public. She should have told him about Spencer when they were outside, but now the moment had passed. It was too late, and she'd lost her courage.

CHAPTER 14

Isaac

The Motul TT Circuit in Assen was one of Isaac's favorite courses, and he was looking forward to the race on Sunday. There were so many terrific places to pass on the track that suited a variety of bike manufacturers in different sections, meaning that anything could happen. Some circuits, like the Sachsenring, favored the acceleration of the Hondas, while others, like the Red Bull Ring in Austria, were geared toward the top-end horsepower of the Ducati or the KTM's. But Assen had a little something for every manufacturer. Most years, Assen produced highlight reel overtakes and active racing that excited fans worldwide.

Like the last few races, Vince had spent today practicing like a man possessed, with little care for his personal safety. He'd say it was about testing limits, but to Isaac, it seemed reckless. It wasn't much different from Vince's usual level of aggression, but to someone who knew him as well as Isaac, there was a knife-edge difference.

For all his anger, Isaac was worried about his brother, so he decided to try talking to him. He waited outside at the boundary between their boxes as Vince returned after FP2, his leathers scuffed from a bone-jarring accident this morning. The man must be a walking bruise.

"I still don't like the set-up." Vince stopped his bike near Isaac and dismounted without a flicker of acknowledgment. He strode into the box, pelted his gloves at the wall, and turned to his waiting pit crew with a shout. "Do your damn job and fix the bike."

Isaac half-turned away in disgust. A private word with Vince now looked impossible. This was none of his business, but it was like watching a train wreck. Horrible and messy. Isaac couldn't look away when he needed to see the damage.

Ripping off his helmet, Vince threw it at one of his mechanics, who caught it with a look of surprise. Isaac had never seen his brother so incensed. In the garage, everyone stopped and stared, as shocked as Isaac. On Luka's side of the box, the crew tried to look busy while they took in Vince's show.

"These tires are shit. The grip goes way too soon. Did someone adjust the top speed of the bike? It doesn't go fast enough on the straights. The acceleration is fucked." Vince sounded like Xavi, not like his usual calm and professional self. Isaac took a breath and backed away.

Through the garage partition, Vince's comments carried loud and clear as he continued to rant. Someone needed to help his brother calm down. Isaac would have tried, but with the way things were between them, he'd only make it worse. Something other than the bike or its tires must be bothering him, and Isaac doubted it was the championship. Vince didn't consider him a genuine threat, and no one else was close enough in the standings to leave him this stressed.

After their second busy day of practice and qualifying, there still hadn't been an opportunity for a private word with Vince. He hadn't answered Isaac's texts asking to talk and hadn't answered the door to his trailer today between FP3 and FP4 or this afternoon after qualifying. No surprise, but Vince must be avoiding him.

After dinner, Isaac left Anna and Catarina at the table on their own and followed Vince to the bathroom. If he couldn't get his brother to agree to talk, it was time to escalate his efforts and force the issue. After checking that they were alone, Isaac locked the door so they wouldn't be disturbed or have reporters zeroing in on their talk. It wasn't anyone else's business.

He waited for Vince to finish and ambushed him near the sink. "Look Vince, can we just make up already?"

"You still seeing that girl?" Vince leaned back against the counter, his arms crossed.

"Her name is Anna, and you know I am." Isaac drummed his fingers against his thigh. Already he was frustrated. Why couldn't his brother be reasonable? "Can't you just admit that you crossed a line when you spoke to her at mom's? You need to apologize. Anna's a terrific girl, and if you got to know her, you'd like her too."

"She's got secrets," said Vince.

"We all have secrets. That's a ridiculous reason."

"What do you know about her?" challenged Vince.

Isaac's eyes narrowed. Vince looked smug. What did he know? "What secrets in particular?"

"You should hear what Spencer says." Vince wouldn't meet Isaac's eyes. "It's bad."

Isaac took two steps forward, his fist clenched at his side. "Spencer has been talking about Anna? Since when are you two such buddies? You used to think he was a pretentious ass. Tell me what he said. I'll handle it." He bit off his words, surprised at the hot flush that rushed through him. Was this because Anna preferred Isaac to Vince?

Vince gave him a long look, perhaps trying to decide if Issac was serious. "He says that for twenty Euros, she gives blowjobs behind the trailers. He brags about being a regular. Apparently, you almost caught them in Germany after the race."

Isaac's mouth tasted like bile as he stepped forward, his body quivering with his intense reaction. That bastard. Wait until he got his hands on Spencer.

Vince leaned back. "Don't kill the messenger. Spencer is the one talking shit. Not me. He says she's been two-timing you since the second race of the season."

"There's no way." Several times lately, Anna had come back upset and hadn't told him what was going on. Spencer bothering her was a real possibility. Secret blowjobs were not.

"Spencer's been harassing her." Isaac would bet money on it after what the Aussie had been saying. "I can guarantee he doesn't like that she turned him down and picked me instead. We'll have him reprimanded and charged with sexual harassment."

"How do you know Spencer is lying?" Vince's dark eyes bored into him.

"Because I know Anna, and she'd never do that. Someone has been upsetting her. I just didn't know who. Either she's heard Spencer, or he's said inappropriate things to her face." Isaac ground down on his molars. "I bet it was the latter." It was difficult to speak through his red haze.

Vince stared at him. "Whoa. Take it easy. No need to hulk out. You know her best." He tugged on his ear.

That's what he always did when he was thinking. Isaac took deep breaths and gave him time.

"I'm sorry I listened to Spencer and his stories instead of talking to you." Vince's tone had changed, but it wasn't the apology Isaac wanted. It seemed like Vince was simply placating him.

"Don't get mad at me again, but you accepted the lies as true because you were jealous." Isaac had never been closer to punching his brother.

"I said you could have Anna. I wasn't interested. How could I be jealous?" Vince's voice was sharp, but he seemed surprised.

Suddenly it became clear that Vince wasn't jealous because Anna chose him, but because Vince thought she'd taken him away. This was about him, not Anna. This talk wasn't going according to the script Isaac had rehearsed over the last twenty-four hours.

"No," said Isaac. "About me. You're jealous that Anna spends so much time with me." How could his brother think that Anna could replace the bond they had with each other? His love for Anna was different. Not a replacement.

"What the hell are you talking about?" Vince's eyes skated to the side again, looking past Isaac to the door. "You got your apology. Let's call it a day." He stepped toward the exit.

Isaac grabbed Vince's rock-solid arm, rigid with tension. This wasn't easy for either of them, but they weren't done. Not when everything between them was still unsettled. He needed to make him understand. "Our whole lives, I've gone along with whatever you wanted. I trained when you trained, and I rode when you rode. I race because that's what you wanted me to do. My life is all about you and what you want." He took a deep breath, waiting to see if his brother answered.

Vince remained silent, his face closed and unfathomable.

Isaac continued. "We're in our thirties and still live together like college roommates. Not adults. I don't even have a home now that I moved out. Just some place I'm staying. That's not right. I need to figure out my own life and stop living yours." He'd said bits of this before but had never said it all. He wanted Vince to understand. "You might not need more than racing, but I do. It's not enough."

Vince turned around and washed his hands. He looked up as he turned off the water and met Isaac's gaze in the mirror. "Training without you is kinda lonely."

Isaac nodded, some of his anger deflating. "I'd still rather train together most of the time, too. I miss having you as a friend and training partner. But you have to accept Anna. It's non-negotiable."

Vince faced him and raised his eyebrows.

"She's the one, Vince. We need more time, and she's got stuff to work out with her ex, but she's a big part of my future. We're in love."

Vince tugged on his ear again and looked at the floor. "I'll apologize. Tonight."

Isaac hugged his brother, as always surprised to discover that though he was the younger brother, he was so much taller. Vince had always seemed larger than life, someone with authority and to look up to, but he was just his brother. And like anyone, he was fallible and only human.

"I'm sorry things have been tough the last few weeks. I've missed you too." Vince squeezed back, tighter than Isaac remembered him doing before.

The two of them returned to the table together, causing Anna to shoot Isaac a questioning look, but he smiled to let her know everything was fine. She'd known about his plan to talk. They both sat down. "Vince has something that he'd like to say." Isaac watched his brother, hoping he'd follow through with a proper apology.

Catarina pursed her lips and rose to her feet. "Want me to go?"

Anna shook her head, and Catarina returned to her seat. She looked thoughtful. Vince seldom said sorry. She must not have heard the rumors either, or she would have reported Spencer.

"Anna," said Vince, "I'm sorry. I was jealous of the time you spend with my brother, and I said crude and unwarranted things. I was out of line." His dark eyes held contrition. "I don't deserve it, but I'm hoping you can forgive me and give me a second chance. I should have trusted Isaac's judgment."

"I accept your apology" Anna's voice tightened, and her eyes glistened.

Isaac could tell she was emotional about Vince's change of heart. She picked up her ice water, the ice cubes clinking, and drank. It was time to change the topic, though he would have to tell her about Spencer's accusations. She liked Catarina, but Anna wouldn't like anyone to be there when he told her. Besides, this was too personal to talk about in public. She might get upset. It might even set off another meltdown.

How could he tell Anna that Spencer was spreading rumors about her? Isaac didn't want to cause her pain. She'd done nothing to deserve this malicious gossip. Maybe he could take care of it without her having to know. He would confront Spencer after the race tomorrow, before the summer break. Isaac would let him know any further harassment wouldn't be tolerated. That way, there could be a fresh start when they returned in August. Anna didn't need to be involved in something so unpleasant. She didn't need to be hurt any more by awful people.

The next day, during the race day warm-up session, Isaac couldn't look at Spencer. He wanted to punch the smug asshole in the face. Of course, he wouldn't. He didn't believe in resorting to violence, but he needed to speak to Spencer privately. It took all his willpower not to confront him. He wanted this dealt with, but it wouldn't be appropriate to talk to the Aussie on the grid. He'd aim for the hotel, after the race. The sooner he warned the man to leave Anna alone, the better.

•   •   •

Sunday, with an hour left before the race, making sure the camera crews were around, Isaac walked out the front of his box and into Vince's. They'd planned this last night. His brother was dressed in his leathers and watching the tail end of the Moto2 race on the screen. With Isaac's arrival, Vince jumped to his feet and strode across the garage. They stood around for a couple of minutes, making small talk about the race as they watched the last lap together on a different screen. Veterans, rather than up-and-comers, dominated the Moto2 championship, so they knew the contenders well. At the end of the race, the brothers shook hands. At least one camera was aimed in their direction.

"See you on the track," said Isaac with a wink.

"May the best man win," said Vince with a toothy camera smile.

"Maybe that will be me today," said Isaac. "I can't let you steal all the headlines."

Vince shoved his shoulder playfully.

Their banter felt so civilized after the angst of the last month.

A smile tugged at Isaac's face as he left. A weight had lifted from his shoulders since last night's conversation with Vince. He would deal with the Spencer issue after the race and, hopefully, leave this problem behind.

For now, it was time to get into his pre-race routine and shut everything else from his mind. He'd never found himself in this position before. As he put in his headphones, he grinned. He was second in the championship before the summer break. He'd made up with his brother, and when he shot a look at Anna across the crowded garage, his heart leaped at her answering smile. She was happy for him. How had he gotten so lucky?

Pre-race proceeded as planned. The hum of activity washed over him, and he tuned it all out. Today he and Vince were both starting from the front row. The weather was sunny and warm, though not as hot as the previous two races in Barcelona and Germany. He'd be glad for the break and time at the beach—he just needed to focus for one more race. Then he was free for a month. Maybe time alone would be what Anna needed to open up about her past. He still had no idea what had happened to her parents. Had they died?

Isaac stared down the track at the first corner, visualizing sweeping around the corner at the front of the pack, imagining where he'd have to position his bike to get the holeshot. Vince started across the row on pole, meaning Isaac would have to cut across Fabiano's path to shoot to the front.

All three riders on the front row typically started well, so Isaac needed to pay attention to Fabiano's Ducati or risk crashing. He amended the picture in his mind. He might need a couple of corners to let his tires warm up, and then he'd pass the Duc. And his brother. The surge of adrenaline hit him hard as he waited intently on the starting grid.

The flagmen came out on track, but he didn't watch their movements—they were irrelevant. He kept his gaze locked on the starting lights. When each one had gone out, it would be time. The bike mattered, the track mattered, but the lights were key. He needed his start to be perfect.

Isaac clenched all his muscles as the last light disappeared. He sprang forward with faultless timing. Fabiano's Duc roared on his left and they left Vince behind. Over the years, there'd been the odd time when his brother had had mechanical trouble or mistimed the start. Not often. But today, it must have happened again. Isaac surged ahead of Vince.

Heart racing, Isaac ignored his senses that screamed to brake for the first corner as they thundered toward turn one, all twenty-eight riders on the track braking for the hard right. Waiting a fraction longer to slow the bike, he aimed for the inside of the lane. He leaned hard, squeaking by on the inside, sitting Fabiano up, slowing his rival for a split second. It was enough.

Isaac darted ahead and took the holeshot, rocketed around the Struben corner, powered down the back straight, flicked through the quick left-right-left-right, through the Timmer chicane, and wound onto the start-finish straight still in the lead. His pit board registered P1, L26, and #16 0.1. Fabiano was still the closest rider. Isaac put his head down and forgot everything in his quest to have a flawless race.

Isaac's concentration never wavered from hitting his exact speed, angle, and braking mark for each corner, curve, and each straight. Starting from the front of the grid and riding alone made it easier to stick to the line he wanted on the track for the best drive and to reduce the wear on his tires. Too bad he'd never qualified well before this year. For most of his MotoGP career, he'd spent the early laps fighting through the pack for position while the leaders escaped. Not since his final year of Moto2 had he had this kind of clear track.

He spared only a fraction of his attention for the sounds of other bikes or the feel that another rider was close. Vince should be on his ass, but the sound of multiple bikes not far behind grew fainter and fell into the distance. His pit board flashed at the edge of sight each lap. P1, L10, #16 6.5 sec. Exhilaration ran through him; he'd left them in the dust. This race was his to win. He just needed to keep his mind sharp, not let it wander. Focus.

Every twist and turn, Isaac led, but he didn't let up. Lap after lap, he maintained his rhythm and groove. He'd left the pack far behind but couldn't afford to let his concentration waver, or he'd be picking himself out of the gravel. Flying through the start-finish straight, this time his pit board read P1, L3. Three laps to go. Partway around the first corner section, something broke through his intense concentration. The race had been red-flagged. Stopped.

His brain whirring, he ran through scenarios as he slowed his pace. Would they call the race finished as they were more than two-thirds the total race distance, a rule used in the Moto2 and Moto3 levels? Would they restart the race, a three-lap sprint? His time advantage would be gone, though he'd start at the front.

Sitting up as he rode slowly back toward pit lane, he glanced at his dash. Maybe there would be a team communication to explain. Nothing came. He waved at the cameras and at the stands full of spectators as he continued the lap at a slow pace. A few other riders cruised past, looking as confused as he felt; they too acknowledged the fans in the packed grandstands. Nobody congratulated him because nobody else knew what was going on. Had he won?

Many of the fans stood on their feet. They weren't looking toward the track, but staring at the gigantic screens displaying the race feed. Maybe he needed to check out the same information.

Isaac flipped up his visor and slowed further to watch one of the giant screens. The race was over, and they'd declared him the winner.

He fist-pumped the sky, jubilation roaring through him. His gaze flipped to the scoreboard. Isaac Vasquez, MotoGP race winner. He'd done it. Tears trickled down his cheeks, soaking into the lining of his helmet. He'd actually won. It didn't seem real yet. After almost ten years at the top level, he'd given up on seeing this day arrive. One thing marred the exhilarating moment. Why had the race been called? It hadn't been the weather. Somebody must have crashed. His blood chilled. For the race to have been stopped, it must be serious.

That's when the realization hit like a hammer blow. Vince's name wasn't on the official scoreboard. Coming to a complete stop, Isaac vaulted off his bike, ripped off his helmet, and ran toward one of the TV screens where everyone had been staring. He skidded to a stop as the broadcast replayed the accident.

Behind him, five riders had been vying for position, and they all wanted the podium—Luka, Vince, Fabiano, Yoshi, and Spencer. From the drone camera angle, even in real-time instead of slow motion, the accident seemed inevitable.

Spencer had fallen behind and become desperate not to be left by the others. He'd tried to pass from too far back with a dangerous move and clipped Yoshi's wheel. They both went down. Yoshi landed on his back and his bike bounced across the track, pieces raining down. The bike catapulted into a Honda rider on the track around the corner in the next section, knocking the rider over. The second Honda rider had ridden into the gravel trying to avoid pieces of the accident but continued, as had Fabiano. There was no sound on the screen. Isaac had trouble breathing. Had the flying motorcycle smashed into Vince?

Isaac needed to see the incident again to be certain. Willing the outcome to be different. He watched while it replayed from several angles and sank to his knees, his helmet forgotten. Vince had been the rider taken out by the careening motorcycle. The replay continued, and Isaac struggled to comprehend. Vince lying motionless, surrounded by marshals who'd placed the medic sign, signaling they needed trackside medical. This was the nightmare they all avoided thinking could be reality.

Motorcycle racing was a dangerous sport. People died.

No matter how many times they showed the replay, in the end, Vince remained motionless.

The wail of an ambulance got Isaac to his feet, struggling to see the ground through his blurred vision. When he looked up, he didn't recognize the sobbing person on the massive screen. Then he realized it was him. He was the man sobbing. What had happened to Vince? Was he dead? Paralyzing fear shot through Isaac as his blood turned to ice. Over the years, he'd seen half a dozen riders die, even lost a friend in Barcelona in 2016. But he'd always thought Vince was invincible.

It was several minutes before Isaac pulled himself together. The ambulance had already left the stadium, and the cameraman had moved on while the network showed a subdued celebration in parc ferme as Luka and Fabiano arrived. No smiles and jubilation today. Isaac couldn't look at the screen anymore.

His legs shaking, he returned to his bike, which was no longer running. Without a starter, he had to abandon it. He pounded the bike's tank in frustration and headed to the nearby paved path that ringed the far outside of the track, behind the safety fence. He looked down the length of the fence. Where were the marshals? This was going to take too long. Not knowing his brother's condition was choking him.

He hadn't gone far when a marshal rode up behind him. "Want a ride back?"

Isaac nodded and, without a word, hopped onto the small bike behind the orange-clad race volunteer. Dread settled in his chest. What would he find when he returned to pit lane?

His heart clenched as Angel and Anna met him wearing serious expressions. Tears streaked her face. It must be serious.

"Vince?" Isaac hopped off the bike, patting the marshal's back in thanks. Isaac stared at Anna and Angel, waiting for their words as he held his breath, bracing himself for the worst. Please, let Vince be alive.

"Alive, but unconscious," said Angel, holding up his hands as though to prevent Isaac from chasing down the road after the ambulance.

"Is it critical?" Isaac clutched Anna's icy hand in his, needing her support. Vince was alive. He needed to get to the hospital. Isaac would rather do that than conduct post-race interviews or sign autographs. He needed to be there for his brother.

"I don't know if I can talk to the media." His throat ached with worry. A camera crew had already trained their lens on their conversation. Vultures. He kept his back turned and his voice low. "Any news from the med center?" His voice shook, and Anna squeezed his hand again. He'd forgotten that he was holding hers. His knuckles were white, so he forced himself to relax his grip.

"They skipped the med center and took him directly into the city to the hospital. The track medic said, at the very least, he has a concussion," said Angel. "His vitals are stable. Don't worry, your brother is a warrior." He gripped Isaac's shoulder, hard enough to almost hurt. "I've arranged a quick podium and a ride for you two to the hospital."

Isaac shook his head, preparing to refuse, but the look in Angel's eyes told him it was pointless to argue.

The older man continued. "Your contract says you have to do the interview, but everyone will understand if you keep it short. No autographs."

Isaac took a deep breath. He could keep it together that long. "Thank you. Let's get this over with."

Podium. He'd forgotten that he'd won the race. Without Vince there to celebrate, this victory was hollow. Isaac tuned out the swarming cameras and the crowd of reporters as they made their way into parc ferme. He would focus on these essential pieces of his job, then go to the hospital.

Isaac didn't remember the words he spoke to the media. It was a blur from the time he answered their questions to the moment he stood on atop the podium accepting the first-place trophy. He raised the trophy over his head. Removing his winner's cap for the Spanish national anthem, he stood at attention—separate from Luka and Fabiano. Afterward, the two of them sprayed each other with champagne while he half-heartedly shook his bottle and took a single sip. He tried, but he wasn't in a celebratory mood. Everyone must understand.

Soon he could leave the podium, and Angel escorted Anna and Isaac to a waiting car that drove them to the hospital. For all their hurry as they rushed inside the well-lit ER that smelled of disinfectant, there was no new information. Vince's head injury was serious, but he was stable. The doctors wouldn't know more until he woke up—which could be minutes, or it could be days.

The three of them sat in a row. Waiting. While noises in the busy ER continued around them. Hours passed without news. Anna fetched water and sandwiches nobody wanted to eat, and they settled in for a long night.

At midnight, Angel left, saying, "Text me if you hear anything. No matter the time."

Isaac nodded and sent another message to his mom, telling her to sleep if she could and that he'd update her in the morning or as soon as he heard anything. He willed his brother to hang in there. He needed Vince to be okay.

CHAPTER 15

Anna

Anna closed her eyes for what felt like only moments, but when she startled awake, the sun shone in the windows at the far end of the hospital waiting area. She stretched. They'd been in the hard plastic chairs all night, waiting for an update on Vince's condition. Being here like this brought back memories of her grandmother's accident when Anna had been twenty-one and close to graduating from university.

There'd been sleepless nights and cramped muscles then, too. She stood, her back cracking as she massaged her kinked neck. No matter what country it was in, hospitals were always uncomfortable. Isaac's head leaned against the wall where he slept with his feet braced on the floor, his long legs stretched out. At least he was getting some rest.

She sighed. Shouldn't they have heard something by now?

She glanced at Isaac again, checking that he was still asleep. Grabbing her wallet, she scuttled downstairs to get herself tea, coffee for him, and something quick for their breakfast. He was still sleeping when she returned, so she set his breakfast pastry on the side table next to him while she sipped her steaming beverage.

She glanced up when a white-coated doctor entered the room. She hadn't seen this one before. His gaze settled on Isaac, and the doctor moved toward them with purpose, so she rested her hand on Isaac's shoulder and whispered, "Honey, wake up. The doctor is here."

Isaac's eyes fluttered open. It took a second for him to react. Perhaps he was figuring out where they were and why. He yawned and stood stiffly, looking as though he was bracing himself for what the doctor would say, his feet shoulder-width apart. He took a deep breath. She took his hand and squeezed. Vince had to be all right.

"You must be Isaac Vasquez," said the doctor with a thin-lipped shadow of a weary smile. "The daredevil younger brother. It's a wonder both of you haven't been in hospitals more often." No-nonsense directness oozed from him. At least they might get the actual story from someone like him, rather than medical run-around and partial answers.

Isaac tightened his grip on Anna's hand and attempted a smile. "How's my brother?" She tried to radiate positive vibes, hoping the news was good.

The doctor said, "He's awake and doesn't seem to have any cognitive impairments. Physical symptoms include deep tissue bruises, a fractured collarbone, and two fractured ribs. The only issue is his diplopia, or double vision. I understand that he's suffered from this condition twice before. Concussion symptoms are cumulative, so we don't know how long it will take him to recover." He listed the injuries matter-of-factly. Most of it didn't sound too serious, though head injuries were always difficult to gauge healing time.

"The last time he had double vision, he worried it might be permanent," said Isaac. "Is that likely?" Through their joined hands, she felt his body stiffen.

If Vince couldn't see to race, his career would be over.

"We have no way of knowing at this stage." As a professional, the doctor's face gave nothing away. "We're recommending that your brother shouldn't fly right now. The noise and busy environment at both the airport and onboard the plane would be too much stimulation in his condition. He will also need a fair bit of help at home for the next while."

"I'll be there. I live with him."

Isaac's quick answer took Anna by surprise.

Not that he wouldn't want to care for his brother because, of course, he would, but because Isaac had moved out. Perhaps during the early recovery, staying with his brother at the villa made the most sense. It didn't seem the time to ask, but where did that leave her? It had all just happened, and she and Isaac hadn't discussed their living arrangement again. Not Portugal and the beach for certain. Was she supposed to move in at Vince's too, or would she be going back to the Inn? She squared her shoulders. Isaac could help Vince and she could support Isaac. She'd do whatever she could to help.

"He won't want to stay here." Isaac looked out the window, perhaps considering their options for returning to Spain from the Netherlands. "I'll rent a car. It's only a two-day drive to get home."

The doctor nodded. "We can discharge him tomorrow, allowing you to make travel arrangements tonight. Would you like me to take you back to see him?"

"Yes, please." Isaac dropped Anna's hand and reached for the coffee she'd brought him. He turned to her. "I'll be back in not too long. We'll go back to the hotel afterward, figure out a car, and get cleaned up."

"Maybe more sleep too," she said. Dark shadows ringed his eyes, and he needed to shave, but he looked better than earlier. Waking up was a positive first step in Vince's recovery. She was exhausted, and she wasn't the one who had raced yesterday. Isaac must be ready to drop.

His wan smile said it all as he left, following the doctor down the hall where they disappeared.

She was happy for Isaac that his brother was alright. Vince couldn't race with double-vision, but it had gone away before—hopefully, it would again.

•　•　•

An hour and a half later, they returned to the hotel, and Isaac flopped onto the bed. He'd kicked off his shoes but was otherwise still dressed.

"I just need a minute, then I'll get undressed." He closed his eyes.

Before Anna could speak, his deep, even breaths showed he was already falling asleep. She should leave him be—he'd dropped off so fast. She couldn't sleep like that. Slipping into the bathroom, she took a quick shower, washing the smell and feel of the hospital from her skin. A million small things to do ran through her head as the hot water rushed over her and down the drain.

Once out of the shower, she texted Angel. *"Don't know if Isaac told you. Vince is awake. Battered and bruised. Has a concussion. We'll get the hotel to let us into Vince's room later today to collect his stuff."* It wasn't her place to mention the diplopia.

She was about to lie down to rest despite the daylight seeping in through the edges of the blinds and curtains when her phone vibrated. She debated ignoring it, but it might be something important. Picking it up, a pit formed in her stomach. She didn't want to, but she should answer. She slid into the bathroom, where she could speak without disturbing Isaac. Her eyes ached, and she longed to sleep, but this was Adam's work number. Had he gotten her new number from Sandra?

"Hello." Despite the privacy, she kept her voice quiet.

"Oh my god, Anna. You answered. It's about time." Adam's self-important voice was just how she remembered. "How've you been, Babe?"

"What do you want?" She didn't want to talk to him if he was going to chit-chat and not get to the point.

"Sweetheart, that's no way to speak to someone. You're being rude again." Adam's rebuke and overly familiar term of endearment caused a stab of pain in her temple. He was a headache even long distance.

"I've had two hours of sleep. You probably should speak to my lawyer, anyway. What do you want?" Her patience was already wafer thin, and she regretted answering.

"I miss you," he said. "And I was wondering how long it will be until you come home from Texas or whatever ridiculous jaunt you've gone on."

His words grated on her nerves as he continued.

"I don't want you to regret selling our place and ending things whenever you come to your senses."

At least he didn't know she lived in Spain. Her entire head now pounded. "Adam, I'm not coming back. We're over. Not just right now. For good. What happened?" Before he answered, she said, "Tiffany dumped you. Didn't she?"

There was a pause that told her she'd struck the truth.

"I want you to come home."

Did he believe his own lies? She deserved better than Adam. How had she ever put up with this pretentious idiot?

"You just want to keep living in my townhouse for free. You need to move. If you have nothing essential to tell me, next time, call my lawyer." Answering had been pointless.

"Anna, don't hang up. I'll sign the papers, provided you meet me in person. No lawyers, just me and you."

That was the last thing she wanted. "Why?"

"I want you to look me in the face and tell me it's really over."

"It's over. You cheated. You don't love me. Give up, move out, and if you have questions, talk to my lawyer. I'm blocking this number." Her hands were shaking as she hung up and made it so he couldn't call from work again. A sense of satisfaction suffused her. She'd stuck up for herself and handled the conflict on her own.

Her head pounded as she came out of the bathroom, plugged in her phone, and lay down, resting her hand on Isaac's chest, which rose and fell in even rhythm as he slept. Laying next to him was peaceful. The two men were the same age, but that was where the similarity ended. She hadn't dared to think too far ahead with Adam, but even after just a few months, she couldn't imagine her life without Isaac. He respected her and gave her the care and love she'd always hoped for. Closing her eyes, she fell asleep.

•   •   •

A wave of relief washed over Anna when they pulled into Cervera in the rental car two days later. The excruciating road trip was over at last. Vince, with his battered body, had been in pain for the duration. He hadn't complained but had been snappish and bossy. She excused him for his poor manners because she probably would have been similar—if not worse. Two long days in the car had been enough for all of them, though Isaac had been patient, with never a harsh word in response to Vince's foul humor.

That evening, once they'd settled Vince at his place, Anna and Isaac returned to their rental house to collect their belongings. At last, they had time on their own.

"Adam called the other day." Her voice was even and calm.

"What did he want?" Isaac said as he grabbed a stack of shirts from his drawer and shoved them in a duffle bag. A pile of shorts followed. He packed everything.

"He wanted to convince me to come back to Seattle. So he didn't have to move out of the townhouse."

"Have you seen my running shoes?" Isaac said, looking around the empty closet.

His lack of reaction surprised her. Her first feeling was hurt, but she looked at the bigger picture. Isaac was so wrapped up in Vince and his recovery that perhaps her information seemed unimportant. She felt foolish for bringing it up. Maybe she was making too big a deal out of Adam's call. Next time, she'd only bother Isaac if something significant happened. She'd handled this already, and he was busy with more important things.

For the first few days back at Vince's, Anna tried to help Isaac by cooking, getting groceries, and running errands at the market, but Isaac had to return to the market and cook when Vince requested a recipe that Isaac knew how to make, and Anna didn't. Vince made several other food requests that she was unfamiliar with, and Isaac found her looking up recipes.

"I've got a great recipe," he said. "I can make those things. They're Vince's comfort food. I don't mind."

Isaac took over the cooking, and she reminded herself that it was one of his favorite things. Perhaps he needed it to unwind.

Several times Anna tried to write, but Vince always interrupted, at first looking for Isaac or asking her to pass on information. Sometimes he sat and asked questions about her manuscript. She appreciated the interest, but not the constant distraction.

If he wasn't talking to her, Vince often played loud music or brought his computer to the living room or on the patio to listen to old races. With his vision bothering him, he couldn't play video games or watch movies, his usual pastimes when he wasn't training or working out. He couldn't read either, but that one he didn't seem to mind. He must be stressed out and bored, maybe even looking for company, but he made it hard to concentrate.

It was impossible for Anna to get into a groove with her writing. Vince was used to constantly training and had far too much energy. She felt for him, and it was his house, but the feeling swelled within her, and she wanted to be left alone. Though self-imposed, she was under a deadline, as time kept ticking and November edged closer every day.

Just in case, she updated her CV and bookmarked a few jobs she would be qualified for, including two that she might be able to stay abroad and work remotely. Maybe there would be a way to make an income while she finished writing and querying. She wanted to stay with Isaac, not return to America. A long-term, long-distance relationship was doomed.

Anna's frustration and the feeling that she was unproductive and, in the way, grew each day. She needed to finish this story and move on to revisions and preparing query materials. Not only was she nearly thirty and yet to do something worthwhile in her career, but the end of November loomed, increasing her sense of urgency.

On the fourth day since returning home, she went to Isaac.

"Can we talk?" She had difficulty speaking, knowing he might not like what she was about to say. Even if they'd never argued, the possibility tied her stomach in knots.

"Uh-huh," he said absently, glancing up from the website on diplopia treatment and remedies where he'd been reading. His eyes returned to the article before she spoke, which made her gut clench tighter. He'd been off since their return home, and she didn't understand why. Vince was improving, but Isaac seemed more worried, not less.

Anna tried to keep her explanation brief, so she didn't lose the rest of his attention. "There are two things. First, I don't have the funds to stay in Spain and off work past the end of November." He knew that, but what else she had to say needed context.

He still faced the screen. "You don't need money. I can pay your rent, or maybe we should move back here where it's free."

"I believe in paying my share." She didn't want to take advantage of Isaac the way Adam had taken advantage of her. Besides, this was Vince's house, and he hadn't invited her to live here. Though she and Vince were getting along better, it was still awkward being here all the time. She would have stayed at the rental house for a little longer, but she didn't want to sleep there without Isaac, who wanted to be near his brother in case he was needed at night.

"I was thinking about the rental," Isaac said. "We aren't there anymore. I thought I'd call them today and let them know so they can rent it to someone else."

"I don't want to live with Vince." Anna blurted the truth.

Isaac's jaw set. "I'm not asking you to live with Vince, but I can't leave him."

He wasn't understanding. She took another tack. "If you don't want the rental anymore, we should give it up." That wasn't what she'd come to talk to him about.

Isaac stopped reading and swiveled toward her with a slight crease between his brows. Maybe he sensed that she was unhappy. "Do you want to leave?"

"No," she said, hurt that he would even ask. Her chest tightened. Of course, she didn't want to leave him. "It's not about me and you."

She took a deep breath. "Adam will only sign the papers from my lawyer if I meet him in person. I don't want to, but if I don't, the sale will take too long. Maybe I could meet him in Texas with my lawyer. If it means the house sells, I can afford the flight and pay my share of our rent. Wherever we end up."

"When were you thinking of going?" he said.

"The last week of the break," she said. With Vince's slow improvement, Isaac couldn't commit to coming with her, even if his support would be welcome. He also could be back in full training mode right before the next races. It wasn't the best time for him to travel.

"That's a good idea," he said. "What's your other problem?"

This was trickier to explain. Something about being here in Vince's house where she didn't feel like she belonged was preventing her from writing. She had time but no inspiration. Constant interruptions also inhibited her efforts. There was nowhere here to call her own. She decided to just lay out her thoughts.

"I can't write here." She held her breath, scrutinizing him as she waited for his answer. "I can't get in the zone."

His attention focused on her again. "You could go to the beach house in Portugal."

"Without you?" Her brow tightened. She hadn't considered leaving him behind.

"I might make it at some point. Vince's bruises are a lot better, and his bones are healing. His headaches are less, and he says his vision is improving, even if it's still double." Isaac didn't sound convinced.

"Maybe your mom could help or take over for a week," said Anna, biting her lip. Isaac shouldn't bear this burden on his own. "She's already offered, twice."

"He's my responsibility," said Isaac, his voice leaving no room for argument. "He needs me. After I ignored him and moved out for over a month, it's the least I can do. He might not have crashed if he hadn't been pushing so hard and under so much pressure to win."

"You were under almost the same pressure." The words popped from her mouth.

"It's not the same. He's the champion. Plus, I need to take care of him." Isaac's disagreement shut down the conversation. "I worry about him being here alone."

She didn't agree. Was there something she was missing? Isaac was right to have moved out, and since the accident, he'd gone the extra mile. Vince had been an ass—and sometimes, he still was. If she'd been in Isaac's place she wouldn't have been as quick to forgive and forget. Arguments lingered and built up if there wasn't proper resolution. Not just an apology but actual amends were required. That was how her brain worked.

"You're sure you don't mind if I go to Portugal on my own?" said Anna, considering the possibility. She'd be lonely, but probably productive.

"Of course not," said Isaac. "Your goal for the break was to finish your story. That's important, and I don't want to impede your writing. You should go."

The beach house would be peaceful. There would be fewer interruptions, and swimming would feel amazing in the heat of the day. Summers in Spain were hotter than she was used to after living in the Pacific Northwest her whole life. Portugal would be similar, but with the ocean nearby.

Here, Vince's restlessness and misery weighed on her emotions. An escape seemed ideal, except that she didn't want to leave without Isaac. Though she'd spent years living on her own and could look after herself, everything was better together. She liked the idea of Isaac joining her later. If she worked hard, she could finish the draft of her story, and there might still be opportunities to spend quality time together while she tackled revisions and lined up an editor for the fall. Still, it might be longer than a week. What if Isaac didn't come?

So she wouldn't feel so disappointed, she ran through scenarios. She'd come to Europe to write, not to fall in love, even if she was trying to succeed with both the writing and her relationship. Even if Isaac didn't come for two more weeks, he'd be there for the last ten days.

It seemed like a workable solution.

"If you'd like, I can drive you to Barcelona tomorrow to catch a train," he said, his eyes flicking once more toward the screen and his research.

CHAPTER 16

Isaac

Isaac wandered the house, still feeling distracted as he gathered his book and his keys. His mind kept circling back to his last conversation with Anna before she'd left on vacation. The details weren't as clear as they should have been. He'd been so worried about Vince spiraling into depression because of his injury, that Isaac hadn't been able to think straight. Anna had left at his suggestion, but he couldn't recall exactly what he'd said. He frowned, unable to escape this new worry. He hoped she hadn't been offended.

He should have told her about Vince's past, even if nobody outside the family knew the secret.

Time seemed to drag without her around.

He headed upstairs to collect Vince for an appointment.

"You're so mopey and miserable," said Vince as Isaac drove, taking his brother to a follow-up with a specialist in Barcelona. "You're not regretting staying with me, are you?"

"Of course not," Isaac snapped without thinking. "What makes you think I'm moping?"

"You've been wandering the house for the last three days like you don't know what to do with yourself. I don't need you to look after me twenty-four seven."

His brother's words got him thinking. Isaac wished that he'd been able to go with Anna to Portugal to frolic at the beach and make love on the patio under the stars, not to mention swim in the warm ocean. Cervera was inland and hot. He'd been looking forward to being at the coast since the Portimão race in April. But it just wasn't the right time, not with Vince's injury. The uncertainty about his brother's condition weighed on him. Even more, Vince's mental health needed monitoring. If he couldn't race, they might have a problem.

Throughout the drive and during lunch, he couldn't shake the idea that he might not have made the best decision when he'd sent Anna away alone. Vince didn't think he needed full-time care, so why had he stayed? Isaac could remind Vince about his eye exercises, drive him to appointments, cook, and keep him somewhat entertained, but if this appointment turned out well, Vince might need him less.

Isaac leaned back in his chair, resting his head on the wall of the specialist's waiting area as he considered what came next after the summer break. He hoped Vince could race the second half of the season. Once racing resumed, his time with Vince, if he was still recovering, would be reduced and he and Anna could spend more time together again. Plus, Vince had a championship to defend.

"Good news," Vince said as he left the doctor's office. His smile was wide and genuine.

•   •   •

Isaac's mom stopped by the house a couple of days after Vince's positive appointment, and she seemed surprised to find Isaac on his own.

"Where is your Anna? I would love a proper visit this time," she said as she expertly chopped a whole chicken with a boning knife. "Down in the village?" They were cooking another of Vince's favorites for dinner.

"I sent her ahead to the house that we rented on the beach in Portugal." Isaac couldn't keep the disappointment from his voice. "For our summer holiday." It sounded lame. He wasn't sure why he couldn't ask for help and join her, but the words stuck in his throat. What was wrong with asking for something for himself?

He counted the days since Anna had gone, surprised to discover it had been a week already. No wonder he missed her so much he ached.

"Not much of a holiday with you here and her there," said his mother as she arranged the pieces of chicken in a glass dish with spiced rice and chopped vegetables. "I'd be happy to stay with Vince for a week or two. My schedule is flexible now that I've retired."

"Maybe later. Vince is my responsibility," said Isaac, turning away to pour another glass of sparkling water. He didn't want to have to explain his guilt. Vince might not have had the accident if Isaac hadn't pushed him so hard to succeed and prove himself still the champion.

"The way I see it," his mother said, stopping what she was doing. "Vince is my son, therefore, also my responsibility. He's injured, his soul is hurting because he's scared he will lose what he loves, and he's alone. Other than family, racing is all he has."

"Ma," Isaac interrupted. "I know. That's why I'm the best person to be with him. I understand better than anyone else. He lost almost two years after his arm took forever to heal. Which is why I moved in. I stayed with him through all four surgeries and the long road to recovery. I saw the toll. I was the one on suicide watch." He looked down to find he'd clenched both fists.

"I'd hoped Anna was the one to make you see that there is more to life than Vince and racing," said his mom as she threw their dinner in the oven, closing it with a bang. "She's got more substance than Isabella who bolted at the first sign of trouble."

Her words were like a splash of cold water on his face, a wake-up call. It was strange to hear something that had been on his mind come from his mother's mouth.

"She has. Anna's perfect for that mom, but she's trying to finish writing a novel and was having a difficult time concentrating while here." He'd forgotten about the connection between Isabella and Vince's difficult recovery years ago. Their breakup had been another reason he'd stopped dating.

His mom pursed her lips and raised her eyebrows, though she didn't speak. Not yet.

Her lack of opinion threw him off, so he babbled additional explanation. "Vince is bored because he can't do anything he likes. He followed Anna around, talking. He didn't know what to do with himself. It was much better than being nasty, and I'm glad he was trying to get to know her, but you know Vince. It's all-or-nothing with everything. I appreciated his effort, but I think she was frustrated." Anna was like his brother in the all-or-nothing department.

"Maybe after the way Vince spoke to her last month, she found it uncomfortable to be around him so much." His mother looked at him sideways. "He was awful. I was so embarrassed that a son of mine would speak like that to a lady, especially one you love."

Her voice had taken on a mother lecturing tone that she'd seldom used on him since he was a teenager.

"Vince apologized, and he meant it." Isaac shrugged, returning to the fridge to avoid making eye contact. His mom had a way of making him see his shame. Had he been thoughtless? He hadn't considered that Anna might still be bothered by Vince's behavior prior to Assen, but his mother had always been perceptive.

His mom stepped away from the counter and pointed at him with a piece of celery. "You've always been such a good boy, so easy-going. I'm not sure we were always fair to you." She sounded regretful as she returned to her salad-making.

"What do you mean?" Isaac frowned. "You and Dad were fair."

She stopped chopping and set the knife down with a sigh. "We always made sure Vince's talent didn't go to waste, that he had every opportunity, but we didn't mean to let him overshadow you. Your needs are as important as his, and we should have made that clear. He's never been your responsibility. You're his brother, not his parents or caregiver, and not his partner."

Her words were a lot for Isaac to digest, so he turned away to set the oven timer, opting for a slight change of topic.

"Anna is also away because she's worried about paying rent in the fall and winter and has to sell her old place in Seattle. Her lawyer is in Texas."

"Doesn't she understand that you'll take care of her?" His mom squeezed his face. "You have more money than you know what to do with, all those contracts for millions, and you've hardly spent a Euro."

His mother's words triggered a forgotten item and his blood ran cold. In the panic over Vince's accident, he'd forgotten his plan for after the Assen race. He hadn't spoken to Spencer. Guilt surged through him, making his stomach churn. He'd let Anna down even if she didn't know. That wasn't taking care of her. He'd been taking her for granted and forgotten the one thing she needed most.

Just then, Vince wandered into the kitchen, his hand trailing along the wall as a guide while he walked. A patch on his functioning eye forced him to use the other. The specialist earlier this week had been optimistic that Vince was on the road to recovery—it would just take time. Isaac hoped that his vision would soon return, good as new. Vince had one arm tucked in a sling to immobilize his fractured collarbone, but his injuries no longer limited his mobility, even if he hadn't been cleared to train. The three of them moved outside to the patio where they sat and drank wine while they waited for dinner to bake.

As the evening progressed, they told stories about his father, he and Vince sharing their favorite childhood memories and his mom reminiscing about the early days of her marriage when she and his father had first fallen in love. They'd been inseparable. He and Anna could be like that. His mom smiled, and her voice softened when she talked about playing music and dancing in the kitchen while they cooked. Isaac had always wanted a relationship like his parents'—they'd provided an excellent example of a close and loving couple.

They hadn't talked like this before, just the three of them. It felt cathartic to talk about the happy memories without the fresh, raw wound of his father's passing. Isaac missed him, but life continued. Though he was having a wonderful evening, the one thing missing was Anna. If she'd been there, it would have been perfect.

Before his mom left the next morning, she took him aside. "Just call me when you're ready for your vacation. I'll stay here. Vince and I will get along fine." Standing in the driveway, she waited for his answer.

"I will," Isaac promised, his voice cracking with surprising emotion. They weren't empty words. He would figure shit out and go to Portugal before it was too late. He didn't want to lose Anna. Now that he was seeing clearly, he was afraid he'd been dismissive in sending her away with no time frame for his arrival. He'd neglected to keep her in the loop about this thinking, cutting her off from the worries in his mind.

He hoped she didn't think he was like Adam, who had taken her for granted for so long. Had his behavior before she left driven a wedge between them? She'd said nothing of the kind, but he didn't like wondering if he might have caused a problem. He'd fallen in love with her and needed to make this right.

"Don't wait too long," said his mother, giving him a hug that interrupted his thoughts. She climbed into her car and leaned out the window. "Women don't like to be left hanging for long with no time for them and vague assurances. Trust me, I know."

Her words stayed with him the rest of the morning, and Isaac struggled to be present for his brother. Agonizing thoughts of Anna and Spencer and how to handle the situation still swirled in his head. A phone call to Australia wouldn't mean much. He had to confront the jerk in person as soon as they arrived in Finland and force him to stop his harassment. It was unacceptable.

"I'm going for a run. You okay for a bit?" Running would clear Isaac's head and give him a respite from his busy thoughts.

Vince nodded, his mouth down-turned the way it had been since the accident. "Hey. I've been meaning to ask. Did you and Anna have a fight? Is that why she left? I'm here if you need to talk."

It was kind of him to ask.

"Nope. She just wanted to get away for a bit and focus on her writing. When I talked to her a couple of days ago, she mentioned that she's been productive there." That had been yesterday or the day before? No, it had been three days. He owed her several messages and a call.

"The story she's writing sounds interesting," said Vince. "Has she talked to you about it much?"

"Some," said Isaac. "She doesn't say much because she doesn't want to spoil it for me when I read it. I plan to as soon as she says it's ready."

"I'm glad you found someone smart and talented. Someone with passion," said Vince. "You were right from the start. She's perfect for you. I'm sorry I was an ass and didn't see it immediately."

"I told you she was amazing," said Isaac with a smile. His Anna was one-of-a-kind.

"So, really, why are you here?" Vince tugged his ear. "You should be in Portugal."

"You need me," said Isaac. "I don't want to be anywhere else." As soon as the words left his mouth, they felt like only partial truth. He also wanted to be with Anna. He had trouble sleeping without her. His bed had been cold, and her positive vibe had uplifted everyone in the house, though he'd only noticed after she'd gone.

"Other than out for a run." Vince gave him the first hint of a smile since they'd returned. "And maybe with your girlfriend on a beach holiday. But other than that." He shrugged. "It isn't like before you know. I'm recovering. There's an end in sight." He grinned. "No pun intended."

Vince seemed to be telling the truth. It hit Isaac like a gut punch. This *was* different.

"Right." He checked his runners were double-knotted. "Back in an hour and a half."

Isaac went for a long run, working up a good, hard sweat as he tried to empty his mind. It didn't work but provided some much-needed clarity as he tried to figure out what to do with the snarl in his life. Maybe he should look for his own place to live—somewhere to buy, not rent. He'd stay with Vince while he was needed, but that wouldn't be much longer. If he was honest, Vince didn't need him all the time now. He would be fine if Isaac left. His brother might get bored, but since when did that cause irreparable damage? He needed help with driving and errands, but there was no reason their mom couldn't help.

Isaac didn't want to get Anna's hopes up about having a home because he didn't know how long it would take. Until he could surprise her with a house, he would keep this plan to himself. He would make sure there was office space for her, one with windows overlooking the beautiful Spanish countryside and a door that locked. He would show her she was special and that he respected her need for a place to call her own.

Bounding up the stairs after his run, searching for a pen to make a list of what he planned to deal with, he came across his forgotten therapy journal. He'd shoved it in the drawer to hide it from Vince last spring. He hadn't made an appointment in months, nor had he recorded many of his thoughts. Turning the small blue notebook over in his hands, he opened it to the second page and read what he'd written in March, the day he'd met Anna.

'I love Vince and cherish these years we've had together. Training and traveling the world, from racetrack to racetrack. He's my best friend. But when we stop, he'll still be the brightest star in motorcycle racing history. What will I be? Vince Vasquez's little brother. I need to find out what else I can be. I want more. There has to be more to life than living for my brother.'

His written words hit him hard. He'd wanted to find out who he was without his brother and had made strides toward that, but he wasn't done. Coming back here after the accident, he'd backslid, giving up what made him happy. He'd fallen into his old role as supporter and wingman without a life for himself.

Anna was one piece of reorganizing his life. Buying his own home would be a second. The third was to act on what he'd decided about next year. He would tell Anna in person as soon as he joined her and discuss it with others later. Riding back with the race marshal after Vince's accident, he'd reached a final decision. He'd finish out this year and retire.

Isaac had set out hoping to win a race, and at last, he had. His racing bucket list was complete, and he didn't need to prove anything to anyone. What if he'd been the one lying in a hospital bed with broken bones? He'd avoided thoughts like that for his entire career, but it was time to face the facts. Racing was dangerous.

Though Isaac hadn't been willing to admit it, living with the fear and uncertainty was too much to ask of a long-term partner. It couldn't be easy to be married to a motorcycle racer, always afraid that the next accident would be devastating. He'd never had a serious injury, and he should quit while he was ahead. Luck wouldn't always be on his side.

He wouldn't tell anyone else yet, except Angel and LCR Honda, who needed to know. He owed them time to make arrangements with a new rider as a replacement next year. They wouldn't be able to keep his decision from the press forever, but even a month would give him time to break it to Vince. No matter the eventual outcome of Vince's recovery or the championship, Isaac was done. He flipped the journal to the next page and wrote the date before scrawling a brief paragraph.

"I've defied the odds too many times and Vince's accident opened my eyes. I won't be able to have a family and spend my life with Anna if I throw it away on the track. There is more to life than racing."

As he read the page, the decision seemed more real.

When he went downstairs to cook dinner, he left the journal on the desk. He would keep writing and working on himself. He owed it to himself.

Isaac hadn't felt this way about racing when he was younger—life at the track had been all-encompassing and all-consuming. He enjoyed riding fast, and he liked to win. It had been simple. He couldn't quite remember when that had changed, but it probably had a lot to do with his father dying and being unable to make plans for the future. He took out his phone and studied the lock screen photo.

He and Anna had taken a selfie, pressed cheek-to-cheek, grinning. He longed to drop everything and go to her, but that would have to wait. He still had responsibilities, and it was difficult to put himself first, but he was trying. He needed a few more days to get everything in order.

•   •   •

It was one thing for Isaac to decide to put himself first, another to put it into practice. He took longer runs and increased his conditioning on his road bike. Just because Vince couldn't train yet, didn't mean he should let himself go. He wrote in his journal daily, forcing himself to write his thoughts instead of tamping them down to ignore.

He dreaded the phone call to Angel, but he forced himself to make it. When he hung up, his hands shook, and some of the weight had lifted. He'd done one of the hardest jobs. Angel hadn't seemed surprised at his decision and wished him well.

It was official. He was retiring after Valencia. Eleven races from now.

Next, he called his mom and arranged a two-week window for her to stay with Vince starting this Friday. It would be up to Vince if she stayed longer. The last thing he did before packing was to call Catarina's mother, Lily, who was a real estate agent.

"This is Isaac Vasquez," he said. "I'm headed out of town for a couple of weeks, but I'd like to hire you to find me a house and property, at least half a hectare. I'd like to buy in this area."

"That's wonderful," she said. "What do you have in mind?"

"Somewhere close to Vince's but with flatter land, so I can make a beginner dirt bike track," he said. "And a house big enough for a family, including a guest suite for my mother to live in someday."

They discussed other criteria, like the office with a window, while she took notes.

At the end, Isaac said, "Please keep this conversation confidential. I'd like to surprise my girlfriend, and I don't want Vince to hear that I've bought a house until I tell him myself."

"I understand," the older woman said. "Keep it on the down-low, as Catarina and her sisters would say. Consider it done. I'll let you know when I have a shortlist of places to show you."

Isaac hung up and looked around his room, taking stock. Though he'd technically moved out, his belongings were here again. It left an ache inside that Anna was able to take all of her things. Everything she had still fit in a single suitcase and the airport tote bag she had when she arrived. He was lucky. His room had a decade's worth of memories. She'd once mentioned a storage locker with colored glass dishes from her grandmother. He'd be sure to buy a cabinet where they could be displayed in the new house. The idea of making her happy made him satisfied.

He considered sending Anna a text to let her know he was, at last, joining her, but decided instead to let his arrival in Portugal be a surprise.

CHAPTER 17

Anna

Returning from her afternoon swim, Anna slung her beach bag onto her shoulder as she trudged up the path. The water had been refreshing and the beach house had been everything she'd hoped, but the ten days she'd spent here had also been lonely—especially at night when she wasn't writing. She'd had nightmares that featured Spencer, ones that left her crying, shaken, and unable to get back to sleep. When she slept next to Isaac, she felt safe and unsettling dreams hadn't been a problem.

Eventually, she'd gotten up to work on her book, taking some time to enjoy the sunrise. Early this morning, she'd written the ending, and tightened it up over tea and breakfast.

She was excited about the story, though it was much darker in tone than she'd expected. Thoughts of darkness brought her back around to worrying about Spencer. How would she avoid him when they returned to racing? If it wasn't for Isaac, she might have quit her umbrella girl gig. Money or no money. The reason she loved being at the racetracks was because he was there and he loved it. She'd even become a fan of the sport.

Yesterday she'd expected Isaac to call or text, but once again, he'd been silent. She could have called him, like every time they'd spoken so far, but she wanted to give him a chance to make the first move. She didn't want to seem clingy when he was helping his brother. He might be too busy to talk to her. Maybe she was bothering him too often when he had more important things to think about. There'd been several bouts of insecurity recently, with thoughts that maybe Isaac wasn't head over heels, even if she was. Maybe she'd misread the situation, and she'd simply been convenient. That didn't feel true, but it was her worry.

These thoughts bruised her heart.

She kicked a rock as she left the beach and watched it skitter along the shoreline path. In the ten days since she'd arrived in Portugal, she'd averaged ten hours a day writing her story. Her modern fairytale was complicated, rife with both beauty and horror, and she was proud of what she'd accomplished. She'd written an entire book-length story from beginning to end.

She'd sent Isaac a text mid-morning to share her accomplishment, but he hadn't replied. Had he become so wrapped up in Vince and his old life that he was drifting away? Perhaps the distance made it easier for him to let her go. It would be easier to bear than fighting and breaking up, but no less painful. She left the beach and strolled up the stairs toward the house on the cliff overlooking the ocean.

The beach property was perfect, and Portugal was lovely. It should have been an ideal vacation but, without Isaac, it was lacking. Being here was something she and Isaac had planned for the two of them. Since the day she arrived, when she'd stocked up at the market, she had gone nowhere else to take advantage of her holiday. All she'd done was write and wander down to the water for a swim every afternoon. It had been more like work than a vacation. Maybe tomorrow she should celebrate the end of her book by doing touristy things and enjoy herself with something new. She could find some more gelato, too.

She wasn't sure what remained to eat in the house for dinner tonight, but she didn't feel like going out, so she'd have to find something. Tomorrow she'd get groceries and let her story sit for a few days before starting revisions. Maybe even a week. She'd leave it longer if she could, but her fall deadline still loomed. She'd read that editing advice somewhere, that taking a break allowed you to have fresh eyes when you read over it the next time.

Maybe that was the same with people. If you were away, you saw things differently when they were around again, like the expression that absence makes the heart grow fonder. Turning the last corner of the windy stairs up from the beach to the rental, she looked up. A man sat on the front stairs of her beach house. She took only another step before the realization of who it was sunk in, and she bounded up the final stairs. She arrived at the top as Isaac jumped forward and swung her up and around in her favorite kind of Isaac hug. He felt like he always did and she exhaled a deep breath, all her doubts and worry expelled.

He squeezed her tight. "I missed you. I'm an idiot and should have come sooner. Will you forgive me?" He set her down and met her gaze, waiting for an answer.

A smile tugged at her lips, and she pulled his mouth down to hers. The familiar tingle of electricity ran through her, stronger than ever. Absence hadn't strengthened her feelings. She was already all-in.

"I missed you too." She'd missed the warmth of his eyes and the way his smile lit up the world, making everything better. She stepped back, suddenly self-conscious of her sandy, sunscreen-covered skin that had left her sticky.

"You aren't getting away from me yet," he said, tugging her closer and kissing her again. The faint scent of his peppermint soap enveloped her, and she inhaled. Everything about being with Isaac took the edge away. She felt safe, something she couldn't remember feeling anywhere else since her grandmother had died. She'd been silly to doubt.

When they came up for air, she said, "Shower with me? I'm covered in saltwater, sunscreen, and sand. You know how I hate feeling gritty."

"A shower. Now you're talking. I'm hot from the road." Isaac returned to his car and hefted a suitcase from the trunk while she waited before going inside into the air-conditioned interior together. He leaned into the car and grabbed his phone, glancing at the screen.

"You finished your story." He grinned. "Congratulations."

"That's why you didn't answer," she said, a wide smile taking over her face. "You were driving." She turned, unlocked the door, and led Isaac toward the master bedroom and the ensuite's double shower.

The shower was about getting clean, and they didn't linger.

After drying off, Anna leaned into Isaac again, kissing him again while his arms wrapped around her. She wanted to touch him everywhere and remind herself that he was real. Despite her urgency to have him inside her, she let him take the lead. His slow, thorough kisses made her toes curl and her insides warm while the electric buzz on her skin everywhere he touched set her heart racing.

When they fell naked and entwined on the bed, she was beyond thought and lived in the moment, enjoying the physical sensations. Isaac took her away from the noise in her head better than anything else. The world fell away when they were together.

"Mi Corazon, I have news," Isaac said sometime later when they lay in a loose tangle on the rumpled bed while he traced circles on her shoulder. "How would you feel about me retiring next year? I wanted to tell you in person, but I talked to Angel yesterday and made it official." He stiffened as he spoke. He might be worried about how she'd take the news.

She marveled that her opinion mattered.

"You decided not to take the contract extension," she said. "That's brave. If you're happy with the decision, so am I." If he retired, they would probably still watch the races, but then she wouldn't have to fear for Isaac. He had said little before now, but Vince's accident had left him ashen, and she'd known leaving the sport had been on his mind even before the crash.

"I think racing is too dangerous for me now. When Vince was laying there, not moving, I couldn't breathe. I can't stand the idea that one day that could be me, and you'd be the one scared out of your mind. I never want to do that to you." Isaac's warm brown eyes were serious. It couldn't have been easy to reach this decision.

"Will you race the rest of this season?" She couldn't imagine that he'd throw away his excellent season or break his current commitment.

He stroked her hip. "I'm under contract for this season, but then I'm done."

"What will you do afterward?" She bit her lip while she waited for his answer. This type of intimacy was unfamiliar territory. They hadn't talked about their future beyond the racing season.

Isaac cupped her jaw in his hand, making her melt once more as he stared into her with milk-chocolate eyes. "Maybe we can figure some of that out together. I want you to stay with me. I want us to have our own place. My love, my house will not be a home without you inside it. I won't keep living with Vince. I hadn't realized how much I love being around your positive energy until you were gone. Vince said I was moping." He gave a rueful laugh.

"You were busy this week," she said. "I should have asked you about Vince. How's his eyesight?"

Isaac chuckled. "Vince is on the mend. He might not be ready for the first race in Finland, but probably the following one in Silverstone the first weekend in August. Yesterday, his doctor cleared him to train."

He hesitated, his face sobering. "I owe you an apology about the way I let you leave."

Her breath caught at his unexpected words even if they had already made up. "It was for Vince. He's your brother. No apology required."

He shook his head, his eyes serious. "Vince is important, but I can't let him be first all the time. I slipped into an old habit, and I shouldn't have let you leave without me." His voice took on a more distant quality. "I thought I had to put Vince first. It turns out, I was wrong. Sometimes I should come first. I've done it for so long, I expected it was my burden."

"What made you come to your senses?" Her heart fluttered at the way Isaac trusted her with his secrets and his fears. If only she could explain everything on her mind. She shoved the stray thought away— she'd tell him later. She didn't want anything negative to ruin their holiday.

"Mom set me straight. She reminded me how much I've given up for Vince already. I couldn't risk losing us because I was busy trying to look out for him. He's a grown-ass adult and doesn't need me like that. It won't happen again." He smiled and pounced on her, pinning her to the bed. "Unlike other things that are going to happen a lot this week." His kiss knocked everything else from her head.

The rest of their holiday in Portugal flew by in a whirlwind of activity and happiness. They visited Faro, Lagos, and a bird sanctuary. They rented kayaks and paddled them through caverns along the shoreline among the stone outcroppings that littered the turquoise ocean. In the afternoons, they swam, laughed, and sought shade. Isaac cooked delicious food, and they ate out for a few nights, enjoying the atmosphere in the local restaurants.

A few times, Isaac signed autographs for children when he was recognized, but they spent most of their time alone. One night, they made love twice on the patio with the stars above in the inky sky. Anna had never felt closer to anyone than she was to Isaac and couldn't remember a better vacation.

The second to last night, Isaac offered to fly to Texas with her as support.

"I'd rather that Adam not meet you. But I'd love for you to be there." She dreaded seeing Adam because it would remind her of the years she'd lost.

"I promise to stay out of the way. This is your battle, and I'm confident you can deal with him." He bought another plane ticket while upgrading hers at the same time.

"I can fly economy," she said with a shrug.

"I can't," he said with a smile. "We're flying business class."

•   •   •

Anna and Isaac left the beach house on the morning of July 25th and drove up the rocky coastline to Lisbon, where they caught a flight to Texas. She felt like a world traveler these days, back and forth across the ocean. Not long ago, that would have been unthinkable.

The day after their arrival, they planned to meet with her lawyer, and then the following day, fly to Helsinki to meet the team for the race at the KymiRing.

To Anna's surprise, when she and Isaac arrived at the airport in Austin, a camera crew waited at Arrivals. They followed her and Isaac while they collected their bags and their rental car—hovering in the background. It seemed strange to receive that much attention. Who had tipped the media off where they would be? Maybe they'd been seen leaving the airport in Lisbon.

The film crew's presence was intrusive and put her on edge. After the break and time away, she'd forgotten what it was like, always having paparazzi following. The last time they'd been in America, it had also been extreme. Being here was something that had nothing to do with MotoGP, racing, or even Isaac. This was her private business. What could the media possibly hope to see? She did her best to ignore them, but the feeling of being watched persisted. The TV crew may have hoped for a better story than driving straight to a downtown hotel for the night, but that's all they got.

The next morning, Anna and Isaac arrived at the lawyer's office on the eighteenth floor an hour before Adam was due. He hadn't agreed to meet with the lawyer present, but Anna wasn't willing to meet with him alone. Her lawyer had booked a conference room for the meeting. Anna took a breath. She wouldn't be on her own facing Adam. She'd be with Janice.

"Isaac, this is Janice Mulberry. Janice, this is my boyfriend, Isaac." Anna made the introductions.

"You're the motorcycle racer who has won Anna's heart," said Janice as she shook his hand.

"She's the reason I'm having my best season ever," he said with an amiable smile. "My crew chief always reminds me that a happy racer is a fast racer."

Warmth filled Anna. He hadn't told her he attributed some of his success to her. The two of them talked while Anna blocked out their words, trying to prepare for dealing with Adam, practicing conversations in her head. As the time for the meeting neared, Janice's assistant brought her a folder with the necessary paperwork. Everything looked to be ready, and Janice reiterated that according to Washington state law, Adam shouldn't be able to claim any part of the townhouse.

Isaac squeezed Anna's hand and excused himself for a walk, leaving fifteen minutes before the scheduled meeting with Adam. After Isaac departed, Anna spun her ring, twirling it around and around, reminding herself to breathe, and gave herself an internal pep talk. She could do this even if it would be difficult. Even with support, she didn't want to see Adam but was doing this to get the money sooner. And, more importantly, for closure.

She filled her water glass while she waited. The room felt too warm.

An angry male voice at reception was the first sign of Adam's arrival. Maybe coming here had been a mistake.

"What the fuck, Anna?" he said, storming into the room. "Lawyers?"

Janice's assistant, Marjorie, hovered in the background. She mouthed the word, "Security?" to her boss, who gave a slight shake of her head. Her lawyer's confidence bolstered Anna's spirits. She took a few extra seconds to regain her composure after Adam's entrance.

When Anna didn't answer, Adam continued. "When you sent me the address, I thought you had given me the address of your apartment. You misled me. This isn't where you live. I thought I was clear the last time we spoke. No lawyers." He stood over her, waiting for her to apologize.

She took a deep breath. She wouldn't.

Janice took over. "Mr. Chaddley, please sit down. She indicated a seat at the table across from herself and Anna.

Adam scowled when he didn't get an answer to his remarks and stalked across the room like a petulant teen. He yanked his chair away from the table, slammed it down, and sat. He leaned back with his arms crossed over his chest. Anna was familiar with his pose of disapproval.

Anna's chest felt squeezed, and it became difficult to breathe. She concentrated on each inhale and exhale, twisting her ring under the table. She had to keep from having a meltdown. This was too important. He couldn't hurt her, and this could be their last confrontation.

"The least you can do is acknowledge me. You're being inconsiderate. I flew all this way to see you. Look at me." Adam leaned across the table, snapping his fingers near her face.

Anger gave her strength. How had she put up with his behavior for so long? She looked in his direction but didn't meet his gaze.

"Mr. Chaddley, please address your remarks to me. I'm Janice Mulberry, Anna's lawyer. You've received several letters from me regarding Anna's property in which you reside."

"You mean our property." He banged the surface of the table, creating a loud slapping sound.

Adam was probably trying to set off a meltdown. He was well aware that anger and confrontation were triggers and that she was sensitive to noise. Anna wouldn't give him the satisfaction, the colossal jerk. Who acted this way? No one mature or loving. She was better off without him, which he confirmed more every minute.

Anna closed her eyes and counted in her head to five. Then, looking up, she directed her gaze at Adam and looked him in the eye. Maybe this was why she'd needed to come.

"I don't appreciate your tone. You're being a bully, and I'm tired of this behavior. We were together for four years. Not once did we discuss marriage, and we broke up because I caught you cheating. If it hadn't been then, it would have been soon because I was tired of being taken for granted. Your case is a lost cause, and you know it, or you wouldn't have come all the way to Texas. Sign the damn papers so we can be done with it. Relinquish your false claims on my property and agree to move out so the sale can proceed. We're over." She kept her face expressionless and her voice calm, though sweat seeped from every pore. He would respond better to logic than emotion.

He blanched at her blunt words and uncrossed his arms, shifting in his seat. She'd cut him off mid-bluster, and it appeared he was unsure what to say next. He cracked his knuckles loudly, the sound echoing in the room.

"When do I need to be out?" Adam shifted once more.

Her lawyer answered. "You have ninety days from today. Anna has been kind in allowing you to live on her property rent-free these last months and won't insist on rent for the final three months, provided you sign the papers today. She's very generous in allowing you to stay while you make arrangements to live somewhere else," said Janice. "If you have not vacated the premises by October 25th, court bailiffs will remove you and your possessions."

"I'll be out." Adam scribbled his name and the date on the legal documents, writing so hard he almost ripped the paper.

Janice slid a second page in front of him. "Your copy too."

He signed in an angry scrawl, finishing with a flourish, and shoved himself back from the table. He dropped the pen. "What I don't understand is why Texas? What brought you here?"

Anna's heart thumped hard in her chest. Let him think she lived here. She didn't take her eyes from Adam's. "You'll never know because it's none of your business."

With a clenched jaw and a sharp nod, he spun on his heel and left.

Janice lifted the receiver of an office landline phone at the back of the room. "Marjorie, please ensure Mr. Chaddley leaves our offices and alert building security that his business with us is concluded." She turned to Anna with a nod. "Well done. We got what we needed. Do you think he'll be out before the date required?"

"I think so. It seems like he believes for the first time that we're not getting back together."

"It impressed me how well you spoke up for yourself," said her lawyer. "I almost felt like I wasn't necessary. You're better off without someone like him."

When Anna was sure that Adam had gone, a few tears of relief escaped. She'd held onto them long enough to take care of this chapter of her life. With the paperwork in place, she just needed to sign the papers Janice had drawn up, authorizing her firm to act on Anna's behalf in the townhouse's sale in Seattle. They wouldn't list the place until it was empty, but she'd sleep better knowing that it was arranged.

She'd love to list it sooner, but she couldn't count on Adam not to sabotage their efforts. It was best to wait until he was out.

Once and for all, she was free.

She texted Isaac. *"It's done. Come pick me up, please."*

His reply came through right away. *"You okay?"*

"Strangely, yes. I'll tell you about it in person."

He arrived minutes later, having not gone far. They thanked Janice and headed outside to walk back to the hotel.

"So," said Isaac. "What happened?"

"He got angry, and I dealt with him, anyway. A personal victory." She breathed a sigh of relief. That would be the last of Adam. As her grandmother would have said, 'Good riddance to bad rubbish.'

She related the rest of the details to Isaac.

"It must feel good to be done with him. He's an idiot to have treated you the way he did, but I win because I get you." Isaac smiled and took her hand as they walked back to the hotel.

CHAPTER 18

Isaac

Isaac didn't wait long after their arrival in Finland to find Spencer for a chat. He'd rehearsed what he would say several times over the last few weeks. This couldn't be put off again, and it was going to be unpleasant, but he wasn't going to wait for an opportunity, he would make one. He took the first shuttle to the track, changed, and then waited for Spencer by the Australian's trailer behind the garages. The second shuttle would be along soon.

Spencer's steps faltered when he spotted Isaac. He nodded and turned to climb his stairs.

"I need two minutes." Isaac kept his expression neutral and his voice calm, despite his anger. "For a word. In private."

"I'm due on track soon," said Spencer. "Come back later."

"We can do this here and now, or in private. Your choice," said Isaac.

Spencer smirked. Probably a show in case someone else was watching. "I guess you can come inside. I have two minutes, but then I need to change." He shrugged as if it didn't matter and continued up the stairs.

Isaac followed and pulled out his phone before closing the door. "I'm recording our conversation. I'll talk. You listen." He took a breath. "You need to stop spreading false and slanderous rumors about my girlfriend."

"Big man," mocked Spencer. "Coming to protect her honor. She's just some chick. Why do you care?"

Isaac ignored his dismissive remarks. "She doesn't know that I've heard what you've been saying. Don't talk to her. Don't look at her. Better yet, forget that she exists."

"Or what?" said Spencer, his eyes flicking to Isaac's phone in his clenched hand. He smirked again, as if daring Isaac to share the conversation.

"Or next time, she will have you charged." Isaac's molars ached from his jaw clench. There was so much more he wanted to say but he kept himself under control.

"The bitch made it up," said Spencer, as he turned away. "I didn't do anything to her that she didn't want."

Without warning, Isaac shoved the other man against the wall, his arm across Spencer's throat. For all Spencer's bravado, Isaac was taller and had fury on his side. There was more to this than words even if he didn't have proof. "She didn't tell me anything. Vince told me about the filth you've been spreading. If you think this will be your word against a helpless young woman's, you're wrong. Vince and I are both on her side now, and you will pay if you hurt Anna again." His entire body shook with fury. "We'll have you banned from racing permanently. The Vasquez name carries weight."

Spencer must have believed what Isaac said or at least finally understood the seriousness of the conversation.

"Anna who?" he said, all trace of the smirk gone.

"Thanks for your time." Isaac left, not turning off the recording until he was out of Spencer's trailer. More weight fell from his shoulders. He should have had this confrontation with that jerk before the break, but now it was done. While concerned that Spencer might have done something more serious than spread false rumors, he hoped that the man would stay away from Anna and cease all harassment.

Isaac took a deep breath to calm himself and headed into his box through the back door and shifted into work mode. Anna and Angel both shot him concerned looks when he arrived trackside, so he may not have let the encounter go completely, but he thrust it from his mind and focused on his job for today, practice and preparation.

This week, the buzzing reporters had zeroed in on the fact that Vince hadn't come to Finland, making this a prime opportunity for Isaac to make up points in the championship, if he could hold young Luka at bay. Maybe they needed an angle for their articles. Racing without his brother reminded him of Vince's long-ago arm injury that hadn't healed at first. Those had been bleak days for his brother and strange days at the track without Vince. They'd trained and raced for so long together that it was odd to be without each other.

Luka—a future champion in the making—was looking better with every race. This was his rookie year. Next year, Vince would need to beware. It didn't bother Isaac to think of the racing rivalries continuing without him. He'd had a fantastic run and was finishing with his strongest season—one that exceeded his wildest dreams.

Isaac's mid-break return to conditioning served him well. He finished the race first—his second win in a row. While wins, neither of his victories felt complete. He wasn't complaining about the fifty points, but they didn't feel like true tests of his racing abilities. One win he'd earned because Vince had crashed and the second because his brother hadn't been there. It would be a landmark if and when he took a victory going head-to-head against Vince.

Two weeks later in Silverstone, Vince returned, but his conditioning was behind the others after seven weeks away from racing, and he wasn't yet on par with his usual fitness level. Vince had won a couple of races at the famous British circuit, but he couldn't run the same pace as Isaac, Luka, and Xavi, instead finishing fourth, five seconds behind the front trio.

Isaac's third consecutive victory felt like the first real one. Vince was the first person to congratulate him after the Silverstone race, stopping his bike alongside Isaac's, to shake his hand before Isaac continued on to parc ferme. During the podium celebration, after the Spanish anthem played, he caught his brother's eye, and the two of them exchanged matching grins. Let the cameras wonder about that. For

Isaac, it seemed like a dream come true as he stood on the top step of the podium.

That night, Vince and Catarina joined their party, staying until late. When a tipsy Isaac made his way back to his room with Anna tucked under his arm, his face ached from hours of smiling.

Everything in his life felt perfect, on and off the track.

•   •   •

Monday morning, Isaac and Anna sat at their airport gate to head home for a week and a half before the next race in Austria at the Red Bull Ring. He and Anna would stay at their rental place but had plans with Vince for dinner mid-week at his place and at theirs on Saturday. The casual dinner plans felt more like old times and brought a smile to Isaac's face.

While they were waiting, his phone rang. Isaac didn't recognize the number with a Spanish area code but answered anyway. "Hello, this is Isaac."

"Hi, Isaac. This is Lily Navarro, Catarina's mother. Is this a good time to talk?"

"Sure," he said. "We're boarding a flight home in half an hour, but I have a few minutes. What have you found so far?" With his peripheral vision, it was obvious that Anna perked up listening.

"There are three properties for sale near Cervera that fit your criteria at this time. All with at least a hectare of land and with beautiful homes. One house has been renovated, one has had some remodeling, including a gorgeous kitchen, and the third needs some love and attention, but has a lot of potential."

"Could we look at them one day this week?" It would be helpful to see all three and compare.

"I have appointments tomorrow. How does Thursday look?" She sounded hopeful.

Isaac covered his phone and said to Anna, "Are you free to look at houses with me on Thursday?" Her eyes widened, and she nodded.

"Thursday it is. Just send me the time and addresses by text or email, and we'll be there."

"Perfect," Lily said. "I'll set it up and send you an email with the listings and information."

"Thanks. See you Thursday." He would need to let Vince know his plans about moving so he didn't hear it from another source, as so often happened in small towns. It probably wouldn't be a surprise that his relocation would become permanent.

CHAPTER 19

Anna

In Austria, Anna walked, daydreaming about the houses that they'd looked at last week, and making pro-con lists in her head for her favorite two. One needed renovations and one didn't. She came to a dead stop in the service lane behind the garages along pit lane, looking up as a vaguely familiar Moto3 rider blocked her path. She stepped to the side, and he moved to counter her, holding his arms out, not letting her pass. She went on alert, her palms damp. She'd seen him drinking with Spencer several times, one of his younger cronies.

"You're Anna, right?" He glanced over his shoulder, looking around. He was only about twenty years old with an entitled frat boy look about him. He was one of the few riders who spoke English without a trace of a European accent. Another American maybe.

"Yes." She didn't like how he scanned her from top to bottom and that when he spoke, he stared at her chest.

He shuffled his feet. "I've got twenty Euros. Do I pay before or after?" His hand dipped into his pocket.

"Before or after what?" What the hell was he talking about?

"My blowjob," he said, leaning in, clearly checking that their conversation wouldn't be overheard.

The idea rammed her heart into her throat, and her stomach clenched. She needed to get away from this creep. Spencer had probably put him up to this. Just when she'd thought he couldn't go lower.

"I have no idea what you're talking about." She tried pushing past him.

Spencer's friend matched her side-step, blocking her path once more. This time he grabbed her arm. Panic rose in her at the unwanted contact and the implied threat. "Spencer said you would take care of me between practices or races. If the price has gone up, I'm okay with it. You look like you give good head." His words confirmed who was at the root of this encounter.

Her eyes overflowed. "You must be mistaken." She ripped her arm from his grasp. Her chest heaved as she said, "This must be Spencer's idea of a joke, but it isn't funny." She escaped and dashed into the back of the LCR team garage where he was unlikely to follow. She leaned against the wall, trying to get control of her tears as it became hard to breathe. She fought the oncoming meltdown. Her lungs ached, and she pressed the back of her icy hand in turn against each of her flaming cheeks. She didn't want everyone on the team to know that she'd been crying.

Reminding herself that she didn't have to deal with things like this alone, she slunk into the box and caught Isaac's eye where he was debriefing after his FP2 session with Angel.

Isaac must have seen her distress because he stood up immediately. "I've got something I need to take care of. Can we continue this in the morning?"

"I think we've covered everything," said Angel glancing in her direction. "You're free for the evening. If I think of something else, I'll send a text, or we can talk in the morning."

"Thanks." Isaac strode across the garage to meet Anna. He lowered his voice as they moved further into the back where they could be alone. "What's wrong? Are you okay?"

An image of Spencer's ugly leer flashed through her mind and with it, the ghost of his hand on her throat. She should have shared what had happened in Germany and now it was too late. How did she explain her lack of action?

Trembling, she related what had happened just now. As she spoke, the vice around her chest increased, and her words became gasps. She didn't use any names, afraid of what Isaac might do. Her tears came rushing back, and it took hard work to meet his blazing eyes. By the end of her account, she was sobbing.

"Spencer has gone too far," growled Isaac. He was furious, even if it wasn't directed at her.

Her head shot up and her eyes narrowed. "How did you know Spencer was involved?" Her words came out as a yell, and she clamped her lips together, the meltdown sneaking up no matter how hard she tried to keep it at bay.

Isaac tried to pull her into a hug, but she stepped back.

Through her blurred vision, his flinty eyes met her stare and remained hard as he looked away first. He'd known. Her heart drummed against her ribs, and she fought the urge to run away. Isaac might not know the extent of Spencer's actions, but he'd heard something, perhaps rumors, and hadn't told her.

"Let's go to my trailer," he said. "I can see you're upset. You can calm down there."

Upset was an understatement. Calm down? She'd been blind-sided, so she fixated on anger instead of fear, lashing out. "How long have you known?" Her voice emerged louder than intended despite her gasping breath.

Isaac reached for her again, and she crossed her arms, tight to her body as she tried to control the shaking and stepped further away. "How long?" Her voice shook as she wrapped her mind around his lack of surprise.

"Just before Vince's accident," he said, the words dragging one at a time. "Spencer told Vince last spring. When my brother and I made up in Assen, he told me. I thought I'd handled it."

"Handled it? You've had almost two months, and you didn't think to tell me what was being said?" Her voice rose again, and her chest tightened to the point she couldn't draw a breath. She couldn't believe they were fighting.

"Anna, my love. You're distressed. Let's go somewhere quiet where we can talk." Now he looked rattled.

She hadn't meant to make him upset, and it just made the out-of-control feeling worse. "You had no right to keep that from me. It's dishonest. You tell me to trust you, but you kept something that concerns me, to yourself. That's not fair." She wasn't being fair either, she had kept her encounters with Spencer from him, but she couldn't make herself stop shouting.

"I'm sorry. I didn't want your feelings hurt or to make you upset. I was trying to help. To save you from having to talk to Spencer and make him stop harassing you." He remained calm while her emotions churned.

"Too bad. Spencer's terrifying and gross. You withheld information." She wasn't sure she was making sense. Why hadn't she listened and gone somewhere else? She clenched her fists at her sides, trying not to flail. This was as bad as she'd been in a long time.

"You withhold things," he said, a flush sweeping over his face.

Defensive anger surged through her body. He was right.

"Things about myself or my past," she spoke between sobs. "Things that embarrass me. I don't want to talk about Adam taking advantage of me. Or what happened to me as a child. What my parents did."

Isaac stepped back, his eyes wide. She was still being unfair. She'd never told him anything about her parents. That wasn't something she ever spoke about. Instead, she wielded her past like a weapon—her words sharp-edged.

"No, but..." began Isaac, his face paler except the hectic spots on his cheeks.

"Not but. This is different." From the contrite look on his face, he was sorry he hadn't shared what he knew, but she was still angry.

"Can I explain?" He took on a pleading tone.

"Not right now. I'm going to be on my own for a bit. Maybe stay with Catarina."

"I'm sorry. You're right. I should have told you." He stretched a hand toward her. "Don't go away upset."

Anna flinched. "Please leave me alone. I need to think." She ignored Isaac's outstretched hand and stricken face. She wanted to be alone. Not only was she upset about Spencer and his rumors, but she'd lashed out at Isaac and didn't know how to take it back.

She ran for his trailer and locked the door before sliding to the floor and letting the meltdown continue, wracking sobs and screams that overwhelmed everything for the duration. She wished she'd let Isaac hold her, but she was too embarrassed to go back. He hadn't followed, respecting her wishes.

When she was once more under control, she washed her face and sent Catarina a text, grateful she had another friend. Her hands still shook, and her throat felt raw.

"*Had a fight with Isaac. Can I stay with you tonight?*"

The reply was quick. "*Of course. My door is always open for you. Where are you?*"

Her hands shook as she typed. "*Locked in Isaac's trailer.*"

"*I'm still at the track. I'll come get you. We can go for dinner.*"

Anna twirled her ring and leaned her head back against the wall.

Another text came in. "*Girl's Night. You can fill me in.*"

"*Thank you.*" Anna didn't have long to wait before there was a tap on the door.

"It's me," her friend said. "Are you okay?"

Anna opened the door, grabbed her purse, and the two of them climbed into a taxi. It was a relief to get away without seeing anyone. The MotoGP riders were still busy signing autographs.

After a subdued dinner, she and Catarina returned to the hotel, and they went up to the hotel room that Anna shared with Isaac. She needed to collect her clothes and her toothbrush but didn't want to run into Isaac alone. She wasn't ready to speak to him—afraid all she would do was cry or make things worse. She was ashamed of how she'd reacted to news about his help.

She listened at the door, but inside was quiet, without sounds of the TV or of movement. It seemed empty. She flicked on a light and gathered her belongings, stuffing them into her suitcase. She hurried so she wouldn't be interrupted. Already she was as much ashamed as angry. Maybe she should stay and talk things out. Try to explain she'd already been upset and had handled her meltdown poorly.

When something was difficult, she gravitated to Isaac. More than anything she wanted one of his hugs.

They headed downstairs to Catarina's room. Catarina hadn't pushed her for details about Spencer, but her friend had been livid about the blowjobs for money stunt. Several times, Anna tried to talk about the elevator proposition and the assault in Germany by the trailers, but her throat stuck, and her voice failed. She was too embarrassed by how she'd handled things on her own. She should have reported him.

Seeing her distress, Catarina said, "You can stay with me the rest of the weekend and in Cervera too if you want. I have room. When you're ready to tell me the rest, I'm here."

Her friend's kind words brought Anna's tears back but after watching a familiar rom-com and thrusting everything heavy from her mind, it was time to sleep. She still had race duties tomorrow and Sunday, which meant she would have to face Isaac and apologize for her outburst.

After they were ready for bed and the room was dark, it became easier to talk. In halting stops and starts, she told Catarina what Spencer had done, starting with Indonesia and ending with Germany—everything she'd been too scared to tell Isaac. She'd been terrified of what he might do to Spencer. Of course, Isaac wasn't like that, it was just her fear.

Now that Anna was thinking more clearly, it became obvious that she'd done what she'd accused him of doing. Kept important information to herself. Maybe she wasn't meant to be close to anyone. Would she end up alone? Her late-night self-pity wasn't helping.

"You need to report Spencer," said Catarina, interrupting Anna's spiral. "What he's doing needs to be on record. He's popular and good looking and keeps getting away with it."

There was a long pause. Would Catarina continue?

Catarina's voice was softer when she resumed, almost too quiet for Anna to follow and she strained to listen. "I left the racing circuit eight years ago because of Spencer and one of his friends. I got sick of the constant harassment and of watching my back. I didn't report them and he's still hurting people."

"What if no one believes me?" said Anna.

"I do and the other women will believe you. You might not be the only one he's hurting. Isaac believes you and so will Angel. Think about it. It doesn't have to be right now, but I don't want keeping it to yourself to be something you regret."

"Do you regret it?" Anna's voice dropped to a whisper.

"Yes. Especially when I hear your story. He's still taking advantage of his position and his popularity. Who knows how many others he's hurt? If you want my support, I'll go with you."

"I should have said something," said Anna, her voice hoarse and filled with sadness. She sniffled and reached toward the box of tissues, fumbling until she'd located them. The room grew quiet, the silence broken when she finished wiping her tears and blew her nose.

"I know," said Catarina. "What are you going to do about Isaac? I don't agree with what he did. He should have told you. But he's one of the good guys, and he was trying to look out for you." She yawned. "Sorry."

"He's not just good, he's amazing. He wants to buy us a house. I love him but I don't think I can go back unless I tell him everything. It wasn't right that I was hiding what happened. My past as well as my problems with Spencer."

"That's fair," said Catarina, "If you're going to expect that Isaac should tell you everything, you should do the same."

"How do people do that? Just open up and trust?" It was something that Anna had always found difficult. Without her grandmother, she'd had no one. Until Isaac.

"When it's the right person, you just do. Take a leap of faith," said Catarina. "You two seem great together and he's completely besotted with you. But, ask yourself one thing. Could you live without him and be okay? Is he your person?"

Anna didn't answer. Life without Isaac would be bleak and lonely. "I have to be brave and talk to him. How do I tell him about everything and not wreck his race day after tomorrow?" Anna spun her ring in the dark.

Catarina made a snorting sound. "That's rubbish. Do you think he'll be at his best if you aren't speaking?"

Anna didn't answer. Her friend was right. Her grandmother would have told her to march downstairs and make up with Isaac.

"My advice? Pull up your socks, girl, and go tell him everything."

"Thank you for listening," said Anna.

"That's what friends do." Catarina yawned again. "I'm going to get some sleep, and you should too. Talk to Isaac in the morning." Her breathing changed into deep, even breaths as she fell asleep.

Anna lay staring into the darkened hotel room while Catarina slept, and the night stretched onward. Tears leaked from the corners of her eyes, and her head ached from too many tears recently. She didn't want to wait until morning.

She didn't want to lose Isaac over this and let Spencer ruin what she'd built for her life. If it hadn't been for Isaac and Catarina, she wouldn't have anyone. They were good people, and her life was better for her first gamble, that of coming to Spain. She needed to keep going, be strong, and talk to Isaac.

Gathering her courage, she slipped out of bed and collected her bag. She used the blue glow of the digital clock, which read 2:15 a.m., to scribble *"Thanks,"* on the hotel stationery by her bedside lamp and tiptoed out the door, her shoes in hand.

The hotel was quiet at this hour and her footfalls were silent on the blue and white carpet. The halls were bright after the dark room, and she blinked several times while her eyes adjusted. Not wanting to chance another unwanted encounter on the elevator, she opened the door to the stairwell and listened. Inside was dead quiet. She trotted up the two flights of stairs, her steps echoing, and exited on the eleventh floor.

Anna stopped at the door to her hotel room, almost losing her courage. Isaac was probably sleeping. She turned, about to leave, then caught herself. She was still making excuses to keep people at a distance. It had to stop.

She swiped her room card and eased the door open. She closed it behind her, taking pains to remain silent so she didn't startle him. For all her care, Isaac sat bolt upright as she neared the bed. Maybe he'd been having trouble sleeping too.

"Anna?" His voice was tired and scratchy.

"Yes." She'd come to talk, but her feet seemed fastened to the floor. What was she waiting for? Isaac clicked on his bedside lamp, flooding the room in an ivory glow. "Did I wake you? I'm sorry. Should I come back another time?"

"Please stay. I'm so sorry, Mi Corazon."

She sat on the edge of the bed, taking a deep breath, before settling beside Isaac. "I'm sorry I yelled. I was so upset I couldn't think straight. I lashed out at you, even though you didn't deserve it. By the time I ran, I wasn't thinking straight. I was already melting down."

"I know. It was difficult to see you like that, but it doesn't change how I feel."

His words helped her overcome her worry that she'd ruined things between them. "I needed time to think." She chewed on her lower lip. "You were right. I've been keeping difficult things from you too. I'm sorry."

He scooted closer. "Don't be sorry about needing time. Unless you've come to break up with me." He swallowed when she didn't say anything. "Have you come to tell me it's over?" His voice broke.

She shook her head. Her mouth felt like it was filled with sand, making it hard to speak. "Never. But I have things to say too. Please don't interrupt because if I stop, I might chicken out again. I didn't tell you because I was scared to talk about what happened. I wanted to pretend it didn't happen." She waited for his nod of acknowledgement.

He took her hand, lacing his fingers into hers, giving her a dose of courage.

She took another breath. "Spencer has been scaring me since the spring. Threatening me. Propositioning me. In Germany, he clamped his hand around my throat and choked me. I should have told you. I should have asked for your help." A hot wave of guilt swept over her.

"Why didn't you?" Isaac's voice was soft. "Why were you so scared to tell me?"

"I'm not sure," she said, picking at the quilt instead of looking at him.

"I think you know." His voice was calm and steadying. He slid forward and took her other hand, his touch gentle, making her feel precious.

"I'm not worth making a fuss over." It wasn't much more than a whisper, but it was the truth and one of her biggest fears.

"You are worth it to me," said Isaac. "You're worth everything to me."

"You don't really know me." Anna trembled all over. "There are things I don't tell anyone." About her parents for instance.

"After five months, I know enough." Isaac wrapped his arms around her, sharing his heat, but more importantly, making her feel wanted.

He kept his voice soft—soothing. She hadn't realized that she was crying again but everything was a blur when she looked up. "I've never felt like I've been worth it. When I'm with you, I forget sometimes. I left Adam, quit my job, and came to Europe to write. I wanted to treat myself like someone important. I'm trying to live up to what I want and work toward making a living doing something that I love. But it's hard to break old habits of self-doubt."

"You still want to be with me?" Isaac's voice had become more confident.

"Yes, but I have two conditions."

"Let me hear them."

"Ask questions. I'll tell you the truth about anything you want to know. Not just right now, but from now on. I'm just not good at knowing where to start. Sometimes I'll be scared of my memories, but I'll say so, and try."

"I can do that." He kissed her temple. "What's the second?"

"Leave Spencer alone unless he does it again." Isaac's body stiffened. "I'm not ready for the fuss it would make to report him. I want to avoid him and forget about everything he said and did. It's just for a couple of months—for the rest of this racing season. Then, I'll report him and we'll be gone."

"I'm going to be upset when I hear what else he did, aren't I? That's another reason you kept it from me."

"Yes. I was afraid to throw you off your season. Do you promise that you will let it go? At least for now."

"I love you. I don't agree with this, but if it is what you want, I will. We can avoid him, and I'll abide by your wishes."

"Thank you," she said, turning into his arms while he held her close.

Safe in his arms, she told him everything that Spencer had done.

"I want to hurt him. Or to have him arrested." Isaac's words were at odds with his soft voice.

She remained silent. While she wanted Spencer behind bars, she wasn't ready to accuse him in public.

"We got this." Isaac held her for several minutes before she undressed and tucked herself into bed, lighter inside than in a long time. Isaac kissed her, slow and tender, and wrapped his arm around her. He still radiated warmth and acceptance. As her head hit the pillow, her last thought was that, with Isaac's help, she would let him know all of her. The good, the bad, and the insecure.

• • •

The next three weeks flew by in a flash with races each weekend. A whirlwind trip to Austria, Italy, and then back in Spain for Aragon—

one of the two races the Vasquez brothers considered home races, and the fans had turned out in droves.

Every couple of days, Anna made a point of sharing something new with Isaac about her life, and they used it as a starting point for more conversations. She found it difficult to share about her parents, but she was working up to it and told bits of her childhood. The more she did it, the easier it became to let Isaac in, their connection becoming deeper.

The championship remained up for grabs as Isaac finished second in all three, while Vince won two and finished third in the other. They were both riding more consistently than ever. On race weekends away from the garage and the track, Anna ensured that she was never alone.

CHAPTER 20

Isaac

Anna's revelations about Spencer's obscene behavior hadn't left Isaac's mind. Rage filled him whenever he thought about them, but he'd made a promise, and he stuck to it. Spencer had kept a low profile since their talk, but deep down, Isaac didn't believe this ugly business was over. Sooner or later, Spencer would do something again. Isaac just needed to bide his time, and then he'd make sure the asshole landed in jail.

Isaac parked his car in front of his new house. The offer Isaac had put in had been accepted two weeks ago, at the beginning of September. It was hard to believe that he now had his own home, where he and Anna could plan their future. Their place had a gorgeous deck, an updated kitchen, and spacious airy rooms. He'd hired a local company to paint the interior in soft browns, blues, and greens that he and Anna had chosen.

He glanced at his phone, checking the time. His mom and Anna were late meeting him, but should be here soon. They'd gone for lunch together to get better acquainted, and Anna had texted to say that they were on their way. He stepped out of the car and wandered over to the fence that separated the parking area and the garage from the lower property. The gently sloped property with an expanse of flatter area below was perfect for his planned riding academy.

When his mother's car arrived, it was clear that the two of them were getting along from the way they chatted back and forth as they headed toward him. He'd seldom seen Anna so relaxed around anyone other than himself or Catarina. Having Anna comfortable and accepted by his family, including Vince, made his plans feel that much more attainable. They didn't have to accept her, but it was better that they did.

He welcomed the women, unlocked the house, and held the heavy wooden door open. His mom patted his cheek on the way past into the open entryway. Was she up to something, or just thinking of more embarrassing stories? He'd hoped she'd gotten that out of her system at lunch.

"Anna can give me the tour," she said with a cheerful smile. "You can go check where you're going to build a track. I can practically see you mapping it out already. Run along. We brought cold drinks, so join us on the patio when you're done." She continued into the house.

He quirked an eyebrow at Anna, who gave him a slight nod. If she was fine with his mother's plan, then so was he.

Isaac smiled and did as his mother suggested. He only had the beginning of an idea and hadn't worked out all the details, but he'd decided to start a riding academy for kids without a lot of money. Individualized lessons of this type were usually too costly for regular families, but he'd provide the bikes, riding equipment, and instruction. Wealthy families dominated much of racing—his own had been an exception. Vince had been seen as a prodigy, and a rich trainer had taken an interest—first in Vince, then in Isaac. Now, he wanted to pay that forward. He hoped his family name would be enough to bring in students—maybe half a dozen to start.

After planning both an intermediate and a beginner's course in his mind as he wandered the slope below the house, he was almost back to the house when he caught his mother's voice floating through the warm air.

"It was wonderful to get to know you better today, mi querida. You're good for my Isaac." She sounded happy. At least she hadn't nagged him about grandkids yet. Or at least not lately.

He continued to approach but couldn't hear Anna's quiet reply.

"You are one of the first things or people that my boy has chosen for himself. I'm glad he's looking out for himself first for a change. I do not know why he never put himself first, but I see him trying. You must be the right incentive. Be patient if he backslides again and forgets himself to put Vince first, you might have to remind him from time to time. He's been doing it for so long, it is second nature."

His mother had noticed that he was trying to do things differently, and he was glad she didn't seem to mind the change. Until recently, he'd always thought that his parents wanted him to put Vince first. But maybe they'd just been grateful that he'd been easygoing, and later that he wanted to get involved in racing too. It had meant there hadn't been scheduling conflicts, and they had all traveled together for race weekends.

It made it easier for Isaac that he had his mother's support in planning his future.

●   ●   ●

The temperature dropped with the fall weather that turned the leaves golden on the tree-lined hills around Cervera. Spring was Isaac's favorite season, but fall was a close second. This was the last weekend at home before four races on the next four weekends. These races were referred to as the fly-aways, and he and Anna wouldn't be coming home in between races for a change, as these races were in Asia and Australia—too far to travel back and forth. He didn't like leaving so much undone in the new house, but they would finish furnishing a few rooms in the house when they returned.

Isaac shifted gears, thinking about the upcoming trip. The championship was still close, and for the first time, he considered what it might be like to win. It wouldn't change his decision about retirement, but it might help his academy plans. After this series of fly-away races, the final race of his professional career would be in Valencia, Spain—where the season's last race was always held. It was time to let the team announce his replacement.

Anna was upstairs revising her story when he jumped on his road bike, pedaling out of the driveway, and headed for his new meeting place with Vince for their last training ride before departure. He would talk to his brother today.

•   •   •

"I've got something to talk to you about," said Isaac when they reached the halfway point of the twenty-four-kilometer loop where he and Vince had stopped for a short water break after the long series of hills they'd ridden.

"You bought a house. You going to get married?" Vince stared out at the fall countryside. It was difficult to read his opinion from his expressionless face.

"Probably, but I'll have to ask her first. Probably do that in Thailand." Isaac shot his brother a nervous look. "This is something else. Something more immediate." He took a swig of water. There was no easy way to say it, so he just did it. "I'm retiring at the end of the season."

"What about all the offers? It's your best season ever." Vince turned to look at him, this time, his voice rougher than usual.

Isaac still couldn't get a read on him. "It is. I've been having a blast on the track this year. But, I told you I need more than racing. This is it. I'm done after Valencia. I declined the offers."

Vince shook his head as though he didn't understand.

"Your life is racing," said Isaac, needing to get through to his brother so there wouldn't be more hard feelings between them. "Mine used to be, but now it's something else. I want to settle down. Be home every night unless I'm on holiday. One of these days, I want a family."

"I can't say I didn't see this coming since you met Anna." Vince held up his hands. "I'm not blaming her. If your heart isn't in racing anymore, it's time to stop."

"Thanks for understanding." A lump formed in Isaac's throat.

"I don't know what I'll do after," said Vince. "I try not to think about it. Luckily, with my new contract, I've got another four years to figure it out." He grinned and grabbed his bike, heading out to resume their ride. "Race you back?"

"I'm thinking of opening a riding academy," said Isaac. "You could come work for me when you retire one day." It was hilarious that he could be his brother's boss. In reality, they might be partners, or his brother could do special riding workshops. He followed Vince and mounted at the edge of the paved road.

Vince laughed, giving him a sideways glance just as they took off in sync, pedaling side by side. "I just might. In the meantime, I'm going to try to keep winning as long as possible."

"Of that, I have no doubt," said Isaac as he surged ahead, spurring Vince to speed up so he wouldn't be left behind. His brother never changed, and Isaac didn't want him to. "And don't worry, I still plan to train a lot. I'll have to keep you in shape to earn your millions."

As he biked, Isaac's thoughts turned to how the conversation had gone. Without the accident earlier this year and even the misunderstanding about Anna, Vince might not have understood Isaac's decision, but now his brother seemed to accept that for the first time, their lives were about to diverge.

While the idea of ending this phase of his life made him a little melancholy, it was more than balanced by the excitement of possibility.

CHAPTER 21

Anna

Anna's first trip to East Asia had been in April, and now she was flying to Japan. She wiggled in her seat and checked that her book was accessible before fastening her seatbelt with sweaty hands. Despite all the flying this year, take-offs and landings still made her nervous. This was also going to be a sixteen-hour flight, which meant that even in business-class, it would feel like an eternity.

Next weekend was a race in Thailand, followed by one at Phillip Island, Australia, and then one in Malaysia before they would have the long flight home for the final race. Thinking of the end of the season and the future gave her a fluttery feeling in her stomach. For all that she and Isaac were closer than ever, there were still several unknowns in her life that had to be addressed. She'd love to stay in Spain, but she would need to renew her travel visa.

When the plane left the gate to taxi down the runway, she grabbed her book and focused on it until they were far above the ground. Isaac gave her a knowing look, squeezing her arm, and she smiled back.

Isaac started out the Japanese race weekend at Motegi on a tear—setting lap records during practice—and was in the best form of his career. She'd never seen him so dominant in practice. It boded well for the race. Many had met the news about him not returning next year with incredulity, but he seemed at peace with the decision, and had no trouble answering the dozens of questions posed by the media. She'd worried that his brother might have more difficulty with the news, though Isaac had mentioned that the conversation had gone well.

Vince crashed in both FP2 and FP3. He wasn't injured, but his slower lap times meant he had to come through Q1 and Q2 while Isaac earned his first career pole position. On race day, Vince recovered to finish first, and Isaac came second, again.

Thailand was gorgeous, with warm and sunny weather, unlike the torrential rains of Indonesia in the spring. The race had been going well for both brothers until Vince crashed on the second lap. Anna caught her breath, watching the screen until he jumped to his feet, and with the help of the race marshals, got his bike upright. He remounted and chased the rest of the field, gravel falling from his machine for the first couple hundred yards. She was thankful Isaac was getting out after this season. He'd defied odds in not having a major injury before now.

Vince carved his way through the pack of riders like a scythe and looked to be a threat for the podium despite his fall as they swept down the home-finish straight into the final lap. Isaac led with Luka in second, while Vince and Spencer fought for third. Their battle was where the camera focused, as it was a contested fight. Anna wished they would go back to Isaac at the front as she became nervous whenever she couldn't see him for extended stretches of the race. Anything could happen and she might not know. She wiped her sweaty palms and hoped he didn't crash.

Typical of Vince's usual aggressive style, the duel came down to the last handful of corners as they traded positions three times before Vince's tires gave way. He'd used up the grip coming from behind after his crash. His head was in his hands after he slid off the track, but he appeared uninjured. His accident perhaps distracted Spencer, who crashed a second later, leaving Fabiano to steal third, crossing the line with a skyward fist pump.

Vince's DNF, combined with his missed race after the break, left Isaac in the lead for the championship for the first time as he crossed the line in first. He'd led this race at the Chang International Circuit from start to finish. Anna hoped he could carry this lead through the last three races. Racers were superstitious, so she wouldn't say anything, but there was a real possibility he could win the title.

For the days between the races in Thailand and Australia, Isaac and Anna rented a thatched cottage on the beach in Thailand where they spent most of their time lounging in the shade with their books, swimming, and making love. It felt like this was how life was supposed to be when on holiday. No stress. No worries, and lots of quality time with the person she loved. She couldn't imagine a better place to spend her thirtieth birthday. Six months ago, she'd dreaded this landmark, but with the changes she'd made to her life, turning thirty no longer bothered her.

On their last night in Thailand, she and Isaac strolled down the white sand beach at night. It was dark and quiet, without city sounds as their beach was remote and away from the more popular tourist resorts. They were far enough from city lights that the sky was covered in a blanket of stars. Isaac had probably paid a fortune for a romantic getaway like this, but she'd learned he didn't need to worry about money and that he liked to spoil her. He'd surprised her with the announcement that this trip was her main birthday present.

Despite being independent, she was happy that he wanted to treat her to such things. Still, she'd feel better about money when her townhouse sold. There had been no further trouble from Adam, who was scheduled to move in a few weeks. Though meeting him in Texas had been difficult, closing that chapter of her life had been satisfying and important.

"What are your plans after the racing season is over and your umbrella girl career is over?" said Isaac, interrupting her thoughts as they walked hand in hand along the water's edge.

"I've finished the edits my editor suggested," said Anna, thinking of her story. "I should be ready to query soon. I want to find an agent and try the traditional publishing route. It might take a while, but once my townhouse is sold, I have time. I just need one person to love my story and share my vision."

"Is it ready for me to read?" Isaac squeezed her hand. He'd asked several times, but she'd put him off, afraid he might think her story was too dark or wasn't any good.

"Do you still want to?" She gave him a sidelong glance.

"Of course." They walked a little farther, the sand soft and still warm beneath their bare feet as they listened to the gentle lapping of the waves on the beach.

"That wasn't what I meant about the future," said Isaac after a few minutes of silence. He stopped and took both her hands. "You are my other half, my soul mate, or as we say in Spanish, media naranja." The words sounded sweet and melodic when he said them. "Will you stay with me in Cervera? Marry me and make the new house our home." The reflection of the stars and moon gave his eyes a pale glow.

His words didn't surprise Anna, but she found herself still blown away. Her heart raced, and tears of happiness welled up. It must be a dream. "I want to stay. With you."

"Mi Corazon. Marry me and stay in Spain. If you don't want to live here, I'll come to America if you prefer, but I want to share my life with you. I want to read all your books and make love to you whenever I want. I want to decorate our house together, watch MotoGP on TV, or visit Barcelona or Aragon to cheer for my brother. We'll get the best seats and dress like super-fans in Vasquez colors."

Anna threw herself into his arms and kissed him until they were both breathless. More than anything, she wanted to stay in the beautiful house in Spain with Isaac. She'd hoped that she might, but hadn't let her fantasy get carried away in case she was wrong.

"Is that a yes?" Isaac spun her in a circle, a grin on his face.

"It's a yes," she said, feeling like her heart might burst from joy.

He pulled a ring from the pocket of his shorts. Its diamond caught the moonlight and seemed to steal it as it sparkled white and silver when he slipped its cool metal onto her ring finger.

• • •

Anna and Isaac arrived in Melbourne, Australia late the next night after having spent four extra days in Thailand. She kept their engagement news quiet until Isaac shared it with Vince and his mother. Anna sent Catarina a text the next day before they joined the others in Australia, eager to share their good news in person.

"Can we meet before going to the track in the morning? I want to show off my engagement ring." She'd told Catarina already but showing her would be fun.

"Sure. Meet at 8:15 for breakfast? We can chat and take the second shuttle."

Anna held out her left hand, admiring her exquisite ring. She couldn't wait to show it off to her friend. It was a circular diamond solitaire on a vintage-inspired band of white gold that must have cost a fortune. Isaac's choice was beautiful.

Isaac came up behind her and wrapped his arms around her as he nuzzled her neck before releasing her with a kiss. "If you don't like the ring, we can exchange it."

"I love it." She hugged her hand against her chest in a fist.

He laughed and spun her around for a deeper kiss.

"Angel wants me at the track with the first group. The British Racing Network wants to talk to him, so he needs to finish with me early. You'll be fine to come with Catarina a little later?" She found it sweet that he checked with her for signs of unease.

"Of course," she said. There'd been no further incidents with Spencer for two months and he should be busy in Australia as it was his home race, which meant extensive media coverage. There would likely be extra interviews, time with extended family and friends, as well as publicity events. She hadn't seen him since their arrival, which was what she preferred.

Anna and Isaac went downstairs together, and he kissed her quick, heading for the shuttle sitting at the curb out front. At the door, he spun and called back, "See you soon." Neither of them could stop grinning about their engagement. She felt giddy and couldn't wait to give a play-by-play of the walk for Catarina.

As she turned, Vince, also on his way outside, stopped with a friendly smile. "I'm glad you said yes."

After returning his smile, she said, "You knew?" It didn't surprise her he'd been in Isaac's confidence. She looked down at her stunning ring, still not used to seeing its sparkle on her hand.

"Welcome to the family." Vince surprised her by stepping forward to kiss her on either cheek. She'd never been that close to him before and was touched by his genuine display of affection. A few months ago, that would have been impossible.

"Thank you," she said, feeling emotional at his inclusion.

He checked his watch. "I need to go, but I'd love to host an engagement party when we get home. See you at the track. Enjoy your breakfast with Catarina." He jogged out the door and caught the shuttle just before its departure.

How did he know she was meeting Catarina? Maybe they talked away from the track more than she'd thought. Interesting. She'd have to ask Catarina. Maybe he'd seemed more content the last couple of months for a reason.

Anna strolled to the restaurant and poked her head inside. Half a dozen umbrella girls sat together at a large table on one side of the room. Nobody she was comfortable hanging out with. The professional models had their cliques. She, Catarina, and a couple of others were not included. Several younger riders, mostly in Moto2, sat in groups of two and three. No Catarina.

Anna reached for her phone to text her friend, but her phone wasn't in her back pocket. She must have left it upstairs in the room. She sighed. It would feel weird to be without her phone all day and she decided to run upstairs to retrieve it since Catarina wasn't here yet. She would be quick.

Hurrying into the elevator, she rushed upstairs to the ninth floor and collected her phone from the desk where it had charged overnight. She glanced at the screen before she returned to the elevator.

Catarina had sent a message fifteen minutes earlier. *"Running late. Down at 8:25."*

That was in two minutes. Just enough time to return downstairs. In the elevator, Anna tapped her foot when it slowed and stopped on the fifth floor instead of the main level. She didn't want Catarina to have to wait. When the doors opened, to her dismay, Spencer stepped inside. He blocked her exit and tapped the button to close the doors. Heart pounding, she moved to the far side of the elevator as it descended. Her mouth dry, she stared straight ahead. Maybe he'd get the message that his presence was unwanted.

"Well, well, well. If it isn't the American girlfriend." He said it the way Vince had said it at a press conference months ago, as though she were repulsive. "Don't worry, Honey. I have no interest in you anymore."

She raised her chin and didn't answer. Without looking, she spun her grandmother's ring. She'd tried so hard to avoid being alone with him. At least the ride would be over soon and she could escape. She would be safe in the lobby with the milling action and other people.

The elevator slowed, stopping on the third floor, and she breathed a sigh of relief. When the doors slid open, she expected another hotel guest to enter—someone to keep Spencer from doing something more than talking. Instead, the hallway was empty. Spencer lunged toward her and yanked her out of the elevator before she understood what was happening. He must have pushed the button for this stop, and she hadn't noticed.

"What the hell?" She tried to get away, but he twisted her arm behind her painfully. With his other hand, he covered her mouth while he propelled her forward, forcing her down the empty hallway. Behind them, the elevator doors closed, and it resumed its descent.

The third floor was the fitness level, the pool wasn't open yet at this hour, and most of the hotel was filled with MotoGP riders and their teams. Most would be downstairs at breakfast or already at the track. With Isaac and Vince both already gone, only Catarina would wonder where she'd gone. There was no one to hear her scream.

They were alone and Spencer could make good on his threats without fear of interruption.

Her phone buzzed. Probably Catarina. One-handed, she tried to answer, to give a shout of distress, but her phone fell from her hand with a thud, landing on the carpeted floor, and Spencer kicked it in the opposite direction. Her eyes flooded with tears. She struggled to free herself but only succeeded in causing sharp pains to shoot up her arm and into her shoulder. Once they turned the corner, Spencer released her mouth, and in one quick motion, scooped her over his shoulder. He wrapped a heavy arm around her thigh. His touch made her stomach churn.

"Let me go. What are you doing?" She kicked and flailed, trying to get loose, hoping someone else would appear. She'd welcome anyone, even if this was an embarrassing position.

"Stop moving, bitch." He smacked her ass hard enough to sting. "We're going someplace to talk where we won't be interrupted."

She didn't believe he only wanted to talk.

Fear constricted the blood to her brain, and thinking became difficult. All she wanted to do was run. The taste of bile filled her mouth. "I have nothing to say." She kept struggling, but he was too strong, and he continued to hold her in an awkward position. "Let me down." She pounded on his back as hard as she could, but he didn't seem affected. He was one of the bigger riders, and she couldn't escape.

Her hopes plummeted. She hadn't answered Catarina's text. Her friend might wait a while before worrying and searching. Tears filled Anna's eyes as she continued to squirm, trying to free herself—to no avail.

Spencer carried her into the family change room and did a quick check, still carrying her over his shoulder while she continued to holler and pound. Maybe someone on staff would be around. The hall remained empty, and they were alone in the private room. The click of the door lock echoed.

Giving her another sharp smack, he released her and shoved her as her feet hit the tiled floor. She fell to her knees, banging them hard enough she winced. Scrambling to her feet, she tried to get past him to unlock the door. He lunged and got a vise-like grip on her left arm.

"Not so fast, Missy. We have unfinished business. How about that blow job? Or maybe you'd like me to bend you over and fuck you."

With her right, Anna smacked his face as hard as she could, stinging her hand, the impact jarring her arm. Her engagement ring must have spun to face her palm as it left a bloody gouge on his cheek. The expression on his hardened face turned her insides to jelly. The blow only seemed to have made him angry. She quaked inside. She'd be lucky if he didn't hurt her this time.

He backhanded her across the face. The impact stung like fire and the metallic taste of blood filled her mouth. Her lip split and her cheek smarted. She was having trouble breathing and felt like her chest was being squeezed in a vice. Her breath came in gasps, and it became difficult to focus as the panic took over. Flailing, she made contact, scratching the side of his face, leaving at least three angry tracks.

Spencer grabbed her hair and dragged her to the counter, smashing her forehead hard enough to leave her dazed, seeing stars. She went limp, but he held her in place. He fumbled first with the zipper of her shorts, then his, as he kept her pinned down. Her sobs made it difficult to breathe, and his voice grew far away as his rough hands shoved her into position.

"I like it rough," he whispered in her ear, his hot breath on her face. "Resist if you want."

That was the last straw. She was losing control fast. If she didn't fight harder, it would be too late. Her shorts and underwear had pooled near her ankles. Now or never. She struggled and tried to push herself away, succeeding enough to draw a full breath for the first time.

"This is going to be quick. I want you so bad." He smacked her ass again.

Inside she fought to maintain enough of presence of mind to continue to fight. She screamed loud enough it hurt her throat and rattled the mirror on the wall—a long continuous sound she couldn't control.

The intensity must have startled him. As his grip loosened, still screaming, she elbowed him in the gut, driving her arm back with force as she launched away from the counter. As he staggered away, she slid down the wall and sat, hugging her knees, still screaming and sobbing—her meltdown in full swing.

Spencer stepped back, a look of revulsion on his face. "Freaky bitch. You're not worth it." He pulled up his shorts, crouched down, his nose almost touching hers. Squeezing her face, he wrenched it up to force eye contact. "If you tell anyone, next time I find you alone, you'll be sorry." Releasing her, he fixed his clothes, and looking like nothing had happened, he strode out the door.

Unable to stop, she continued to cry and scream, her throat raw and painful.

She wanted to lock the door and hide, but her legs wouldn't move from where she was frozen in place. Sometime later, struggling to cover herself, she tugged up her shorts, even if she couldn't fasten the zipper with her trembling hands. Later, she would be grateful she hadn't been raped. Right now, she couldn't think or do anything except cry and shake.

CHAPTER 22

Isaac

Isaac finished his debrief with Angel and sat watching the TV screen in the Honda garage as the Moto3 riders finished their FP1 session. Once they cleared the track, he'd have ten minutes before his session started. He and Angel had discussed strategy for the practice and determined which types of tires they would use, and now his crew chief was busy doing the scheduled interview.

With a few minutes to kill, Isaac absently picked up his phone. There were several text notifications from Catarina. That was odd. He seldom got messages from her. Maybe to congratulate him on the engagement, but the timing was off. She would know he was about to be on track. Checking the latest, he grew alarmed. Holding his breath, he scrolled back to read from the start—sent over thirty minutes ago.

"Anna's late for breakfast. Any idea if she's running late?"

"She's not answering her phone."

"Did she forget our breakfast plans and go to the track with you?"

"What room are you in? I'll go knock." He checked the time signature with growing concern. That one had been sent twenty minutes ago. The updates continued every couple of minutes.

"I can't find her anywhere. Not sure what to do. Still no answer."

"I missed the second shuttle. I'm getting worried."

Five minutes ago. Catarina must be frantic that not only was Anna missing, but she also hadn't gotten a hold of him.

"She's not here. We're Room 923," he sent back, his forehead tightening as his disquiet grew.

Isaac called Anna, but she didn't answer—it went straight to voicemail. He hung up and sent her a quick text. *"Call me. It's urgent."*

Clutching his phone, he set off through the garage to the service lane where the emptied second shuttle was leaving. No Anna. Where could she be? Something was wrong.

It was a long shot, but maybe she'd forgotten her phone in the room and missed her messages. Maybe she'd arrived and headed into his trailer, though it wasn't like her to have left without meeting Catarina. He trotted up the stairs, unlocked the door, and stuck his head into the darkened interior. She wasn't there.

"Not on the shuttle. Checked the trailer. Not here." Biting his lip, he updated Catarina.

He thought for a second. *"Did you try the washroom?"*

"Three sets. Nothing." came her speedy response. *"I'm out of ideas."*

Where was Anna? What had made her miss her breakfast plans? It wasn't like her to disappear. A bright yellow taxi passed him and stopped outside the factory Yamaha team's garages. Spencer jumped from the vehicle and ran up the stairs into his trailer to change. Late. He'd also missed the shuttle.

"I don't know what else to do. I'm freaking out." Catarina wasn't the only one.

Pieces fell into place and Isaac's blood ran cold. Spencer had something to do with Anna's disappearance. Isaac would deal with him later, but in his panic, it was more important to find Anna. What if she was hurt?

He ran to the taxi, reaching it just before it left. "Can you take me back to the Ramada Hotel?" At the driver's nod, he jumped in the back seat, still wearing his riding leathers. Isaac couldn't sit still, so he fidgeted with his phone as the car headed for the quick trip on the highway. He checked the time. Shit. Just before nine. He was supposed to be on track any minute. He called Angel.

His crew chief answered the phone on the first ring. "Isaac, where'd you go? I leave for five minutes, and you're gone."

"Anna didn't arrive on the second shuttle. I think something happened."

"Isaac, where are you?" His boss sounded impatient.

"I'm in a cab, headed back to the hotel."

At first, there was silence, then Angel cleared his throat. "I can cover for the first half of the session. I'll say you are indisposed, but you need to get back, or you will forfeit your time for FP1."

"I know." Was his departure rash? Isaac was about to find out.

"No matter how you and that bike fly, if you miss the entire session, not only will there be questions, but you'll be in Q1 tomorrow afternoon instead of Q2. You could start from the back of the grid and give yourself an insurmountable task for the race."

"I know," Isaac repeated. He'd worked so hard to put himself at the top of the standings this year with top-notch qualifying and consistent racing. Ordinarily, he'd never miss a crucial timed session. "Something is wrong. I'll get back if I can, but Anna comes first." He hung up and stared out the window, willing the car to go faster. His chest tightened for the rest of the five-minute drive, the feeling of dread growing.

His phone buzzed with a new message from Catarina.

"She doesn't answer in your room. Still nothing."

"I'm on my way. Cab should be there in two minutes."

He leaned forward. "Excuse me, can you drive any faster? It's an emergency."

He tapped his phone to pay as soon as the car stopped. Catarina met him at the curb as he flung open the door and hopped out.

She didn't greet him or waste words. "The first thing I thought of when I couldn't find her and she didn't answer, was Spencer." Her voice shook, and she blinked back tears. "That's why I stayed and kept searching."

Isaac had never seen his friend so upset.

"Thank you. Spencer is at the track. He came late." It was difficult to speak in full sentences with his fear barely contained.

"The hotel won't tell me his room number. I tried. What if he's done something and locked her in there?"

"We'll find her. Tell me what happened. From the beginning." He projected confidence he didn't feel. Panic would solve nothing.

"I was running late," said Catarina with a shuddering breath. "And texted that I'd be down at 8:25."

"Did she reply?" It would help to pinpoint when she'd disappeared.

Catarina shook her head. "One of the other girls said she saw her by the door of the restaurant at about 8:15, but Anna didn't stay."

That was about the time his shuttle had left. "How about the hotel staff?"

Isaac struggled to keep his voice calm. That was almost an hour ago. His Anna could be upset or hurt. He needed to find her.

"Nothing. Maybe Spencer found her alone in the lobby," said Catarina.

Isaac shook his head. "Too public. He's been careful never to be seen with her." It helped that Catarina was aware of the entire problem with Spencer. Isaac paused, trying to recreate what had happened in his mind. "She left the restaurant. Maybe she went back up to our room to get her phone, and he found her before she answered your first text."

"I'm so sorry I was late." Tears slid down Catarina's cheeks.

"It's not your fault. This is on him. We might have to check floor by floor. His room could be anywhere." Isaac opened the door for Catarina, and they entered the hotel. Crossing the lobby, he pushed the button to summon an elevator. "I'll check our room because I have the key. Maybe she was too scared or upset to answer the door when you knocked. Or she put on headphones. Music is calming." He hoped that's all that had happened, even if he didn't believe it.

Behind where they stood, a woman spoke to the front desk clerk, "I wanted a sauna but there was someone screaming on the fitness level. You need to check it out. Someone needs to see if they're okay." She looked concerned.

Isaac and Catarina shared a glance and hurried into the elevator when at last it arrived. He stabbed the button for the third floor. When the doors opened, they rushed out.

Anna's purple phone lay on the floor next to the wall. He grabbed it. There were dozens of text notifications from himself and Catarina. Trotting down the hall, they passed the pool and turning the corner, the sound of sobbing became clear.

"Oh my god," said Catarina, covering her mouth. "She's still crying?"

"She's having a meltdown." Isaac broke into a run, skidding to a stop in front of the family change room at the end of the hall.

Bursting through the door with Catarina on his heels. Anna's tear-streaked face looked up, and her look of terror subsided. Even in this state, she recognized them. She closed her eyes and took a couple of shuddering breaths, trying to regain control.

Isaac sat beside her and moved her into his lap where he wrapped his arms around her. He held her close, feeling her relax an infinitesimal amount.

"What can I do?" said Catarina, speaking Spanish.

"I don't know how the law works in Australia," said Isaac, speaking calmly despite the welling volcano of anger inside. He had to keep it together, or he'd frighten Anna more. "But tell the concierge to call the police." He turned back. "Sweetheart," he whispered as he smoothed her hair with one hand. "Was it Spencer? Did he do this?"

She didn't seem able to answer verbally yet, but she gulped and nodded.

This time, that bastard would pay.

Not leaving, but calling the front desk, Catarina said, "This is an emergency. There's been a sexual assault on the third floor in the family change room. Call the police and send medical."

Minutes later, a harried-looking man dressed in a burgundy hotel blazer arrived at the door near Catarina. "I'm the hotel manager," he said, a look of concern on his face. "The police are on their way." From a distance came the sound of an approaching siren outside the hotel. It stopped out front. "I've told security to pull up surveillance footage for the elevator and the third-floor hallway."

Anna's tears slowed. Her face remained blotchy, and her lip was swollen and split. A purple lump was growing on her forehead. Rage filled every fiber of Isaac's being. Spencer had hit her. Isaac remained on the floor, his legs still on either side of her, his arms wrapped around her in a full-body hug.

"What happened?" said the hotel manager.

Anna lifted her head and directed her gaze at Isaac's hand. "Austin Spencer attacked me and forced me in here where nobody could see us."

The manager took in Isaac in his riding leathers and the young women in their team clothing. "Spencer? The Australian racer?" From his wide-eyed look, the man was shocked by the news.

Isaac nodded. "We'll be pressing charges." Anna stiffened in his arms. "We'll help," he said, "But he can't get away with this again. He hurt you." She leaned back against him with a sigh and nodded. He looked at the hotel manager. "It will help if it's caught on camera."

Two police officers in black and tan uniforms arrived minutes later, a paramedic in tow. Isaac helped Anna move from the floor to the hallway, where it wasn't such a confined space. There were too many people for the small change room. The manager blocked off the hallway, closing it for the duration of the police stay.

Isaac took Anna's hand, standing beside her while she told the officers what had happened.

"Austin Spencer tried to rape me." She'd recovered her poise and could speak for herself. She explained she was on the spectrum and had been overwhelmed by the assault. "It's the first time my meltdowns have ever been helpful." She bit her lip as she stared at the floor.

"Helpful?" said one of the police officers, glancing up from her notebook. "He smashed your head on the counter and hit you."

Isaac wasn't sure the officer believed Anna's story.

Anna must have thought the same thing. Her body stiffened and her fire returned as she spoke. "He attempted to rape me, but we fought. I elbowed him in the stomach and screamed so loud, he might have worried that he'd be caught, so he left. My screams saved me." She met the officer's gaze. "I was really loud." She took a deep breath. "When I slapped him, my ring cut his face. Can you get DNA from it?"

"Indeed, we can," said the first officer. "I'll send someone over to collect it."

The second officer swabbed her ring, dropping the sample into a sealed bag. Then, he took photos of the change room and of Anna's face, showing her swelling goose egg, split lip, and the purple and red bruise forming across her cheekbone. Bruises bloomed on her wrist as well, so the officers took additional photos. Once the damage had been documented, the paramedic carefully checked her injuries and passed her an ice pack.

"Do you have any idea where Spencer would have gone?" asked the first officer.

"To the track. He and I are supposed to be at the same practice." Isaac glanced out the window toward the Phillip Island circuit. The practice was more than half over.

"Who are you?" said the officer with the notebook.

"Isaac Vasquez, Anna's fiancé." Saying the word brought out his protective side, and he slid his arm around Anna's waist. She shot him a grateful smile.

After collecting all the pertinent contact information from Isaac and Anna, the police and paramedics left, promising to take care of everything else. One of the officers accompanied the manager to collect the security footage.

Catarina left after she hugged Anna. "I'll see you later."

Isaac returned Anna's phone, and when she saw the time, she gasped. "You need to go back to the track. You're missing FP1."

"I'll head back to the track later for FP2. I want to stay with you for a while." He watched the seagulls swooping over the nearby shoreline. The track was closer to the ocean than any of the others that they raced. Because he'd missed FP1, he hadn't set a time for the session and risked a poor starting position. It would be the first time this season he hadn't automatically qualified in the top ten.

Taking a breath, he ran through the familiar course in his mind. It settled his jittery nerves, which would help Anna stay calm. Besides having a hill, it ran anti-clockwise, like COTA, Aragon, the Sachsenring, and Valencia. It would be difficult to beat Vince here, with or without this problem with Spencer that remained foremost in his mind.

"I'm going to the track." Anna's announcement surprised him, slowing his walk toward the elevator. Her voice was hoarse. Maybe they should get her some tea.

"We can wait awhile." He searched for signs of continued distress, but she'd calmed down. While her injuries would discolor her face, he was thankful that they were no worse.

"I won't ruin your championship hopes. We can't let Spencer affect the outcome."

"I don't care about the race," Isaac said. Right now, it didn't matter.

"You need track time if you're going to fight for the win on Sunday." She nudged him toward the elevator, her jaw set in a stubborn line.

He'd never loved her more than for this selfless resilience after the attack.

"I'll have to go through Q1 either way." He shrugged, then pushed the button to call the elevator. He wouldn't change his decision to come back, even if he could.

"You'll get into Q2. A top-six start. I have faith." She smiled as the doors opened and tugged him inside. "Let's go."

"What's the hurry?" He narrowed his eyes. Why was she rushing back to the track?

"If we're lucky, Spencer will be arrested today, and they'll disqualify him from the race on Sunday. I don't want to miss that. If we go now, I can watch the cops arrive." Her jaw flared. She wasn't quite as fine as she insisted, but if she wanted to see Spencer arrested for closure, that's what they would do.

It might help her sleep tonight, knowing Spencer was behind bars. Isaac nodded and took her hand as they headed for the exit. Besides, it would be satisfying to see Spencer in handcuffs.

CHAPTER 23

Anna

Anna got her wish. Just before FP2 that afternoon, a police car pulled into the service lane and parked behind the Yamaha boxes. Two officers stepped out of the vehicle and were joined by one of the senior racing officials, who must have been waiting for them. The governing body of the MotoGP races must have been notified of Spencer's impending arrest.

While the three of them shook hands, Anna hustled down the stairs of Isaac's trailer and hurried through the garage. She seldom interrupted Isaac when he was working, but as she trotted through, she said, "They're here."

Isaac followed her along the edge of pit lane where Catarina and Angel joined them from the other Honda garage. Vince trailed behind to watch the show as well.

They arrived just in time.

The two officers who had been at the hotel this morning were on site.

"Austin Spencer?" said one, looking at the Yamaha motorcycle racers going through their prep for the second practice session, which would start in less than ten minutes.

"Yes." Spencer turned from where he was speaking with his crew chief. With his back toward pit lane, he didn't notice the audience out front, or he might have been more concerned. "I'm Austin Spencer. How can I help you? Autographs for your kids?"

"I'm afraid not," said the second officer. "We're here to place you under arrest. You'll need to come with us."

"Arrest?" Spencer scoffed, stepping back to show a scowl on his typically smug face. Turning to face the police, he caught sight of Anna beyond the Yamaha garage.

Meeting his eyes, she crossed her arms across her chest and nodded.

"I don't know what you're talking about," he said, attempting to bluff his way out of trouble. "I have no idea what she told you, but it was a pack of lies."

"You're charged with sexual assault, gross indecency, and attempted rape," said the first officer.

The racing steward spoke as well. "We have suspended you for the weekend while they investigate this matter. Effective immediately." The short man with the MotoGP logo on his white polo shirt handed a piece of paper to Spencer's crew chief.

The chief scanned the document. "What have you done this time, Spencer?"

"Make it go away," Spencer pleaded. "This is my home race. Half the fans in the stands, are here to see me."

His boss shook his head. "Not this time. I'll be making a call to the Yamaha head office. The police are making formal charges, so you will be suspended by the team and manufacturer. If found guilty, Yamaha will terminate your contract."

The officer lowered his voice to speak to the crew chief.

Anna edged closer to hear the police officer's quiet words.

"A full investigation will follow his incarceration. We have security footage, DNA evidence, and there may be others who come forward once he's behind bars. He's going away."

Blood drained from Spencer's face, and he looked from side to side. No one on his team looked in his direction as they returned to busy work.

"You're under arrest. Please hold your wrists in front of you," said the second officer. "I'd like to caution you that any statements you make may be used as evidence."

Anna noted that their wording differed from the Miranda Rights used in America, but that the meaning seemed similar.

"This is your fault, bitch," Spencer snarled at Anna. He lunged and was caught by the officers. Heart racing, she held her ground, maintaining eye contact.

"Sir, I caution you not to resist arrest," said the female officer. "Or that will be added to the charges."

"I should have hit you harder." Spencer's face turned a lurid shade of red as he sneered, seemingly unable to stop himself. "If I ever catch you alone, you'll wish you were dead."

Anna stepped back at the pure hatred that blazed from his eyes. The entitled ass had believed he could get away with what he'd done.

"Don't worry," said the second officer. "After what we just heard, we'll recommend no bail." He fastened the first metal cuff with a clink.

Anna watched with satisfaction as they cuffed Spencer's wrists and hauled him toward the police car. When the sound of the car door closing in the service land indicated that he was inside, she smiled, satisfaction filling her. At last, this was over. She returned to work.

•   •   •

The headlines the following day were all about Austin Spencer's arrest. By afternoon, just before qualifying, three more young women had accused him of sexual assault and rape. His career was over, and he should spend years in prison.

Anna waited with the crew in the garage for Isaac to go through Qualifying One, the first time he'd been relegated to that session this season. She'd chewed on her thumbnail until it was sore, more nervous than Isaac. He'd assured her he wasn't worried—prior to this year, he'd almost always been in Q1, and he was familiar with the feeling and the strategy. He'd also topped the timesheet in FP4 only minutes ago. He had race pace but needed a fast lap to send him into Q2.

Only the top two riders of the seventeen taking part in Q1 would advance to Q2 to compete for positions in the front four rows of the race. Qualifying ran two back-to-back sessions of fifteen minutes, which took a different skill set than racing. It wasn't about consistency or long-term strategy, just who could go the fastest for a single lap.

The teams saved new soft tires from their allocated number, specifically for qualifying, as they had better grip and speed in the brief sessions. Isaac wouldn't be able to use new soft rubber more than once in Q1, so he could save a fresh soft rear one for Q2, if he got through. Many other riders would just be happy to get into Q2. He wanted to make the front row. Saving a soft tire was a gamble.

Angel sent him out on a lightly used soft tire to start. It wouldn't have as much grip as a new one, but Anna hoped it would be okay. She followed Isaac on screen, clenching her pen like a weapon as he sat up and rode within the speed limit to the pit lane exit before accelerating onto the track. One of the KTM riders stuck to him like glue as they accelerated to do a quick out-lap to warm up the tires and the bike.

On Isaac's first full-speed lap, he rode into turn three too hot and ran out of bounds, canceling his lap time. Several other racers set fast times, including one from the younger Wilson brother on a second Yamaha that might be enough to advance. His time would be hard to beat.

Isaac's second full lap time shot him to the top of the timesheet for less than thirty seconds before it was bettered. Sweat dripped down Anna's back as Isaac entered pit lane, where he hopped off his bike while the quick-moving team changed the rear tire to fresh rubber. It was frustrating to have him wait for the final six minutes of the session before remounting and returning to the track. She wiped her palms and didn't speak until he'd finished his out-lap.

This time, a young Ducati rider and the same KTM rider stuck to Isaac's back wheel, hoping for a tow. They followed him, letting him slice through the air so they could attempt to emerge from his slipstream down the final straight before the finish line. They would try to slingshot from behind to beat his time at the last second.

On the first hot lap, he bettered his previous fastest time, but his trailers beat it by hundredths of a second, knocking him back to third. Two more riders flew to the top of the leaderboard while he was in the first section of the next lap. The stalking KTM ran out of bounds, unable to keep pace with Isaac on his flying Honda. The Ducati rider stayed in his slipstream and beat him by thirteen-thousandths of a second and shot ahead. There was a roar of dismay from the stands. This year, underdog Isaac had become a crowd favorite.

Isaac remained in third with time for one more lap. First to sixth were separated by only a quarter of a second. There was no room for error, or he'd be starting the race no better than thirteenth.

With bated breath, Anna watched while he threw himself through the course one more time. She kept one eye on the official scoring order on the edge of the screen. Tuning out the Marcus Birch and the other commentators, she focused on Isaac, seeing some of what he saw via the mini onboard camera on the back of his bike. He was tucked in and flying through the corners.

The screen switched to a different view, showing him slide through the final corners with both his elbow and his knee scraping the track—Vasquez style.

"Go, go, go," she muttered. "Don't crash."

"You've got this, my boy," Angel said under his breath.

She couldn't take her eyes off the screen as the entire team willed him to succeed.

Qualifying well would make the difference between fighting for the win tomorrow and damage limitation mode, letting Vince back into the championship. Now that Isaac was ahead in the standings, he might win the season. Not that they had ever discussed it outside of a press conference, but he had to be feeling the pressure.

The checkered flag was out, meaning that only the riders still on course for their final lap could improve their times. The rest were done already. Isaac lost the trailing Duc when the rider couldn't run the

Honda's pace. It was all on Isaac now. He needed a last lap fast enough to beat at least one of the two riders at the top of the timesheet.

After the third interval of four, he still had a quarter of a second lead on their interval time, the screen showing his lap time in red. He was on pace to place first. He could do this.

As Isaac crossed the line, the pit crew erupted in a loud cheer and the fans crowded in the stands roared. He'd set a new lap record and qualified first, moving on to the second session with the top riders. Anna sagged in relief. If he hadn't advanced, she felt like it would be her fault, though he would never say or think it. With the pace he'd shown, he would have been in Q2 already if he'd stayed at the track on Friday.

There wasn't much turnaround time between the qualifying sessions. Isaac stayed quiet in the box, sitting at the back with his air pods in, remaining in race mode while he focused on what he could control this weekend. He seemed impervious to her emotional roller coaster.

Angel directed the crew to mount a new soft tire on Isaac's bike for the first part of Q2, their gamble of saving two having paid off. He had one for the first half of the session and the one they'd saved for the second half when all the riders would be in full time-attack mode.

Isaac left the instant the session started, a determined look on his face.

Anna's heart was in her mouth, watching the riders on course once more. Vince appeared to be an unstoppable force on this counterclockwise track as well, throwing down the gauntlet with a lap time only two-thousandths off Isaac's lap record. With ten minutes to go, someone would surely beat his time.

When Isaac came in for the mid-session tire change, she took a deep breath. He didn't look right or left, but departed as soon as his bike was ready. This part was make or break. As usual, it came down to the final laps. Some riders finished, settling for places on rows three and four, but those that had timed things to perfection had one more lap and remained on track. This included Luka, Xavi, Vince, and Isaac.

Isaac was listed sixth so far and Vince was on pole. Vince crossed first of the final four, staying at the top, but smashing the previous best by four-tenths of a second—an unheard-of margin, even for such a dominant rider.

Xavi's lap looked set to equal it for the first half, but he bobbled coming through Lukey Heights at turn nine. That left Isaac and Luka swooping through the long left turns at eleven and twelve before they thundered down the Gardner Straight toward the line. The front end of Luka's bike wobbled, wasting valuable fractions of a second. Isaac flashed through the finish two-tenths shy of Vince's record, setting a personal best and second overall—teeing up another Vasquez showdown.

CHAPTER 24

Isaac

Isaac usually paid no attention to anyone or anything on the grid as he listened to music until the last possible second, using it to drown out distraction. Today, he spared a glance for Anna holding his umbrella, her engagement ring sparkling in the sunlight. He caught her eye and winked. He was grateful to share his final MotoGP races with her. After today, he had only two more professional races, and he intended to enjoy them.

He got away clean, following Vince through the first several laps, trading places several times with Luka. This allowed Vince to pull a couple of bike lengths in front and stay there. Isaac found his rhythm and was feeling good. He was planning when to put a move on Vince when out of nowhere a seagull smashed into his bike—one of the random Phillip Island hazards.

Somehow, he kept his bike upright, and on the track as he shook off the unexpected collision. But he lost time and Luka shot ahead. With only three laps remaining, Isaac was alone and in a safe third place. He accelerated to get back on terms with Luka, but the kid sped away. After two laps, Isaac conceded. He couldn't catch him. At least he hadn't crashed. Finishing third meant another valuable sixteen points in the championship.

Vince won again, gaining nine points on Isaac, whose lead had shrunk to a slim margin. Isaac needed a solid finish in Malaysia, so he'd be leading going into the final race. While he led the overall standings, part of him expected Vince's rally. He wouldn't be surprised if his brother won—he was the only twelve-time world champion for a reason.

With Spencer in jail, Anna seemed happier. Isaac hadn't realized how much it had affected her day after day, just being on guard. That wasn't the only positive news. Her lawyer had let her know Adam had vacated the townhouse before the specified date, and her firm had listed it for sale. Things were coming together in their lives.

The Malaysian Grand Prix at Sepang was the last of the 'flyaway' races, and Isaac was looking forward to returning home afterward for ten days before the last race in Valencia, Spain. He couldn't wait to sleep in his own brand-new bed.

The Sepang race weekend proceeded like clockwork. Angel and the crew had the bike in top form, and Isaac qualified in third—another front-row start. The Sunday forecast had been for a mix of sun and showers, but they awoke to a gorgeous blue-sky day without rain clouds. Perfect for racing.

The first two-thirds of the race went well, and Isaac was in the mix for a podium finish, once again battling with Luka and Vince. For a split second, he hesitated, his mind wandering, and the next, he catapulted through the air. He landed hard on his back—the airbag inflating and preventing serious injury. He lay still in the gravel for a few seconds— the wind knocked out of him. A dust cloud hung over him, floating while he caught his breath. He smashed a fist to the ground. Damn.

He sat up, trying to rein in his emotions. Despite the crash, he was alive. The inattentive moment could have caused something so much worse. He couldn't dwell, needing to put the crash from his mind.

Shuffling to his feet, already feeling where bruises bloomed, he stood and took stock. Nothing seemed painful enough to be broken or sprained. He determined he was fine and moved farther from the track and took a couple of deep breaths, before checking to see if he could remount.

He glanced up the track, though all the riders had disappeared around the next bend in the track. He needed to salvage anything, even a point or two, but there was no possible way. His bike was destroyed, scattered into five or six pieces. He kicked the nearest chunk as he trudged toward the safety fence and the path beyond while trackside marshals dragged his shattered bike away. He took a breath. He'd had amazing luck all season. This crash had been due, but it wasn't the end of the world. At least he was uninjured. Still, if only he hadn't lost concentration. The championship had been there for the taking and if he wasn't careful, it would slip from his grasp.

By the time he arrived at pit lane, the race had ended, and Vince had won, again.

Isaac did a quick calculation in his head. With his DNF and Vince's twenty-five points for the win, he and his brother were tied with four hundred points each. Everything would come down to the final race. If Isaac won, how would Vince behave?

•   •   •

Just before midnight, on the night before the championship showdown in Valencia—which was being billed by Marcus Birch as #VasquezShowdown—Isaac jumped up to answer the knock at their hotel room door. It was late for visitors so it must be important. Vince stood in the hallway, with his hands shoved deep into the pockets of his jeans. He must not be able to sleep either.

"Can we go for a walk?" His brother said. "I want to talk to you about something."

"Sure. Let me tell Anna." Isaac poked his head into the bathroom where Anna was brushing her teeth. "Vince asked me to go for a walk. I shouldn't be too late." He kissed her cheek, grabbed a sweater, and left with his brother.

They took the elevator to the parking garage.

"I thought we were walking," said Isaac as the doors opened underground.

"There's somewhere else I want to walk so we can ditch the cameras," said Vince.

They climbed into his car, and they drove to the Circuit Ricardo Tormo where the race tomorrow would be held, the last of Isaac's career. Vince parked, and they strolled side by side near the quiet track on the paved path outside the safety fence. They'd shared a lot of memories here, having been on the racing circuit since they were teenagers. It seemed fitting that Isaac's last race was on Spanish soil.

Vince must have something particular on his mind, but at first, he didn't speak.

Twice he tugged his ear and seemed about to say something, but so far, the silence had been unbroken.

After half the circuit in the chilly November night, lit only by the overhead lights at distant intervals, Vince said, "Do you think you'll miss it?"

"I'll miss you and yeah, there will probably be times I'll miss racing." Isaac had made peace with his decision and could discuss it calmly.

"Do you regret not signing again? Retiring at only thirty-three?"

Isaac shook his head. "I'm ready for something different." As he ambled, he cataloged the turns and his crashes over the years. At least they'd never been serious. Looking back, he didn't think he'd ever pushed himself as hard as this year. He'd been the one to play it safe. Well, relatively safe, no motorcycle racer lived a conservative life.

He and his brother walked until they were across from the final turn before the start-finish straight.

"I want you to do something for me," said Vince, slowing his pace.

"Sure," said Isaac. This must be the reason they'd come. It would probably be about training, the riding academy, or the future. He hoped Vince would miss him next year, too.

"Tomorrow, I want you to try to win." They stopped.

Isaac laughed. "Of course." His breath plumed in the frosty air.

"No. I mean it," said Vince, his intensity boring into Isaac. The overhead lights made his skin look ghostly and pale and reflected off his dark eyes.

"You're going to let me win?" Isaac frowned, feeling his forehead tighten. That didn't seem like Vince.

"No way," said Vince, waving his hands. "Of course not, but if I win, it has to be because I deserved it. Victory is cheap if it's handed to me. If you can win, do it. Fight for the championship. I'm going to go all out, and you should, too."

Isaac said nothing.

Vince continued. "Don't get mad at me, but I think you crashed during the last race because subconsciously, you expected me to win. You lost your concentration, and your race went to hell."

Irritation flashed through Isaac, only to dissipate in seconds while he resumed walking, Vince trailing. Isaac hadn't looked at it that way. He'd just seen his accident as unlucky, but Vince had a point. His head hadn't been in it. Not enough for a victory. After fifteen meters, he halted once more and faced his brother. Crashing in tomorrow's race wasn't the worst outcome.

"What if I win?" Isaac's voice cracked. He didn't want to wreck their relationship over something so silly as a race, no matter how important.

"Then you'll be the champion this year, and I'll be happy for you. You deserve it as much as I do." Isaac tried to interject but Vince barreled on. "Don't get me wrong. I love winning. But you're my only brother, and we've done this together for so long. The least I can do is to be a gracious loser."

Isaac raised his eyebrow. "Can you?" While he said it with a teasing tone, there was some truth to his question. Gracious losing wasn't his brother's strength.

Vince laughed. "That's fair, but for you, I can. You're family. To win, you'll have to beat me. Promise you'll try."

Isaac studied his brother. "It won't ruin our friendship?"

Vince held out his hand. "I promise. Brothers before victory."

Isaac shook his brother's hand and pulled him in for a hug. He swallowed. "I promise to give it my all." His voice cracked. This was one of those times that Vince's words had been not just a pleasant surprise, but a gift. "May the best Vasquez win."

CHAPTER 25

Anna

Anna read in bed, waiting for Isaac to return to the hotel. Her eyes grew bleary, and she yawned, surprised his walk with Vince was taking so long. They'd been gone for two hours already. Tomorrow was race day, and they could sleep in a little, but still, it was late. In the morning, they also had the Hero's Walk and autographs sessions. Whatever had brought Vince to the door must have been important. He, too, would want to be at his best tomorrow.

The MotoGP race was the final and main event of the weekend—held after the Moto3 and Moto2 races. The media circus had been more distracting than ever, with cameras following the riders at all times and extended autographs sessions with hordes of excited fans. With Vince and Isaac tied, the championship was still up for grabs. In most years it had already been decided before the last race.

She yawned again, determined to wait up, but fading despite her nerves about Isaac's last race. She put in her bookmark and was about to flick on the TV, when Isaac opened the door.

"You're still up," he said with a smile. "You waited."

"Of course," she said. "I wanted to make sure everything was okay."

"Vince shocked the hell out of me," he said, shaking his head. He kicked off his shoes and sat on the end of the bed.

"What did he say?" She held her breath, hoping Vince had been decent.

Isaac shrugged. "It was almost unreal. He drove us out to the track, and we walked around the outer edge. It was completely quiet, like when we were young. We used to walk the tracks at night together. Tonight, we walked and talked, like old times. Just as we got around, near the finish, Vince told me to try to win the race."

"Of course, you'll try." She sat straighter, offended that Vince would suggest that Isaac wouldn't give it his all. "It's not like you were going to throw the championship." She took a better look at Isaac's face. "Were you?" She took an incredulous breath. "You wouldn't have done that."

He shrugged again. "Not on purpose." He tossed his sweater onto the chair in the corner. "I'll be right back and then I'll tell you the rest." He disappeared into the bathroom for a few minutes to get ready for bed before sliding in beside her. "Get the light?"

She flicked off the reading lamp and moved into the warm circle of Isaac's arm, resting her head on his chest and shoulder. She didn't want to push, confident he would explain.

The darkness settled around them, and it was a couple of minutes before he spoke. "Vince said I crashed last time because I didn't think I could win. That I lost concentration and let him win. Subconsciously, maybe I did." His voice sounded thoughtful, but he hadn't tensed up. This might not be news.

"Do you think it might be true?"

She felt him nod before he said, "Deep down, I might have been trying to put Vince first again. More than anything, he wants another championship."

"Don't you?" Her eyes adjusted to the dark, and she was able to make out Isaac's face. She searched for any signs of distress.

Isaac's eyes remained open, staring at the ceiling. "I never thought I'd win. I didn't expect to even be a contender."

"And now?" The pale seam of light that snuck in under the door reflected from his eyes. "You're the Cinderella of the year."

He laughed. "I hadn't pictured myself as any sort of princess."

"I just mean the underdog. Isn't that how they're billing you?"

"It is." His arm tightened around her. "I want to win," he whispered, like he was trying out the sound of the words, still barely able to believe it himself.

"What do you think is different this year? Why now?"

"Vince said it was the bike." He sounded unhappy again.

"That was before, when he was being an ass. He doesn't believe that in reality. What do you think?"

"I think I'm happier and know better what I want. It's helped me focus." He kissed her. "You're a big part of that, but it's as much because in going after you, and putting myself first, I think I also did that on the track most of the season."

"Then that's what you need to do tomorrow. Win for yourself. You've worked so hard all year, and you deserve it every bit as much as your brother, if not more. He already has twelve championships."

"You're biased." Isaac kissed her. "I have a feeling you aren't used to putting yourself first, either. You can remind me to put myself first sometimes, and I'll remind you."

"I'll try," she said in a whisper. "It's tough to break lifelong habits, as you know."

"Who did you put first? Everyone else?" said Isaac. "I still know next to nothing about your family, other than you were raised by your grandmother who hoped someday you would be a writer."

Anna didn't say anything at first. "My parents didn't want me."

"That can't be true." The words popped out of his mouth.

He must be thinking of his own parents. Carmela was warm and loving, and from the sound of it, his father had been supportive and kind. They'd been a family that put their sons' needs and futures ahead of their own.

"I don't want to make tonight about me," she said. "Adam used to say I did that." He'd never understood that sharing her connection was her way of relating to situations.

"I'm not Adam and I can't sleep, anyway. Talk to me. Tell me about your childhood. I want to listen." Isaac's arms tightened.

Her heart ached with old wounds, but she trusted Isaac. "I was a difficult child who was intense and cried a lot. I hadn't been diagnosed yet, and my parents struggled to figure out what to do with me, so I made myself unimportant. I didn't want to be a bother. I tried not to ask for anything, even hugs or attention. When I was diagnosed with autism, it became clear that I needed more than many neurotypical kids. My parents didn't have any money, and they fought about me all the time."

"How old were you?" Isaac's voice seemed far away as she slipped deeper into the memories.

"Eight. I don't think they realized I could hear their arguments, or how much I understood. But I did." She took a deep breath. "The walls were paper thin in the apartment. My dad said I wasn't worth the extra money they would need to spend on therapy and doctors. He wished I was normal." Her voice had become a whisper. She'd told no one her father's words, not even her grandmother.

Isaac's arm tightened again. "That's awful. At least your mother must have thought you were worth it."

She wished that were true. "Not for long. My dad left soon after that and my mom couldn't cope on her own. When I was nine, she got fired for leaving her job when the school called, insisting that I be picked up early. I'd had a problem with another student and gotten upset. A meltdown."

She paused and wiped the tears that leaked from her eyes, and her chest tightened. She'd never shared this part with anyone, either.

"My mom packed up my clothes and grabbed a couple of my favorite books. She drove us to her mother's house and rang the doorbell. Right on the porch, she handed my suitcase to my grandmother." Her voice caught as she continued. "My mom said, 'You wanted a granddaughter. She's not worth this much work. She's all yours.' Then she walked away."

Isaac squeezed her gently. "Have you heard from her since?"

"She didn't call or write, though she sent my grandmother emails from time to time, and she never visited. When I was thirteen, I snuck onto my grandmother's computer and searched through her old messages. Not once did my mother even ask about me. When my grandmother died, my mother came to the funeral but treated me like a stranger, like she was lost in her own grief. She left immediately afterward, and we haven't spoken in all these years. I don't even know where she lives." Anna's tears released in earnest, great wracking sobs that shook her body. For all the tears, speaking of the past was a cathartic release.

"I want you," said Isaac, tightening his grip. "Mi Corazon, you're wonderful. I think you are worth it a thousand times over. It's perfect that we found each other."

His simple statement reminded her that in her new life—she was valued and loved. It was time to let go of the pain in her past. She had a new family.

•   •   •

Anna stood on the starting grid. Isaac was in P2, and Vince was on pole. Even their final race would begin side-by-side. She glanced at her soon-to-be brother-in-law, his face a mask of total concentration. Catarina grinned back at Anna, her face aglow with excitement. This race would decide who was this year's champion. Twenty-two races, and it was still undecided, a reporter's dream.

Anna's heart fluttered, and she wiped her palms against the bottom edge of her shirt, gripping the umbrella to keep it steady on her last umbrella girl gig. They were into the final minutes, between the sighting lap and the final pre-race warm-up lap. The countdown clock ticked down the minutes until the season's finale. Isaac's eyes were open, but his focus was elsewhere. She glanced from him to Vince and back. Isaac's face mirrored his brother's. They'd never looked more alike, wearing twin masks of concentration as they blocked out the rest of the world.

With one minute left, the non-riders cleared the grid, leaving only the racers.

A pushy reporter called to Angel as they returned to pit lane. "Are there team orders from Honda? Do the bosses have a preference on who should win #VasquezShowdown? Do they prefer Vince and the factory team to win?"

Angel kept walking.

The reporter persisted. "Does Isaac have free rein to go for the win?"

It had never occurred to Anna that Honda might have a preference between Isaac and Vince, and her heart thumped hard against her ribs.

Angel turned and spoke into the mic. "If there were orders, they relayed nothing to me. The guys will sort it out on the track." He continued into the box with his clipboard and stared at the screen, waiting for the start.

Anna turned for a last look before entering the box where they'd watch from the screen with the race commentary. With a rev of engines, the riders departed for their final warm-up lap. This was it.

CHAPTER 26

Isaac

Isaac's fingers twitched as he sat on his Honda, staring down the track as the riders took to the grid for what was his last time. He'd woken up this morning with a sense that he had a date with destiny—a tingling sensation that settled in his bones—a certainty. This was going to be his day.

Once the starting lights flickered out, he'd be in his last race, and he took a moment to take that in. He didn't look at Vince or at Anna. This was up to him. His worldview shrank to just him, the bike, and the track ahead—as it did on his best racing days.

When the red lights disappeared, he hit the throttle, and his motorcycle shot forward, timed to perfection. Beside him, Vince got off the line equally well. They shot down the long start-finish straight with the pack of twenty-six riders roaring behind. Vince got the holeshot, braking into turn one. Setting his jaw, Isaac stuck his wheel almost to his brother's as he forced himself to be patient, slotting into second, feeling the rush of an exhilarating start and the press of bikes behind.

This was another counterclockwise track, Vince's specialty. Isaac clenched his teeth as he focused on running a pace fast enough to warm up his tires, especially on the left-hand side where they'd get the most use. He couldn't push too soon, or he'd risk crashing, and he steered through the Doohan corner, flicked through the quick corners of four, five, and six before flying down the short back straight, twisting through the tight section from turns seven through eleven. Then he thundered through the swooping curves of turns twelve and thirteen before braking hard for the final corner and racing down the start-finish-straight to end lap one.

After that, most of the race was a blur. It was apparent that he and Vince were in a class of their own today, leaving their opponents behind. Checking his pit board as the laps ticked off was automatic and helped him stay grounded. He hadn't shown Vince a wheel, but he stayed with him, pushing his brother to buckle under pressure. It didn't happen, which was to be expected. This was a win Isaac would have to earn.

He watched, ready to pounce on a mistake, a slip, or for Vince's tires to lose their grip and create an opening. Lap after lap passed, and there hadn't been an opportunity to pass. Vince's race remained perfect, and Isaac matched him, move for move and lap for lap. Sweat trickled down his face and pooled at the base of his neck. His muscles grew fatigued, but he ignored the discomfort.

With three laps remaining, Isaac dove up the inside on the tight, technical section, taking the lead for the first time. The brothers traded places four times on that lap, with Vince regaining the lead as they powered down the start-finish straight to start the penultimate lap, headed for the Aspar corner where Isaac outbraked his brother, forcing Vince's bike to stop with almost no space on the track. They bumped together but somehow, they stayed upright and on course.

Isaac's arms shook, his heart lodged in his throat as he swept through turns two and three, expecting a countermove. He wasn't disappointed; he knew his brother's racecraft better than anyone. Vince flicked it into the lead in the Angel Nieto corner at turn six and accelerated through the turns, braking hard for turn eleven, where Isaac regained the lead. It lasted only seconds before he and Vince swapped positions again, with Vince at the front as they powered down the long straight to start the final lap.

Twice more they switched, like a dance with complex moves orchestrated to perfection. Isaac wasn't sure who would win anymore, but his final race was the most fun he'd ever had on track—win or lose. It felt like a perfect race. No matter what, it was the best way to end his career.

Vince led going into the final three corners. Isaac needed to mount one last challenge. Victory needed to be earned, now more than ever. Still, there was a split second where he almost hesitated. There was no shame in second. Second was a fabulous result for both this epic battle and the season. What if pushing on worn tires threw the race away?

Ignoring the doubts, Isaac slid through turn twelve right on Vince's rear wheel, holding his breath and digging into his reserves. To his surprise, there was the tiniest opening, as Vince ran a few centimeters wider than usual at turn thirteen, leaving a small margin of unclaimed track on the inside. His tires must also be worn.

Remembering the conversation with his brother last night and his feeling of destiny this morning gave Isaac the courage to leap ahead. In the blink of an eye, he wedged his bike into the minuscule gap, forcing Vince to lose momentum, sit up, and drift farther out onto the track.

Isaac shot ahead and braked hard for the final corner, stuffing his bike around the apex. He couldn't remember the last time he'd taken a breath. Still expecting a retaliatory move from his brother, Isaac powered through the short run toward the finish line, accelerating for all he was worth. Vince tried to pull out from his slipstream and slingshot to victory, but Isaac had the faster drive and the more direct line. Neck and neck, wheel in wheel, they roared across the line, slicing the air at almost the same time.

They both looked skyward toward the scoreboard. Neither knew who'd won. It had been so close.

Isaac's name sat at the top. Alone.

A roar rose up from the crowd and filled his chest with their thunder.

He'd won the last race and the overall championship. Tears streamed down his face as he reveled in the moment and tried to accept that his victory was real. He flipped up his visor as he slowed his bike while he waved to the stands, doing a partial lap that ended in front of the packed Vasquez fan club stands—screaming and cheering spectators in red and blue waving flags. The grandstands rocked with their celebration. It was almost unbelievable. He'd won.

When he stopped his bike, his brother parked at his side.

Vince passed his bike to a marshal and ran toward Isaac, then he shook him by the shoulders. "That was a fucking exceptional race, little brother," he shouted. "Congrats on being the 2029 MotoGP champion." Then they hugged.

Isaac didn't have a specific celebration planned, something cheesy and elaborate like Vince would do, and for a second, he regretted not coming up with something fun. Angel and his crew had wanted him to plan a trackside celebration for the fans and the cameras, but Isaac had refused to speculate about winning. He'd been afraid to jinx his race, however, Vince had prepared. Several more race marshals dressed in orange vests dashed up, one holding a duffel bag that he passed to Vince. Another took Isaac's bike and kept it running while he dismounted.

From the bag, Vince removed two sleeveless T-shirts that read, Isaac Vasquez MotoGP Champion 2029. He pulled one on over his leathers and tossed another to Isaac, who removed his helmet, and tugged on the large shirt over his leathers. Next, Vince removed a custom, gold-painted helmet with #1 on it and passed it to Isaac. "I had one made to your specs." He wore an enormous grin.

Hands shaking from adrenaline, Isaac tucked the new helmet under his arm while his brother stuck a #1 decal over the existing number on Isaac's bike. Only the champion could display number one.

Tears streamed down Isaac's face once more, overwhelmed by his brother's generosity that showed more than anything that he'd been genuine in his desire to be brothers first and foremost.

"What would have happened if you'd won?" said Isaac, giving his brother a second hug amid the ever-circling camera crews.

Vince winked. "I had a different duffel prepared for that with shirts for both of us. My theme was twelve plus one. Seems it wasn't meant to be. Not yet. Maybe never." He shrugged. "I'm thrilled you won. It was one of the most fun races of my career. What more could I ask?" Vince's eyes shone, and his toothy smile stretched across his entire face.

His happiness was genuine.

Isaac jogged to the safety fence and tossed his old helmet into the stands for the waiting fans, followed by his sweaty gloves. They could be souvenirs. Then he put on the new helmet, claimed his bike from the waiting marshal, and jumped on. Vince collected his bike and the two of them headed to parc ferme where Anna and their teams waited to celebrate.

"Who was third?" Isaac said as they rode up pit lane.

"No idea," said Vince. "Probably Luka. That kid's going to give me nightmares in the off-season."

Isaac laughed. "Anna and I will cheer for you to get your twelve plus one, next year."

•   •   •

The party continued after the champagne-soaked podium presentations, and on into the night back at the hotel.

It wasn't until well after midnight that Isaac, Vince, Catarina, and Anna sat at a table together, about to wind the night down and return to their rooms, when Angel strolled over to the table and flopped into an empty chair.

"That was the best race I've ever seen," he said, slurring as he thumped his scotch onto the table. He turned to Isaac. "How did you know you could make that last move?"

Isaac stayed where he was, leaning back with his arm around Anna's shoulders. "I woke up this morning and knew I could win."

"Like it was destiny," said Vince with a nod. "I've felt that, but not this morning. I think I knew the entire race, that if I screwed up even once, the race was yours."

"Destiny. I like the sound of that." Isaac shared a look with Anna, who smiled. She felt like a part of his destiny, too. He stood. "Time for us to say goodnight." He smiled at Vince. "Thanks," he said to his brother. "For everything."

With that, he and Anna left together, arms wrapped around one another.

EPILOGUE

Anna leaned back in her corner office, massive windows on two sides letting in ample natural light and overlooking the seared Spanish countryside. It had been hot this June. She sent her most recent chapters to the printer, collected them, and stapled them together, ready for tomorrow. Setting them beside her computer, she clicked off the background music.

This space had been designed for her, and she loved it. Her grandmother's flower paintings hung on the front wall, and the two interior walls were lined floor to ceiling with bookshelves that she spent her leisure time trying to fill.

Isaac had surprised her over the winter with a trip to Seattle to retrieve her book collection, which he'd asked her lawyer to box up and add to the storage locker with her keepsakes from her grandmother, including her antique glass collection. It was so like him that he'd remembered her off-hand comment about her special belongings. He'd also purchased and refinished a solid walnut cabinet with a glass front that he'd placed in the dining room of their new house, where she displayed her colored glass.

On special occasions, they used her beautiful dishes, and she was ecstatic to feel connected to her grandmother again. This was a life her grandmother would have been overjoyed for her to have.

Anna stretched, not quite ready to get up yet, listening to the faint sounds of Isaac and his teenage students on the property below, their dirt bikes slowing as they returned to the shed for the night. She often timed her day of workshops and writing to end at the same time Isaac finished, so they could spend the evening together.

It had taken Anna six months to find an agent to work with for her completed first novel, *A Spell of Dance and Silence,* but she'd just submitted her revisions, and her agent hoped they would soon find a publisher. Anna was excited to think that soon she might be a published author—a dream come true. She'd spent the months querying while they planned their small wedding for the break in the racing season, coming up in three weeks.

After all, they needed Vince, the best man, to be available, as well as his not-so-secret girlfriend, Catarina, who was Anna's maid of honor. Vince and Catarina had surprised everyone, except Anna, through the spring when they'd revealed they were a couple. She'd had her suspicions that the two of them had been more than friends for some time.

In March, when the new MotoGP season had started, Isaac had been restless, as everyone had expected, but only a little. He'd trained with Vince over the winter, pushing his brother to peak fitness again, but never regretted his decision to retire. After all, he insisted there was more to life than racing.

Spring races in Jerez, Barcelona, and Portimão had been easy to travel to, as had a race weekend in Germany where they'd watched Vince defend his title, making him an eighteen-time 'King of the Ring.' In the overall championship, he was in a dogfight with Luka for the title. Anna had a feeling that Luka might win this one. The kid had been on fire, almost unstoppable, and for once, Vince had his own distractions, though from what he said, he'd never been happier.

Anna had just finished the draft of a new story, one about a woman who had accidentally wished herself back in time five years where she had a chance to make different choices. For herself, she no longer wished to be anywhere or any time else. Her life with Isaac was everything she once had dreamed of, and more. She no longer felt like a passenger on her journey through life, but a driver who no longer wished for any life but her own.

ACKNOWLEDGMENTS

My husband and I moved into our current house in the fall of 2009, blending our two families to make a new one. Soon after, Rob discovered the Speed Channel and started watching motorcycle racing. He had raced once in his youth, before deciding it was too expensive and too dangerous. From the other room, the races sounded exciting, and I found myself drawn in time after time. It became our thing. We sorted out the various leagues and levels, becoming fans of MotoGP racing, the lightweight, intermediate, and premiere classes.

It wasn't long before we needed to watch all the races, not just some of them that we happened across. So, we bought an online video pass to the MotoGP website and have made it a ritual to watch all three levels for all eighteen to twenty races per season. We also watch practices and qualifying sessions. If you know me, you won't be surprised at the level of my obsession. For fifteen years, we've followed our favorite racers since they were teenagers, emerging on track with Moto3 and making their way through the ranks to the top level of MotoGP.

I want to thank all the MotoGP racers, their teams, and the league for providing us with countless hours of entertainment. I wrote *Racing Towards Destiny* in the summer of 2022, just as my racing obsession kicked up another notch. We rewatched older races, starting over where we began, but this time with a deeper understanding and a different appreciation for the skill, talent, and strategy involved.

While my story is entirely fictional, many characters were inspired by my favorite riders, including several sets of brothers that race at the highest level. For each pair, one is more successful than the other, which led me to wonder about their family dynamics. A special thanks to Marc and Alex Marquez, Aleix and Pol Espargaro, Brad and Darryn Binder, and Valentino Rossi and Luca Marini. They'll probably never know they inspired this story (which is in the process of becoming a series), but they did.

Many people are involved when writing a book, so I want to thank the two wonderful writing communities I belong to. Thank you to the Creative Academy for Writers, the online community where I find workshops, support, and writing friends. Special thanks to those I spend time with at the Surrey International Writers' Conference and who come to book fairs and book launches where we buy each other's books. I want to have a special shout-out to Stacy Sakai, who first beta read *Racing Towards Destiny,* Bonnie Jacoby, Keay Francis, Leslie Wibberley, Sarah Neeson, and all the others from TCA who help by making writing less solitary.

The second community I wish to acknowledge is the group of Black Rose Authors who ARC read, provide blurbs and reviews, and celebrate successes small and large. A special thanks to those who have read this book, or supported me in another way, including Anna Daughtery, Cam Torrens, David Buzan, Diane Hawley Nagatomo, Gail Ward Olmsted, Gary Gerlacher, Karen K. Brees, and Susan Sage. Thank you to Reagan Rothe and the Black Rose staff who patiently answer my questions, promote my books, and to David King who designed my gorgeous covers.

Also, thanks to my critique partner Benjamin Brockway for reading this story's early, rougher version. I accept his ribbing about the romance in my books because he's willing to read my stories, even when they aren't his preferred genre, and he always provides useful and insightful feedback.

A giant thank you to my weekly critique partner, friend, and editor Tracy Thillmann. She deserves credit for wading through my word echoes and rough drafts and for giving me suggestions on how to improve my story at more than one stage.

As always, I've saved my friends and family for last. Thank you to Ann Marie, Ari, Ashlie, Bonnie, Celine, Christine, Cindy, Dani, Diane, Dom, Ella, Janis, Jen, Jenny, Jim, Joanne, Julie, Kirsten, Laurel, Laurie, Leslie, Lilian, Linnea, Mary, Melissa, Michelle, Natalie, Roberta, Robin, Sandi, Sheelagh, Shelley, Stacy, Susan, Tina, and Violet, for coming to book launches or buying my advance author copies immediately, making me feel like I have fans who get excited to read my books.

Thank you also to my cousins, my sister, aunts and uncles, and other family who read and recommend my books. All your support and interest is appreciated. Another special thanks to my husband Rob, my mom (Cheryl Jennings), my step-kid (Kayde Gibson) for promoting my books at the library where they work, and my daughters (Laurel and Hayley Dabb) for reading my stories and supporting my need to write. I love you.

Chapter 1

Sometimes change is infinitesimal, slow. You don't notice its icy fingers wrapped around your throat, stealing your breath, your beliefs, changing who you are until you don't recognize yourself. I was in the middle of such a change before the accident. The slow erosion of myself, into nothing.

I hadn't been behind the wheel in two years, not since the accident. I didn't like to be reminded of those dark days. Few career women in their early thirties don't drive, but walking kept me from another harrowing driving experience. Plus, I'd discovered that I enjoyed the fresh air and exercise.

I crossed the Museum lobby and nodded to the recent hires at the Information Desk, though I'd never spoken to any of their fresh, youthful faces. I stepped into an empty elevator, heading up to the peace of my office and lab.

"Hold the elevator," came the call from across the lobby.

I ignored the request. Christopher, the conservator of our museum, raced toward the closing door, shoved his arm inside, and slid in beside me. I rolled my eyes. I'd almost escaped, but hadn't been fast enough. Trapped beside him, his heat radiated toward me and I scooched sideways. He wore running clothes and his dark, wavy hair dripped with sweat. His muscles looked hard, the kind only dedicated athletes or gym rats achieved. I hoped he planned to shower before work.

"Hey, Lizzie." He smiled, the dimple appearing in his cheek.

My teeth ached with the effort as I maintained a neutral expression. I was not, nor had I ever been, a Lizzie. I hated that nickname. My name was Elizabeth, which suited me—serious, classic, and a little stand-offish. The latter may not have suited me when I was younger, but it did now. I'd been burned too many times to let people get close to me. Life had been filled with harsh lessons.

I nodded to be polite. Being around Christopher was a constant struggle to maintain professionalism. What I really wanted to do was yell, "Leave me alone. I don't need anyone." More than anyone else, he brought out the worst in me. Why wouldn't he take a hint and leave me alone?

"Cat got your tongue again?" He leaned across me and pressed the button for his floor. "My magnificent presence has once again rendered you speechless." He winked.

The elevator ride lasted an eternity. How long did it take to get to the fourth floor?

He smirked.

I raised one eyebrow, but he knew I wouldn't respond. Even before I stopped talking, I hadn't spoken to him. Not since his brother Brandon had disappeared without a word of explanation. Why start now?

"Oh, Christopher."

His mincing tone meant to mimic my voice as he clutched his hands to his chest, caving in his broad shoulders in an attempt to appear feminine.

"You're so handsome and strong." He batted the long dark lashes that fringed his ice-blue eyes. "I'd love to meet with you after work. I don't want to be around anyone, but I find your magnetic charm irresistible."

I cast a withering glance in his direction. Other women fawned over him. He'd probably been told those exact words last week. He could have been charming if he wasn't loud and annoying. Half the time, what came out of his mouth was so full of expletives that I had to filter them out in order to listen. If I spoke, I couldn't imagine it would be to him. He'd never told me anything I wanted to know, like where the hell his brother had gone. Not that I'd asked. I'd been too proud.

Our colleagues at the museum left me alone. They were content to send me emails and receive answers the same way. But not Christopher. Christopher intruded upon the peaceful setting of my office and harassed me for details in person. He was the only person in my professional life who cared that I couldn't speak. His ridiculous remarks seemed designed to elicit a response, but I didn't give him the satisfaction.

"I'll see you later, Lizzie. I have a couple of questions about the new shipment from the Middle East, and something personal." He stepped off on the fourth floor. "I'll come chat after I've showered."

I gritted my teeth. I couldn't wait.

His tall frame strode from the elevator and he turned to blow me a kiss. Why hadn't I reported his outrageous behavior to HR? I didn't want him to know I'd enjoyed his attempt, though after he was gone, I allowed myself an amused smile. I continued to the sixth floor where my office and lab were located. Maybe I should install a punching bag in the corner and bring workout clothes. It might help after encounters with Christopher. I could work on my left-right-knee-roundhouse combinations.

I couldn't wait to get to the lab that had become my sanctuary. The lab access was through my office. One side of the room had a custom-designed, painted chart of the most recent theory of human evolution. The tree-like diagram of the origins of the human race and their relatives took an entire wall. Seeing it made me smile because it reminded me of the part of my life over which I had control.

They'd hired me fresh from grad school, where I'd received my PhD in Paleoanthropology, and three summers of co-op jobs at the Smithsonian. My job was to create and maintain a display at the brand-new museum here in Portland, meant to one day rival the famous exhibits at the Smithsonian in Washington, DC, or the American Museum of Natural History in New York City.

Scientists used to think Neanderthals in Europe and the Middle East had died out, replaced by more advanced, modern humans moving out from Africa in a single wave.

Now, scientists acknowledged that multiple waves of anatomically modern humans had interbred with Neanderthals and older populations of early humans in several parts of the world. It shouldn't have been a surprise. Anyone who'd seen certain hockey players in the eighties could have recognized a Neanderthal brow ridge. Who knew what DNA lurked within the human species, waiting for selective pressure to force the next wave of evolution? Part of my job was to bring these modern ideas into the new exhibits.

Once I would have discussed these ideas with my boyfriend Brandon over tea in my office after work or over dinner at the cozy restaurants with good food that he always seemed to locate. Or I would have chatted online with my friend Jeff. We'd been close in grad school, but my job was here and he was across the country, in New York. It had been easy to drift apart, through geography and circumstance. The biggest factor in my lost friendship had been my husband, Eric.

It was hard to maintain a long-distance friendship with someone you weren't allowed to see or talk to. I missed sitting and talking about men and movies. We'd had almost the same taste in both, but now it had been years since Jeff and I had a conversation. The gulf had become too immense to bridge. Without a friend, I talked to myself or to my cat. Ember didn't mind, she just purred. Now she was the only one to hear my voice.

After the accident, I hadn't set out not to talk. I just had nothing to say. I'd become lost in my thoughts, trying to cope with my snarled mess of feelings. Then I didn't want to speak. It took months before I realized I couldn't anymore. It had been two years, and I still hadn't spoken in the presence of another person. I hadn't been injured, but the trauma had inhibited my voice. It infuriated my therapist, Dr. Maeve Fossey. We'd been unable to find a solution. We were scheduled for another fruitless appointment tomorrow. She talks. I type.

I read my emails and replied to everything that needed attention. It took an hour, but it would ensure uninterrupted peace afterward. In my office, I was accessible, but in the lab, everyone recognized I was unavailable. Barring an emergency, everyone would leave me alone. Hitting *Send* on the final message, there was a knock at the door. Before I could escape, Christopher barged inside. He'd changed into dark blue jeans and a t-shirt, his work uniform unless he was meeting with the Board, which was the only time he wore a suit and tie.

"Lizzie, perfect." He closed the door and the room shrank. His big personality stole most of the limited space. "Glad I caught you. Downstairs took longer than expected because there was a problem with a water leak in the Modern Technology display. I expected you would have escaped by now."

I shot him a sharp look at his choice of words, so close to my thoughts when I'd heard his knock.

"I had an unusual phone call last night. Once I would have talked to Brandon, but I want your opinion."

At the mention of Brandon's name, the world closed in and it became difficult for me to hear the rest of his words. Maybe there wasn't enough oxygen in the room. I had trouble concentrating and my vision blurred. My face burned and I willed myself to keep the tears at bay. Christopher continued talking but trailed off when he realized I wasn't listening.

"I'll pick you up at seven. I'll explain then."

I wanted to refuse his invitation, but I was too upset to protest.

His expression was thoughtful, as if I'd said something he hadn't expected, though I hadn't said a word. Maybe my discomfort was written on my face.

I expected him to mimic my daze or pretend to dab at imaginary tears, but he didn't.

"You okay? Do you need to sit down?"

I shook my head. My palms were sweaty, and I crunched them into balls and shoved them deep into the pockets of my white lab coat. I didn't want to go. I couldn't spend that much time with Christopher. Trying not to be obvious, I took calming breaths.

"Look Lizzie, I wouldn't ask if it wasn't important. Please?" All traces of his usual jokes were gone.

I'd have done anything for his brother at one time—before he'd disappeared from my life without an explanation. For Christopher too.

"I know you don't like me," Christopher said.

At that, I looked up and tried to focus. Not that I didn't like *him*. I didn't want to like anyone.

His voice was quieter and less abrasive than usual. His pale blue, almost silver eyes looked sincere.

"But I'm out of options. Please eat with me."

I panicked again and shook my head. Eat? That wasn't a meeting. It sounded more like a date. I glanced down at my jeans, comfortable walking shoes, and lab coat.

"You don't have to change. It's not a date," he said, interpreting my glance.

He'd said *'Please'* twice. I couldn't recall hearing that word cross his lips before now. Maybe I hadn't paid attention. Despite my feelings, I was the slightest bit curious. I shrugged and nodded. Sighing would be rude, so I kept it to myself.

"Thanks, Lizzie. I appreciate your overwhelming enthusiasm. I'll see you at seven." His blue eyes twinkled—his good humor restored.

What had I gotten myself into? I already regretted my decision.

When he showed himself out, I moved into the lab and retrieved the most recent box of fossils to arrive. I wanted to forget Christopher, banish him from my mind. Dr. Maeve said my favorite coping mechanism was avoidance. With a hint of defiance, I opened the box and sorted the contents. Most were casts of bones or bone fragments, but one box contained original fossils from the Middle East that were close to a hundred thousand years old. The Middle

East's proximity to Europe, western Asia, and Africa made it the perfect place to find evidence of mixed populations of early humans and some of the rarer species that had become extinct. This Mesolithic study was for the next exhibit I was developing.

I stayed in my lab for the rest of the day, removing Christopher from my thoughts, until my phone chimed with a notification.

"Ready?"

I didn't know he had this number. He'd never used it before, as far as I could remember. I'd changed my number because Eric used to scroll through my messages, looking for reasons to be angry. It had been easier to start fresh. This number had been for family and work only. How could I reply and get out of dinner?

Christopher tapped on the window.

He was in my office. There was no escaping.

I shrugged and rotated my neck, the muscles tight from the precision of measuring, labeling, and identifying the fragments of fossilized bone. I glanced at my phone—seven-ten. How did that happen? I was late. He'd been patient. Leaving the box, so I could resume tomorrow, I jotted a few quick notes, shut off my computer, and turned off the lights before I joined him in my office. I needed a few minutes for my brain to change gears.

As I locked the door and joined him in the hall, my unasked question about his brother returned to my mind. Something he'd said had stuck with me all day and I wanted an answer.

"Why can't you talk to Brandon?" I texted while we waited for the elevator. Once upon a time, he and Brandon had been so close.

A strange look appeared on Christopher's face. I couldn't decipher his emotions, and his usual smile disappeared.

"I thought you knew about Brandon." His voice was flat, without inflection.

He looked like he was working up the courage to tell me something difficult. My eyes narrowed. If I'd Googled his brother, I could have known, but I'd avoided even that temptation for the last five years, deactivating my accounts on social media.

"Fuck. I'll just say it. Brandon died. Four years ago."

My body sagged as though I'd been gut-punched and I used the cold stainless wall to steady myself. The taste of bile rose in my throat. All this time I'd imagined Brandon married, living his own happily ever after across town. Successful and alive. I shook my head. I'd been a bitch for thinking the worst of him.

"After your breakup," Christopher said, "He disappeared from everyone. Worked all the time. Didn't talk to anyone. Kinda like someone else I know."

I couldn't look at Christopher, but his voice continued as though from a distance. It seemed calm, which was shocking considering the topic was his brother's death.

"A couple of months after you two argued, he slipped into a coma and never woke up. At first, we had hope, but he stayed like that for a year. By the end, there were no longer signs of brain activity. We turned off the machines. He wouldn't have wanted to stay like that on life support."

For Christopher, this was old news and the pain would be more distant. Not forgotten, but squished down to a manageable level. Would my pain become dull, blunt? Today it was like twisting knives.

I rewrote Christopher's words in my mind. The argument that led to my breakup with Brandon had been minor. After that, his brother ghosted me, blocked my number, and vanished. I'd waited outside his house twice, but I hadn't seen him. Later, I'd been so wrapped up in my own problems with Eric that I hadn't heard about Brandon's coma or death. Tears pricked at my eyes and this time, a few escaped. Christopher could mock if he wanted. I didn't care. I'd cared about his brother. With partial success, I smothered my feelings so I could ignore them. Dealing with them all at once was too difficult.

The elevator doors opened at the bottom and we stepped out. I reeled—his words like blows. Coma. Dead. I'd spent all this time wondering what would have happened if we'd stayed together. How things would be different. They'd have been the same. I'd be in mourning, and still voiceless, since that was my response to trauma.

With this new grief surrounding me, the memory of the accident hijacked my waking hours. I slipped back to my moment of crisis, the flood of memories overwhelming my mind.

There was a clarity in the headlights. I discovered that in the moment with the blinding lights, screeching tires, and jarring crunch of sound, that while I didn't want to die, I was resigned. White light rushed toward where I was frozen and time stopped. When I'd viewed photos of the wreckage online, I didn't understand how anyone could have survived. As the driver, it was my fault. I shouldn't have been the one to live.

"Lizzie, are you okay?" Christopher's voice came from far away.

I nodded, numb. We walked out of the museum as I relived when I'd walked away from the twisted, mangled metal. My old life had died in that infinite moment, transfixed by the lights, and with it my voice.

Chapter 2

Christopher and I strolled a few blocks to a restaurant, the air warm in the May evening. In this part of the city, most restaurants had outdoor sidewalk patios—so many interesting places to choose from. It was a beautiful evening, ripe with the promise of the approaching summer. Outside was better. I had more space and fresh air. I could tell from his frown that he was concerned, but he'd asked to talk and I would try to listen, despite the shocking news that brought back my trauma. Once again, my mind flashed to Eric and the night that had changed my life.

As we walked through the door, I recognized where we were. I'd been here before when it had served Italian instead of Indian. The scent of rich spices filled the air, bringing me back to the present, and I inhaled their fragrance. I was starving. I couldn't remember my last hot meal. For convenience, I ate a lot of salads and sandwiches. Once more, I breathed in the heavenly aroma. I couldn't wait to eat.

A server in black pants and a white blouse led us to a quiet table in the back with dim lighting. It wasn't supposed to, but it seemed like a date. To a stranger, we might look like a cute couple, though Christopher and I were mismatched. But they say opposites attract. He's tall and I'm short. He's dark, I'm fair. His face was made to laugh, while mine was serious. I've always been the kind of person who everyone says would be pretty if only I'd smile—the worst compliment ever. Despite all those differences, from the outside, it might look like we fit. I glanced toward the door, wondering if I could bolt or if Christopher would follow.

"Still not a date," Christopher said under his breath as we sat.

The way his thoughts followed mine was uncanny. Was I so easy to read?

Our server said, "Can I start you off with drinks?"

"A bottle of red," said Christopher. "Do you have a recommendation?"

I didn't drink alcohol, so I handed my wine glass to our server and shook my head. He inclined his head and accepted it without pause.

Christopher chuckled. "Never mind. What's on tap? I'll get a beer instead. Lizzie, you want a beer? A cocktail?"

I shook my head and held up my water glass.

When our drink order was settled, Christopher said, "I didn't know you don't drink. Was it the accident?"

I started. I had forgotten that he'd know about it, but I didn't want the conversation to be about anything personal—especially not the accident—so I shook my head. It took up too many of my sleepless nights. I couldn't let it take my days, too.

He lifted my phone from the table and handed it to me. "Tell me."

"My mom drank. She died. I don't. Why are we here?" Impatience surged through my veins.

"Let's order first. I'm starving. If you're wondering what's good, it's all as delicious as it smells. Sometimes I want one of everything on the menu."

I dreaded the ordeal of ordering in person. Most of the time, I ordered takeout online to avoid the embarrassment of silent pointing, which made me feel so useless. Sometimes I wanted to talk, but when I tried, nothing came out. Dr. Maeve said that I wasn't trying. That deep down, I didn't want my voice. She said I needed to find the right incentive.

I studied my menu and flipped it closed almost right away. Christopher was staring, but I was determined not to fidget under his gaze.

"Well, Lizzie. What're you getting?"

He leaned back in his wooden chair, the picture of ease and relaxation, while I dripped with sweat, a side effect of extreme anxiety. I hoped it wasn't obvious.

I pointed to the two items I'd chosen.

When our server returned with ice water and a pint of his chosen IPA, Christopher ordered. "The lady will have the lamb madras curry and I'll have butter chicken. We need two orders of vegetable samosas, an order of naan, and a side of basmati rice."

Grateful he'd handled my order with so little discomfort, I sipped my ice water. Why was he being so considerate?

"*Thanks,*" I texted. My tense shoulders loosened a little.

"I suppose I should explain." He took a long drink of beer, then set it on the coaster. He adjusted it to sit in the exact center before speaking. "I didn't know you were unaware of what happened to Brandon. I apologize. He'd said it was a rough breakup, and I respected both of you enough to stay out of it—give you space. It was none of my business. I thought you would've heard what happened to him through others at work. I didn't consider how little you interact with people and I'm sorry I upset you."

I shrugged, watching him play with his fork.

"I didn't handle it well at first, either. I had a rough couple of years. We all need to escape. Hence the women. Though, as you may have noticed, I quit some time ago."

I hadn't noticed. As usual, I'd only noticed things I wanted to see.

I nodded, suspicious of his motives for taking me out for dinner. He was the last person I'd date, if I dated. Which I didn't. That would require being close to someone.

Christopher took another sip. "Last night, I got a strange call. Someone called for Dr. Winters. I seldom use that name outside work, even though I have a doctorate. Then the man launched into gibberish about the serum and needing to restart human trials. He talked fast. Something about genetic enhancement."

Startled into meeting his eyes, I grabbed my phone. *'He was looking for your brother.'* I couldn't type his name any more than I could say it. My fingers felt paralyzed.

"Yeah, I figured that, but he didn't let me explain. It was a brief call. He freaked out near the end. Said he had to go, that they'd traced his line, that it was too dangerous. In the background, there was a crashing sound, then a bang, like a door had been forced open. There was a scuffle, and the line went dead."

My eyes widened in surprise and my pulse quickened. Once, I'd overheard Brandon on the phone. He'd mentioned the pressure to start human trials. I'd asked him about it later. That conversation had been our last.

"I've tried calling back, but it goes straight to an automated voicemail with no name. I didn't leave messages."

I shook my head.

"What?"

"They might come for you if they think you're him."

"Who? Brandon?"

I cringed when he said the name, but maintained eye contact.

"Give me some credit. I blocked my number. But I appreciate your concern for my well-being." He grinned, his dimple reappearing.

My heart lurched at the sight. I didn't want to like him. I'd rather ignore him.

"What I was wondering," he said. "Does any of that sound familiar? Brandon said you remember everything. So, if he mentioned anything odd like that, I figured you'd know."

I must have hesitated or looked guilty because his eyes lit up and he talked faster.

"I knew it. It's years later, but better late than never. The doctors say a drug overdose caused Brandon's coma."

I choked on my water and my hands shook as I set down the cold glass. I couldn't have heard that right. Brandon had been career-driven, health-conscious, and careful. He'd never take drugs.

I shook my head. No way. The room became too hot as my cheeks burned. A tightness constricted my chest as it sucked the air from my lungs. The restaurant became too confining. I had to get out.

"I agree. He didn't do drugs. It wasn't an overdose. His coma had to have been caused by something else. The call may be a clue. I want to solve this mystery and I need your help. Help me Obi-wan Kenobi, you're my only hope."

Ignoring the Star Wars reference, which in other circumstances I would've loved, I shoved back my chair, grabbed my phone, and ran. Christopher called after me, but I didn't listen. I made it outside and two buildings over before I stopped to throw up. I wanted to be left alone, but, of course, Christopher followed. When I leaned forward, one hand on the rough stone wall, he held my hair away from my face as I heaved. He rubbed my back and made soothing sounds I couldn't understand for the roaring in my ears. What if I could've helped Brandon, and I'd let him down?

Christopher handed me a glass of water and a cloth napkin from the restaurant to wipe my mouth. My legs were rubbery, and I shook all over.

My eyes filled with scalding tears, but I didn't let them fall. I took a deep breath and barricaded my feelings away. Since my childhood, I'd taken upsetting thoughts or feelings and visualized them behind a barrier. Sometimes it helped.

He stepped back, his hands shoved deep in the pockets of his jeans.

"I have nowhere else to turn, and I need your help. I won't say another word about Brandon tonight. I had no idea how badly you'd react. I'm sorry. Come inside and eat. You're too skinny. Then I'll drive you home, leave you alone to think."

I was a coward. I didn't know how to help, but I let Christopher take my arm and guide me back to our table. He slid a piece of gum across the table and ordered mint tea to settle my stomach. I allowed him to take this much care of me while he chattered about books and movies. He made it easy for me to just sit. He didn't ask questions or make demands. I'd walked to work, so it was convenient to let him drive me home—I could avoid the darkening streets.

On the walk to his car, I pulled out my phone to text him the address, but he said, "I know where you live. The same place, right?"

I nodded. He'd picked up his brother a few times, long ago. My heart hurt. I wanted to curl up with a romance novel and escape.

At my darkened townhouse, I got out, texted my thanks, and climbed the stairs. I wished I'd left the porch light on. I'd known I might not be home until after dark, as I often worked late. I raised my hand to signal that I was fine, but Christopher didn't drive away until I'd located my key and unlocked the door.

If I hadn't found being around him confusing, it could have been a pleasant evening. I hadn't expected to enjoy his company. I'd felt more normal than I had in a long time. The last two years had been lonely and had seemed like an eternity.

I put down dinner for my kitty and headed for the shower, wishing I could wash my feelings down the drain. It was getting too hard to keep them distant. I had so many regrets in my life and tonight only highlighted them. I'd spent years feeling sorry for myself about Brandon's disappearance, wondering what I'd done wrong. Afraid I hadn't measured up. That I hadn't been good enough. I regretted getting mixed up with Eric. Our marriage had been a disaster. I also regretted the energy I'd spent hating someone who, while over-confident and annoying, wasn't so bad.

Tonight, my house seemed quiet and too empty. My eyes grew tired from reading and I shut out the light, but the silence pressed inward and wouldn't let me rest. I tossed and turned for another two hours. Too many thoughts tumbled in my head, like clothes in a dryer. Around and around, going nowhere. My mind went where it always did when I couldn't sleep—back to the same few jarring moments.

After the accident, my boss advised me to take some time—a leave of absence was usual in these circumstances. Instead, I threw myself into my work, which became my existence. I went through the motions of living. I attended Eric's funeral, but all I remembered were white flowers and the smell of lilies. After the funeral, I avoided my family. They meant well, but despite the tragedy, it didn't affect their lives the way it did mine. My family misinterpreted my wall of numb silence as shock or sorrow. They didn't know that guilt consumed me. Or relief. Or guilt about the relief.

I couldn't remember the last time I'd laughed. It must be years, but it had nothing to do with the accident. It dated back to the beginning of my marriage, when I'd let myself slip away, becoming a cringing, fearful husk without friends. I was ashamed that I'd made such poor choices. I didn't want anyone to learn what I'd hidden the last four years, locked in the prison of my mind. The real secret was now six feet under.

In moments like this, I believed that keeping secrets had led to one thing. I was alone. I didn't have anyone to lean on, to confide in. Alone didn't have to mean lonely, but I was. Nothing seemed to fill the gaping hole inside.

"I'm still ashamed, Ember." I stroked her soft fur. She didn't open her eyes, but a rumbly purr emerged. "Eric hurt me and before that, Brandon. When you let yourself care about people, they have the power to hurt you. I don't know how much more I can take. Being alone is too hard."

In desperation, I jumped out of bed and grabbed a piece of amethyst from the top of my dresser. A couple of sessions ago, Dr. Maeve had brought out a tray of stones and asked me to select a piece to be my worry rock. I'd thought her request silly, but harmless, and had complied. My gaze had settled on the purple crystals as if they'd spoken. I had expected nothing to come of it but had taken it home. I reviewed her words as I gripped the crystals in my hand.

"All my hardest clients choose something special," she'd said. "Stones have properties to heal our minds. This may relieve your anxiety. Hold it when you're sleepless and overwhelmed."

I didn't know how it worked, but she wanted me to think of better times and believe I could get through this rough patch. I'd tossed it there weeks ago, skeptical of its use. I'd been unhappy for so long, but news of Brandon's death was the last straw.

What did I have to lose? Something had to make a difference. It was worth a shot. Tears leaked from the corners of my eyes as I stared at the ceiling and clutched the purple stone to my chest, its sharp edges etching the palm of my hand. My feelings were impossible to keep at bay at night.

With Ember curled into a tabby-sized ball of fur near my hip, I whispered.

"I don't know how to change anymore. I'm so alone."

As I squeezed the stone in my fist, I shuddered and suppressed a sob.

"I wish I had a mulligan so I could redo my life."

Find out what happens next in *The Wish.*
Available in paperback, ebook, and audiobook.

ABOUT THE AUTHOR

Award-winning author Lena Gibson is a storyteller as an elementary school teacher and keeper of the family lore. She holds a First-Class Honors degree in archaeology, with minors in history, biology, geography, and environmental education from Simon Fraser University.

A voracious reader from childhood onward, Lena seeks wonderful books in which to escape. Because of her passion for different genres, she combines elements of many in her writing. As an adult newly recognized with autism, she often creates characters that reflect this experience.

When Lena isn't writing, she reads, practices karate, and drinks a ton of tea. She resides in New Westminster, Canada, with her family and their fuzzy overlord, Ash, the fluffiest of gray cats. You can learn more at lenagibsonauthor.ca.

NOTE FROM LENA GIBSON

Word-of-mouth is crucial for any author to succeed. If you enjoyed *Racing Towards Destiny*, please leave a review online—anywhere you are able. Even if it's just a sentence or two. It would make all the difference and would be very much appreciated.

Thanks!
Lena Gibson

We hope you enjoyed reading this title from:

BLACK ROSE writing™

www.blackrosewriting.com

Subscribe to our mailing list – *The Rosevine* – and receive **FREE** books, daily deals, and stay current with news about upcoming releases and our hottest authors.
Scan the QR code below to sign up.

Already a subscriber? Please accept a sincere thank you for being a fan of Black Rose Writing authors.

View other Black Rose Writing titles at
www.blackrosewriting.com/books and use promo code
PRINT to receive a **20% discount** when purchasing.